The grinning sk̲ull̲ ... ... completely preserved skeleton, which ruled out plague victim or any leftover from antiquity. There was no sign of any shred of clothing. When the corpse had landed on its back on a bed of dried mud and ancient refuse, it had been naked. Unless the corpse had been taking a bath at the moment the bomb fell, this most probably ruled out wartime blitz victim, although blast had been known to strip victims to the buff. The possibility could not be dismissed just yet.

But these factors the three experts in death absorbed almost subconsciously. What they were staring at in the glare of the arc-light was the yellow tinge on the bones and a similar discolouring of the surrounding area.

'Slaked lime,' said DS Dalton.

'Indubitably,' said Professor Dart.

'Murder,' said DCI Armstrong.

Former national newspaper foreign correspondent and celebrity interviewer, Victor Davis lives in London. He is the author of two previous novels, *The Ghostmaker* and *Queen's Ransom*.

GETTING
AWAY WITH IT

Victor Davis

ORION

An Orion Paperback
First published in Great Britain by Victor Gollancz in 1999
This paperback edition published in 2000 by
Orion Books Ltd,
Orion House, 5 Upper St Martin's Lane,
London WC2H 9EA

A CIP catalogue record for this book
is available from the British Library.

ISBN: 0 75283 398 7

Printed and bound in Great Britain by
Clays Ltd, St Ives plc

Acknowledgements

This novel covers incidents that take place over a long period of time and involves a number of fields of expertise. I could not have completed it without being steered on numerous occasions out of my blunders and into the right paths.

I gratefully acknowledge the guiding hand of Sergeant Charles Owen of the City of London Police.

The lovely old Ealing comedy *Hue and Cry* figures significantly in my story and I'm grateful to its director, Charles Crichton, aged eighty-seven when we spoke, for telling me something of its location shooting in the City of London and on Bankside. I also thank John Herron of Canal + Image UK Ltd., at Pinewood Studios, who loaned me a pristine copy of *Hue and Cry*.

Bruce Watson, science supervisor (archaeology) at the Museum of London Archaeology Service, was a tremendous help.

Local historians Mr C. H. Ryall and Mrs Audrey Ringrose (no relation of my hero, Commander Thomas Ringrose!) first alerted me to the facts surrounding the real-life Eltham murder that plays its part here. I thank them.

My friend, the opera singer Melinda Hughes, supplied me with a graphic description of what life is like in an exclusive girls' school. The things those girls get up to!

Lastly, a heartfelt word of thanks to Hazel Orme, editor of this and my two other published novels. Hazel doesn't let me get away with anything.

This one is dedicated to the memory of my brother,
John Michael Davis.

Behind every great fortune lies a great crime.

Honoré de Balzac

BOOK ONE

Chapter One

While the British trooped wearily to the polls on 9 April 1992, at the end of an ill-tempered general election campaign, two men arrived at the front door of a middle-aged couple in the village of Colney Heath near the cathedral town of St Albans in the county of Hertfordshire. They had a tempting bundle of crisp, crackling fifty-pound notes in their hands, and had arrived in response to a Van for Sale advertisement in a magazine.

Acting out their roles as ordinary buyers, the men made a cursory inspection of the couple's pale blue and white Ford transit, and made a brief pretence of haggling over the asking price.

But there was never any doubt that the vehicle was ideal for their wicked purpose and they determined to have it.

A deal was speedily struck – so speedily that it would be difficult but, as it proved in this case, not impossible for the couple later to identify the purchasers from photographs they were shown by officers of Britain's anti-terrorist squad.

The cash was handed over in exchange for the keys and vehicle documents, and the satisfied couple waved the two men goodbye as they headed off towards the M25 orbital road.

As the unsuspecting vendors turned their backs and went indoors, a long period of anxiety and terror was about to begin for them.

For the two men, members of the Irish Republican Army from South Armagh – one believed to be a farmer in his mid-thirties and the other an electrician nine years his junior – twenty-four hours of intense, murderous activity, for which until this day they still have not been called to account, lay ahead.

They took their new purchase to a secure address some-where on the twenty-mile drive into the north London sub-urbs. Here a crude bomb, weighing up to one ton and composed of a satanic mixture of fertilizer, fuel oil and ammo-nium nitrate, designed to produce a violent shockwave, was loaded into the back.

The following day was a Friday. Normally, the end-of-week exodus from the money-churning mills of the City of London's financial district begins early and is completed by seven p.m. But not on 10 April.

The high-commission earners from the merchant banks and bond-trading floors were in euphoric mood. At that hour the pubs and wine bars were still doing brisk business as the lingerers celebrated the unexpected election victory of the Conservative Party, which had hitherto left them free to trade hindered by minimal regulatory shackles.

Later, on that early-spring evening, the two Irishmen care-fully parked the van outside the Baltic Exchange, a heavily ornamented Edwardian building in St Mary Axe in the heart of the City. Security cameras positioned on neighbouring buildings caught the two hurrying away, heads down in their hooded anoraks to frustrate identification.

When the pair were safely clear of the area an imprecise warning was telephoned to railway staff across the River Thames at Waterloo station.

Twenty minutes later, at nine-twenty-five p.m. and before the threatened City area had been accurately pinpointed by the police, the van exploded with devastating effect.

A crater fifteen feet deep was instantly created in the road-way, revealing traces of an old Roman road and tearing out sewage and water pipes, gas lines and electric cables as if a crazed surgeon had gone to work on a supine patient's entrails. The Baltic Exchange seemed to bloat under the force of the blast and then shatter. The front doorman, aged forty-nine and working overtime, was instantly killed, as was a fifteen-year-old girl waiting in a car for her father, and a twenty-nine-year-old securities dealer, who had been drinking with his colleagues.

The appalling blast roared through the narrow grey canyons, gathering debris and spreading out to thunder against some three hundred buildings, shattering stone, brick and marble, and sending millions of glass shards hissing through the air.

Inside the multi-storey buildings, the raging beast of dust-thick air plucked down false ceilings and ducting systems, swept desks, filing cabinets, computers and late workers against far walls.

That night, ninety-one of them were injured.

Chapter Two

During the following few days the press and television news-casts carried many pictures of the devastation to the City's more outstanding buildings and those occupied by the most famous companies – the Commercial Union building, the NatWest Tower, the Hong Kong & Shanghai Bank, the Union Bank of Switzerland among them.

The cameras also pointed sadly at the almost total ruin of St Helen's Church, which had stood for nearly seven centuries in Bishopsgate, having survived the Great Fire of London in 1666 and the German Luftwaffe's bombing campaigns during the 1939–45 war.

Apart from its Nigerian owners and tenants, no one fretted overmuch at the damage to nearby Abura House, an undistinguished post-war structure of seven storeys in multi-occupation, the tenants including an American bond dealer, a venture-capital group and the Nigerians themselves, who seemed to have interests in many spheres.

When it was originally raised on blitz ruins in 1955 as offices for HM Customs and Excise, Abura House had been named

Fletcher Hall, marking the site where in medieval times had existed a guild of fletchers or arrow-makers.

In the sixties, the building had proved too small and inconvenient for the customs men and they had moved on. The building then underwent several changes of ownership and usage, and in the early eighties the weather-worn blue plastic panelling of the façade, which had been inspired by the decorative ideas of the Festival of Britain back in 1951, was replaced by modern glass curtaining and an updated marble entrance hall and canopy.

After the facelift, the original builder would not have recognized the place.

This fact was later to have extraordinary repercussions that no one could have foreseen.

In an assessment of the IRA devastation, bomb damage experts noted that these post-war structures may have lost their fragile façades in the blast, but the steel-and-concrete skeletons beneath had withstood the thunderclap much better than the older buildings, with their timber floors and internal plaster walls.

So the Nigerians now had on their hands a sturdy skeletal building that remained uninhabitable while they sought compensation from insurance and government sources. At first they were content to await the arrival of their money and use it to restore the building to its pre-bomb state and function. During this hiatus they were pleasantly surprised to be approached by the Montemar Bank of Spain and asked, 'Why bother? We need a foothold in London. Leave the reconstruction to us.'

The Nigerians received a sum considerably in excess of what their own surveyors had said Abura House *intacta* was worth on the current property market, and happily allowed themselves to be bought out.

The directors of the Montemar Bank of Spain were lying to the Nigerians. They had no intention of restoring Abura House. They immediately ordered the drawing up of plans to demolish the building, excavate the site to provide underground parking and erect a state-of-the-art architectural show-piece of twenty-two storeys above ground.

Finalizing these plans and having them accepted by the demanding City of London Corporation's Planning and Transportation Committee and English Heritage took three years. Finally, in 1997, the scaffolding and the blue plastic dust screens went up and the forty-two-year-old bomb-blasted building was poised to come down.

Chapter Three

Before demolition of Abura House began, there had been an extremely distasteful incident – carefully kept out of the newspapers – involving the City Corporation and the construction tycoon, Vernon Gatling, who had failed to win the demolition and reconstruction contract.

The last time Gatling had figured in the list of Britain's richest men his fortune had been put at £460 million. These lists were always wildly inaccurate, since they were composed by journalists taking desperate guesses when they could not access the true figures. But there was no disputing that, give a million or two, Vernon was awesomely rich.

He was not, however, entirely a self-made man. His father Frank (always known as Gunner, a reference to the famous Gatling gun with which he, incidentally, had no family connection) had first made significant family money from post-war demolition and reconstruction. From this foundation Vernon had created an international construction empire and had broadened out into the building and ownership of hotels, holiday resorts, shopping malls and skyscrapers. The so-called Gatling SkyCities in New York, Chicago and Rio de Janeiro were his monuments.

Vernon was aggressive – as aggressive as any American. For

a while he'd revelled in notoriety in America for a headline feud with the city fathers of Beverly Hills in Los Angeles. He'd shocked the filmland enclave by producing the blueprint for yet another Gatling SkyCity with a proposed site on a corner of Rodeo Drive. He must have known he was pissing in the Santa Ana wind, though, and that the usual bungs to officials would not work: the city fathers had never yet made an exception to the zoning laws permitting such a high-rise building in Beverly Hills. The construction industry suspected the whole farce was a case of Vernon Gatling having fun to keep boredom at bay. He had made his pile through dogged drive and head-down determination, and conflict played an essential role in his amusements.

From early on in his confrontation with the City of London Corporation, it was apparent that Vernon was, once again, pissing in the wind, although on this occasion there was no fun on his agenda.

Deeper passions, as yet unsuspected, were in play.

He as good as accused City of London planning officials of accepting favours to use undue influence with the Spaniards and their architects to steer the Abura House contract towards a rival.

The three Common Councillors, who comprised the unofficial court of inquiry, were puzzled. Vernon Gatling's tender to the Spanish bank's architects had been received six weeks past the deadline. That wasn't his gung-ho style at all. When they summoned him to the Guildhall, he arrived in a truculent mood flanked by two lawyers who appeared less than happy with their client's stance and their brief. On his behalf, they demanded that the whole bidding process be taken back to the beginning, with the existing contracts declared null and void while Vernon Gatling's accusations of collusion between the successful construction rival and the Corporation officials were further investigated.

Apart from being affronted by the slur on the good name of their officers, Corporation members were baffled by the tycoon's vehemence. After all, given the size and extent of Gatling's global operations and holdings, the new building in Bishopsgate was minor league, even taking into account that the Corporation had upped the plot-ratio in line with its policy to prepare the City for global competition.

At the confrontation Gatling banged the table in a bullying manner not appreciated by the City gentlemen. The glass tumbler covering the neck of a water jug jumped and rattled.

'Would you kindly not do that,' said the chairman icily. 'With all your experience of the construction industry, Mr Gatling, I simply don't understand why on this occasion you were so laggardly with your tender.'

'When the work was put out, I was bluesail fishing off Cuba with my daughter,' said Gatling irritably. 'My contracts people simply failed to appreciate the significance of Abura House, which has undergone considerable alteration in recent years. Until I returned and spotted its exact address on the published tender documents, I had not linked the property with its original name – Fletcher Hall. After all, it was a long time ago.'

'What was a long time ago, Mr Gatling?' The chairman struggled to be patient with him.

'When my father let me build it. Fletcher Hall was the first time he trusted me to take charge of a large construction project. I was only twenty years old.'

'You're telling us,' said the chairman slowly, 'that the building is of great sentimental importance to you?'

'Yes, that's it,' said Vernon Gatling, nodding vigorously. 'Enormous sentimental importance. I really should be the one to put a new building on that site. Tradition and all that . . .'

The committee members were a study in incredulity. The chairman said explosively, 'Mr Gatling, nursing a sentimental attachment to a building is one thing and quite understandable. Most of us save that for our old schools. But taking it so far as to impugn the integrity of officers of the City Corporation in order to get your own way is totally unacceptable.

'You have produced nothing but unsubstantiated rumours of the flimsiest nature and we have dutifully squandered our time looking into them. Unless you and your advisers have anything more germane to offer, this committee intends to terminate this inquiry forthwith. Enough of our energies have been wasted on this slur. We must insist that you withdraw your allegations. Your legal advisers must have told you that what you have implied is actionable and we will not hesitate to grant our officers permission to initiate such proceedings as they see fit.'

The trio watched cold-eyed as Gatling's lawyer leaned over and whispered into his ear. The face of the tycoon grew grimmer and his lips compressed. Across the mahogany, they could see the blood disappearing from his tightening nostrils and hear his teeth grating.

Finally, they watched him stomp off to a side room to confer with his unhappy mouthpieces. The committee waited.

On Vernon's return, they observed him attempting to re-arrange his menacing face to appear chastened. The look did not come easily. Massive wealth means never having to say you're sorry.

But now Vernon spread his arms in a gesture of surrender. 'All right, gentlemen, I admit I got carried away.' He attempted a boyish grin. 'My advisers are right and I am wrong. I withdraw without reservation anything I said that reflects on the Corporation and its servants. It's just that Fletcher Hall is so close to my heart and the honour of building the new one would give me immense pleasure. Is there any remaining prospect of a review of the tenders?'

The chairman shook his head. 'I'm afraid not, Mr Gatling. We have satisfied ourselves that our officers have behaved correctly at all times and that the winning contractors are qualified to carry out the work in accordance with City of London building regulations. We have no cause to intervene on your behalf with the Montemar Bank of Spain. The matter is closed.' The chairman snapped shut his file. 'I would add that it is in everyone's best interest that this unhappy business is buried and forgotten.'

Much later, when a young writer named Gervase Meredith was floundering with the research for Vernon Gatling's unofficial biography and had prised out of a member of the City Corporation committee an account of these proceedings, that last remark assumed a haunting resonance.

The fracas with the City Corporation meant little in itself.

Just another spoilt bigshot who, for once, couldn't have everything his own way.

No one at the time detected the desperation that lay behind Vernon Gatling's ill-judged slander of the Corporation's officials.

In truth, he nursed as much sentimentality for Fletcher Hall as he would for the rebuilding of a public lavatory.

BOOK TWO

Chapter One

Sometimes late at night when only insomniacs are watching, or in the afternoon when mothers and the unemployed have joined the glum television audience, it is possible to catch a repeat screening of the first of the celebrated Ealing comedies. It is called *Hue and Cry*.

In 1946 Laurence Varnish saw the black and white film eight times at the Elephant and Castle picture-house in South London when it was first released. He was in it.

Naturally, Larry Varnish never bought a ticket. Like all his mates, he'd creep round to the side of the cinema alongside the railway arches where the ticket-buying mugs queued out of the rain, insert his wire hook into the crack between the emergency double doors, draw it upwards, snag the inside push-bar and tug until the doors clicked open. Then, in a commando crawl that he'd seen in many a war movie, he'd slither into the auditorium and surface, a picture of boyish innocence, comfortably ensconced in a red plush sixpenny seat.

This was known to one and all as Bunking In. What else were the kids to do? There was no money about.

The tactic did not always succeed. If the po-faced box-office lady in her smart crimson uniform said she'd sold only a dozen tickets for the early show, and the manager could see even in the gloom that there were at least twenty people in the auditorium, he did not have to look far for an explanation. Then all hell would break out as the young street-rakers ran every which way to avoid his wrath.

If you were unlucky enough to feel his Frankenstein grip on

your shoulder before you could charge headlong at the exit door and burst forth into daylight and freedom, you could accept the good hiding – what was 'good' about it? young Larry wanted to know – or accompany the fuming manager to his office while he summoned the police. No kid in his right mind took this option. The police meant angry parents. The police meant an appearance at the Tower Bridge juvenile court. The police meant Borstal, if you had previous convictions. You took the walloping.

The miserable old sod of a manager didn't even give the third option – which you were offered across the road at the rival Trocadero cinema – of doing penance by taking the Brasso and yellow rags and polishing the circle rails and the long narrow ashtrays screwed to the backs of the seats. Cleaning staff were hard to come by in 1946.

Larry was neither walloped nor arrested. When the ushers' torches began criss-crossing the stalls seats, like the wartime searchlights of recent memory, seeking out the young miscreants as if they were Heinkel bombers, he knew it was time to forget his special movie for a while and concentrate on personal survival.

Larry could leap those curving rows of plush chairs like a champion hurdler while the manager and his staff, wrong-footed at every aisle, cursed as the little will-o'-the-wisp ducked and dived, jumped and scampered and fell unwelcomed into legitimate patrons' laps before breasting the exit doors with the kamikaze's cry, 'Banzai!' This last was not particularly appropriate but what did Larry care? The triumphant howl sounded good.

And the hurdling was excellent training for similar encounters that were to come later when the City of London police had come to identify him as Vanishing Larry.

Despite all the obstacles put in his way, Vanishing Larry was still able to bunk in at evening performances and disappear into audiences too big for the manager to count by the light of the flickering movie.

'Here I come,' he'd hiss at his mates, giving them a few moments' warning as the screen showed a mob of street urchins charging along Bankside where Shakespeare had once toiled, and up on to Southwark Bridge. Larry remembered so well Mr Crichton, that funny bloke who was the director, shouting, 'Run, you little buggers, run!'

Take after take they had run their hearts out for him, supposedly in pursuit of a gang of villains, although no one had bothered fully to explain the plot at the time. He'd had to wait until the picture reached the Elephant and Castle for that.

And in the scampering mob of local kids, who'd been hired as extras for a shilling a run, you could catch just one glimpse of Larry's slum-pale face, mouth open in a shout (probably 'Banzai!' but the soundtrack was later redubbed) as he whizzed past the camera at a distance of eight feet.

'I'm a blinking star – just like Errol Flynn,' Larry would declare, to a chorus of farts and other rude expressions from his mates.

Larry had just left school at fourteen and was hauling beer crates at Barclay Perkins' brewery, a few yards down the road from where he'd had his moment of movie glory.

What with the upset of the war, his dad away in the Kate Carney, and one thing and another, no one had bothered overmuch to see that Larry Varnish emerged from the school system fully rounded for citizenship. But at least he could read and write, and he was bright enough to know that there must be more to life than hauling crates and the promise of all the free beer he could drink on the brewery premises – when he was old enough.

Sometimes there were long delays between camera set-ups while *Hue and Cry* was being filmed, and cast, crew and extras would idle away the time in the shell of a bombed Thames-side building on the north-east end of Southwark Bridge where the film's climax was to be shot. One of the actors, a cropped-haired man playing a plain-clothes copper, was popular with the street urchins. He made them laugh with his stories. He knew Will Hay and George Formby.

But it wasn't this acquaintance with the popular film comics of the day that grabbed Larry's attention. The geezer seemed to know a lot about London. He sat on the river wall, pointing out the house where Sir Christopher Whatsisname, the bloke who built St Paul's Cathedral, had lived, the spot where

Shakespeare's plays, none of which Larry had ever seen, had first been staged, and a boozer, the Anchor, that had a secret bolthole for smugglers behind the sliding oak panelling of an upstairs room. The tide, as brown as Mum's Oxo gravy, was ebbing, and the actor pointed out a couple of barefooted boys foraging in the mudflats on the far side of the Thames. 'They're called mudlarks. They're looking for old coins, anything from the past.'

Then the actor, who was a bit on the flowery side when he wasn't being a stern upholder of the law in the movie, did something that was to seal Vanishing Larry Varnish's fate. He scuffed the heel of his size ten Metropolitan Police-issue boot into the dirt alongside the river and said dreamily, 'Who knows what tales the shades of the Romans beneath our feet would have to tell if only they could?'

Larry was genuinely flummoxed. Romans? What Romans? From what he'd seen in the movies, the Romans were a bunch of Eyeties who ponced around showing their knees and racing chariots. What had they to do with London?

Larry voiced his bafflement. 'You're having me on. We had the Normans not the Romans. That's what they told us at school. Battle of Hastings – ten sixty-six.'

The actor laughed. 'You must have gone to a funny school,' he said, not unkindly. 'The Normans are practically newcomers. Long before them, the Romans practically founded this place – Londinium, they called it. They were here for more than four hundred years.'

Larry didn't give him an argument, which he might have done if it had been one of his own mates. The actor had a posh voice, which meant he knew what he was talking about. The man dug his heel in again. 'Almost anywhere around here, if you went down deep enough, you'd find the evidence.'

'What kind of evidence? Dead bodies?' asked Larry. He felt a stirring, a whisper of interest as if phantoms were already rising from the earth, tugging at his newly acquired long trousers – his long 'uns – to claim his attention.

The actor patted the pudding basin haircut that Larry's mum gave him every three weeks and said gently, 'No, my boy. They'd be merely bits of bone by now. "Golden lads and girls all must, as chimney-sweepers, come to dust."'

'Blimey!' said Larry, impressed at the vibrant delivery. 'So what would you find then?'

Oh, masonry, crockery, pots, burial urns, that sort of thing.'

'No treasure?' Larry was disappointed.

'Some. Jewellery. Coins. The occasional Roman miser's hoard, I daresay. In fact, there's an ideal opportunity to look – probably the only chance there ever will be – right now.'

'How's that, mister?'

The actor made a sweeping motion with his hand. 'Look around you and weep for the imperial splendour that is gone. Since the blitz, the City of London has lain mostly in ruins, waiting for the money to rebuild. They brought in Italian and German prisoners-of-war to clear the surface rubble and dump it in Essex – which seems an appropriate role for Essex. The last POWs have just been sent home and, until the rebuilding begins, Londinium lurks temptingly just beneath our feet.'

Chapter Two

After the film-crew had wrapped for the day and Larry had trudged home to the Buildings for his tea, he told his parents what the actor had said about the Romans. His father immediately told him the joke about the Italian tanks that had only one forward but five reverse gears and his mum said, 'You be careful of them actors. Bunch of nancy-boys.'

Like Larry himself, neither parent had any notion that the Romans had ever been in London. His mum said, 'You're as daft as your father. You want to wake your ideas up, sonny Jim.' Then wistfully to her spouse, whom she had just insulted but who was serenely rolling a fag with the aid of his Rizla machine, she added, "Do you remember, in the silent movie days, when I took my mum to the Canterbury to see *Ben Hur*? The silly old cow thought the thing was real. She really showed me up. She screamed so much I had to take her outside. She said that Ramon Novarro could have made a fallen woman of her any time he liked!'

The boy could see he had failed to impress with his newly acquired historical knowledge so he shut up. But his imagination had begun to stir.

The following Sunday, Larry crossed the Thames from the south side and took a stroll around the City. He had been raised in a townscape torn asunder by war and hardly noticed the ruins any more. Now, looking closer, the place was as the actor had described – acre upon acre of empty sites, with cellars laid bare, and shattered office blocks, warehouses, shops and churches. Here and there, the remnants of a building were identified by a small plaque erected by its pre-war occupants. The offered information somehow did more than the sight of the ruins themselves to make Larry sad. He was just beginning to be aware of the bustling life that had existed around him when he was a baby, and which had all been untimely snuffed out.

The war had been over for almost a year but you could still catch in your nostrils the whiff of damp, crumbling mortar and the acrid tang of sundered iron gas-pipes. Chickweed, London Pride and other anarchic plants were pushing up everywhere. Not that Larry could identify any of them. He was a child of the Smoke. He knew tomato plants, because his father attempted to cultivate them in window-boxes, and orange blossom, because his mum had her wedding headdress wrapped in tissue paper on top of the wardrobe, but that was the extent of Larry's horticultural knowledge.

The streets were deathly quiet. Apart from the presence of caretakers and the nightly detail of guardsmen at the Bank of England, in 1946 there were few surviving City buildings in residential occupation.

In Cornhill, Larry came across an intriguing sight. He leaned on a low brick wall and for a while watched a small group of young people, not much older than himself, working in what had once been the basement of an office block. They had marked off areas with lines of pegged string and were carefully cutting a series of narrow trenches across the former basement floor, scraping tentatively with bricklayers' trowels or using small stiff-bristle brushes to clear away surface earth.

A makeshift card nailed to a wooden post told passers-by that they were watching volunteers with the Roman and Medieval London Excavation Council at work.

Larry was disgusted. What a bunch of pussyfooting wankers. They'd never find a Roman at that rate. They needed a squib up 'em. He felt like shouting, 'Get some picks and shovels, you daft buggers, and put some elbow grease into it!' but thought better of it.

As if Larry's indignation had been carried on telepathic waves, a young man took up a mattock and began hacking at the packed earth. That's more like it, thought Larry, an idea forming.

Larry's imagination had been fired by the actor in a manner that none of his schoolteachers had ever achieved. He had gazed across the Thames and shivered. He'd had a similar thrill before the war when his mum took him to a pantomime at the Lyceum up West. One minute he'd been gazing at what he thought was a solid curtain and then something wonderful had happened. Coloured spotlights had been switched on and the curtain – gauze he could now see – became invisible. Beyond it lay a magical kingdom of castles and gingerbread houses with twinkling lamps. And now across the Thames another light had been switched on. He marvelled in his mind's eye at the charging chariots, the plumed helmets and dazzling armour of the centurions, the imperial columns of the palaces, the coliseo and towers of Ancient Rome he had seen at the pictures. Larry was entranced.

He had a long, hard think on the walk back home by way of London Bridge. A day later he joined the public library just round the corner from the Jolly Gardeners where his uncle Teddy had been playing in a darts' competition when the doodlebug hit and killed them all. The lady librarian was amused at this Cockney youth's inchoate thirst for Roman London and found him the right dusty books. Larry was particularly interested in anything with illustrations.

'Wonders'll never cease!' said his dad, when Larry arrived home with four formidable volumes. Larry grinned self-consciously and retreated to his bedroom, where the pictures of the Millwall football team in their baggy shorts gazed down from the walls.

'The little bugger's up to something,' said Mr Varnish darkly to his wife.

Which, in a way, was true.

Chapter Three

Larry soon learned the difference between Roman and Saxon coinage, what a wall faced with Kentish rag-stone suggested, that storage pots were called amphorae, what form an apsidal structure took or an hypocaust. He was particularly keen on the coins and the photographs of museum-quality necklaces, amulets and bangles.

Much later, after he went missing, everyone agreed – often reluctantly – that untutored Vanishing Larry Varnish had an uncanny feel for the historical landscape, a sensitivity that could not be taught in any university lecture hall. He simply had the same God-given gift that had led the Victorian hustler, Heinrich Schliemann, to the mound of earth that turned out to be the lost city of Troy.

Everyone also agreed that if Larry had received a decent formal education he would have ended up as a professor of archaeology instead of what he became – a mystery.

Larry continued to check out the advance of the small trenches across the Cornhill site and one Monday morning he set the alarm and was on the five-thirty a.m. tram, among the boisterous charladies who were on their way up to the City to scrub and polish the offices and marble halls that had survived the bombing. The chars were a randy lot. His torch and trowel almost fell out of his second-hand battle blouse when Big

Fran, a blonde heavyweight old enough to be his mother, took a handful of his crotch without a by-your-leave while the rest of the fruity cows in their knotted headscarves laughed and cheered. Vanishing Larry Varnish was a nice-looking boy with his shining eyes and a body that was becoming very manly, what with that crate-lifting and all.

It was still dark when Larry slipped over the wall in Cornhill and picked his way towards the trenches. If he expected to find treasure, he was disappointed. But his torch beam alighted upon four decorative coloured tiles that were still *in situ* and he did not hesitate to get his trowel under them and prise them out. Some pieces of terracotta pottery had been placed in a cardboard box and he took those, too. Then he went to a caff for his breakfast before moving on to a day's hard graft at the brewery.

That evening he heated the glue pot his dad used when he was repairing the family's shoes and, on his mum's kitchen table, tried in vain to make a whole pot of the pieces the way he had seen it illustrated in the books the lady librarian had found for him. Half the bits were missing.

The tiles seemed a better bet. He cleaned them off and took them to the Caledonian market. No one wanted to know.

'There's no call for 'em, son,' said a trader in cutlery.

'But they're genuine Roman,' said Larry. 'They're very historical.'

'Historical. Hysterical. Who cares?'

Finally, Larry found a trader, touched by the boy's fervent enthusiasm, who lent a sympathetic ear. 'Anything Roman, take it to McKintock's of Pimlico,' he advised.

Hamish McKintock's shop was an establishment in Lupus Street. 'Antiques' was painted in Tudor script on the fascia board, but peering through the grey grime of the windows all Larry could see was junk furniture piled high.

A bell tinkled as he stepped inside and a portly man in an alpaca jacket and polka-dot bow-tie emerged from a back room. Larry handed him the tiles for inspection. 'They're Roman, mister. Guaranteed.'

McKintock shot him a sideways glance. 'Hmm. Guaranteed, are they? By whom?'

'By me, sir.'

The dealer smiled indulgently. 'Now how can a young feller-me-lad like you guarantee any such thing?'

Larry hesitated. This was trickier than he had anticipated.

McKintock stood waiting, the tiles in his hands. His striped shirt had double cuffs and gold links.

Finally, Larry admitted, 'I dug 'em up on a bomb site.'

'Ah,' said McKintock. He added, 'You'd better come in here and tell me all about it.'

The man led Larry into his office and shut the door. On the cluttered desk was a black Bakelite telephone. Larry eyed it with alarm. 'Don't worry,' said McKintock, reading his expression, 'we'll keep the police out of this.'

Over the next twenty minutes, the dealer wormed the story of Larry's new-found obsession from him. 'I thought I'd try to make some money out of it,' he ended lamely. 'I thought I'd be a sort of mudlark – but on land instead of up to my arse in mud in the river.'

McKintock shook his head in an understanding way, but he said, 'Well, you haven't made much of a start. These tiles are practically worthless. I couldn't give you more than five shillings for the four.'

Larry was shocked. 'But they're Roman.' The words had become a mantra.

'Yes, they are,' said McKintock. 'But you have a great deal to learn. Not everything Roman is valuable. As it is, I'm being more than generous. There's a man at the Guildhall Museum who rejoices in the title of Inspector of Excavations. But he's known to one and all as Old Tuppenny. Do you know why that is?'

Larry shook his head. 'I haven't the faintest, mister. I've only just started in this game. Why's he called that?'

'Because,' said Mr McKintock, leaning forward and tapping Larry knowingly on the tip of his nose, 'he's a swindler. He tours the sites where builders' workmen are digging and he offers them a reward for anything of interest they might find. And that reward is always just two miserly copper pennies, which they take gratefully because most of them are bog Irish or illiterate or both and don't know any better.

'Look here,' he said, pulling down a volume from a sagging shelf. He flipped the pages and turned the book towards Larry.

'If you want to make a career out of plundering historic sites, you'd best get to know what to look for. These are engravings of the Roman emperors. I take it you have no Latin?'

'That's what they spoke, isn't it?'

'Yes. And wrote.'

McKintock looked into Larry's unlined and guileless face in silence for a while as if he were trying to come to a decision. Larry felt his bum begin to itch under the searching gaze and he shifted uneasily in his seat. Finally, the dealer said, 'Can I trust you, Larry? I mean *really* trust you?'

'Oh, absolutely, sir. You can rely on me.'

'Have you ever been in trouble with the police?'

'No, sir. I swear.'

'If you've lied, I'll find out . . .'

'On my mother's life,' said Larry.

'Right, then. I'm going to take a chance on you. I can see that you're a very shrewd boy. You've quite correctly recognized the potential for the discovery of relics that the bombing has created. The trouble is that the museums are greedy. They want it all for themselves. There's no room for the poor old private buyer – and he's the chap I'm here to help.'

Larry was watching Mr McKintock's hands. He'd never seen such well-shaped, clean nails, not even on a girl. Now one immaculate nail on a forefinger was tapping the cover of the book he had taken down. 'I'm going to lend this reference work to you. I want you to take it home and look after it. You'll find it a great help in identifying any coins you may dig up. You won't be able to read the Latin inscriptions but if you compare the heads stamped on the coins with the engraved heads in the book you should be able to identify the emperor in whose reign the coin was minted.'

Larry said, 'Oh, that's terrific. I can come to you then?'

'You'll come to me with everything,' said Mr McKintock, staring Larry straight in the eye in a fashion that again made him uneasy. 'You stay clear of Old Tuppenny. Besides coins I'm looking for figurines – little statuettes – glassware and jewellery. Roman women in London often wore gold fertility symbols in the shape of men's cocks round their necks. They have a modest value.' He turned a page. 'See, here's a photograph of one dug up in Colchester.'

Larry blushed.

'As for the coins, they'll most likely be from the reign of Nero – you know, the chap who is supposed to have fiddled while Rome burned, although I have my doubts – Trajan, Vespasian or Claudius. The Claudians won't be worth a dime a dozen. He reigned for thirteen years and the mints churned out coins by the million. The most valuable are the scarcest, the ones minted during the shortest reigns. For instance, look for an emperor named Galba. He managed to hold on to his title for only eight months.'

'Blimey,' said Larry. 'What was it – cancer?'

'Cold steel,' said Mr McKintock. 'Bumped off by his own soldiers because he forgot to pay their wages. Which reminds me . . .'

The dealer took out his wallet and extracted a big floppy white five-pound note. Larry had seen them before but never actually handled one. It was three times what he earned each week at Barclay Perkins.

Mr McKintock handed it to him. 'You can shut your mouth,' he said. 'It's quite genuine. Unlike the Emperor Servius Sulpicius Galba, I believe in paying my troops.'

Larry gulped. 'Wow! Thanks, mister.'

'But don't run away with the idea that those tiles are worth anything like a fiver. This is what you might call an encouragement. In an unofficial way you are working for me now. It's our secret. If you get caught you don't know me. Agreed?'

This dead world was too much for Larry Varnish to take in at one go but he had the books and he was a quick learner. Thus began his lone assault on the sixth of the City of London's acreage that had been made uninhabitable by the bombing.

He journeyed regularly across the river on the charladies' all-night trams and speedily built up a collection of hand tools that he cached in the hulk of a fire-blackened insurance company headquarters near the Mansion House.

At first, he followed the progress of the legitimate archaeological teams, even breaking into their locked huts to use their tools instead of going to the bother of collecting his own. But the archaeological programme was underfunded and understaffed and excruciatingly slow in uncovering whatever lay beneath the basement floors that now lay open to the skies. In his nocturnal raids Larry was not so inhibited by the rigours of science and scholarship. He dug in with a fury and filched more tiles and mosaic, some clay pipes and some damaged green-glass flasks that were actually medieval rather than Roman, and on one glorious occasion a handful of third-century coins of modest value.

Mr McKintock had instructed him in the do-it-yourself method of cleaning these. Larry took his mum's caustic soda from under the kitchen sink and made a solution in which to soak the more corroded of the ragged-edged coins. For those that were tarnished rather than corroded, he had a more surprising method. He took a bottle of his dad's Guinness and poured it on.

'I'll be blowed,' said dad. 'I hope you've got the price of another bottle.'

Larry had. McKintock was not paying him a fortune but the extra bunce certainly encouraged him to press on.

Inevitably, the archaeologists began wailing that their sites were being plundered by unknown vandals and the City of London police were alerted to keep a lookout. In the early hours of one March morning, the culprit was hacking vigorously at the earth alongside the remnants of a Roman wall near Cripplegate when the beam of a torch fell upon him.

'Oi! What are you doing there, you little fucker?' bellowed a uniformed policeman from the road up above. Larry grabbed his tools, yelled, 'Banzai!' and took it on the toes across the wasteland.

Over the following months the coppers became quite used to the shout of 'Banzai!' as Larry took flight. He hopped and leaped from one ruin to the next like a demented gazelle, racing nimbly along tottering walls and down alleyways of ankle-twisting loose stones. Early on, he arrived at a comforting truth: the coppers were reluctant to follow because it would bugger up their nice shiny boots. And the malefactor wasn't exactly a master criminal who was going to earn them a commissioner's commendation.

Nevertheless, the cops did not give up entirely. On another occasion he was ambushed as he came up on to the pavement. In their high helmets, City of London policemen towered seven feet and more, and cast monstrously elongated shadows under the street-lamps. That is what saved Larry. The tip of the lurking copper's shadow touched him and instantly alerted him to imminent danger. He began running for dear life and the cop managed only to catch him with one painful clout around the head from his rolled waterproof cape before Larry leaped a wall and made his escape. He shouted 'Banzai!' even though his lungs were screaming for mercy. He had become a lover of tradition.

Around this time the exploits of the young buccaneer became a topic of conversation among the cops and the Guildhall museum people. He was beginning to make his mark in their lives. Consequently, the beat coppers were ordered to keep a sharper eye out for the nimble rascal, and soon Larry realized that the authorized diggings were becoming too hot for his nefarious activities. He had to find sites of his own.

He turned to his hunters for the solution. He prowled the City of London Museum until he found a map of third century AD Roman London with an overlay showing the townscape of the 1940s. He made a rough sketch. None of the staff gave him a second glance. He appeared to be just another scruffy student.

With this as his guide, Larry began to select the most promising sites for a dig. And now that Schliemann-like instinct came fully into play. He chose only spots shielded from the road and where the concrete floors of the bombed buildings were already cracked. On his first burrowings into the ground he came up with a battered marble bust of what looked to him like a ringleted cherub. Mr McKintock gave him £15 for it. A fortune.

Stone urns and the occasional time-worn figurine followed, along with eroded spearheads, bone knives and a regular supply of coins, all correctly patinated. Larry couldn't believe how careless the Romans had been with their money. Mr McKintock told him, 'Most of it was hidden, not lost. The Romans in London had a great deal of trouble with the Christians and then the Saxons,' he explained.

'Wankers,' said Larry.

'Indeed,' said Mr McKintock, fishing in his wallet for Larry's whack.

Chapter Five

In 1952, when Larry was nineteen, the authorities were finally able to put a name to the young pest.

Larry, haring across the desolation, was still too fast for the puffing, heavy-booted coppers so one night they brought in the dogs who'd been on the way back to the kennels after chasing burglars in Temple Gardens. The mutts cornered him when he was on the way to his tool cache. 'It wasn't bleeding fair,' an aggrieved Larry said later.

One large Alsatian clamped his mouth around his sleeve and wrestled him to the ground. Larry was terrified. He had a desperate vision of the dog bounding away with his much-cherished forearm in his mouth. He wasn't to know that the animal had been trained not to bite hard unless you gave him trouble. 'Gerroff!' he screamed. 'Help! Get him off!'

The cops stood back watching and laughing until Larry wet himself. Having taught him a lesson they hauled him to his feet and off to the cells. They were chagrined to find that he was empty-handed. They thought of stitching him up by planting some tools about his person so that he could be charged with 'going equipped' for housebreaking but the dog-handler was a bit of a nark, keen for promotion and keeping his nose clean, so they decided not to risk it. Instead, Larry appeared before the Guildhall magistrates on the lesser charge of trespass.

A begrimed Larry mumbled a plea of guilty.

'Anything known?' asked the head beak.

'Nothing, your worship,' said the court inspector.

'Hmm,' mused the beak. 'I see Varnish was arrested at six in the morning on a bomb site. Was he sleeping rough?'

The arresting officer coughed, and said, 'No, sir. He fits the description of a man who is suspected of having vandalized various archaeological sites within the City boundaries.'

'Then why isn't he charged with these offences?'

The court inspector butted in again, 'Varnish has not admitted to this, your worship, and we feel there is insufficient evidence to proceed on such a charge.'

The beak wagged a finger at Larry in the dock. 'Whatever you're up to, young man, I suggest you cease forthwith. Your luck has just run out. Fined two pounds.' Eyeing Larry's sorry-looking clothes, he added, 'One month to pay.'

Thanks to Mr McKintock, Larry had the cash in his sky-rocket. He was in the clerk's office paying his fine when a burly sergeant accosted him and said, 'There's a gentleman wants to have a quiet word in your earhole.'

He took Larry by his chewed sleeve and marched him down the hall to a room where a skinny, greying man, in wire-rimmed glasses and a tweed jacket with leather patches, was waiting.

'Professor, meet Vanishing Larry Varnish,' said the sergeant, giving him the nickname that henceforth would be his. 'This is the little fucker – if you'll pardon the French – who thinks he's the Scarlet Pimpernel.'

Turning to Larry, the sergeant said, 'This is Professor Willoughby from the museum whose stuff you've been half-inching.'

'You don't know it was me,' said Larry sullenly.

'Don't you get lippy,' said the sergeant. 'Everyone knows it was you, you little turd. Anyway, why isn't a lad your age in the Army doing your national service? Doing your duty for your King and Country? Are you a deserter or something?'

'Had a spot on my lung,' said Larry.

'Crafty little bastard,' said the sergeant. 'I bet you got someone from the TB ward to take your medical for you.'

Professor Willoughby was looking anxious and a trifle nervous. He was unused to the daily rough and tumble of the lower orders. 'Er, thank you, Sergeant Rumble. Perhaps you would kindly leave me to have a word with our young friend.'

The sergeant stalked off muttering, 'Friend! I'd give him friend!'

The door banged closed and Larry looked warily at Professor Willoughby. He was reassured to see that the man appeared almost apologetic for having set the sergeant on to him. 'Why don't we go across the road to Lyon's teashop for a little chat?' said the professor hesitantly. 'That would be best.'

'Am I still under arrest?' asked Larry.

'Oh, dear me, no. This is, uh, entirely voluntary. This is by way of being a meeting on neutral ground, so to speak.'

He didn't seem such a bad old geezer. They dodged the traffic, and over tea and a Chelsea bun, the professor said, 'You know, Larry – may I call you Larry? – I'm the man in charge of the diggings. It is the most exciting work. This will be the last opportunity we shall ever have to create a complete picture of the way those men and women who came before us all those centuries ago lived their lives in this great city.'

He waved his hand in a wide sweep almost hitting a passing nippy in her frilly apron. 'Soon, all these acres – more than fifty of them – will be once again covered in buildings. Ground will be ripped up and the pile-drivers will drill deep. Modern building techniques will ensure that the secrets of the centuries that still exist at this very moment in the earth will be obliterated. The builders will complete the work that the German bombers started. We're in a race against time to avoid a whole layer of civilization being lost to us for ever.'

'With respect, guv'nor, it looks to me like you're already losing,' said Larry.

Professor Willoughby sighed. 'There you have it, young man. I need all the help I can get. I'm only one jump ahead of the bulldozers. This may come to you as a surprising suggestion, given your appearance in court this morning, but I was wondering if you would care to join us rather than carry on with that frightful night-time foraging and fleeing that the police say you have been doing for so long.'

'I was only fined for trespassing,' said Larry. 'They can't prove I nicked anything.'

'Quite so,' sighed the professor again. 'But wouldn't you feel happier going, er, straight and helping in a noble enterprise?'

'How much does this enterprise pay?' Larry wanted to know.

'Most of my young people are volunteers. My total budget is a pittance. It works out at less than three thousand pounds a year. The City fathers are, shall we say?, not exactly enthusiastic supporters of the project. They are more interested in getting the buildings flung up to provide a rateable income. They are businessmen looking for profits not amphorae.'

Larry was proud that, thanks to the library books, he didn't need to ask the meaning of amphorae. 'They'd change their tune if you dug up a bloody great pile of gold and silver stuff,' he said stoutly, trying to cheer up the old geezer. 'You'd get all the bunce you needed then.'

The professor smiled wanly. 'I don't wish to dampen your enthusiasm, young Larry, but I'm afraid that's just a romantic dream.'

Larry said, 'Most of your young people – the ones helping you – they're my age, aren't they? But they're still at school?'

'That is so. Most of them are studying at London University.'

'They're all well-off? Get pocket money from their dads?'

'A certain amount, I'm sure.'

'Well, I've been earning my own living since I was fourteen. I still get paid less than seven quid a week at the brewery and my mum collars three quid of that for my keep. I can't afford to be a volunteer. Volunteering is for people who eat even when they don't work.'

Professor Willoughby looked glum. 'Yes, I understand the problem.' He gazed into his teacup, thinking. 'Then perhaps you could promise me this. I'll give you a phone number where you can reach me. I think we have established that you have a special eye for promising sites – and an enthusiasm, no matter how undirected. I'm sure there are many places where you would like to dig but do not have the equipment. Why not ring me and tell me where they are? I'll give you a map with grid references. There'll be no need to use your name. This will be between us. You just say something like, "Julius Caesar here," and I'll know who it is.'

Larry started giggling. 'Blimey, you'll think it's some loony from Epsom calling.'

'Another thing. If you find anything that you know is important, I want Julius Caesar to ring, describe the object and give the exact location where it was found. When artefacts are simply filched from a site the all-important provenance is totally lost.'

Larry stopped giggling. That suggestion made him nervous.

'Don't worry,' said the professor. 'I won't like the idea that you've carted off something of historic value but at least I'll have a proper record for the survey.'

'What about the rozzers?'

'I'm afraid you're on your own as far as they're concerned. I have no power to stop them trying to catch you but I promise never to betray any confidence that Julius Caesar might entrust to me. Is it a deal?'

The professor watched Larry's face scrunch into thoughtful mode, the jaw rolling and the eyes narrowing into a kind of wince as he mulled over the ramifications.

'You'll be keeping faith with the Roman Empire that gave us our laws and much else,' encouraged Professor Willoughby. 'You'll personally be re-establishing a link with the spirit of the last Romans who ever trod the earth where we sit at this very moment.'

'Yeah, I like that,' breathed Larry. 'It's really historic, isn't it? It's like being one of them explorers in Africa who discovers a lost civilization.'

'Exactly so, Larry. I think you're a good boy at heart. You'll do it, then? Could you manage another bun?'

Thus began the strange symbiosis between the hard-pressed archaeologist and the Cockney street-raker. Vanishing Larry Varnish nobly denied himself any further plundering of Professor Willoughby's digs and Julius Caesar became a regular caller.

Over the crackling line of a telephone system that still had not entirely recovered from its wartime pounding, Larry would direct the archaeology teams to where, as he put it, 'I've got a feeling in me water you'll win a coconut,' and dutifully list his own finds.

Professor Willoughby would often sigh over these, and on one occasion sighed so hard that Larry took pity on him. 'I tell you what, guv'nor, if you went along tomorrow and walked fifty paces east of your dig in Eastcheap, at the foot of that wall where the rusty gas meter's still hanging, you might find a bit of sacking wrapped round your birthday present.'

Professor Willoughby's birthday was months away but he was there at first light. Trembling fingers delicately pulled the sacking aside to reveal a first-century oil lamp in almost perfect condition, with Pan-figures sweetly gambolling in the clay surface. He could have cried for joy.

Larry did not mention this giveaway to Mr McKintock nor did he mention a bronze coin he uncovered in a pile of charred debris in Botolph Lane. It was in superb condition, with traces of a silver coating still adhering to the base metal, and had almost certainly been salvaged in centuries gone by and kept as a curio by someone in the seventeenth century. The debris originated not in the blitz but in the Great Fire of London.

Julius Caesar said to Professor Willoughby, 'Guv'nor, I've got a bit of a puzzle here. I've found this coin with not one but three faces on it. Ring a bell?'

'Ah, is the wording legible, Almighty Caesar?'

'Clear as anything.'

Professor Willoughby said, 'Let me make a guess. Does it say "Carausius et fratres sui"?' He spelt it out, letter by letter.

'Cor, spot on,' said Julius Caesar. 'That's really impressive.'

'The three faces belong to the emperors Carausius, Diocletian and Maximian. A splendid find. The words mean, Carausius and his brothers, or friends.'

Julius Caesar gave him the map grid reference in Botolph Lane, and Professor Willoughby said, 'It's third century. Carausius was a bad lot. He was a soldier who usurped the emperor's throne in Britain and came to a sticky end.'

'From what you tell me, guv'nor, that's how most of 'em ended up. Them Romans didn't fuck about with probation and time off for good behaviour, did they?'

'There is much evidence to support what you say,' said the professor gravely. Despite the thieving, he was really warming to Larry and his chirpiness.

Chapter Six

By 1953, Vanishing Larry Varnish was a legend. Even the City of London coppers had to laugh at their own clumsy attempts to apprehend him. The dry-as-dust concerns of archaeology did not fire their blood.

By now it had become something of a bloodsport to winkle out Larry from whichever burrow he was plundering and watch him flee over the rubble, arms windmilling, leaving the cry of 'Banzai!' floating on the sooty air. Now that they knew his identity, they could have primed the Met to raid his home in Southwark but the effort seemed out of proportion to the likelihood that Larry would have been so foolish as to keep incriminating objects on the premises.

In fact, they would have found just one arrest-worthy item –

the three-head Emperor Carausius coin that Larry had made his personal talisman. To disguise its origins, he got his dad to solder a tiny eyelet to the edge and hook it on to the ribbon of his Western Desert campaign medal. Larry wore it almost daily on his lapel. 'Here, you daft git, I'll need that back on Armistice Day,' said Dad, who was not otherwise bothered at this ill-usage.

On the charladies' special – buses since the old rattling trams had been abolished – Big Fran and the girls had long since tired of teasing and molesting Larry. Early one morning, as the bus made its way along the Borough High Street, Big Fran eyed Larry speculatively and said, 'Have you got a girlfriend yet?'

For a moment Larry nervously supposed she was nominating herself. 'No one special,' he said guardedly. He was, in fact, still a virgin although burning splints under his black and broken fingernails would not have dragged this from him.

'I want you to meet my girl, Lorraine,' said Big Fran. 'You'll like her. She's just eighteen and working at the Prudential. All the boys are after her but there's not one of them as nice-looking as you.'

'A right little Tyrone Power,' cackled one of the girls.

Larry wanted to say, 'Julius Caesar, please,' but the old bag wouldn't have got the joke.

Larry was invited to Sunday tea at Big Fran's tenement flat up the road from the Borough tube station. There was no husband – he had been killed at Anzio – but there was Lorraine, five foot three of bosomy, fair-haired determination and loveliness.

After tea she said there was an Esther Williams' movie she was dying to see. Larry took the hint. And off they went – no Bunking In now that he was grown-up – to see *Easy To Love*, which bored him silly but the title was clearly meant as the second hint of the day.

Four months later he and Lorraine were married at St Joseph's, the Catholic Church in Redcross Way. She had three bridesmaids and a pageboy, and in the unavoidable absence of the bride's father Larry's dad had been obliged to contribute towards the wedding.

The newly-weds moved in with Big Fran. No one thought it polite to recall that on several witnessed occasions, in the recent past in a public place, the mother-in-law, no matter how impishly intended, had been decidedly over-familiar with the bridegroom's nether regions.

Lorraine, brisk and purposeful with a well-paid clerical job, was just what Larry the dreamer needed to give his rackety life some ballast. Proudly he showed her his three-emperor 'medal' and she listened in amazement to the tales of his adventures in the ruins of the City and of his love affair with the Romans.

She learned all about his fleeting appearance in *Hue and Cry*, about Old Tuppenny, Professor Willoughby and Mr McKintock. But Larry thought he'd best save until much later an account of the one time he had been apprehended when he had earned a police record.

Before agreeing to start a family, Lorraine resolved to shape up her lovable dope of a husband. She told him, 'That McKintock's almost certainly been chiselling you. And how much longer do you think you can carry on playing Vanishing Larry Varnish? Haven't you noticed? The rebuilding's begun – and about time too. In a couple of years all those plots will be smothered in concrete. Then there'll be no more Roman knick-knacks and no more money, apart from your brewery wages.'

Lorraine had a plan: 'You go to McKintock and you tell him he's got to take you on full-time. You want proper wages. No more handouts from his petty cash box.'

'Why should he do that? I've already got a proper job.'

'No, you haven't. Stuff the brewery. All that's doing is sending you home every night with beer on your breath. Think about it. The building contractors are moving into most of those bomb sites now. With their machinery, they'll be turning up all sorts of stuff that, on your own, you could never get at in a month of Sundays. You can give up going with Mum on the early-morning buses. You'll do better if you become Old Tuppenny's rival. You tour the sites every day and make friends with the workmen. With your Mr McKintock's backing, you'll be able to offer them a sight more than Old Tuppenny for anything they dig out. Then later, when the City's rebuilt and there's no more stuff to be had from that quarter, McKintock can keep you on as his assistant in his shop. Christ knows, it sounds to me as if he's made enough out of you already. He should fall over himself to take you on.'

Lorraine had read the future with precision. Mr McKintock took a week to mull over Larry's hesitant proposal – which he deduced correctly had been instigated by the spunky little wife – and agreed.

Even when the Roman diggings ran out, Larry would still be a willing worker, now surprisingly knowledgeable on antiquities – and learning more all the time. Mr McKintock, even with his preoccupation with acquiring a personal fortune, had taken to him. There was a sort of flawed purity about the lad. Mr McKintock could never quite get out of his head the thought that Larry should be singing in a choir.

Chapter Seven

Once Larry Varnish began his daily swing around the City sites, Old Tuppenny was out of business. He stood no chance in competition with Mr McKintock's money and Larry's sheer likeability. Even the site foremen, who should have chased him away, tolerated his presence (and sometimes sold him finds of their own). And Julius Caesar was still able to telephone Professor Willoughby occasionally with information for his survey.

In the following year Larry was overjoyed for the professor when his colleagues in archaeology, who'd been digging patiently in Walbrook for three years, first uncovered a semi-circular structure and then the entire outline of a late-second-century temple where Roman soldiers had once worshipped Mithras, the god of light and strength.

For a rare moment, the fusty subject of archaeology was news for the popular press and queues formed to view the revealed wonders. Meanwhile, the builders contracted to move on to the site were tearing their hair out at the enforced delay in their plans and concocting a scheme to shift the whole caboodle to be reassembled on a site more convenient for public exhibition.

Highly excited, Larry dragged Lorraine along. She kept muttering, 'For Gawd's sake, calm down. You'd think we was off to meet the Queen.'

They took their turn in the line and she gazed down into the pit at the uncovered foundations of the Mithraeum. Her cornflower blue eyes opened wide and she said, 'I don't believe it. You've dragged me all this way to look at a pile of bloody stones. You know, there are times when I think your dad's right: you're doo-lally.'

'No, no,' said Larry, jumping up and down. 'It's wonderful. It's historical. Just think! Romans once knelt on this spot and worshipped their pagan god.'

Lorraine, a stalwart Catholic girl, looked up sharply. 'Do you mean to say they weren't Christians?'

'Well, they were later on, but not when this temple was built.'

'So this is where they made their human sacrifices, is it? Disgusting, I call it!'

'No, Lorraine, you've got it all wrong. No humans. They'd only offer up animals – pigs, sheep, chickens, that sort of thing.'

'Oh, so that's all right, is it? Torturing dumb animals? Your Romans sound like a bunch of Nazis to me.' His wife turned her back on the revealed wonders and marched away, her new Dolcis shoes making an ill-tempered clackety-clack over the rough paving.

Larry could see that his vision was not shared. He accepted this with fortitude. His mates were the same. Anyone who missed a Millwall home game for an afternoon at the poxy reference library in the Walworth Road ought to see a doctor.

He took Lorraine to the teashop where he had gone with Professor Willoughby but she wasn't to be mollified with sweet tea and a pork pie. Across the tiny table, she shook her neat head and said softly, 'They're just heaps of useless old stones, Larry. You're wasting your life.'

Larry wanted to explain. He looked at her sadly but kept silent. If only he had the words, like Professor Willoughby and that actor geezer . . .

Over the following weeks Larry followed the Mithras story in his evening paper. Building work on the site had come to a halt – at a cost to the office-block developers of half a million pounds, so it was rumoured – until the decision was taken to lift out the remains of the temple and re-site them in Queen Victoria Street where they would not impede any further the advance of Mammon.

One of Larry's new contacts was a site foreman named Denny Fling, a Dublin man who'd actually volunteered for service with the British Army during the war and had become a regimental sergeant-major nicknamed by the rude soldiery RSM Fling, the Bullshit King.

Fling had worked on several City rebuilding projects and had already done one modest deal with Larry for what turned out to be five Vespasian coins and a post-Roman fuming pot in fair condition. He was now overseeing a new site clearance and office construction in Bishopsgate. In the seclusion of the site hut, Denny lit the Primus and brewed tea strong enough to dissolve the spoon. He said, 'You can't stay long. I'm workin' for a coupla them time-is-money fookers. They'd skin a turd for tuppence. If they poke their heads through the door, you pretend to be lookin' for work.'

Larry sipped his tea and said, 'Jesus, Denny, give us some more milk.'

'Ach, you fooking Cockneys. Gave me nothing but trouble in the Army. Always dodgin' the column.'

'That's what Cockneys are for,' said Larry comfortably, gazing round at the wooden walls that were already covered in work schedules, safety regs and a pin-up of Diana Dors in an angora sweater. He mentally compared the size of Miss Dors's bristols with Lorraine's – his wife faring quite favourably – and passed on. Again his eyes came to rest. 'What's that drawing?'

'Something the guv'nors stuck up – droppin' us all a hint, I suppose. You'll find copies have gone up on sites all over the City. Since that Mithras find, all the contractors have been scared shitless that we'll stumble across another historical heap of stones and fook up their on-time bonuses or bring the penalty clauses for late delivery of the building down on their heads.'

Curious, Larry carried his steaming mug over to the wall. The drawing was a David Langdon cartoon reproduced from *Punch* of 6 October, 1954. Larry had never heard of the humour magazine that featured widely in dentists' waiting rooms. When he had had a toothache once he had gone to the Guy's Hospital dental school where the luxury of free magazines was not indulged.

Langdon's cartoon showed a group of labourers gathering on a City building site where work was about to begin. Their foreman was saying, 'Start about here and the first man to find a Roman temple gets docked a quid.'

'It's historical. They should be proud to find such a thing. Rotten sods,' said Larry.

He was still indignant when next he telephoned Professor Willoughby. 'It's up on every contractor's noticeboard in the City, guv'nor,' said Julius Caesar, echoing Denny Fling. 'Isn't there a law against pulling that sort of stroke? Incitement, or something?'

'I very much doubt it, Caesar. I fear our enthusiasm – yours and mine – for the Roman world of another time is a subject only for comedians' jokes and the wretched films of Mr Cecil B. De Mille,' mourned Professor Willoughby.

'Fuck 'em,' said Caesar.

'Quite so.'

Vanishing Larry Varnish's defiant cry was the last sound Professor Willoughby ever heard the Cockney utter. Later, he was destined to recall the words for the police after he spotted the paragraph in the London *Evening Standard* and telephoned them.

Chapter Eight

Larry was not on the telephone and Mr McKintock had refused to let him distribute the telephone number of the Pimlico shop to his contacts. 'I must retain my deniability,' said the dealer. 'I can't be linked to those pilferers. You'll have to think of something else.'

Reluctantly, Lorraine had allowed her young husband to distribute among his bomb-site coolies her extension number at the Prudential headquarters in High Holborn. 'You'll get me the sack,' she said.

'No, I won't. I promise. They're all blokes who use nicknames – like when my dad puts a bet on with our street bookie. If any of them ever rings, he'll give a nickname and ask for me to get in touch. You'll only be on the blower for a matter of seconds.'

The call that came from the Bullshit King was as straightforward as Larry had promised. When Larry arrived in Bishopsgate, he skirted the area warily to make sure the bosses weren't on site. Denny Fling's team were pickaxing old walls still standing to a height of twelve feet and a mechanical scoop was loading the rubble into the metal-sided trucks. Six men were salvaging old bricks, there being a severe shortage at the time.

Denny spotted Larry standing on the periphery and gave a jerk of his head, indicating the hut. Inside, Denny produced eight corroded coins.

'That's your second lot from this site,' mused Larry. 'Did you get them from the same spot?'

'Sure,' said Denny. 'They're coming out of loose soil in a pit. We've cleared out the top rubble but we're still using shovels because we can't get the digger down there until we clear those walls away.'

Larry felt his Schliemann antennae stirring. 'Can you give us a look?'

'Don't be so gormless. There's a couple of the architect's pen-pushers on the site today and the poxy bosses could show up. Give me some money for the coins and then you'd better piss off before they find you.'

Larry handed over one of Mr McKintock's white fivers, pretty certain there wasn't going to be any ultimate profit in the transaction. But Mr McKintock could afford a bummer every now and then, and Denny was worth encouraging.

But what monopolized Larry Varnish's thoughts as he scampered away was not his employer's impending disappointment but 'the feeling in his water' that the Bishopsgate site might be the Troy of his dreams.

Lorraine's mum was still catching that charladies' pre-dawn special up to the City. 'Give us a call when you get up?' asked Larry, who hadn't been on a raid for many months.

Both women wanted to know what was going on. 'It's a feeling I've got – a feeling I might be on to something a bit tasty,' said Larry, and refused to elaborate.

On the early bus, it was Lorraine's mum who now took the teasing. 'Can't take liberties with him now he's married your Lorraine, can you, Fran?' screeched one female bruiser.

'I can't see our Fran letting a little thing like that stop her,' yelled another, along the length of the bottom deck.

'I hear it's not such a little thing,' added a third, to a chorus of ooohs as all the laughing women swivelled to stare openly at Larry's fly-buttons. He snapped his knees together and they all howled.

Larry grinned and took the joshing. It was his mother-in-law's turn to blush. 'Dirty old cows!' he shouted, as he jumped off the platform at Gracechurch Street and headed directly for Bishopsgate. He'd have to use the tools on the site. He assumed his own cache had long since been either discovered or stolen.

Larry stood for a while in shadows to make sure there were no busybodies about. Then he took a running jump at the wooden hoarding fronting the street and soared over. He landed with a thump on rubble that was piled and awaiting removal.

He headed directly for the equipment hut and wrenched the padlock, hasp and screws from the woodwork with the jemmy he had been carrying up his sleeve. He selected a pick and shovel, carefully quartered the ground and began searching for the pit Denny Fling had mentioned. He tried to use his torch as little as possible while he was at street level and as a consequence found the pit by falling into it. He gave a sharp yelp as he rolled to the bottom, where his progress was abruptly halted by a shallow wall only the depth of two bricks.

The purloined tools had landed on top of him. He shook them off before remembering the need to avoid clatter in the silence of the pre-dawn when only the occasional newspaper van and beat bobby passed on the street above.

Larry took the pick and shovel to the far end of the depression. He calculated that the pit was more than fifty feet in length and thirty feet wide. He crouched and directed the beam of his torch slowly over the ground at a height of a foot or less. He began trembling so violently that he had to stop for a minute, catch his breath and clear his eyes, which had begun to water in his rising excitement.

To confirm his first impressions, he repeated his action with the torch, the low light throwing into relief every bump over which it crawled. 'Banzai!' he breathed. He could detect two rows of small mounds in regular alignment. He walked between them, arbitrarily chose a spot in the impacted earth and plunged in the spade. Thirty minutes later and two feet down, the shovel's tip screeched against something hard. Larry stooped and, with his bare hands, clawed aside the grit and earth. He wiped his palms down his trousers and shone the trembling torch. 'Banzai!' he breathed again. The brickwork flooring still shone pinkly after sixteen centuries.

Larry's stomach churned and his head sang. He swiftly refilled the hole and tamped down the earth. Thanks to his library books and his examination of the layout of the Mitbras temple, he knew exactly what to look for. He moved over to one of the low-lying mounds in regular alignment and frenziedly cleared the top clay with the side of the shovel until he reached stonework. He ended up staring at the remains of the base of a stone column that had once supported a wooden roof.

His suspicions confirmed, he raced back to the end and studied the wall of earth and rubble that confronted him. He noted that it ran in virtually a straight line from side to side. 'Balls! Wrong end,' he muttered and trotted the fifty feet to the other end, which appeared to bow outward. 'It's a fucking apse!' he whispered. 'I'd bet money on it. Old Willoughby's going to have a baby when I tell him.'

He began to excavate. He actually gagged with the tension when a sunken block of masonry began to reveal the top edges of lettering carved so deeply into the stonework that even the natural erosions of time had failed to obliterate them.

He straightened up for a moment to wipe his dripping brow and stopped abruptly. He realized suddenly that he was no longer having to peer through the gloom or use the torch. In his obsessive covering of the site he had allowed the dawn to arrive unnoted. 'Blimey!' he swore, gazing up at the lightening sky. He had to get out fast. He threw earth back over the stone, hurriedly cleaned off the pick and shovel, scraping them with the sole of his boot, and returned them to the hut. There was nothing he could do about the dangling padlock.

Cautiously, Vanishing Larry hauled himself up the hoarding to eye level and scanned the street. He had to wait ten minutes before the pavements were clear and he could vault over and return to the twentieth century.

Chapter Nine

Lorraine had never seen him so agitated. 'For Gawd's sake, sit down. You're making me dizzy,' she complained. But Larry Varnish continued to dance around her mum's living room waving his arms above his head and singing, 'I'm the history man, the mystery man, try and catch me, if you can.'

He stopped only when his waving arms came near to sweeping Big Fran's Rock of Ages and its covering glass dome off the mantelpiece.

He checked in with Mr McKintock and handed over Denny

Fling's coins. They were received, as expected, with a marked lack of enthusiasm and Larry went off to scour Pimlico for an art shop. He needed some essential supplies before his next foray into Denny's domain. He did not tell Mr McKintock of his find. Time for that when he had confirmation of his great discovery.

Back home, Larry stripped to his white vest and crawled into bed. It was six p.m. 'Give us a shout at eleven,' he told Lorraine and Fran. 'I'll be out tonight.'

Big Fran was not happy, 'Are you going out burgling, Larry Varnish? Is that what those early-morning bus rides have really been about? 'Cos if they were you'll break my Lorraine's heart – which'll be nothing to what I'll do to you.'

'No, no. Nothing like that, Fran. It's archaeology not burglary. It's historical,' said Larry, stepping back a pace. He'd never understood why Fran was half as big again as her daughter. 'I think I've made a discovery – but I have to make sure.'

A little after midnight, Larry threw an ex-Army battlepack, loaded with his gear, over the hoarding and swiftly followed. The padlock hasp on the tool hut had been repaired but Larry wrenched it off once again and helped himself to the tools he needed.

He headed directly for the stone block where he had glimpsed chiselled wording before he'd had to rebury his find and depart. Now he toiled by starlight, freeing the stone facing from the clay and using a yard broom from the hut to brush it clean in a manner so ruthless that trained archaeologists would have cried out in anguish.

He used his fingers to scour out the letters. He trained the torch beam over them. They were Latin, all right, but they might just as well have been double Dutch as far as Larry was concerned. Anyway, Professor Willoughby would be able to tell him what they said.

Larry rummaged in his pack and fished out a large sheet of tracing paper. He used carpet tape to attach it section-by-section to the block, making sure it lay flat against the stone facing and the lettering. Then with care, in contrast to his digging ferocity, he took a soft pencil and made a complete tracing of the Roman lettering.

He stopped to drink a cup of hot tea from the vacuum flask that Lorraine had filled for him, and then he turned to the semi-circular shape visible in the earth. His body thrummed with electricity. He felt energized with the strength of ten men.

For the next two hours he needed every ounce of it. At some time in previous centuries some heavy masonry had fallen in upon the surrounding area and clearing enough of it to one side so that he might examine what was creating the semi-circular impression in the earth took him dangerously close to a new dawn.

Finally, he was confronted by a square stone slab set flat against identifiably Roman brickwork. It would not budge, not even when Larry managed to get the tongue of the pickaxe between slab and brick and levered. The only result was that the narrow brick began to crumble.

So Larry went like a Fury, hacking away at the tenacious clay to undermine the slab. He came out of the hole sweat-drenched and once again applied leverage. He'd remembered something from the books. The last of the Romans in Britain had buried their treasures to prevent them being looted by the marauding Saxons. And this upright slab gave every appearance of having been put in place to conceal . . . what? Still it would not budge. 'Fuck!' said Larry. Panting, he hacked at the mortar around the slab's edges. It was slow work and his arms ached from wielding the pickaxe. He raced back to the hut to find chisels, a club hammer and an old sack to muffle the noise.

He shot a desperate glance at the sky. He couldn't go on much longer. It was Saturday morning and Denny's gang would be arriving for the usual half-day shift before they all disappeared to the pubs and the football terraces.

He stood, cursing the slab. 'Move, you bastard, move!' And, once again, inveigled the pick head between wall and stone. This time the thing tilted with a small groan as the London clay surrendered a fraction of its centuries-long grip. The gap was now two inches at the top and Larry was able to insert the entire head of the pick and haul on the handle, employing his total bodyweight. The slab sullenly conceded another six inches – enough for Larry to be able to insert the torch and gaze down into the ruptured darkness.

He whimpered. Caught square in his beam was a rectangular niche in the Roman wall and standing in that niche was a perfectly preserved bronze figurine some fifteen inches high, wearing a funny little hat.

Vanishing Larry Varnish knew with unshakeable certainty that he had found his Troy – the remains of a second pagan temple within the ancient walls of the City of London. Dug out, the semi-circular mound would prove to be the apse and the lettered stone block the altar. The crusted figure, which his torch now made radiant, was the graven image of a god those long-ago warriors had worshipped.

Larry reached in. If it was fixed to the ledge in the recess he was fucked. He had to get off the site within the next twenty minutes. The first of Denny's gang would be arriving at seven.

He strained to reach down, tongue between his lips, his chin grazing the top edge of the slab, his eyes turned upward at the lightening sky. He grunted. He twiddled his fingers spider-fashion, searching blindly, fingertips waggling and seeking gentle contact with the hat and head. He strained further, his chin pressing hard into the tilted slab so that it made a red mark, but he couldn't manage any further advance towards the object in its niche. Still swearing, he tore off his old battle blouse and shirt and plunged his naked arm back into the slot. He could have wept. His fingers still failed to reach their goal.

Larry came out of his struggle with a start. Christ! Denny's blokes would be unlocking the access gates at any moment. He put his shoulder against the sloping slab and shoved it back into the upright position against the wall from which he had so painfully prised it. He raced across the site and threw the borrowed tools back into the hut – no time to clean them – and clambered over the wall, almost falling on two middle-aged male pedestrians.

'Sorry,' he mumbled, clutching his precious pack to his chest and tottering for a second. 'I had to take a leak.' He took to his heels before they could reply and jumped on a number 35 bus at the traffic lights.

Chapter Ten

Larry excitedly described the figurine with the homely little hat that had been almost within his grasp. 'It sounds quite pretty, I'll give you that,' conceded Lorraine. 'What's it made of?'

'It's a bit dirty. So would you be if you'd been standing around like a lemon for the past couple of thousand years. But I'm sure it's bronze,' said Larry.

'When you get it home I'll run it under the tap.'

Larry almost howled. 'Lorraine, don't ever suggest a thing like that. You can flick your feather duster over it. And that's all. You have to leave the crap on this kind of stuff. It's called the patina. McKintock'd go spare if you touched it.'

'All the same, I bet it'd look nicer after a rub with a spot of Brasso. Those bleeding arty-crafty collectors must have dirt trailing all over their houses,' sniffed Lorraine.

She wanted to know how much the little god would be worth.

'I'll tell Mr McKintock that I paid twenty quid for it. But it's not the money I'm interested in. I'm going back to dig it out and get another look at the rest of the site. You know that Mithras thing I took you to see? Well, I think I've found something like it. I'm going to ring Professor Willoughby on Monday.'

'You be careful,' warned Lorraine. 'You know you're not supposed to be in those places. You'll get yourself into trouble.'

'Nah,' said Larry. 'They'll be so bloody grateful for what I've found that they'll forget all about that. Though poor old Willoughby will be sighing a lot more than usual when I tell him about the little feller who's gone missing from his perch.'

Larry pulled out his tracings and unfolded them. 'This is the proof of my discovery. I took those letters off a bloody great stone that I think was the altar. It's Latin, all right. I only wish I could read what it says.'

He stowed the sheets in the bottom of a chest of drawers.

'I've got to go out,' he said. 'I need some new batteries for this torch and a couple of car jacks.'

Larry Varnish repeated his performance of the previous day. He had his evening kip while Lorraine sulked because she'd wanted him to put off his site raid to take her Saturday dancing at the Streatham Locarno. 'If your bleeding statue's been there since the year dot, it wouldn't make much difference if it stayed there one night longer,' she whined. But the excitement of discovery had Larry tightly in its grip. The little god was calling him and could not be denied.

Big Fran had just finished giving Lorraine a home perm when Larry emerged from the bedroom yawning, scratching and wrinkling his nose at the chemical stench of the setting lotion. The women weren't talking to him.

Wordlessly, Lorraine made up his flask of tea and pursed her lips in rigid disfavour when he attempted to kiss her before slipping away into the balmy early spring night.

Memory of that brief moment of coldness towards her husband was to torture Lorraine for many years to come and often send her into spasms of body-shuddering sobs. 'If only I'd known . . .' she'd whisper futilely. But, then, Vanishing Larry Varnish didn't know either.

Denny Fling's Saturday-morning shift had not bothered to repair the lock a second time. Perhaps they've realized nothing's been nicked and think some tramp's using the hut as a dosshouse, thought Larry.

He helped himself to the tools he needed and once again confronted the slab. This time, though, he had two borrowed car jacks to insert into the gap. He jammed them between slab and wall and began working their ratchets. Painfully, the dark mouth began to widen, like that of a terrified patient with the dentist poised above. Larry hacked furiously at the packed clay at the base of the slab to speed up the process.

Twice he plunged his bare arm into the gap before he made first contact. Finally, gloriously, he felt something at his fingertips. 'Banzai!' he breathed, as his arm slid down and his fingers wrapped firmly around the head of the figurine. He knew immediately the statue was not fixed in place. It rocked to his touch.

Slowly he drew the god out of the niche and upward, taking infinite care not to scrape him against the slab that had protected him since, perhaps, the time of Christ. Larry had goosebumps.

He drew the figure into the light and a long, shuddering 'Ohhh!' escaped involuntarily from his dust-filmed lips. Tenderly, he cradled the statue in his arms the way a young father cradles his new-born baby. And, like a young father, Larry found himself weeping. Perhaps Lorraine, his mates and his mum and dad would understand him now. He'd done something important. He wasn't just playing silly buggers, as his dad had complained. He'd had a dream come true, just like people in the pictures.

He completed his investigation of the slab, satisfying himself it concealed no further treasures. Then he dug vigorously into the clay until he hit a sleeper wall that must have once acted as foundation for the columns supporting the roof. In sinking trial holes to establish the location of the temple aisles and arches, Larry sifted out a further selection of badly eroded coins and slipped them into his trouser pocket. But there was nothing else to match the grandeur of the little god.

No matter. He felt he was working for Professor Willoughby now and not Mr McKintock. This was historical, and Larry felt fulfilled.

He was just congratulating himself on discovering what looked like the site of the temple's own well when a small scattering of loose earth slithered down the bank and ended up at his feet.

He looked up to see a dark figure silhouetted against the dawn sky. 'Blimey!' he gasped, and turned to run. But a second figure was already down in the pit, blocking his exit.

'So you're the bastard who's been breaking in,' said the figure sharing the pit with him. 'What do you think you're doing?'

The figure took two steps towards him. The man was

carrying a brickie's hod cross-wise in front of him, just like Little John about to knock Errol Flynn off the log in the Robin Hood film.

Larry twisted wildly looking for an escape route but they had him blocked off. For a moment he thought they must be plain-clothes policemen. 'There's no need for violence,' he squeaked.

'Isn't there?' said the one in the pit, taking a step nearer. And Larry was no longer so sure.

The one up top spoke for the first time. 'You're well out of order. You're that fucking Vanishing Larry Varnish, aren't you? We've heard all about you, you little prick.'

'Look,' Larry lied desperately, 'I haven't nicked anything. In fact, I've done you a big favour. You could be famous. You could be in all the papers next week.'

'What the fuck are you talking about?' said the one up top. He now had Larry blinking in a powerful torch beam, the picture of a man getting the third degree in a James Cagney film.

Larry shaded his eyes to try to get a look at his captors. They were in shadows. 'I've found a Roman temple all on my own. We're standing in it. It's a wonderful thing. It's historical,' he shouted up.

'The fuck it is.'

'No, really. I'm not kidding. Let me show you. There's even a little statue. I bet that when we get Professor Willoughby from the City archaeological team down here tomorrow, he'll tell you exactly the same.'

'The hell he will,' said the man with the hod, who was now only five paces from him. 'This site's being prepared for a new building. We're not going to lose our bonuses because a heap of stones stops work while a mob of fucking eggheads come round drooling over them and tossing off. The moment we get the bulldozer down here, this lot gets cleared away.'

'*What?*' An outraged Larry forgot his fear of the two strangers. 'You can't do that! The Romans once stood here. Centurions in their helmets and armour with their chariots waiting outside. It's – it's – it'll be like destroying St Paul's Cathedral.'

'You're talking through your arse. What would a little toerag like you know about such things? You're just a thief. They ought to lock you away for a couple of years. That'd knock the bounce out of you.' The too-good-for-the-likes-of-you sneer in the hod-man's voice was like a goad in Larry's flank.

'I've been learning a lot,' said Larry. 'Reading books and stuff. I know what I'm talking about.'

From up above, the man cut in, 'Never mind the fucking testimonials. What are we going to do with him?'

Larry drew back defensively. He had only his lightweight torch in his hand. The little god was lying wrapped in a piece of sacking at his feet. The man above him said, 'We should, by rights, take you by the scruff of your dirty neck and drag you along to the nick. But if you promise to keep your mouth shut about all this Roman crap we might be inclined to let you go.'

The other man said, 'Bollocks. The little bastard'll never keep his word. He could ruin us.'

'Look, mister,' said Larry, 'I don't want to ruin anybody but you've got to see we have to do the right thing here.' He repeated his mantra. 'It's historical.'

And with that Larry took his chance. He ran at the man with the hod, feinted left and swerved to the right, succeeding in outflanking him, but was momentarily impeded by the protruding hod's long handle.

Vanishing Larry Varnish made a leap for the centre of the nave of his beloved temple and could hear the man up above shouting, 'Get the bastard! Stop him!'

Larry shouted, 'Banz—' But something happened before the cry could finish leaving his throat. The temple foundations spun wildly as if they had been mounted on a turntable and his torso appeared to get ahead of his madly pumping legs.

Unaccountably, his face plunged into the soft ground and crumbs of earth filled his mouth, nose and eyes. What a bloody silly thing to do, he thought as the light went out.

Chapter Eleven

Lorraine and Big Fran were ready in their Sunday best for morning Mass and still Larry had not come whistling up the stone stairway. 'That husband of yours is turning into a bloody idiot,' said Fran. 'He'll be late for his own funeral.'

Later, Big Fran could have washed her mouth out with carbolic soap for saying that.

The two women gave up waiting for the man of the house, cleared away the breakfast things, left Larry a note and went off to church. The note was still on the kitchen table when they returned. The cooking of the Sunday roast was immediately forgotten.

'I don't like it,' said Lorraine.

'Neither do I,' said her mother. 'Could he have bumped into some mates and gone to the Skinners for a pint?'

'Without letting me know? He's not like that, Mum.'

Fran had to agree. Larry was quite gentlemanly and, when he wasn't being teased by the girls on the charladies' special, nicely spoken considering where he'd been brought up.

For the next two hours Lorraine and Big Fran scoured all the likely public houses without success, shouldering their way through the boozy, hazy throngs in the public bars. They knew he didn't have the money for saloon-bar service so they didn't bother looking beyond the cut-glass screens that separated the nobs from the mobs. When chucking-out time came at two p.m. they returned to the flat subdued. The note was still untouched. Lorraine began to snivel.

Big Fran got down to cases. 'It's a bit early for waterworks. Did he say where he was going?'

'All I know is he was very excited because of something he'd found in the City. Something historic, he said. But you know what a daft bugger he is about all that. It was probably just another one of his brainstorms. He said he was digging out a statue. He was hoping to get a bit more than twenty quid for it. But, honestly, it sounded to me like you wouldn't stand it in the kharsi. It was one of them things where you leave the dirt on it. I ask you!'

Big Fran said crisply, 'If he went back for that, he's been nicked. Or broken a leg or something.'

'Oh, sweet Mother of Mercy,' said Lorraine, twisting her tearstained handkerchief. 'What shall we do?'

'First we hide these tracings,' said Fran. 'They're obviously knocked off. Then, if he hasn't shown up by teatime, we'll have to go down to the Borough High Street nick and see if he's in trouble.'

The next twenty-four hours were a time of deepening bewilderment for the two women. Neither the Metropolitan nor the City of London police had any knowledge of Larry Varnish's whereabouts. The two forces checked with each other and checked the hospitals. No Larry.

When he was still missing on Monday afternoon, a Metropolitan Policewoman called on the wife, who was hysterical, and the mother-in-law. The female rozzer's questions were uncomfortable. What kind of work did he have that took him out of the house late on a Saturday night? Wasn't he also known as Vanishing Larry Varnish? Wasn't he notorious for stealing from sites of antiquity?

'He's an antique dealer. He's very knowledgeable about the Romans,' said Lorraine loyally. 'And he wouldn't harm a fly.'

The policewoman didn't argue with that. The City dicks had spoken quite fondly of him. Larry was more a source of amusement than anger. No record existed of anything he had stolen over the past seven or eight years and, therefore, nothing had ever been logged in the Crime Book that would have damaged the force's clear-up rate.

Larry was not officially listed as a missing person until Tuesday. Everyone's best guess was that the silly bugger had fallen in a hole and broken a limb or worse while ferreting around for something to pinch. The problem was: where to start looking in the vast acreage involved?

In view of Larry's past history the job fell to the small City of London force. Beat coppers were ordered to keep a lookout. Site workmen were drawn into the search and the three

London evening newspapers spared Larry, a nobody, a few paragraphs.

Typical was the *Evening Standard*. Under the modest headline VANISHING LARRY VANISHES this item filled a column end:

City of London police are appealing to all building workers to watch out for a 22-year-old man who may have been lying injured on a bomb site for the past three days.

He is Laurence Varnish, of Douglas Buildings, Marshalsea Rd, Southwark, an amateur archaeologist who is known as Vanishing Larry because of frequent brushes with the police when he disappears into the ruins to avoid arrest. He is known to trespass on blitz sites looking for antiquities.

His wife, Lorraine, 21, said today, 'We are sick with worry. Larry went out on Saturday night and we haven't seen him since. We think he may be lying trapped where no one can hear his cries for help.'

For the next week Big Fran's flat seemed jammed with sympathetic bodies. Larry's parents and the parish priest practically moved in. The policewoman called every other day to assure the bereft family that everything was being done. Some of Larry's mates risked having their wages docked by taking days off to roam likely sites. Mr McKintock stayed away and made no communication then or ever again.

Professor Willoughby paid a visit to the tenement flat to express his concern. Big Fran eyed the stick-thin figure and thought he could have done with a large helping of her steak-and-kidney pudding.

The professor wasn't sure how to reach a rapport with these unschooled women. It soon became apparent that they had little enthusiasm for Larry's obsession and he felt obliged to come to Larry's defence. He said hesitantly to Lorraine, 'You know, Mrs Varnish, your husband was, er, is a remarkable man in many ways. He has an uncanny instinct for the topography of an ancient site. Most enviable. Far sharper than my own. In other circumstances, given a less disadvantaged start in life, there is no knowing to what heights he might have risen in the academic world.'

Neither Lorraine nor Big Fran knew the meaning of 'topography' but were not about to display their ignorance to this gentleman.

For a fleeting moment Lorraine was tempted to show him the tracing paper. But this, she decided, would only make matters worse by openly branding her husband a thief and losing the toff's sympathy for his presumed plight.

On the sixteenth day, the policewoman telephoned the priest and together, uncomfortably, they appeared on Big Fran's doorstep.

The policewoman insisted on making a cup of tea for everyone while the priest got the dazed women seated. Then she took Lorraine's hand and said, 'There's no easy way to say this, Mrs Varnish. But if Larry is out there we think he must be under a collapsed wall or something similar. In any case too much time has gone by. There has simply not been the slightest trace of him. The search has been very extensive but the job has been made all the more difficult because your husband preferred to work at night when there were no witnesses to his coming and going who might, in normal circumstances, have pointed us in the right direction.'

Big Fran, all her usual bombast missing, said fearfully, 'Are you telling my Lorraine that Larry is dead?'

The policewoman nodded. 'It must all be over by now. His flask of tea would long since have run dry. Let's hope that whatever happened was swift and merciful.'

Away from all the tears, the policewoman was called in by the detective chief inspector who had studied her reports. 'Any chance there's more to it?' he wanted to know. 'Run off with his fancy woman? Found a pot of gold and pissed off to Tahiti?'

She shook her head emphatically. 'Not a chance, sir. He hasn't been married long and his wife is very pretty. A love match. There's no suggestion of another woman. He's a bit of a tea-leaf but harmless. Whatever he was, it doesn't seems to have stopped everybody liking him. Even Professor Willoughby was practically in tears – and Vanishing Larry has been stealing his artefacts for years.

'You watch, before they finish rebuilding the City, poor Larry's maggoty body will come to light from under a stone and the coroner will be able to mark it up as death by misadventure.'

The DCI tossed the file into his out-tray. 'Fair enough. Do you have a boyfriend, Carol?'

BOOK THREE

BOOK THREE

Chapter One

The hired image-makers named it the Land of Grasse, which at least raised a snigger among hopheads who couldn't spell. It was really the perfume department and was known among the staff at W. O. Wilkie's – WOW! to Knightsbridge shopping junkies – as Pong Passage. Perfume was a speciality at WOW. They took a world view. The challenge was to find a leading name they didn't stock.

If you were merely headed for the food hall and the pork sausages, Pong Passage was a classic, marble-splendoured example of that English taste for self-inflicted humiliation. A male so crassly unbriefed as to enter Wilkie's emporium by the Basil Street entrance deserved everything served up to him.

You'd think, as an act of mercy if not a gesture of male comradeship, that before you gave the fatal first push on the art-moderne chrome doors the attendant Cossack would take hold of your arm, jerk you out of your trance, and hiss into your hearing-aid, 'Don't do it, sir. The bitches are ravenous for red meat today.'

But, hey, he's a Cossack. Right? Sadism goes with the territory. So he merely watches with snap-shut lips and inner joy as you blunder towards the ambush.

You push in and there they are, waiting in two disapproving lines like a very superior court of crows. The incipient smiles of warm insincerity on a dozen sets of perfectly drawn carmined lips freeze and, at first sight of you, fall away and transmute into a dozen frowns of disapproval. They edge back in unison, putting a little more of their shiny glass counters between you and them in an unspoken gesture of genteel distaste.

Immediately you feel like a bum. You edge past the purveyors of Guerlain and L'Air du Temps and collide with the icy stares of Paris, Nina Ricci and Agnès B. You just know that these coiffed, glossed, burnished harpies can see right through your clothes to the hole in your Y-fronts and the fluff in your navel.

Their stares say that they know you have *dank places* about your person but you needn't think they're going to step forward on their shiny dominatrix heels, take aim with their chic squirty vials and grant you absolution with a five-second burst of some heavenly fragrance.

Oh dear me, no. They are not going to waste their samples on so obvious a loser, a man who wears trainers and mail-order polyester reinforced trousers. And, what's more, a man who so obviously cannot afford to keep a mistress or two and is therefore in no position to shower his sweet babes with an occasional litre of those rich essences from the gaudy fields of Grasse. The No Sale sign, unmistakable, uncompassionate, unrelenting, hovers above your unworthy skull.

They tap impatiently on their counter tops with blood-red nails shaped like Gothic windows, anxious for you to be gone. You have the criminal look of a man who buys perfume *only from duty-free shops in airports*. So hurry along, little man, and have done with you.

This ritual degradation is an equal-opportunity hazard. Men who have failed the test in running the gauntlet of Pong Passage have their female equivalents: women in shellsuits (unless they are foolish Americans who cannot be expected to know any better), floral leggings, market-stall jeans. They will receive a condescending squirt but only on humbling, grovelling request and only if the recipient can endure the hooded, patrician gaze guaranteed to bore through the top garments and expose, for the entire court of crows to see, the grey bra, the chainstore knickers and the spider tattoo on the left buttock beneath.

So be off with you, too, my good woman. Your, hmm, companion was last seen in search of, ah, pork sausages.

Tabitha Gatling was not aware that such social minefields existed. For a start, when she stepped out of her cab in her St Laurent button-through, she expected the Cossack to be holding the door and adopting a suitably servile manner. Then, while she paid off the cabbie, she took it as a natural law that he would race ahead of her to throw WOW's doors wide in welcome.

Tabitha swept in like an empress, her gaze coolly embracing the length of Pong Passage. At the sight of her, the crows not already hitting on socially acceptable customers visibly remembered their posture, picked up their aromatic wares and ventured into the walkway.

In the distance Tabitha spotted Finula already playing the wide-eyed dope, sniffing at the bottles like one of the bloody Bisto Kids. Tabitha hoped she wasn't going to overdo it.

The Givenchy crow took first tilt at Tabitha. Would *modom* like to experience a soupçon of the latest *parfum*? 'No, *modom* would not,' said Tabitha crisply. She needed to move further into the centre of the hall where more customers were concentrated. Tabitha needed an audience to create confusion while Finula swooped.

Tabitha decided on the Rive Gauche crow. She was younger than the rest of the harridans, perhaps not yet as armour-plated against future shock. Tabitha turned the full glory of her smile upon her.

The young crow raised her atomizer spray. 'Perhaps a test sample, madam?'

'Hmmm, I'm not so sure that stuff's guaranteed to do the trick,' mused Tabitha.

'Trick, madam?'

'You know,' said Tabitha, disconcerting her with a vulgar wink, 'get a man so horny he has your kit off before you've had time to ask his name.'

The young crow looked uncomfortable. This was not a proper confidence for a saleslady to be sharing. 'If you'll raise your wrist . . .' she suggested, hurriedly changing the subject and directing the nozzle.

'Darling, that's for the suburban ghastlies. Did you ever know a man whose kink was to screw wrists? No, of course not.'

Tabitha watched the professional geniality on the girl's painted face begin to turn into something more wary.

'If you want to give me a squirt where the next randy bugger's liable to be sticking his big nose, then try this.'

She had her top three buttons undone and the dress spread wide before the crow could object. Tabitha flicked the frontal clip on her Rigby & Peller brassière and tugged the cups aside. The contents plopped out and bounced against her ribcage. 'There, put it between my juicy mammaries,' she said.

Tabitha noted with pleasure the agonized look crossing the girl's face. 'Please, madam, this is a public place,' she appealed.

But the damage was done and the objective achieved. Around them all conversation died and commercial intercourse came to a dead halt, as Tabitha had been confident it would. After all, how often did Pong Passage witness a stunning blonde of five foot eight exposing her splendid breasts for all the world to see.

'Well, are you going to put a squirt down in the valley, or what? I seem to remember that you accosted me with the idea.'

'But on the wrist, madam!' cried the girl. 'You must know that that is the convention – wrist or neck. Not on the – the – chest.'

Tabitha savoured that stumble over chest. What had been the first word to come to the crow's mind? Tits, she thought. Time for the raised voice. 'If my body is to be assaulted by strange substances, hurled at me from what looks like an anti-rape CS gas canister, I think I have the privilege of deciding which portion of my epidermis shall receive the blast.'

Tabitha thrust her bared breasts at the girl, who stared, horrified, at the mocking pink tips on the tanned mounds.

'Oooh!' said the shocked women shoppers now encircling the drama.

The crow's poise lay in tatters at her agitated feet. Her surrender was abject and total. She endeavoured to direct the spray of scent while at the same time not appearing to make undue appraisal of Tabitha's booty. The result was an overlong squirt that trickled down Tabitha's cleavage and into her lower regions.

'Please, madam, would you now adjust your dress?' begged the girl. 'You're causing comment among the other customers.'

'I should bloody well hope so,' said Tabitha, who could see some kind of black-jacketed floor manager, arms akimbo at shoulder height like a dance teacher, unctuously easing his way through the throng. 'It's not every day you see a pair of boobs as good as these without benefit of silicone.'

She was buttoning up when the floor manager burst through the ogling crowd. 'What's the trouble here?'

'No trouble,' said Tabitha sweetly, before the young crow could answer. 'I've been sampling the scents. I can't imagine what all these people are staring at. I think I'd better come back when the store doesn't have a crowd of football supporters cluttering the aisles.'

A man among the spectators began to laugh and gave Tabitha an appreciative round of applause. Head high, she headed for the exit and the Cossack.

Five minutes after the crowd had dispersed and the floor manager had hied himself off to Soft Furnishings, another crow gave a well-bred cry of distress. A spectacular crystal flacon was missing from her *parfumerie* display.

'Well, it wasn't that hoity-toity mad cow,' said the young crow. 'We all saw the only things she had room for under that dress.'

W. O. Wilkie's head of security was not seeing events in a kindly light. 'You prick,' he told the serf who'd been on duty in the monitoring room. 'The moment she began her striptease you toggled camera seven in so close you could see what she'd had for breakfast.'

The two men were watching the rerun of the tape.

'Getting your jollies, were you?' said the boss. 'Having a quiet one off the wrist?'

'I just thought it was a strippergram girl. Someone's birthday, or somefink,' whined the hapless minion.

The boss ignored him and was watching the scene progress. 'There!' he said suddenly. 'The dark-haired bint in the bottom left-hand corner.'

Camera seven had zoomed in so closely on the disturbance caused by Tabitha Gatling that the perfume counters in the foreground had all but disappeared from the frame.

'There she goes!' said the head of security. The two men witnessed a hand reach out to snatch the flacon that was the centrepiece of the counter display. They had no record of the thief's face. When she came into full view of camera seven she was heading away from the eye in the ceiling and towards the street exit.

'Cheeky bitch!' said the security boss. 'It's adding insult to injury. She's popped the loot into a Harrods bag.'

The head of security rewound the tape and watched Tabitha's performance for a second time. He froze the frame at the moment when she had opened wide her dress. 'That's one for the office wall,' he grunted. 'I've a mind to slip a print to the *Screws of the World* – Tabitha Gatling out shopping till she drops.'

'You know who this fancy piece is?' asked the serf, surprised.

'Doesn't everybody? I don't know what *Hello!* magazine and the gossip columns would do without her.'

'Then we can have her nicked. She wasn't just stripping for devilment. She was in cahoots with the tart with the Harrods bag. I'd bet on it.'

'Grow up,' said the head of security. 'There's a swamp of shit a mile wide between knowing it and proving it. She'd hire some two-K-a-day brief who'd have your goolies in the wringer ten minutes after you stepped into the witness box. Put it down to experience. The next time you spot a woman auditioning for *Penthouse* force yourself to notice what's going down in the immediate vicinity. Because, if you don't, you'll be nightwatching holes in the road.'

The boss turned off the video. 'Anyway, those two mad cows haven't been as damn clever as they think. They've a surprise coming.'

*

Tabitha arrived back at Cheyne Walk on Finula Colm-Harrington's heels. She brushed past the housekeeper, Mrs Burroughs, with a minimal acknowledgement and raced up the broad staircase to the first-floor sitting room. Mrs Burroughs stared after her, face as tight in disapproval as that of any of the crows of Pong Passage. Now what mischief had the little minx been up to?

Tabitha was panting as she burst through the double doors. 'Did you get it?'

Finula, under her glossy black fringe, smiled like a cat hoarding cream and held the suspense for five seconds. Then she plunged her hand into the Harrods bag and pulled out the crystal flacon. 'Da-daaaaa!' She held it aloft and the crystal caught the lights and sent rays winking around the room. The liquid inside was the colour of sapphires.

'My God, there's almost enough scent there to swim a length in,' said Tabitha. 'Give me a whiff.'

Her friend, daft daughter of a lord Tabitha had taken up as one might adopt the leftover puppy of a litter, carefully scratched loose the sliver of gummed tape holding the elaborate stopper in place and reverently placed the flacon on a low table. 'Now,' ordered Tabitha, 'set the spirit free!'

Finula twisted the stopper loose and hauled it out. Both women stood back. Finula said doubtfully, 'Should we greet the spirit or something?' But Tabitha did not answer. She reached out and gave the flacon a gentle shake. The pale liquid sloshed in the open neck.

Tabitha placed it under her nose and inhaled. She sniffed again. Finula's dark eyebrows were raised in expectation of Tabitha's pleasure. 'Odd,' said Tabitha. 'I can't smell a bloody thing.'

Finula said, 'Here, let me.' She sniffed over the open flacon, made a face and carefully tilted the heavy vessel to pour a drop into her palm. After a moment, she shrieked, 'Omigod! You know what? We've liberated a jar of coloured water – for display purposes only!'

Tabitha stared at her. 'You stupid bitch. This was your dare. Did I go through that pantomime for a glass jar?'

Mrs Burroughs could hear the screaming match from the hall, followed by angry shouting on the staircase and the slamming of the front door as an aggrieved Finula stormed out.

Later, Tabitha slouched moodily into the kitchen and dumped the empty flacon on the work surface. 'Present,' she said to the housekeeper. Tabitha made many little gifts to her daddy's staff to compensate for her many acts of inconsideration. 'It'd look nice with a couple of long-stem roses,' she suggested tentatively.

Mrs Burroughs and Cook exchanged the look that says, 'Have you ever heard anything like it?'

When Tabitha had dragged herself away, Cook said, 'Does she have a clue about the price of long-stem roses?'

'Why should she?' said Mrs Burroughs. 'Her flower bill last month from Moyses Stevens came to more than you earn in a month. It goes directly to Coutts. The bank sends her confirmation of payments. Most of the time she doesn't even bother to open the envelopes. I find them in the wastepaper bin – or on the floor when she can't be bothered to find the bin.'

Mrs Burroughs hefted the heavy flacon. 'Long-stem roses be buggered,' she said. 'I reckon my Charlie could turn this into a nice table lamp.'

Chapter Two

Tabitha Gatling could not cook, sew, weave, keep house, iron or shop reliably for the usual domestic comestibles. While still at school she had once ventured forth to buy a lipstick and had returned with a shooting-stick. She was never able adequately to explain this.

She had never held a paid job. When she was reproached with this she had a flip answer ready – provided by her clever friend Piers Frobisher, notorious gossip columnist of the

Express, who had plucked it from the proceedings of the House of Lords.

Some hoary old politician named Macmillan had been defending friends who, like Tabitha, had swanned cheerfully through life without a job. 'It didn't seem to do them any harm,' harrumphed the old boy, displaying an unfashionable contempt for the work ethic, which he had wisely concealed from the electorate when he had been prime minister and urging everyone to beaver away in the cause of national economic well-being.

Of course, the reason Harold Macmillan's friends and Tabitha did not work in the back-breaking, factory-bench, wage-earning, nose-to-grindstone sense was due to their immense good fortune in having been born to inherited wealth. Earning a crust was a spirit-deadening activity properly left to the lower orders, who should be grateful for the opportunity.

In a wider sense Tabitha worked very hard. She could play a fair game of tennis, ride, ski, swim like a porpoise, dance an eightsome reel, drive fast cars with skill, stay up all night, benchpress 140 pounds, and shop recklessly – as the shooting-stick episode had revealed.

She had been asked to leave her fashionable school in South Kensington at the age of seventeen where she had been, in theory at least, studying for three A levels.

Tabitha was an habitual breaker of school rules. She ate junk food and drank soft drinks in the streets, and was known to take this provocation of her teachers to extremes by pouring her lemon Fanta into an empty Special Brew beer can and openly swigging from that. She defiantly wore jewellery with her school uniform. She occasionally smoked a cigarette in the school environs, even though she disliked the habit. Upsetting her teachers was all-important to her jaded spirit. She was her father's daughter.

To girls of her year she was a legend. The story of Tabitha on the lacrosse field is still told. The school's recreation ground was in Battersea where members of the public had access to the far side of the twelve-feet-high chain-link perimeter fence.

Regrettably, the girls in their skimpy athletics kit were a

magnet for the neighbourhood studs and perverts. Occasionally, when the turmoil in the spectators' trouser-fronts was all too obvious and girls were being upset, the games mistress would summon the police on her mobile phone. Tabitha merely shrieked with laughter.

On the occasion when the legend was born, she had eschewed the divided flannel skirt obligatory on the playing-field so as not to give the unwelcome spectators unseemly glimpses of underwear. She turned up in a flannel skirt from which, undetected by the games mistress, the divide had been removed. When she slyly 'mooned' the perverts with her creamy buttocks, they went into onanistic overdrive. Tabitha wasn't wearing any knickers under that innocent-looking skirt.

Consequently, Tabitha Gatling was the recipient of a great deal of SD – Silent Detention – where miscreants were gathered into one classroom to sit in glum silence for one hour beyond the last class of the day.

Tabitha's crowning achievement as a rebel was to be awarded DPC – Detention Plus Chore – for having leaned from a first-floor window overlooking the street and, with her blouse in disarray, shouting, 'Help! Help! Save me! I'm being tortured by hairy Greeks!'

The Greeks in question were Pythagoras, Euclid, Plato and others. But the passers-by who helpfully summoned the police weren't to know that.

For her DPC, Tabitha was handed a box of tissues and a spatula and ordered to tour the empty classrooms and scrape the chewing gum from the undersides of the desks.

Tabitha stared in incredulity at the mistress who had awarded this punishment. 'Fuck off!' she said, and pushed away the tissues and spatula with such force that the woman toppled backwards over a wastepaper bin and wrenched her back.

Tabitha's father, Vernon, was summoned to see the headmistress and advised that, if Tabitha wished to continue her studies with a university place in mind, it had best be done with a private tutor. The escapade also cost Vernon six thousand pounds for the teacher's wrenched back.

Tabitha had no interest whatsoever in striving for a university education. She considered she'd had more than enough education of the formal kind. She had what she called her 'forays' to keep boredom at bay when not engaged in her other sportive pursuits.

Such a one was the raid on W. O. Wilkie's department store on Finula Colm-Harrington's dare. In truth, Tabitha Gatling could afford to buy enough flacons of perfume to fill a princess's bath many times over.

The coming of the third millennium was proving a wonderful time for a handful of the *jeunesse* such as Tabitha whose family fortunes, founded in the rubble of post-war Britain, had now reached their zenith.

Their fathers and grandfathers had seized their opportunities during the post-austerity years of the aforesaid Harold Macmillan and continued happily making money throughout the sixties from the chumps who had been lured away from life's rat race by marijuana, pop music, love-ins, and flower power, which was no power at all.

The next great surge in the fortunes of these driven men came with the abolition of control over the international movement of money and the arrival of the Thatcher years when making money achieved Himalayan heights of respectability.

By Tabitha's late teenage years, the fortune founders were being reluctantly parted from their wealth by death or infirmity, leaving the fathers of the present generation of golden youth sitting on top of the pile obligingly created for them. The money was theirs to multiply or squander as they chose.

Due to this happy set of circumstances, Tabitha Gatling was that millennium phenomenon, a trust-fund babe, her daddy's only darling daughter.

Chapter Three

Fate decreed that Gervase Meredith was to become the rank-ing authority on Tabitha Gatling's family history. His odyssey began harmlessly enough in the Mayfair offices of *Vanity Bazaar*, the glossy publication read by everyone who was anyone and everyone who desired to be someone.

Often with such publications, the headline is fully formed before a word of the accompanying article is written or even conceived. That was the case here. Someone at the features conference had thrown the headline 'A Babe In Summertime' into the ideas pot and the editor had immediately pulled them out and declared she was in love with those enchanting four words.

Now she was mentally sifting through her stable of the most likely writers to match to this assignment when, through the glass wall of her chic office with the zebra couches, she espied Gervase, one of her on-off freelance contributors, mooching through the editorial floor. He was on the way to Accounts to collect some owed expenses.

She opened her door and shouted sweetly, 'Gervase, get your ass in here.'

He obeyed with alacrity, even permitting himself to be patted fondly on the buttocks as he sidled past the boss and into her lair. If he wasn't about to be bollocked for some foul-up, this meant an assignment.

With one hand, she shaped an invisible headline in the air. 'A – Babe – In – Summertime,' she said slowly, as if reading to an infant.

'I like it,' said Gervase dutifully. Never dump on an editor's idea. Always pretend at least that you're going to give it your best shot.

Yet, for once, Gervase could see the possibilities.

'Could you flush out a suitable trust-fund babe who isn't too busy shagging some smelly pop guitarist, hang out with her and deliver five thousand appropriate words in time for the big autumn issue? It's gotta be light-hearted. It's gotta be clean – no pharmaceuticals,' said the editor.

'Leave it to me,' said Gervase swiftly, before she could change her mind or wrongly detect a lack of enthusiasm. The assignment was a dream. The expenses would be phenomenal. Plus he badly needed the fee that his agent Long John Silver would negotiate. Gervase's bank manager did not subscribe to the philosophy that it was a perfectly proper arrangement in a capitalist society for a gentleman to live with a permanent overdraft.

The editor was in full flow. 'I see the piece capturing the reality of such a girl's life which to outsiders in the workaday world must seem to take place inside the rainbow glow of a champagne bubble.'

'I like "life in a champagne bubble",' encouraged Gervase.

His first problem was that he knew no trust-fund babes, they being notoriously too wallet-zapping to take out. But *nil desperandum*. His pal Piers Frobisher knew more about this privileged circle than anyone alive. And he was just a phone call away.

From his enviable contacts book, Piers plucked the names of three babes. 'Any one of that trio might suit your purpose, old cock,' said Piers generously.

Alas, it was not to be. Two turned Gervase down flat without even suggesting a meeting and he rejected the third after lunching her at Daphne's. She was a monumentally stupid girl who took four calls on her mobile telephone during the meal. He was relieved when the waiter asked her to switch the damn thing off. Any five-thousand-word feature article centred on her braindead activities would of necessity have been cruelly satirical and triggered a call for the return of the tumbril.

'Keep it light-hearted' was his instruction. Gervase wasn't seeking to destroy a young life no matter how pointless. Back he went to Piers.

'You could try Tabby Gatling,' he said, furnishing Gervase with her unlisted number, 'but she carries a health warning.'

'Oh?'

'Very bright girl, but I'm not sure you're her speed. Likes to put fires under people. Takes a lot of keeping up with. On that subject, is *Vanity Bazaar* paying your expenses?'

'Too bloody right they are!'

'If you take on Tabby, you'd better make sure they know what they're in for. She thinks nothing of taking the morning Concorde for lunch in New York and flying back in time for a night of body-shaking among those naughty South London bank robbers at the Ministry of Sound.'

Piers also delivered a caution, which meant little then but assumed a great significance later. 'One other thing,' he said, 'I know you. Randy bastard. If she should take you on as a charity case and let you get your leg over, you'd better watch out for her old man. Tabby is not just the apple of his eye, she's the whole bloody orchard. A penniless hack such as your squalid self has no chance.'

Gervase Meredith left a message outlining his proposal with Tabitha Gatling's answering-service.

He was to learn that her attachment to the telephone was deep and enduring. All the same, she took two days to return his call. He was in bed asleep. He groped for the lamp, knocking over his water glass and cursing. A groggy glance at his watch told him the time was two a.m. but, with effort, he held back his irritation. Gervase needed this girl. He cleared his head and began to soft-soap her.

He didn't get far.

She cut in, 'How old are you?'

'Twenty-eight.'

'Have I interrupted you in the middle of somebody?'

'No. I'm alone.'

'How dismal. What's a slip of a lad like you doing sleeping his life away?'

'It's a habit I've got into.'

'Baaaad!' she said. 'What are you wearing?'

Gervase was naked but to acknowledge it would have opened the door on dangerous territory. 'Pyjamas,' he lied.

'God!' she said. 'I thought *Vanity Bazaar* people had more imagination.'

'I'm a writer,' he said wearily, 'not a male model or a fetishist, Miss Gatling.'

'Tabby. Call me Tabby, like the cat,' she cut in. And before he could say another word, she added, in staccato fashion, 'Just listen. I take it you have a car? Good. Save a life.'

Tabitha Gatling was phoning from some Notting Hill drink 'n' drug joint beyond the Mason-Dixon line of the Westway, somewhere up near the canal. She'd 'blown-out' her escort, as she put it, and wanted rescuing.

'Draw your car up to the kerb, directly opposite the door, keep your engine running and shout to the bouncer that you're there to collect Miss Prism. Then be ready for a fast getaway.'

She was gone before he could voice either doubts or objection. Rescue from whom? Couldn't she get a taxi?

But the sound of the cleared telephone line was his only answer. This was obviously some kind of test. Given her well-chronicled popularity, she could have telephoned a small army of friends and hangers-on. Gervase cursed again, threw back the duvet and swung his feet to the floor. Was she simply having him on? He reminded himself that it was not April Fools' Day.

He found his *A–Z* street guide, and twenty minutes later was heading down Ladbroke Grove. The dive was situated in what had once been an old people's luncheon club, the narrow doorway marked by a neon sign of the kind that was unhooked and taken inside during the hours of daylight for fear of thieves. Gervase wondered briefly where the old people ate now.

In their brief conversation, Tabitha had instructed him to do a U-turn so that his four-year-old Series 3 BMW was pointed back towards town. He did as told and pulled up opposite the doorway, from which issued the skull-jarring thump of over-amplified rock. The flashing purple light identified the dump as Snakes. Judging from the louche knots of the clientele littering the pavement, restoring their hearing and getting some oxygen back into their withered lungs, the place was aptly named. A number of sharply dressed dudes eyed him curiously. Gervase checked to make sure his wristwatch wasn't showing from beneath his sleeve. He needed no inducement to keep the engine running.

He released the passenger-door lock and shouted across to the guardian of the portals, a mountain of beef in black-tie and the obligatory shades that must have rendered him near blind in the gloom.

'Car for Miss Prism!'

The big lummox cupped an ear. 'Wossat, white thing?'

'Car for Miss Prism!' Gervase bellowed again, above the air pollutant masquerading as music.

From behind the man mountain there was a sudden movement. The purple neon bounced off something golden, and Tabitha Gatling, blonde hair streaming in her wake, darted from behind the bouncer and raced across the pavement. As she hurtled forward her long silken legs caught the light. She was encased in a little black dress that barely covered her bum. And she was screaming something incomprehensible.

Gervase barely had time to thrust open the passenger door before she collided with the panelling and threw herself into the seat. 'Go! Go! Go!' she yelled. Her Galahad was about to utter a soothing, 'Take it easy,' when he abruptly changed his mind. A black girl in a light-coloured leather catsuit had detached herself from a dark doorway and was close on Tabitha Gatling's heels. The object glinting in her right hand was not a Gucci handbag.

'Christ!' Gervase swore, and threw the stick into gear. Tabitha was still screaming at him and punching the knob to make sure the door between her and the girl with the blade was securely locked.

The black chick did not waste time tugging futilely at the handle. She took alternative direct action. To Gervase's horror she threw herself on to the bonnet and grabbed a wiper.

'Shake the cow off!' screamed Tabitha.

The girl's face was jammed against the screen, terrifying in its distortion and the intensity of its hatred. The knife was somewhere under her body. Gervase had already started to move forward but now he braked sharply.

'Don't stop! Don't stop! Kill the cow!' screamed Tabitha. God, what had he got himself into here?

The various groups on the pavement were beginning to

advance. They did not look friendly. He knew he had to get out of there before something terrible happened.

The black girl was hammering on the screen in impotent rage. Thank God it was three a.m. now and the road was empty. Gervase put the BMW into a tight lock and surged forward into a tyre-smoking circle. Round he circled three dizzying times before centrifugal force cut in and his outside passenger began to lose her grip in her slippery garment.

Despite the bloodthirsty urgings coming from his hyper-agitated passenger Gervase was also beginning to lose his nerve. The black girl could be severely hurt, or worse, if this madness continued. He braked sharply and that turned out to be the best thing he could have done. The sudden halt jerked her loose, causing her to slide away, screaming obscenities, as she scratched futilely at his paintwork for a hold. She landed in a heap in the road, taking the wiper with her.

He almost ran her down on the return as she struggled to her knees but managed frantically to straighten up and speed away – in the wrong direction. In his rear-view mirror he could see a crowd from the club swarming into the road. He was convinced that if they had managed to block the getaway the pair of them would have been lynched. His heart was thumping as loudly as the music.

He peered into the rear-view mirror again and was relieved to spot the demented girl now on her feet and raging. She couldn't be badly hurt. He released the air from his paralysed lungs and turned with a lighter heart to the task in hand.

A few minutes later he was blundering through the back streets of Paddington with his cargo whooping and cheering to celebrate her deliverance.

He pulled over and looked at her. Despite the relief, he was still shaking. She was laughing. 'What the dickens was all that about?' he snapped – and to hell with offending her. 'You could have got us killed.' He was in no mood for the soft-soap he'd originally intended.

In reply, this vision threw herself across the seat in a theatrical fashion. She said, 'My hero!' embraced him and planted a great mwah of a kiss on his bristly cheek.

He caught a fleeting whiff of a subtle summery perfume and then she slumped back in her seat. 'Know who that was?' she asked, a sly grin sliding into place.

'The black girl? No.'

'It was that bitch Stella Sterling. Sterling, for God's sake. That's a case of sailing under false colours. She was born in horrid Hounslow and her real name is Pound. Pound Sterling. Get it?'

'What is she, a pop singer?'

Tabitha stared at him. 'Does your mummy know you're out this late?' she said.

'Funny,' he said. 'I was about to ask you the same question.'

'Stella Sterling is this year's catwalk queen. Ralph Lauren has anointed her.'

'I seem to recollect reading something of the sort,' Gervase said shortly. 'But that doesn't explain why she was coming after you with a switchblade.'

Tabitha Gatling tucked those long legs under her like a little girl and for the next ten minutes Gervase listened to the first of many convoluted stories that his trust-fund babe would spin for him in the aftermath of some upset or outrage.

In this encounter she had quarrelled with her male escort, a peer's son whom Gervase knew to be a cokehead – scoring some cocaine, he suspected, had been the underlying reason for the visit to Snakes – and she had dumped him. Recklessly, she had stayed behind in this dangerous place when he had stormed out like a petulant boy which is what he was. A few minutes later, she said, Stella Sterling's man had started coming on to her.

'So what did you do?'

At twenty-three, the fine planes of Tabitha's face were firmly in place. She grinned wickedly. 'Naturally I gave him every encouragement. You should have seen Stella brewing up to explode. Talk about Krakatoa. She might be Queen of the Catwalk but I was there to inform her that she is certainly not Queen of the May.'

Gervase shook his head. 'You can't toy with people like that. It's a dangerous game. You can get away with it a hundred times and then . . . Well, it almost happened tonight.'

She was not impressed. She was still laughing but she said, 'Are you going to carry on being Mr Misery Meredith from Morden?'

In Tabitha's eyes, he learned, to be Morden born and bred was the gravest of misfortunes. Morden is deep in the irredeemable suburbs, the last stop on the south London section of the underground railway.

Of herself, she'd admit airily, 'Oh, I'm from Upney,' which Gervase already knew she wasn't. A glance later at the underground map explained all. Upney is one stop beyond Barking – as in barking mad. For her, that map, with its serpentine tangle of lines, possessed a significance that would have escaped most of us.

He started up the car and said, 'I'll take you home.'

'For God's sake,' she grumbled, 'don't I get a drink first? God! You're such a dork.'

'Coffee,' he said firmly, and drove to the all-night stall at the foot of the Albert Bridge. ''Ello, darling,' the old geezer at the urn greeted her. 'You're looking a bit special tonight.' Tabitha's circle of friends was wider than Gervase had thought.

The old geezer nodded at him. 'For a moment there I thought you was in trouble. Is he Old Bill?'

'I'm in trouble all right,' said Tabitha sweetly. 'This long streak of misery is a bloody journalist. He wants to do my life story.'

Gervase thought of correcting her but weariness was setting in and the dazzle from the zillion bulbs lighting the bridge for the delectation of the tourist trade was hurting his eyes. He took his coffee and gloomed silently into it while she chatted happily with the old geezer as if she'd just had ten hours' undisturbed sleep.

'So wot 'ave you done wiv Big Julie, then?' inquired the old man, wiping his counter. Big Julie, alias Julian, was the young viscount with whom Tabitha had begun her eventful evening.

'Gave him his marching orders,' she said. 'The nerve! He started making goo-goo eyes at some hairy-arsed rapper, would you believe?' She had omitted that item of information from the account she had given Gervase.

The old geezer clucked in sympathy like a father confessor. 'You didn't know he was ginger, then?'

Her eyes widened. 'No. Did you?'

He shrugged. 'Big Julie came here one night with a kid. A bit of King's Cross rough trade who took one of my fried sausages and started doin' suggestive fings wiv it. I told Julie to get the dirty little sod to stop. Couldn't 'ave 'im upsetting my other customers. I get crowned 'eads 'ere.'

Perfect! For all his exhaustion, Gervase was already taking mental notes. He resolved to get out more at night. In ninety minutes in this unanchored girl's company he'd gathered enough copy for a London-by-night magazine article.

Gervase looked at Tabitha, one bare arm propped on the spot where the old geezer had wiped away the spilt tea and sausage-roll crumbs. She seemed as at home as if she were propping up the bar at Tramp or Annabel's.

He was intrigued, and he was hooked. Right now he could think of nothing more delectable than to be her shadow throughout the summer, as much for the rollercoaster ride as for the commissioned copy. She was so vibrant, so reckless, so *charged* with the life force. She was irresistible. He decided he would go the distance with her.

Gervase had no intimation then of how far that distance would be.

Her father's home was a stroll of only a few hundred yards back across the river and she wanted to walk, but Gervase was knackered. She grumbled like a little girl being sent to bed early, but he bullied her into the car and drove her in a couple of minutes to Cheyne Walk. She gave him another theatrical mwah on his ever more sandpapery cheek and jumped out.

She turned and leaned back in. He forced himself to keep his eyes raised above her gaping neckline.

'All right, Mr Misery,' she said. 'You're on.'

He watched her push open the elaborate eighteenth-century wrought-iron gate and sashay up the short path. She knew his eyes were on her. Without looking back, she flicked her buttocks like a chorus girl as she opened the front door and disappeared.

He sensed he'd passed a test of the machismo kind.

Chapter Four

Gervase Meredith arranged to meet Tabitha Gatling for lunch two days later at the Oxo Tower.

She entered the brasserie twenty minutes late shaking her head as if she were already despairing of him. 'The *brasserie!*' she said. 'My dear, what can you be thinking of? The chairs are instruments of torture. I've been waiting for you in the *restaurant.*'

'They were all booked up,' he said.

'Nonsense,' she huffed, like a dowager. 'I've taken good care of that.'

And taken care she had. She led the march through to the restaurant where waiters did everything but throw themselves before her feet as they ushered them to a table with a spectacular view of the Thames. On the way Gervase lasered a ray of pure venom at the maître d' who'd earlier told him the place was full.

Settled at last, in what he had to admit were much more buttock-friendly chairs, he asked what had decided her to go along with his proposition. What had been the clincher?

'No clincher,' she said. 'You were on from the start, old Misery. Why do you always assume the worst?'

'You've known me five minutes. Why do you think I always assume the worst?'

She leaned forward over her Caesar salad. 'I know your sort,' she said. 'You're okay but you need taking out of yourself. You're going to wake up dead one day. Then you'll be sorry for what you missed.'

'So you decided I was a worthy candidate to be taken out of himself? That's your mission, is it?'

'Well,' she said, cocking her head so that the blonde tresses drooped on to one shoulder and pretending to eye him judiciously, 'the raw material is pretty unpromising but I don't see why I can't teach you how to kick holes in a few stained-glass windows.'

'I see you've read your Raymond Chandler,' he said.

But she did not get the origin of her own allusion. 'Life's too short for books. Why buy life second-hand when you can afford the real thing? There'll be time for books when I'm really old like you,' she taunted.

He'd taken along to the lunch Millie Moses, a woman photographer whom, he informed Tabitha, would pop up from time to time to take the pictures to accompany his article. When he introduced her, Tabitha asked, 'Where's the war?'

Gervase suppressed a grin. Like most of her breed, Millie lived in combat gear, from clumpy ammunition boots to her many-pocketed khaki jacket. The garb was, he supposed, intended as a feminist statement that women can be as front-line as the men. However, alongside Tabitha, elegant in a cream linen suit, the poor woman looked more like a road-sweeper than a daredevil of the battlefield, which she was. Millie looked very tight-assed as she struggled to maintain on her weathered face an expression of enthusiasm for the assignment.

Tabitha was already becoming the sort of exotic creature either heartily loathed or envied by other women. Gervase made a mental note to have a quiet word with his snapper. A hostile photographer, deliberately using the wrong lenses and angles, can make even the loveliest women look like dogs. He wasn't about to let that happen here. He realized he was already becoming protective of his summertime ward.

As they rose to leave, Tabitha said to him, 'Let's go! You and I have unfinished business.'

He was about to kiss off Millie when Tabitha added, 'No, no. She comes, too. There'll be a picture in it – your first for the article.'

Gervase and Millie followed their anointed babe in his old BMW. They drove to South Kensington and parked on yellow lines in Stanhope Gardens. Tabitha climbed out of her Jaguar XK8 convertible and walked back to talk to them. Gervase had no idea what was coming.

She said, 'You stay here and keep your peepers open.' And to the combat camerawoman, 'Train your artillery on that door.' She indicated the black-painted front door of a stucco-fronted house thirty yards away.

They watched her stride across the road, ring the doorbell then take two steps back as if to make room for the occupier to step out into the open – and into Millie's lens.

Impatiently, their babe jabbed at the bell again and eventually the door opened. She spoke to a maid and a few moments later into view came the sleep-dazed profile – it was mid-afternoon – of Lord Julian, Tabitha's unreliable escort of three nights ago. He was wearing a rather splendid crimson dressing-gown with a Christian Dior logo on the breast pocket and his bare feet were thrust into backless flip-flops.

From the car they watched the conversation hot up, with the recalcitrant viscount becoming increasingly animated under Tabitha's tongue-lashing for his ungentlemanly nocturnal behaviour. Gervase wished he was nearer to catch the angry words. Millie began loosing off a few frames.

Tabitha held her ground a good yard from the doorstep and, unconsciously, Julian was lured further out into the open. When he was practically shouting into Tabitha's face – and could be seen head-to-toe by Millie – the unbelievable happened. Their babe half turned away as if winding herself up and came back swinging. The punch from her balled-up fist caught Julian with a sharp crack on the side of his unshaven jaw. This was no maidenly tap. This was a welterweight putting knockout muscle behind the hook. Gervase sat open-mouthed. He could hear Millie's motor-drive going into a frenzy. A close intimacy with warfare had left her ever ready for outbreaks of violence.

Julian staggered back, tottered, went down on the brass threshold with a thump – and stayed down. Tabitha said something with an air of finality about it and raised both arms in the air in a pugilist's gesture of triumph. The young peer at her feet was giving a close impersonation of a worm. Satisfied, she sauntered back across the road as if she hadn't a worry in the world. 'Was that all right, darlings? Did the earth move for you as it moved for him?' she drawled. She hadn't even broken sweat.

They watched her climb back into her Jag, massage her knuckles for a moment and then vroom away, almost knee-capping an approaching traffic warden as she departed. Her witnesses' mouths were still hanging open. Their eyes went back to the doorstep. A houseboy in a white jacket was helping the groggy viscount back inside. His jaw appeared to be broken.

'There's something wrong with that young lady,' said Millie. 'She's mental.'

'She's a touchy girl,' Gervase said. 'Easily hurt.'

But even while he was quipping he was thinking about the long, cold calculation that had preceded the brief, hot-blooded moment of revenge.

Gervase made a mental note: crossing Tabitha Gatling would be a risky pastime. Best not.

For some days he expected a visit from the police. Tabitha had committed a criminal assault, and Millie and he were both witnesses. He scanned the gossip columns but Dempster and Piers Frobisher had apparently heard nothing. The viscount laid no complaint with the police – presumably because he did not wish his sexual preferences to be bandied about in court as the root cause of his injuries. Millie placed the amazing photographs in her safe, pending *Vanity Bazaar*'s exclusive publication.

Tabitha showed no subsequent remorse. Gervase followed in her carefree wake to her Mayfair hairstylist (twice a week minimum), manicurist (once a week), reflexologist, aromatherapist, psychic (an old fraud called Madame Arletty, a name borrowed, he guessed, from the French actress) and on a numbing four-hour shopping expedition to Sloane and South Molton Streets where he lost count of the number of garments she tried on and discarded. However, he kept a written note of the value of dresses and suits bought. Despite her obvious status as a regular and well-regarded client, she made no attempt to seek discounts. She paid full price for everything. The final tally for this daddy's girl, unleashed with her own platinum charge cards, was £17,500.

In one frock shop Gervase learned just how unselfconscious she was about her body; his impression was reinforced when she related to him, with much relish, the incident of the filched perfume flacon in Pong Passage.

He had been summoned into a changing room to arbitrate between a selection of cocktail dresses. She made him sit on a small gilt chair and judge as the items were slipped on and dropped off at her feet for the saleswoman to pick up later. Tabitha was wearing only a pair of white bikini pants. She was in superb physical condition, with high, rounded breasts and graceful, soaring legs. Her tan was overall. An absolute peach of a girl – at least physically.

At one point in this impromptu striptease, she said slyly and with a complete disregard of the saleswoman's presence, 'I hope you're not sitting there getting horny. I want you to concentrate on the clothes.'

'You're a terrible tease,' said Gervase, clearing his throat. 'You shouldn't do these wicked things to elderly gentlemen.'

'I've been meaning to ask you,' she said. 'Did you have it in mind during our summer odyssey to have your wicked way with me?'

'Certainly not,' he said. The saleswoman, blank-faced, had turned away and was fiddling with coat-hangers.

'Liar,' she said.

He supposed he was, up to a point. But a minefield lay between thinking it and doing the deed. On his own resources, how could he keep up with such a racy creature, no matter how sexually desirable? He'd just observed her spend in half a day more than a third of what he earned in a good year. Ultimate humiliation would be the only possible outcome of making a move on her.

'Look upon me as your amanuensis,' he said. 'Simply here to note your every *aperçu* and witticism,' he added soapily.

'Would you mind giving that to me again in English?' she said. 'Is that what an amanu-thingy does?'

It was the first inkling he had that, despite the commanding accent and the fortune her father had spent on her education, she was deplorably ill-informed in certain areas.

She was simply not academically inclined. She was far too impatient. She was preoccupied in assaulting real life, jemmying open the bloated coffers of her fortune, having too much fun spending the stuff to be bothered with the agonies of the mind.

Her hangers-on and attendant ego-polishers had no interest in looking beyond her beauty and money. They could not have cared less that behind the gloss and the swank there existed a dangerous vacuum.

She was a girl who loathed being alone. The mobile phone was the umbilical to her frenetic world. She'd use it even to call a friend sitting a few yards away in the same restaurant.

In just two weeks of babe-chasing, Gervase was already suffering from Tabitha Gatling overload. He had been seriously mistaken to believe that there could be synergy between them. He found that her unflagging energy drained his own. His phone would ring and against the background hubbub of some 'in' Fulham Road *boîte* he'd hear her shrieking, 'Is that you, Misery? Come and meet the man Daddy says I'll marry only over his dead body.'

From the copy point of view, the invitation was irresistible. However, in those two weeks he was introduced to no fewer than three men who would have to circumvent Daddy's corpse if they were to gain the glittering prize. One was an incorrigible chancer, a Tory Member of Parliament, aged forty-six and just separated from his second wife, another was a coarse-featured bond trader of twenty-five, who earned an astonishing amount of money but really wanted to be an actor, and the last was a sad Greek lad named Perry, for Pericles, whose patrimony, he complained, was being plundered by his avaricious American stepmother. To a table of friends and worshippers swept by gales of laughter, Tabitha kept offering all kinds of blood-curdling solutions to Perry's problem. Each was designed to bring about the offending woman's premature demise.

Gervase concluded that she did not provide sex for any of them. When he learned the story of the mooning on the lacrosse field, the twelve-foot chain-link fence assumed a symbolic role. She *always* kept a fence between herself and those who lusted after her. She was a temptress whose satisfaction came from ultimate non-delivery of her flesh. Could she still be a virgin despite all her gamey talk? It was an amusing thought.

Thanks to her looks and growing glamour, she was already on the mysterious A List, a low-rent social register for our times that publicists consult when they issue free invitations to movie premières, club and restaurant openings, and for the VVIP seats at pop concerts.

Gervase had Millie Moses shadow her at these functions, artfully photographing her alongside the likes of Jack Nicholson, Brad Pitt and Mick Jagger. The usual over-exposed suspects.

Tabitha pouted when her amanuensis sometimes declined to attend these grisly events. She wanted courtiers, but a rapidly weakening Gervase wasn't playing. Besides, his new girlfriend, Nelly Tripp, was beginning to complain of neglect. There was no lack of volunteers from other quarters.

He suspected Tabitha's fury at Lord Julian had had little to do with his having abandoned her at Snakes. More likely, she was under the illusion that she was dangling him and his title at the end of one exquisitely manicured finger when, in reality, her true function was herself to be flaunted as the camouflage for his homosexual trawling. This was a rare rebuttal of her queenship.

During the night at his Walham Grove semi-basement digs ('the garden flat', in estate agent-speak) he started to let the answer-machine take the strain of Tabitha's random calls. She sometimes rang only for a pointless chat. Her greeting was usually on the lines of 'Hello, Misery. Speak to me. What's the word?'

At dawn one morning, he opened his bedroom door to hear the pips denoting a recorded message. He shuffled to the machine and pressed Play to listen to her message timed at two-forty-five a.m: 'I know you're there, Misery. You can't hide in the corner. You're supposed to be at my side, taking down my golden words. But all I get is that awful Moses woman making a bloody nuisance of herself.'

Later, he was to ask, 'Why can't you get along with Millie? She's won international awards for her pictures.'

Tabitha shuffled a bit and then abruptly flared, 'I don't think she baths very often.' He guessed that, more likely, the antipathy had arisen because Millie Moses was a woman of recognized achievement and Tabitha wasn't.

Her message ended, 'We're going to meet Daddy. Call me.'

He did, with some alacrity. He'd not formally asked to meet Daddy for fear of rejection. But he most certainly wanted Vernon Gatling, alias Daddy, to figure in his article.

He'd been hoping that an unforced encounter would occur. Gatling *père*, after all, was the major source of Tabitha's financial well-being.

From various clues in the financial press, Gervase judged that Tabitha's annual income from the trust fund set up by her grandfather 'Gunner' Gatling, and hugely augmented by Vernon, amounted to £180,000 a year. Taking into account the low rates of interest then prevailing on the money markets, he calculated that her trustees must be sheltering in excess of £3,500,000 on her behalf. She also had the use of her father's various homes and estates, and was a non-executive director of several of his companies with appropriate compensations. Her XK8 was a company car.

No wonder she could neither spin nor sew nor had any desire to learn.

Gervase phoned.

Chapter Five

He need not have fretted about his mounting expenses for the journey to meet Daddy. Vernon Gatling sent his personal jet, a sparkling Gulfstream IV-SP, to collect them from Gatwick airport and run them down to Nice in style. A presidential-sized black Merc was waiting to pick them up. 'Nothing but the best for Daddy's little girl,' chortled Tabitha, with glee.

They'd been invited, she told him in the limo, for the Monte Carlo rally weekend. She placed her legs up on the seat in front. She was wearing what he could only describe as an *haute couture* travesty of a school uniform, with a badgeless blazer and a pleated skirt cut eight inches shorter than any headmistress would allow. Standing upright, her knickers were no more than an inch away from exposure. With a *faux*-felt bowl-shaped school hat trailing a dark green ribbon over her loose tresses, she suddenly appeared much younger than twenty-three. The first word that came to Gervase's mind was jailbait. What the hell was she playing at?

The Merc glided past the fort and skirted the huge Antibes harbour with its serried ranks of bone-white yachts. He wound down his window. 'Which is Daddy's?'

'You certainly won't find it slumming among these ghastly rowboats,' she said, genuinely disgusted.

'What are you talking about?' he said. 'Some of these must be worth half a million quid.'

She removed one slim leg from the seatback and kicked him in the knee. Her knickers, he could not avoid observing, matched the green of her hat ribbon. 'You have the taste of a shopkeeper,' she said.

They continued on a full circuit of the harbour. At the stone arch giving entrance to the old town, the driver turned left and took them out on to the roadway on the harbour wall. Suddenly, they fetched up at a stone gateway. On the far side, all was revealed. Antibes has a small hidden harbour within a harbour where only the mega-rich are permitted to berth their great seagoing vessels.

Ten were moored along the quay. Third along, flanked by the mighty yachts of a Saudi prince and a German publishing magnate, was Vernon Gatling's pride and joy, his Italian-built sea-greyhound, the *Black Glove*. It was a thing of sleek beauty and, indeed, cast most other pleasure-craft afloat into the category of rowboats. 'Go on – admit it,' said Tabitha, nudging his knee again. 'There are boats and there are *boats*.'

'The name sounds a trifle sinister. Odd one for a pleasure yacht.'

Tabitha shrugged. 'Daddy's such a tease. He says he'll tell the world one day. He'll be angry if I let the dog out of the bag.'

'Don't you mean cat?'

She gave a short laugh that he could not read. 'Do I?'

The chauffeur trailed them with the luggage on to the balustraded gangplank. They were only half-way up the incline

99

when a man's head and shoulders appeared on an upper deck. 'Tabby!' he yelled. 'My baby!'

The head abruptly disappeared and a moment later reappeared. Vernon Gatling was using the highly polished handrails to slide and skip down to main deck. Father and daughter rushed at each other. Tabitha squealed like an eight-year-old at a Spice Girls concert as Vernon Gatling swept her off her feet, steadying her with one hand firmly embedded in her buttock and causing the back of that minuscule skirt to rise dangerously high. Three crew members watched appreciatively.

Father and daughter's faces collided in a kiss. As Vernon rocked her and swayed like a father soothing his infant at bed-time, his canvas-slippered feet shifted round on the spotless wooden deck. Gervase was taken aback to see the passion behind the kiss. Their lips were parted and, if he interpreted the fluttering of Tabitha's cheeks aright, her tongue was inside her father's mouth.

Unlike the grinning crew, Gervase was embarrassed and looked away, pretending to study the German's floating gin palace next door.

At last Vernon dropped his only child back on to the deck and Gervase turned to be introduced. The two men shook hands firmly but Vernon Gatling was barely interested. Tabitha was now nuzzling into his neck and, in his preoccupation, he afforded Gervase only a fleeting, blissfully blank smile.

The tycoon was wearing beautifully cut cream slacks and a cinnamon silk sports shirt. His smooth tan was of the type that only the super-rich seem able to achieve. His forearms were notably muscular, and he stood a fraction over six feet tall from his yachting slippers to his thick blond-grey mane.

He was chunkily built, with powerful shoulders to match those arms and large hands that looked well acquainted with manual labour. His features were too blunt to be described as handsome but the hair, beginning to retreat, flowed back along the temples and gave him a vaguely Viking air. You could not mistake Vernon Gatling for anything other than a star in his own sphere of activity.

His eyebrows were as straight and quizzical as his daughter's. Tabitha had been a late child. He was now sixty-four years old. When Gervase had asked Tabitha about her mother, she had snapped, 'She's dead. We don't talk about her.' He had immediately changed the subject. His article was not aimed at exhuming family skeletons, although he made a mental note to check Mummy out. What was the problem there?

When Gervase was led off to his cabin on the main deck, father and daughter were still nuzzling each other in a way a previous generation would have regarded as 'snogging' and highly inappropriate. Gervase certainly found the sight disturbing.

He started to unzip his case but the steward said, 'Leave all that to me, sir. Mr Gatling will expect you for drinks in a quarter of an hour on the pool deck. Perhaps you'd like to freshen up after your flight?'

The modernistic furnishings of his quarters were faultless. In the bathroom, a complete range of gentleman's toiletries was arrayed on the marble top. A pale blue box contained a Tiffany razor in hallmarked silver.

'Where's Miss Gatling's cabin?' Gervase asked.

'Oh, she'll be in her usual suite next door to her father. One deck up,' said the steward as he hung Gervase's meagre kit in the wardrobe. The man was making a conscious effort not to catch Gervase's eye. He wondered if that was because of the quality of his leisure clothes or because of the uninhibited behaviour of the steward's master.

While he was brushing his hair Gervase felt a subtle shifting underfoot and when he stepped outside he could see they had just cast off for the short trip along the coast to Monte Carlo.

The afternoon was fine and balmy. On deck, the Gatlings and other male passengers already had drinks in their hands. There was some sort of ill-tempered discussion going on as they watched the shoreline slide past. Gervase heard Vernon Gatling say, 'You'd better take me seriously. Call me a sentimental fool. Say I've lost it. I couldn't care less. The board and the accountants can go fuck themselves. We'll pay whatever it takes.'

The body language of at least two of his companions betokened exasperation. But they all straightened and shut up as Gervase hove into view.

Gatling briefly indicated the men and introduced them as 'my associates'. He made no attempt to furnish their names. They nodded and turned to the view.

Gatling had put on a fresh purple shirt with mother-of-pearl buttons and draped an arm loosely around Tabitha's shoulders. She was still wearing that provocative schoolgirl outfit minus the hat.

Gervase now had time to size up Gatling. He was a hard man to read. His grey-washed eyes were hidden behind arrow slits of flesh. In a world of slipshod speakers he had the careful enunciation of an autodidact who'd taken elocution lessons: heavy on the aspirates and careful to give each consonant due weight.

Tabitha said suddenly to her father, 'Gervase was with me when I slugged Julian.'

And to Gervase she added an afterthought, 'Did that Moses woman's photos come out?'

'So she says. I haven't seen them yet.'

Vernon Gatling looked puzzled. He said to his daughter, 'You set Julian up for someone to take pictures of you breaking his jaw? You realize it's going to cost me thirty grand to keep him quiet. If his lawyers get their hands on the prints it'll be even more. You won't even be able to claim self-defence.'

Tabitha placed her cocktail on the table and began nuzzling his neck again. 'Oh, Daddy, you know you can fix it. You can fix anything. Anyway, old Misery here will want to use one with his article.'

And that's when the ordure hit the air-conditioning.

'Article? What article? What are you talking about?' said Vernon, holding his darling daughter at arm's length.

Gervase looked from father to daughter and back again, his heart already sinking. In his head he heard a jarring note in a major key sound loud and clear. *She hadn't told Daddy about the article.*

Gervase could have shaken her until her lovely teeth rattled. She was just playing with all of them. Her voice adopted a wheedling, little-girl tone. 'Oh, Daddy, don't be cross. Misery here is going to write a wonderful feature article about me in *Vanity Bazaar*.'

Those fleshy slits abruptly jerked wide open to reveal red veins surrounding the pupils. 'Jesus Christ,' he yelled at the hapless Gervase. 'Are you a reporter?'

'Er, not exactly,' said Gervase. 'I write feature articles.'

'But you are a journalist?' Daddy looked decidedly out of sorts.

'Why? Who did you think I was?' Gervase said, taking care not to sound assertive.

'I thought you were just another bloody boyfriend,' he yelled. 'I never give interviews to reporters unless it's about business. I never have reporters in any of my homes, much less have them aboard the *Black Glove*.'

'I'm sorry. I didn't know that,' Gervase said, although he had had a pretty good idea that that was his general policy. In the past Vernon Gatling had use for journalists only when he was trying to float one of his real-estate ventures on the stock market and needed the publicity.

Now, for the first time since he'd met her, Tabitha did not appear in total command of the situation. 'Oh dear,' she fluttered. 'It's all my fault, Daddy. I meant to tell you but it slipped my mind.'

Lying little bitch! thought Gervase.

While this mini-drama was taking place Gervase could not help noticing that two of the 'associates' quietly replaced their glasses on the steward's silver tray and slipped away.

Vernon began to pace like a caged animal. 'My God! My God! I've never allowed the media on my boat,' he said. But Gervase was relieved to see that Tabitha's confession had taken some of the heat off him. Still, Gervase thought, Vernon Gatling would have liked nothing better at that moment than to throw him over the rail and let him swim for Cagnes-sur-Mer, which had just appeared on the port side.

Grimly, Vernon said, 'Come with me.'

Tabitha wailed, 'Oh, Daddy, this is all my silly fault. But there's no harm done. Misery is all right when you get to know him.'

But Daddy wasn't listening. Gervase dutifully followed Vernon Gatling to his panelled state room with its naval paintings and a superb seventeenth-century terrestrial globe that, in passing, Gervase prayed he had not converted into a cocktail cabinet. He was ashamed to admit to himself that Daddy's manufactured voice gave rise to such snobbish thoughts.

The tycoon rounded on the bemused writer and said, without preamble, 'Right. Tell me about this article.'

Gervase did so, leaving nothing out – and throwing in his Good Samaritan act at Snakes as evidence of devotion to his daughter.

Vernon digested all this and for a few moments regarded him in silence. Then he began pacing the state room, absently pulling books from the shelves and smelling the leather bindings before replacing them. While he continued with this odd habit, he said over his shoulder, 'It's going to be a piss-taker, isn't it? Spoilt rich girl with more money than sense . . . more money than umpteen teachers and nurses earn in a lifetime of hard graft . . . chucking it around like Marie Wozname.'

'Antoinette?'

'Right. Antoinette.

'Actually, I don't think *she* chucked it around enough. If she had, things might have turned out better for her.'

Vernon looked at him as if he had come unglued. 'What the fuck are you talking about?' he said.

Gervase knew he was gabbling as he tried to steer proceedings into a low-key chat to establish a civilized relationship. But Vernon was interested only in saving his daughter from the jaws of the media mockers.

'Tabby is going to end up looking like an empty-headed little tart just so you can flog copies of your poxy magazine.'

'No, no. Mr Gatling,' Gervase protested. 'That's not the idea at all. I'm not out to satirize her. It'll be the story of a modern miss – the story of how a girl spends her time when she is not subject to the normal pressures of workaday life. She has a luxury lifestyle but it doesn't have to be presented in a rebarbative light.'

Vernon cut in, 'Don't come here trying to put me down with your fancy words. How much are you worth?'

104

'Compared with you, about tuppence,' Gervase said promptly.

'Lemme tell you something, mister.' The elocution was beginning to slip. 'She's all I've got. Who else am I to spend my money on? Why should either of us be ashamed of that?'

'No reason at all,' said Gervase. 'She's a credit to you,' he added, not at all certain he wasn't lying.

Vernon drew closer and when he bared his teeth Gervase could see that the upper edges of his lower set were gold-lined. Vernon Gatling ground his teeth – a sure sign of harboured secret anxieties, no doubt connected with his high-risk financial dealings.

He said, 'At Tabby's age my old man had me servicing and operating earthmovers, cranes and eight-wheel drives. I spent six days a week up to my arse in sump oil and brick dust. On the seventh he made me learn how to do the books. Well, fuck all that. I don't want Tabby ever to go near that shit. While she's young, I want my little girl to have the things I never had the chance to enjoy. She has a world of time before she settles down. Meanwhile I don't want her coming home to me in tears – ever! – because she's been turned over by some schmuck with a laptop. Anyone who does that to my kid is gonna bitterly rue the day.'

Gervase ignored the verbal muscle-flexing. And it was not his place to lecture Daddy about imparting to his child some parental wisdom and the virtues of moderation. Who was Gervase to presume? He wasn't Tabitha's father. Come to that, Vernon Gatling's behaviour on their arrival had not been exactly fatherly either.

There was a lot more in a menacing vein and at one time Vernon Gatling offered to meet Gervase's fee to forget the assignment. Gervase looked at him amazed. 'Even if I took it, which is out of the question, you'd be wasting your money,' he said. 'My piece will be little more than pseudo-sophisticated fluff which is what *Vanity Bazaar* specializes in. They're not Marxists seeking to undermine the rich. You simply have no cause to fear the outcome.'

The multi-millionaire grunted. He wasn't convinced.

*

For the remainder of the weekend, Gervase Meredith was the spectre at the feast. When the *Black Glove* moored in its prearranged position inside Monaco's tiny harbour the town was already being rendered hideous by the noise of the screaming engines of the Formula One cars as the racing superstars practised on the cramped circuit for the big race on Sunday.

Vernon said to him bluntly, 'Look, I'm not going to upset Tabby by asking you to move to an hotel. For one thing, the town's bursting at the seams – there isn't a coalhole to rent. For another, I accept that you walked into this situation blind. All the same, you're a fucking embarrassment to my business friends, who were expecting to be able to have confidential discussions without a reporter hovering at their elbows with a tape-recorder at the ready. You're about as popular as a dose of the pox.'

'Thank you for your candour,' Gervase said icily. 'Have you seen me with a tape-recorder?'

'It's probably concealed up your tight arse,' said Vernon.

It was no loss for Gervase to undertake to keep his distance from the associates. Huffily he took breakfast in his cabin, and dinner ashore on the roof of Loews Hotel with Millie Moses, who'd had to drive into Nice to find a room.

If Gervase Meredith had known then what he learned later, he'd have been creeping all over that boat, ears, eyes and, yes, tape-recorder on alert to catch every murmur that issued from the mouths of Vernon Gatling and his henchmen.

Meanwhile, Tabitha bounced prettily and apparently unconcernedly between boat and shore, getting Millie access to the pits where she photographed *Vanity Bazaar*'s chosen babe with the glamorous English driver, Giles Mancroft. After the race, which was won by a German and gave Gervase a headache, Tabitha disappeared with Mancroft for the remainder of Sunday evening. Perhaps she was his consolation prize. He had lost a wheel on the eleventh lap. Gervase didn't much admire himself for feeling a twinge that was uncomfortably akin to jealousy.

On Monday morning the *Black Glove* was still in harbour but the associates had gone. And Vernon became much more relaxed. He and Gervase sat on deck drinking coffee and watching the bleary-eyed crews of the other yachts who had partied the night away creeping up on to their decks and preparing to depart.

Tabitha had come aboard some time in the early hours and had still not surfaced. Vernon said he had been playing blackjack at the casino and had won sixty thousand francs. 'Here,' he said, suddenly tossing a bundle of hundred-franc notes across the table, 'you have it. It's a bit embarrassing winning when you've already got more than enough.'

This crude second attempt at bribery riled Gervase as much as the first attempt had surprised him. 'For God's sake,' he said, lobbing the money back into the tycoon's lap, 'stop this nonsense, Mr Gatling. I could make you look extremely foolish if the introduction to my story described how you had attempted to buy me off. Have you thought of that?'

'Have you thought of being dead?' Vernon said, holding Gervase's uneasy stare until he blinked.

Millie hopped a scheduled flight back to London while the Gatling party cruised back to the *Black Glove*'s permanent mooring at Antibes. Gervase was intrigued by one aspect of that first encounter with Vernon Gatling: the total absence on board of female companions apart from Tabitha. Over the years Vernon had been seen escorting a host of desirable women, mostly from London or New York society or from the world of the catwalk.

As far as Gervase could gather from other guests aboard the yacht, Vernon's late wife, Tabitha's mother, the one never spoken of openly, had been named Alice. She'd been 'a home body', he was informed – a stark contrast with Vernon's most regular current escort, the Countess Zoë di Sola, a serial wife, lately divorced from her third husband, an Italian fine-arts dealer who inhabited his own Tuscan palazzo.

Zoë was American, daughter of a Washington political dynasty and brainy graduate of Wellesley College. Each carefully considered marriage had massively enhanced her financial standing. She had embellished the feminist war cry: 'Don't get mad,' she advised the sisterhood, 'get everything – plus legal costs.'

Her barracuda character was not difficult to read, if you could get beyond her amazing beauty and her considerable wit.

Gervase soon learned that, when Tabitha was around, her father's paramours were absent – and vice versa. When he mentioned Zoë's name, Tabitha hissed at him, like a serpent that had been trodden on, 'That whore will get my daddy only on the day bananas grow in Iceland.'

Despite her father's opposition, Tabitha continued dutifully to play the babe game. 'I'll talk Daddy round eventually,' she said confidently. 'We took him by surprise, that's all.'

She allowed Gervase and Millie to accompany her to Ladies' Day at Ascot, to polo on Smith's Lawn, to a ballooning weekend in Normandy, to Wimbledon, where she had a fling with the Australian wonderboy Gosforth Gaines until he unexpectedly went out in the quarter-finals and headed for Qantas and home. Tabitha seemed to be having trouble hitching her star to a champion.

Gervase could do nothing but marvel at the fearful energy she poured into a life that was borderline decadent and would have been completely so if she'd ever given him any reason to believe she used recreational drugs. She also carefully limited her consumption of alcohol. Her life was a high in itself; she was at that enviable stage when every sight, sound, taste and feeling was new. She needed no artificial boosters. Daddy had bought the world for her.

There was a constantly revolving wardrobe, incessant telephoning, the hunt for fresh excitements, the wearying (to him) round of fashionable restaurants and clubs, and a gallimaufry of vile people who attempted to worm their way into her pleasure-soaked circle of intimates.

No one with a living to earn could have sustained the killing pace. He began to wean himself away although the phone calls to him 'for a jolly good goss' came almost daily. Somehow, without anything sexual transpiring between them, Gervase had become her confidant. Compared with the sleazebags who never seemed far from her side, he was a pillar of probity. She never said, but Gervase suspected she knew of Daddy's attempts to buy him off and that he had been the first person to put a dent in Vernon's belief that money will solve all problems.

Chapter Six

Two weeks before publication of Gervase Meredith's article in *Vanity Bazaar* the subject rang for more than a goss. The whole thrill-seeking episode of the 'foray' that she and Finula Colm-Harrington had made on W. O. Wilkie's department store was about to go public.

'Some bastard has sold the story and photos from the security cameras to the *Sun*. Daddy's going to be furious.'

For once Gervase lost his temper with her. 'Never mind Daddy,' he shouted into the mouthpiece. 'My story will be pre-empted. Ruined. Scooped. How could you be so silly?'

'It happened before I knew you,' she said, for once abashed.

For the first time, Gervase slammed down the phone on her. His worst-fear scenario was that he'd find her on the front page of the *Sun* next morning. And, sure enough, his worst fear was realized. There she was, brazenly opening her brassière, nipples emerging, in a hazy frame filched from the security tape. This study sat alongside a headline reading 'Tabby's Titillating Take-off. See pages 3, 4 and 5'.

The *Sun* had given her and the half-witted Finula the lip-smacking treatment as only the *Sun* can. There were more out-of-focus photos inside and a sharper one of a tearful Finula confessing all, with her grim-faced titled parents standing in the background, arms crossed and very cross.

Tabitha herself – 'darling daughter of mega-rich building tycoon Vernon Gatling' – had told the *Sun*'s reporters to piss off, but they had snatched pictures of her emerging from a West London restaurant called the Collection. The camera caught her giving them the finger.

Gervase groaned and buried his head. All in all, it was a total professional disaster for him, wiping out, as it did, his claim to have an exclusive 'take' on the life and times of Tabitha Gatling.

The editor of *Vanity Bazaar* was on the phone at ten sharp, just as he finished ploughing through the morning papers. He closed his eyes and steeled himself for the tirade. Instead, she screamed into his ear, 'Darling, it's a gift from heaven! The *Sun* has given us a curtain-raiser we couldn't buy for a million sovs!'

Gervase opened his eyes again. 'You're happy, then?' He tried to sound as if he had planned the whole *Sun* layout and expected no other reaction.

'Delirious, darling. We must do lunch soon. The *Sun* have made the silly little cow into a real personality. Given her a public recognition factor Everest-high. Our cover story will anoint her as *the* Babe of the Decade. It'll be essential reading for every wannabe in the entire Western world.'

Gervase thought he must be losing his instinct for popular journalism. His editor turned out to be right in every respect.

He kept his word to Vernon Gatling. In print he had not taken cheap shots at his daughter. It would have been too easy to have mocked her and adopted a sternly moralistic view of her headstrong lifestyle that a hundred thousand wannabes were already envying as they turned the silken pages of *Vanity Bazaar*. In the text Gervase made the point that at least she wasn't sitting on her wealth, hoarding it for generations unborn like the parsimonious landed gentry in their cold houses who hated all *arrivistes*. Much of Tabitha's patrimony was filtering down through stratas of frockmakers, shopgirls, waiters, cooks, hoteliers and the like. He made it sound almost as if Tabitha was a public benefactress.

But it was Millie's series of shots showing Tabitha slugging the perfidious viscount (headline: 'How About A Knuckle Sandwich, Darling?') that stole the limelight from his prose and made Tabitha an unlikely heroine for the sisterhood. The lawyers as usual had done their best to take the spice out of the coverage. On their insistence, Julian's face was obscured and the copy referred only to 'an aristocratic creep-about-town'.

There was, of course, immediate and intense speculation in all the popular newspapers as to his identity. His anonymity was preserved for just twenty-four hours after *Vanity Bazaar* hit the newsracks. The battered viscount was grassed up by a porter who'd been cn duty at the Westminster and Chelsea hospital when he'd been wheeled in nursing his purple jaw. This time it was the *Daily Mail* that had the scoop.

From being a rich nobody whose wayward existence was known only to café society and the followers of gossip diaries, Tabitha was suddenly catapulted into the upper reaches of London celebrity. She was in demand for talk shows where her photogenic looks and blithe views on serious feminine issues had studio audiences in hysterics.

She said rapists should have their goolies cut off. Men who controlled prostitutes should have their heads shaven and the word PONCE tattooed on their skulls. A wife-beater should be hung up by the thumbs while the maltreated woman beat the shit out of him with a lead-tipped cane. Alimony dodgers should be suspended in iron cages and exposed to public mockery.

Under those golden tresses lurked demons. And Gervase had played his part in releasing them.

As if in gratitude, she insisted that he should be her ghost-writer whenever she was approached to put her name to a feature article for a newspaper or magazine. 'I tried to do it myself. One bloody word after another. It's hard work and there's too much else on my plate,' she said.

'Scribble, scribble, scribble, eh! Miss Gatling?' joked Gervase, after the Duke of Gloucester sympathizing with Edward Gibbon. But, as with bishops vandalizing stained-glass windows, Tabitha didn't get it.

She was rapidly becoming the Outrageous Voice of Golden Youth but she wasn't prepared to submit herself to the slog of writing. She'd learned at her daddy's knee that you didn't pay a dog and bark yourself.

Gervase leavened her medieval views with some much-needed humour and cashed the cheques.

For a newspaper series she introduced him to a system of female self-defence that was photographed at every stage to illustrate his reports. In her teens she had mastered the physically demanding course with impressive facility. At a North London studio, a converted warehouse, he watched her in her baggy tunic being stalked by her instructor. Gervase already knew the wallop she packed in that right-handed 'knuckle sandwich'. And now she revealed a new trick that was almost balletic. She could spin like a top on either foot while the other leg rose to shoulder level. If the side of that circling foot got up sufficient momentum and made full-force contact with the side of your jaw, you were out cold. He'd seen something similar done during a Thai boxing match. Both she and the instructor wore heavily padded head protectors before they demonstrated this dangerous skill for the benefit of Millie's Nikon.

During their clothes-buying expedition, Gervase had wondered why Tabitha's feet, when she slipped off her smart shoes, revealed callouses like armour plating – her only bodily imperfection. Now he knew. Her toughened feet were formidable weapons.

Tabitha also kept a heavyweight's punchbag in the cellar of the Cheyne Walk house and used her father's gymnasium in the country home, an eighteenth-century pile in Warwickshire called Spear's End. Like many another woman of independent means, Tabitha's physical jerks helped while away the empty hours and were part-substitute for the rigours of punching a time clock and wage-earning.

Apparently, Vernon Gatling had recovered from the shock of Gervase Meredith's sudden appearance in his life. 'Daddy was cool,' reported Tabitha a couple of days after the *Vanity Bazaar* piece appeared. 'He said you were very wise. He was glad you hadn't double-crossed me.' There was still lingering menace in that remark, thought Gervase.

The upshot was that with this stamp of parental approval – or at least an absence of disapproval – Tabitha included Gervase and, more surprisingly, Millie Moses in a weekend party of her intimates, including Finula and a pair of flash lads with impeccable manners, introduced simply as 'Wes and Waxy from the Old Kent Road', who even in their casual gear continued to shoot imaginary cuffs and hitch shoulder pads that they'd left behind in South London.

Gervase drove out to Warwickshire in his old BMW and parked it beside two shining Bentley dropheads that he learned belonged to Wes and Waxy, whose profession was never stated.

Vernon, who was not among the weekenders, had made a superb job of renovating Spear's End. He'd had the good sense to leave the interior in the hands of experts. The furnishings, pictures and antiques were of a piece. The result was wonderfully calming even on Tabitha's ragbag collection of friends. The servants were attentive, the food excellent and the various recreations invigorating and fun – apart from the wretched obsession for charades that country house hosts deem *de rigueur* since that is the hazard one faces if one should be honoured to stay with the Royal Family. The Gatlings were nothing if not socially ambitious.

Gervase was intrigued by Wes and Waxy, who had brought a couple of teenage models of the anorexic. tendency with them. They were enthusiasts for anything on offer but, all the same, they hardly appeared to be the kind of males one normally encountered at these upper-middle-class happenings.

The reason for Millie's presence and an invitation to bring her cameras became clear. Tabitha wanted an album portraying herself in a profusion of expensive creations from her wardrobe, using both the exterior and interior splendours of the restored Spear's End as her backdrop. 'Daddy wants a set of pictures of me,' she explained demurely.

Tabitha, for once, was seeking a freebie. But she hit the buffers with Millie who had more nerve and chutzpah than James Bond.

It was clear to Gervase that the hostess had expected Millie to take out her cameras in exchange for a free weekend among the nobs. Millie had worked with bigger nobs than Tabitha was ever likely to assemble, including the Queen, three British

113

prime ministers and two US presidents. Millie said sure she'd photograph Tabitha at Spear's End – and quoted her the full commercial fee.

'I thought you'd do it out of friendship,' said Tabitha, making a face.

'I'll be as friendly as you like, but my price is still the same. For anyone else it would be time-and-a-half as this is my day off,' said Millie, who didn't know the meaning of day off.

Millie's sarcasm cut deep. For a time, Tabitha looked thunderous and Gervase braced himself to be asked to leave and take his horrible photographer with him. But Tabitha was trapped by her own scheming. She'd had all the clothes and accessories prepared and laid out – and Millie was the only top-hole photographer within hiring distance that weekend.

Like a woman surrendering a cherished birthright, she agreed Millie's price and the rest of the party steered clear of them and the shoot for the remainder of the day. The atmosphere between the two women could best be described as formal.

On a somnolent Sunday morning when only the wretched Finula had gone to church, Gervase said casually to Waxy in what he hoped was a sympathetic tone, 'Do you have to get back to town for an early Monday morning start?'

'Leave it aht,' said Waxy. 'We don't do the business on Mondays, do we, Wes? Thursdays is our best day.'

They both laughed fit to bust and Waxy placed a comradely arm around Gervase's shoulders, hugging him tightly to his side. He had the muscles of a TV Gladiator under that brand new country-check shirt.

Much, much later Gervase remembered Piers Frobisher's mention of Tabitha's bank-robbing dance partners and wondered.

Gervase Meredith's agent rang. John Silver was known as Long John for both literary and ironic reasons. He was five foot one. 'I'm taking you along to see Raymond Dilke,' he said, without preamble.

'What for?'

'So that he can ask your opinion of the Schleswig-Holstein question. Whaddya think? He wants to see you. Ain't that enough?'

'Is it a commission for a book? I've never done a book. I'd like to do a book.'

'You're a sprinter not a marathon runner. You're making a lotta money out of that poor little rich girl.'

'I'd still like to do a book.'

'Okay. Let's see what Dilke has to say. Listen to me: Don't say yes unless I say yes. And don't talk money. This is big-time. You leave the sordid to me.'

'Understood,' said Gervase, wondering why Raymond Dilke, chairman of the publishing giant Chantry's, desired his presence.

'Oh, yes,' added Long John. 'Three pip emma tomorrow and, for fuck's sake, wear a collar and tie. Why do you journalists all dress like shit?'

'We're terrified of being mistaken for agents,' said Gervase, replacing the receiver while he was ahead.

The sherry glasses were out and Raymond Dilke was beaming. Indeed, *chuckling.* 'So this is the young man who has *tout le monde* talking,' said the old boy.

Gervase caught his agent's look, which said, 'Keep your mouth shut and listen to the gentleman, stupid. This is the massage before the message.' He gave a self-deprecating, shy smile and put the glass to his lips. He couldn't think what else to do.

Dilke had been joined by his Old Etonian editorial director who had a head of black bushy hair surrounding a bald patch that few could view because he was six foot three. He joined the beam-and-chuckle routine. Those OEs all thought they were so fucking marvellous, but Gervase knew one thing for sure. Long John, looking up at them like Jaws when he'd just spotted a blonde in a bikini paddling above his head, would make Matzo balls of both of them.

'We're full of admiration, aren't we, Rodney, for the way Mr Meredith has captured the *zeitgeist*, as it were, in his chronicling of the life of that extraordinary girl, Tabitha Gatling?' said Dilke, addressing the agent as if the object of their admiration was not present.

'He's done a grand job,' agreed Long John, nodding sagely. 'Mr Meredith is among the finest journalists of his generation.'

This was news to Gervase, but none the less welcome for that. He nodded modestly but they weren't even looking at him. They knew who needed the schmooze.

Dilke was saying, 'It is apparent to us that Mr Meredith, through his manifest talents, has gained entry into the charmed circles that surround Vernon Gatling and his daughter. We feel he is the right man in the right place to tackle a project that has intrigued us for some time – namely, to publish a full history of the Gatling family.

'Who had ever heard of the Gatlings until recent years? But here we have the family patriarch among the richest men in the world, squiring a remarkable line of beautiful women and wielding a fortune that seems to have been created entirely since the war. Yet he remains an enigma wrapped in a mystery. What does anyone know about him or his antecedents?'

The OE cut in. 'As far as we're aware, Vernon Gatling does not come from old money. So how did he and his father get their start?'

Raymond Dilke added, 'I'll be frank with you, Mr Silver, we first commissioned one of our regular authors for this project. That was three years ago when Vernon Gatling was making headlines over the skyscraper he wished to build in Beverly Hills.'

'Who was the scribe?' asked Long John.

'It was Gus Meldrum of the *Wall Street Journal*, a fine investigative journalist who had previously written two splendid biographies for us. He was properly commissioned and we heard nothing from him for four months. Then he telephoned Rodney here, quite unexpectedly, to express doubts about continuing. He said he had run into difficulties and, in any case, was experiencing domestic problems. He offered to return his advance.'

Gervase saw Long John wince at this.

'Rodney urged him to take time to reconsider – told Gus he was under no pressure from us to deliver. We were quite prepared to put back the publication date. So Gus went off to mull over what Rodney had said.'

'And?' prompted Long John.

'And Fate, unfortunately, took the matter out of all our hands. Gus had been phoning from Los Angeles where he was putting together the chapter on the Beverly Hills saga. Three days after the call, his agent rang to say Gus had slipped in the bathroom and died. He was staying at the Chateau Marmont. There was a rock of crack cocaine on the bedside table. We were shocked. Gus was a family man. A Yale man. A disciplined man.'

'Writers!' said Long John in disgust. 'Always moaning they're blocked. Always looking for a new jolt.'

The mention of writers reminded the trio that Gervase was present. They turned in unison to include him in the proceedings.

'Well, young man,' said Raymond Dilke, 'does the challenge of the Gatlings appeal to you?'

Gervase looked at Long John and received an imperceptible nod. 'If the terms are right, certainly,' said Gervase. 'No question, they are a colourful family. Was Gus Meldrum's intended biography an authorized version?'

'I fear not,' said Dilke. 'Mr Gatling said he was not old enough to deserve a biography – which was a ridiculous thing for a sixty-year-old man of his accomplishments to say – and his ancestors too uninteresting to warrant inclusion. He withheld his blessing.'

'You say Gus Meldrum was four months into it. Do his executors have his research material?'

'It's damned irritating,' said Rodney. 'They say they've

found nothing relating to the Gatlings among his papers. And his widow can throw no light. We know for sure he spent at least a month in England on assignment for the *Wall Street Journal*. He had intended at the same time making a start on the Gatlings. 'There must be something somewhere. Unless the papers have been chucked out accidentally.'

'So Vernon Gatling got his way, after all,' said Gervase. 'He won't have shed any tears over poor Meldrum. I can tell you from personal experience that he hates anyone nosing into his private life. He almost had a fit when he found me aboard his boat. He employs public relations people to see that people like me are normally kept at a distance. When I unwittingly breached the *cordon sanitaire*, he tried to bribe me to drop the *Vanity Bazaar* piece. He's a hard man. I'm okay with the daughter but I don't think I'll get much joy from him.'

'Creep up on him,' urged Rodney. 'In the beginning go to the archives. Follow up with fellow workers and distant relatives. Leave him and the toothsome Tabitha till last. You already have a mass of material on her. She'll make a great psychological study.'

At Rodney's elbow, Long John's eyeballs were sliding sideways in a meaningful manner. He was indicating the door and silently telling Gervase that he should use it. His writer took the hint. 'Well, I think I can leave Mr Silver to settle the details with you two gentlemen. It was a privilege to meet you both.'

Gervase shook hands all round and, under his agent's beam of approval – it was a relief for once to have a writer behaving himself in company – withdrew.

Long John rang him two hours later. 'You're on. Hundred grand advance, sixty now, rest on publication. Expenses as incurred. Go get him!'

Gervase Meredith sat back with a bump. A hundred big ones? His girlfriend, Nelly Tripp, was a reporter on contract to the *Guardian*. To justify that sort of loot, he knew he was going to need help. He called Nelly.

Gervase groaned, 'I can't bear the thought of all that grubbing around for the fucking birth, death and marriage certificates. I hate that side of investigative journalism.'

'You've been spoilt, my lad,' said Nelly briskly. She was small, raven-haired and dynamic. You didn't get to be a *Guardian* reporter at the age of twenty-seven because of your exquisite flower arrangements. Now Nelly was on his case and taking charge.

'Since you've been ghosting for that ditsy bimbo, you think life is all champagne, yachts and dinner at Daphne's. It'll do your soul good to get down to some honest graft. Think of the money.'

'Yeah, I've thought of nothing else,' conceded Gervase. 'You know, this is the first time since my father tipped me out into the wicked world to make a living that I've actually had real cash in hand. And I'm nearly twenty-nine for Christ's sake.'

'Take a tip from me,' said Nelly. 'Don't tell your fancy piece about this project. She's all over you now because you're useful to her. But what you are about to do will definitely get Daddy riled. And if it comes to a choice between you and dear Daddy, there's no contest. She'll discard you minus your goolies faster than you can say Yves St Laurent.'

'I dunno. Tabby's a bit wild but she's not such a bad egg.'

'You're such a prick,' said Nelly. 'Don't you know anything about women? They gravitate towards the money.'

'You're not gravitating towards my money.'

'Who says I'm not? Take me to dinner – somewhere expensive.'

All the same, he decided for the moment to follow Nelly's advice.

Gervase bought a metal filing cabinet, found room for it in his bedroom, and began to fill it with his research material and computer printouts for which Nelly Tripp made herself responsible, being wondrously skilled in the electronic mysteries.

The published material on the Gatlings' business activities was considerable and Gervase spent weeks gathering it in, indexing it and assembling it in chronological order before facing the fag of creating the family tree.

He continued to ghost for Tabitha but she'd become pouty since discovering the existence of Nelly.

'Who was that girl who answered your phone last night?'

'Her name's Nelly Tripp.'

'What a common-sounding Mordenish name. What was she doing in your place at one-thirty in the morning?'

'We are very close.'

'You're fucking her,' said Tabitha flatly. 'And I thought I was the love of your life.'

'Our friendship is of a different order.'

'You've never fucked me.'

'Now don't start that, Tabby. You know you're only teasing. It would spoil our relationship – and what would your daddy say to you being involved with a no-account hack?'

'Bullshit!' said Tabitha. 'What's this Nelly got that I haven't?'

'An overdraft for one thing,' said Gervase.

Tabitha was phoning because she'd been offered an expenses-paid trip to New York for a photo-layout for *Vanity Fair*. 'They wanted to put their own writer, a chick, on the case. I said, "No way. My amanuensis is Mr Gervase Meredith, the distinguished British wordsmith. We come as a pair or we don't come at all."' Tabitha paused. 'I think I just made a *double entendre*.'

Gervase ignored the provocation. 'What's the theme?'

'They propose taking me to Harlem and Newark, New Jersey. The headline is "Babe in the 'Hood". I get to meet a lot of black dudes.'

'Don't you think you'd be better off with an American writer who knows the ground?'

'Listen, you began this babe bullshit. You're included in, buster. Anyway, I don't know why you're playing hard to get. There'll be a fat fee in it for you.'

They flew Concorde. As usual, Tabitha kicked up a fuss about the seating arrangements. According to her, if you weren't placed in the first ten rows, you were social dogmeat.

For Gervase, Concorde was a first and he was disappointed. 'I hadn't realized it was such a cramped little thing. If Britain and France had developed the jumbo jet instead of throwing a billion quid away on this toy for the rich, the economy would be in damn sight better shape,' he complained, as they went sub-sonic for the drop into Kennedy.

'God! You really are a misery,' said Tabitha. 'Why don't you just accept what's on offer in this life? Why do you have to question everything?'

'Because that's what journalists are supposed to do,' said Gervase doggedly. 'It doesn't always make you popular.'

The assignment failed to stir Gervase's imagination. They ventured from the opulence of the Plaza Hotel with a camera team and a wagon-train of style co-ordinators. Tabitha was arrayed in various sets of street clothes and introduced to a number of carefully sanitized groups of 'brothers' in the deprived black neighbourhoods while the magazine's photographers got to work.

Gervase dutifully took notes and supplied appropriate copy about the bodacious babe who was currently outraging a once-again swinging London with her outrageous opinions. It would have been tired stuff back home but the Yanks had yet to be exposed to the pleasure of the full Babe-Tabitha phenomenon.

Tabitha also dragged him to a couple of hellish Manhattan nightclubs where he watched her being hit on by the scions of the Park Avenue set. There was much swapping of telephone and e-mail numbers.

When she flew home, pleased with her conquests, Gervase stayed on. He'd had an idea.

He made a transatlantic call to his newly acquired publishers and said to Rodney, the OE, 'Let me have Gus Meldrum's address and number. I'd like to have words with his widow while I'm over here.'

Over the past week in the 'hoods he'd struggled to decipher the hip slang and mangling of the English language. It was a relief to speak to someone with the beautifully modulated voice of another America.

Gus Meldrum's widow listened politely to Gervase's explanation for his call. Finally, she said, 'I don't know what I can do to help you, Mr Meredith, but you are welcome to drive out. Allow yourself three hours. Sag Harbor is at the far end of Long Island. I'll have some lunch ready.'

Chapter Eight

Gervase was early. For once, traffic on the notorious expressway – 'the longest parking lot in the world' – was moving at a fair lick. The Meldrum home was on the edge of the old whaling town, one of those delightful wood-frame Cape Colonial houses, modern but owing everything to the genius of eighteenth-century architects. Felicity Meldrum turned out to be a plump, greying women in her fifties with a kindly, sad face. Of her three children, the daughter was in medical school and the two sons still at university. Gervase could see why she had agreed so readily' to see him. The house echoed. She lacked company.

She made him sit in a chintzy armchair and she introduced him to a very dry martini. As he sipped, she eyed it almost lasciviously. 'Aren't you having one?' asked Gervase.

Felicity Meldrum smiled sheepishly. 'I have to ration myself. Martinis are the besetting sin of lonely widows. For a time, after Gus had gone, I'm sorry to say I indulged rather too freely.' Her upper lip was trembling.

'If it had been me,' said Gervase stoutly, 'I think I'd have remained blotto for a year. Your husband's death must have come as a terrible shock. He was relatively young, wasn't he?'

'Yes, we'd just celebrated his fifty-second birthday.' He followed her glance to a framed photograph on a sideboard. It showed a stooped man, professorial in appearance, in rimless spectacles and wearing a chef's toque. Gus Meldrum had been presiding at a garden barbecue when the photograph was taken.

Gervase set down his chilled glass. 'From what they told me at Chantry's, his research material on the Gatling family could not be found after his death. I wondered if, after three years, any of it had since come to light?'

Mrs Meldrum shook her short, iron-grey locks. 'He worked on the book here and at the *Journal*. There was a file on every other project he'd ever worked on, except that last one. I was puzzled. I know for a fact he'd already written a great deal of material in his den.'

She rose abruptly. 'Let me show you.' She led the way across polished timber floors to Gus Meldrum's study above the double garage.

'There have been some alterations. Our sons use it now. But the furniture and that old Apple Mac desktop are the same.'

There were football pennants on the walls, a framed photograph of Meldrum receiving the Pulitzer for his *Wall Street Journal* exposé of a particularly avaricious arbitrageur and insider trader, a lithograph of Albert Einstein and two tall filing cabinets much like the one Gervase had recently bought to house his own research material.

'What about the computer?' he asked. 'My girlfriend knows more than I do about this sort of thing, but doesn't all work get stored on a hard disk? Perhaps you need a password to get in?'

'No, there was nothing like that. Gus had the priority but we all used the machine for our various purposes at other times. We found nothing concerning the Gatlings. Not a word. Nor was anything found among his effects at the *Wall Street Journal*.'

'Could he have had another, secret, place? Some writers do. Just to have peace and quiet while they work?'

She said patiently, 'Mr Meredith, Gus and I had been married twenty-eight years. As far as I know we had no secrets from each other. I was outraged when, after Gus's body was found, the police tried to imply that he had sent for a call-girl or had picked up a prostitute on the Sunset Strip and she had sold him dope. Gus and I both occasionally smoked a spliff when we were on our own but we never went near anything more hazardous.'

Gervase stared. 'What prostitute? I was told he was . . . experimenting, no doubt, with crack cocaine and slipped in the bathroom. No other party was mentioned.'

For the first time anger flitted across the gentle face. 'We have only the word of an elderly night porter and the police eventually discounted it. The man gave a description of a young woman in dark glasses, wearing a navy blue beret over jet black hair who, he claimed, asked for my husband's room number.

'The Los Angeles police department searched for this person but came up empty-handed. A severe blow to the temple killed Gus. If it weren't for the presence of the crack cocaine, which I know Gus never touched, I'd have accepted that he fell in the bathroom. It has nagged at me for the past three years that there is something monstrously wrong about his death. I do not even rule out homicide. But nobody wants to listen. They think I'm only interested in an act of revenge by trying to pin a murder on this unknown girl who, they think, was there to provide my husband with nothing more sinister than a little dope and a lot of sex.'

Felicity Meldrum began to cry. 'Oh, I'm so sorry,' she sobbed. 'I didn't mean to do this.'

A stricken Gervase stepped back to the doorway where she had remained standing and hugged her tight. 'That's all right,' he said. 'You go ahead. You're entitled.'

She served lobster tail and salad for lunch. Gervase declined wine. 'Better not. Your traffic cops with their ever-ready guns frighten the life out of me.'

Across the polished old table, he returned to the puzzle that had brought him here. 'Could you have had a burglary that went unnoticed?'

'Just for Gus's research papers? It doesn't sound very likely. Of what value were they to anyone but Gus?'

'Well, there's Vernon Gatling for a start. I know from personal experience that he hates anything published about his private life. Now that he's a prince among the glitterati I suspect he has become ashamed of his humble beginnings.'

Felicity Meldrum said, 'Gus was certainly rebuffed when he requested a meeting with him. And, afterwards, Gatling's public-relations people wined and dined Gus, trying to dissuade him from carrying on with the project.'

'I'd take a bet they offered him money to desist,' said Gervase, remembering his own experience aboard the *Black Glove*.

'That's right, they did,' she said. 'Gus merely laughed. He was a man of the highest integrity.'

Gervase carefully set aside his empty plate and placed his forearms on the table. What he had to say had to be said with finesse. 'Mrs Meldrum, did you know your husband had doubts? He even tried to back out of the deal with Chantry's.'

She stiffened in her ladderback chair. 'I find that hard to accept.'

'I'm afraid it's true. I have it directly from Raymond Dilke. Your husband telephoned Chantry's three days before he was found dead. He mentioned that he had run into difficulties and had domestic problems. He went away to reconsider.'

Mrs Meldrum was clearly bewildered. 'But he had no domestic problems. We were, if anything, indecently happy. He had a fine career and our three children have always been a joy to us.'

'Then he must have been inventing an excuse to get out.' Gervase had to press the point: 'Why would a man of your husband's integrity stoop to such a lie? If he was simply bored or otherwise disenchanted with the project, why not simply say so?'

She sat silently, staring at the sheen on the table-top. Then, tonelessly, she said, 'For the last month of his life he was very subdued. I thought he was overworking. When he went off to Los Angeles to continue his research, he insisted that I shut the house and go to stay with my sister in Albany, upstate New York, for a week or so. I took it that he didn't want me to be rattling around this house alone – all the kids were away at school.'

She raised her eyes and looked into his. 'Are you suggesting there was something, well, sinister in this?'

'Until this conversation,' said Gervase, 'I thought I was engaged in a conventional literary exercise to produce a routine biography. Now I'm not so sure. Your husband's out-of-character conduct . . . your suspicions concerning the circumstances of his death . . . I know Vernon Gatling is a hard man but it's a giant step from persuasion to murder in order to get your own way about something as inconsequential as a book. From your husband's formidable reputation as an investigative journalist, I'd guess he has made enemies in other fields. Employing contract killers is an American rather than a British pastime. Perhaps all this has nothing to do with Vernon Gatling? Perhaps your husband really did have a fall and was not murdered at all.'

The widow said bleakly, 'Yes. We may be allowing our imaginations to get out of hand. We'll never know, will we?'

Felicity Meldrum detained Gervase as long as she decently could, showing him round the pretty town – 'It's hell at the weekend when half Manhattan thunders in' – driving him out to a windy bluff to view the house where John Steinbeck once lived, and giving him afternoon tea before he hit the highway back to the Plaza Hotel.

Her parting words to him were, 'You watch your back, young man. As the saying goes, just because you're paranoid doesn't mean to say they're not out to get you.'

Chapter Nine

Nelly Tripp listened wide-eyed to Gervase Meredith's recital of his encounter with the melancholy widow. 'Right!' she said, snapping back to life. 'We take no chances. We make a copy of everything. We keep one here and one at my place. That bastard Vernon Gatling sounds as if he's been "putting the plumbers in", like Richard Nixon with Watergate, to steal the documentary evidence of a misspent life. Vernon has bonked a lot of women and some of them must have blabbed to Meldrum. Perhaps he hasn't got much between his legs?'

'I can't believe he'd have Gus Meldrum bumped off just to

hide the fact he's got a little dick,' said Gervase. 'I mean, it's out of all proportion.'

'Maybe like his dick,' said Nelly. 'Not only do you not know anything about women but you haven't much of a clue about men, either. I know any number of so-called hunks who are obsessed by the size of their tools. They'd murder for something larger.'

'How come a girl of your tender years knows so much about such things?' said Gervase. 'I thought you were sweet and innocent.'

'Grow up!' said his paramour. 'And help me get started on the copying.'

From the first birth certificates and entries in parish registers that Gervase and Nelly laboriously turned up, they established that in the nineteenth century the Gatlings had lived in Bermondsey, the riverside borough facing the Tower of London.

It was Nelly who came home with the first fragment of gold dust: a photocopy of an entry in a burial register for June 1848, recording the death of the property tycoon's great-great-grandmother, Gertrude.

Gervase took one look, gave a whoop of triumph and hugged Nelly, swinging her off her neat little feet. 'No wonder Vernon doesn't want a biography!' he shouted.

Under the column listing cause of death, in long, spidery handwriting, had been entered the words, 'Death by Judicial Hanging'. Granny Gatling had been just thirty years old and a felon.

There were no further details and Nelly pushed Gervase out, groaning and moaning, to face the grinding follow-up research among the files held at the British Museum newspaper section in Colindale, north London.

The Times finally yielded a brief account of Gertrude Gatling's crime. She was described by the anonymous correspondent attending her trial as 'a female of unusual size, dull and hardened in her stupidity'. She had clubbed to death an older woman, a street orderly named Florrie Tregaskis. They had quarrelled over territorial rights, so the judge and jury were told.

The report kept referring to the accused as 'a pure-finder' without any further explanation of what this trade entailed. It had obviously been a well-known term in the early days of Queen Victoria's reign but to Gervase it was unfamiliar. He made a note to check.

Gertrude Gatling had been described in court as a woman known for her aggressive disposition and ill humours. The jury had no difficulty in finding her guilty nor the judge in having the black cap placed upon his wig and sentencing her to death.

Rolling on the microfiche, Gervase found a nauseating account of the condemned sermon by the ordinary of Newgate Gaol, the Reverend Mr Carver.

The governor's house and the entrance to Newgate, known as the Felon's Door, had been besieged by fashionable people of both sexes waving their tickets of admission and anticipating salivatory happenings. They had not been disappointed.

Lashed by the Epistle to the Romans – 'But after thy hardness and impenitent heart treasurest up unto thyself wrath against the day of wrath and revelation of the righteous judgment of God' – the condemned woman had collapsed repeatedly into the two turnkeys' arms and was each time 'restored to animation' with cold water applied to her bloodless lips so that the clergyman's sermon might continue long and thunderous.

The crowd joined lustily in the hymns and finally departed, gratified and cleansed.

Gervase rubbed his hands in unpitying glee. 'Great chapter!' he said to himself. 'What a find!'

'What the hell is a pure-finder?' asked Gervase, putting down the *Concise Oxford Dictionary* which had failed to enlighten him.

Once again Nelly pored over Gervase's notes. 'It was obviously some kind of nineteenth-century trade. Who do we know with a sociology degree?'

'Half the world,' said Gervase.

Nelly phoned a girlfriend. 'She says try Henry Mayhew's Victorian survey of the London poor. He investigated all the street trades of the time. Off you go.'

Once again Gervase found himself walking round to the borough reference library.

And there it was.

He didn't know whether to laugh at the embarrassment Vernon Gatling had coming when the biography was published or weep at the grinding misery Mayhew's researches had revealed.

'The pure' was simply a euphemism for dog-shit. During Queen Victoria's golden reign this was worth from eight pence to one shilling and two pence a bucket for 'the dry, limy-looking sort'. The buyers were the leather-dressers and tanners whose yards proliferated in Bermondsey. The alkali in the shit assisted in the purification of the goat and lamb skins that ultimately found their way to glovers, shoemakers and book-binders to the gentry.

Reading this, Gervase sat back abruptly in his chair, and said 'Jesus!' so loudly that he earned stern glances from other readers. He had a sudden, vivid remembrance of Vernon Gatling in his state cabin hectoring him and at the same time absently taking down old volumes from his shelves and *sniffing* at their morocco covers.

Vernon knew!

According to Mayhew, there had been some 240 people scavenging the streets, courtyards and alleys of London for the pure, of whom Gertrude Gatling must have been one. Gervase had a vision of a hefty, lumbering woman claiming 'her streets' and fending off any interloper attempting to scoop up 'her' turds.

What had been her victim's transgression? Had Florrie Tregaskis, the street orderly, moonlighted by taking her besom and sweeping up the only thing that stood between Gertrude and starvation? Gervase pictured the woman of 'unusual size' coming upon Florrie surreptitiously collecting the pure, bearing down on her in uncontrollable rage and hammering her into the cobblestones until the blood ran in the gulleys.

Fighting over *dog-shit*! My God! thought Gervase. He found the tableau as hard to grasp as the enormity of African famine.

He ploughed further into Mayhew and at last discovered the

secret of the *Black Glove* that Vernon Gatling might one day 'tell the world'.

The pure-finders were easily identifiable: they carried, for obvious olfactory reasons, collecting baskets with handled lids – *and kept their right hands covered with a black leather glove.*

Gervase ceased making notes and gazed at the dust motes floating in a shaft of sunlight that struck his desk from a window high in the reading room.

Vernon Gatling knew everything about his great-great-grandmother's desperate life and death. That much was certain. What must he feel, as he sits in one of his many penthouses, in the towers that bear his name, looking down godlike on the scurrying workaday mortals of the streets below, surrounded by art treasures, servants and the ever-present fawning entourage? He must still think of her and her grisly end, or why else the *Black Glove* name on the yacht? Was a constant battle raging inside his head, the man of substance and power wanting to forget? The boy from Bermondsey forbidding it and calling him back – a classic case of *nostalgie de la boue*?

He returned to Walham Grove in a queasy state. He told Nelly, 'Thanks a bunch. My stomach's still heaving. I shan't be eating dinner tonight.'

She said, 'Still, you have to admit, it's a corker of a story – from dog-shit to riches in four generations. Vernon Gatling and his flash daughter are going to be severely humiliated when we dump this particular bucket of doo-doo over their heads.'

'I feel a bit guilty about Tabitha. I'm almost her damn guardian,' mumbled Gervase.

Nelly rounded on him fiercely. 'Don't you *dare* feel sorry for that exhibitionist bitch! She'll shuck you off the moment you're no longer of use to her. Just don't you forget that – and don't you dare drop her any hint that we are working on the family biog! Word will zip straight back to Daddy.'

Gervase nursed a fizzy drink in an effort to settle his stomach. He said, 'Do you think Gus Meldrum found out about Gertie and the dog-shit and Vernon threw a moody? Gus was in London for more than a month nosing around after he got the book commission. He was a world-class digger. I wonder if we've followed him down the same trail to where old Gus sighted the first turds in the Gatling saga? And Vernon found out?'

Chapter Ten

Having had his first success among the archives, Gervase was at last galvanized. He no longer required Nelly Tripp's firm shove to eject him from the flat and direct him towards the brooding repositories where the British record their births, deaths and marriages. Gatling was an unusual name – he found only four in the current London telephone directory – and this was a great help as his eyes sped through columns of surnames from an age before computerization.

Swiftly he discovered that Gertrude had had a son, Jack, born just three years before she was hanged. In turn, his first-born was named Alfred (1878–1936) who had a third son, Frank, born in 1910. This was the Gatling whom Gervase was later to learn had been nicknamed Gunner, in honour of the rapid-fire machine-gun invented by an American, Richard Jordan Gatling, which an Anglo-Egyptian army had deployed with impressive effect against the fuzzy-wuzzy hordes at the battle of Omdurman in the Sudan a few years previously.

Gunner Gatling had been Vernon's father.

From their wretched existence in the lower depths of Victorian London, the Gatlings had struggled their way upward. They were men and women of the streets, supreme opportunists forever with a predator's eye for the unconsidered trifles of the imperial city. They were totters, rag-and-bone merchants, scrap-metal collectors. They lived on the droppings of canines and humans. By the time of Alfred's birth, they had owned their own yard in Tanner Lane, Bermondsey.

Gervase went exploring in this dingy corner of South London, a town-planning nightmare of shabby commercial premises cheek by jowl with council flats and warehouses converted into 'loft' apartments for the upwardly mobile. Storage premises for antiques from the nearby Bermondsey Market stood on the site of Gatling's Yard. The manager had never heard of the family, but Gervase was not flummoxed. He'd been taking lessons from Nelly, his very own investigative reporter. 'You go straight to the nearest pub and find the oldest inhabitants,' she had advised.

Gervase found the pub and found the oldest inhabitants – in fact, three of them, two women and a man who had survived boom, bust, depression and blitz. Remarkably, they were all still laughing, God bless 'em. Gervase bought them their favourite tipple and got down to business.

The man remembered Gunner vividly. 'He had this old horse and cart like Steptoe but you wouldn't think he had tuppence to his name. He dressed in rags. In fact, for the Easter parade in Hyde Park, his poor horse was better dressed. Old man Gatling was a nasty bastard. For a dare us kids would run through his yard yelling and screaming and pulling down the stacks of scrap iron. He'd come running out of his hut ranting and raving as if we were robbing him. He wore one of those thick leather belts and if he caught you with the buckle end you knew all about it. He copped me once with that buckle and broke the skin on the back of my head. My mum was furious. There was blood all over my new shirt.'

The old boy sucked on his remaining teeth at a memory suddenly recalled. 'My dad went storming round to the yard. He wasn't the only one who tried to sort out old Gatling but Gunner was a big bugger. It usually ended up with pals having to separate the men. After my dad went for him, I used to kid myself that he was winning when they pulled him off but, looking back, I think his mates pulled him off because old Gunner was getting the best of it.'

One of the two old darlings broke in, 'Walloping the kids wasn't the only thing. He used to treat that horse something cruel. We've all seen him punch it in the head. Really punch the poor beast so that it staggered. He nearly got nicked for it once. Some toff was passing him in Great Dover Street and witnessed him clout the animal because it'd walked on a few yards without getting a giddy-up or something. The bloke reported it to the police. By rights old Gatling should have been up at Tower Bridge for cruelty and put inside. But he got away with it, as usual.'

'How did he manage that?' asked Gervase, signalling the barman for another round.

'Had the police in his pocket, didn't he? They were always up in his office with him pouring whisky down their throats and they turned a blind eye to the stolen lead and copper that passed through the yard. Half the bloody churches and factories in the area lost their lead roofs because Gunner Gatling lived local.'

The ancient trio watched Gervase scribbling on his notepad. 'What's this for, son?' said one of the old ladies who was enjoying her second milk stout and had so far kept silent while she enjoyed her unexpected good fortune.

'I'm doing a family history,' he said carefully. 'A sort of family tree.'

She nodded, satisfied. 'Well, after all we've said about him, you'd better not leave out the old bugger's medal,' she said.

'Oh, yes. I've seen mention of that. An MBE, wasn't it? Awarded for bravery? I haven't yet had time to go through the military records for the details,' apologized Gervase.

'Military records my arse,' said the old girl. 'He was never in the forces. Gunner Gatling was too crafty to get caught for that.'

'So how did he get an MBE?'

'In the blitz, wasn't he. In Heavy Rescue – you know, the ARP, air-raid precautions.'

'So what did he do for the medal?'

'Dunno, really. You ought to ask Percy Start.'

'Percy Start?'

'Yes, he was our local air-raid warden. Once worked alongside Gunner.'

As if she had given a signal, the three put down their drinks, cupped their hands around their mouths and yelled in unison, 'I shan't tell you again – *put that bloody light out!*'

Then they all rolled around in their seats, tears of mirth

following the downward course of the wrinkles in their cheeks. The barman came to see what the commotion was about and Gervase grinned uncertainly.

'Sorry, son,' said the old girl, collecting herself. 'Percy's a bit of a joke around here. If you had a chink in your blackout curtains as much as the size of an eyelash, he'd be bellowing up at your window like a regimental sergeant-major – even when the Germans already had the whole bloody place lit up like a Christmas tree with their incendiaries. Before the war he was such a mild little man. Then they gave him that armband and tin helmet and he turned into Adolf Hitler.'

Gervase Meredith found Percy Start living up the road in a ground-floor, surprisingly graffiti-free council flat. He was eighty-two, had a straight back and cropped iron-grey hair. His ARP helmet was still hanging in his hall more than half a century after the cessation of hostilities.

Clearly Percy was still the sergeant-major and you could see why the yobs had failed to spray-paint in the vicinity of his front door: an ornamental Japanese samurai sword of the type that can take off an arm with one swipe was racked alongside the hatstand.

Percy sniffed with a small tic of disapproval as he stood aside to afford his caller admittance. Gervase guessed the old man had caught a whiff of the alcohol on his breath.

He did not offer any further refreshment but politely seated Gervase in his neat living room. Gervase gave him the family-tree and history spiel and asked about the wartime medal.

'He was awarded it by His Majesty the King for rescuing bomb victims from the debris,' said Percy importantly.

'Where did this act of bravery take place?'

'Somewhere in Kensington.'

'Not here in Bermondsey?'

'No. Frank Gatling began his service with Heavy Rescue here but transferred to a Kensington and Chelsea unit.'

'Wasn't that odd? I mean, you were next to the docks here in Bermondsey. You were much more heavily bombed.'

Percy shrugged. 'Frank Gatling, his wife Cynthia and little Lionel lived in three rented rooms next door to his yard. He transferred to a Heavy Rescue unit north of the river when he moved his family over to a house off Kensington High Street. Better class of neighbourhood, I suppose.'

'Wait a minute,' said Gervase. 'Who's little Lionel?'

Percy permitted himself a tight, indulgent smile. 'I suppose you know little Lionel as Vernon, the man who builds all those skyscrapers, hotels and gambling casinos. Little Lionel has gone up in the world. He's far too grand for Bermondsey nowadays.'

'I can see that,' said Gervase, 'but when did he change his name to Vernon?'

'The name Lionel came from his mother's side of the family. Even as a little boy Vernon hated it. Other boys used to tease him. They said it was a cissy name. They'd call him Lion and challenge him to roar like one. He was always in fights. Luckily for him, he was a tough little fellow – rather like his father in that respect. Neither of the male Gatlings let anyone tread on them. They had ambitions, which I suppose is one of the reasons Gatling Demolitions became so successful immediately after the war.'

Percy was beginning to wander through the byways of memory. Gervase pulled him back. 'You were going to tell me about the Vernon thing.'

'Ah, yes. Unlike most of us, Frank Gatling – I always thought the Gunner nickname inappropriate for a man who had not been in the armed forces – came out of the war in better shape than when he went in. In 1939 he was nothing more than a scrap-metal merchant with a small yard, a horse and a couple of full-time workers. I used to do his books, such as they were. He only let me see what he wanted me to see. Almost immediately after the last siren sounded, he blossomed out as Gatling Demolitions, a big concern. He returned to us here in Bermondsey where his roots were. He took over a huge yard off the Old Kent Road, bought up second-hand bulldozers, cranes and earthmovers at auctions of wartime equipment. And he seemed to have plenty of money to do it.'

'Oh? There couldn't have been much money in ARP work.'

'You've put your finger on it. There were lots of ugly rumours that Frank Gatling had been making money on the black market. There was strict rationing, you know. When the gossip reached his ears, he finally admitted he'd won a sizeable sum on the football pools but had opted for no publicity. He told me, "I've been forced to own up and now I'll get smothered with begging letters. I can't let these lies spread. It's not good for business."

As a kind of public acknowledgement of his good fortune, he said his son Lionel had decided to change his hated name to Vernon. It was on Vernon's Pools that Frank Gatling said he'd had his win.'

'What an extraordinary way to acquire a name,' said Gervase.

'Yes,' said Percy. 'The only person upset was his mother, Cynthia, poor woman. She'd always considered Lionel to be a name that had class. It's awful how little I can remember about her. She was so insignificant alongside her ambitious menfolk. So timid. Half the time I think she was just plain scared of Frank. I can't even remember her funeral.'

Percy Start wagged a sorrowful head. 'She was much neglected. Apart from making money, Frank had one obsession as a young man – ballroom dancing. The only time you ever saw him out of his working clothes was when he went off on a Saturday night to some competition or demonstration, leaving poor Cynthia behind. She had two left feet, or so Frank complained. His regular partner was some fancy piece from a hairdressing salon up Rotherhithe way.'

Gervase brought the old man back on track. 'So before Gatling Constructions came the demolition business?'

'Yes. London and many another town were in ruins, as I'm sure you were taught at school. There was much work for demolition experts and Frank Gatling had learned a thing or two in Heavy Rescue. He was clever. He didn't charge in like a madman, knocking down walls by swinging an iron ball on the end of a crane. Frank would go carefully through every surviving room, cellar and attic of the buildings he was bringing down. For the first time in his life he didn't just have a trade in rags and scrap. He salvaged marble fireplaces, ornamental pillars, sconces, antique baths, old oak floorboards and any other fancy fitment that had been abandoned. He hired a line of railway arches and had all this stuff stacked away against a return of a post-war market. When he'd had the pickings, and the building sites were cleared of the ruins, it was a logical development to move on to reconstruction. And that's when young Vernon joined the business and began to build his fortune and all those glass towers.'

At last Percy Start offered refreshment. Gervase, mouth parched after the alcohol, joined him in the small kitchen where Percy, a widower it transpired, went through the stiffly correct motions of making a pot of tea with tea-leaves from a tin caddy, properly boiled water and five minutes' brewing time. Gervase gratefully accepted two cupfuls.

The emollient brew and the fact that Gervase had put away his notebook appeared to relax his host. As he shook hands to leave, Percy hesitated, then said, 'I think you should go over to Kensington to complete the picture. I'm sure I've only ever known a fraction of it. That football pools story . . .'

'Yes?'

'Frank Gatling may have had a medal but he wasn't always wedded to the truth. No one ever proved he got that start-up money by picking eight draws. I've often wondered . . .'

Chapter Eleven

Nelly Tripp listened to Gervase's recital and said, 'I think your Mr Start is right on the button. Find the money source and you find the man. You should do what he says and get over to Kensington.'

Gervase groaned.

'By the way, Her Royal Highness has been on. She's becoming awfully suspicious because you're not always at her beck and call, these days. I told her you were visiting your mother. The *News of the World* want her to do a piece on the world's ten most fanciable men. You're to supply the copy.'

'How the fuck would I know about that crap?'

'Don't worry. She says she'll supply the names. Guess who comes in at number one?'

Gervase flashed up an instant mental picture of Tabitha in her teasing schoolgirl uniform and Vernon Gatling with his hand pressed firmly into her buttock. 'Easy,' he said. 'It has to be darling Daddy.'

'Right on,' said Nelly. 'They say incest is all right as long as you keep it in the family.'

He wondered if she had inadvertently said something too uncomfortable to contemplate where the Gatlings were concerned.

Emerging from the basement store, the librarian dropped the tattered volumes on the sturdy desk, causing a small cloud of fine dust to billow across the oak surface. 'That should be enough to keep you going for a while,' she puffed, so cheerfully that Gervase Meredith had to fight an internal battle to quell a sarcastic and deeply ungrateful retort.

The pile tottered and toppled, sending thin ledgers skidding towards him. Gervase felt his strength leaking away. This was going to take days, if not weeks. There were six years of ARP and Fire Guard post records, incident reports, casualty reports, each raid meticulously timed from first warning (red alert) to All Clear (white), day raids (key: yellow), night raids (key: purple), parachute flares seen, type of incendiary bomb (phosphorous or kilo magnesium) dropped, location of water and gas main fractures . . .

Despite his initial antipathy, two days' exposure to these dog-eared exercise books, in which many hands had made brisk, factual entries, began to bring about a chastening change in Gervase. He found himself handling with growing reverence these volumes with their broken spines and foxed covers.

The agonies of those terrible times between 1939 and 1945 seemed to rise off the page all the more potently because the language was that of the office clerk and not the poet. Emotion was nowhere to be detected. Here were his forebears at the zenith of their Englishness, disciplined, enduring, brave in a way that sought no fanfare, resolute in a way that begged no quarter.

'Now all the youth of England are on fire,/And silken dalliance in the wardrobe lies,' he murmured.

'Christ, what happened to us?' he said to the empty room. He thought of the hedonistic world of which he had become a chance chronicler. Were Tabitha Gatling and her friends – and, indeed, himself – even of the same species as those wartime stoics in their tin hats? Building a bridge to that heroic age in his imagination was not easy.

He dutifully noted the signatures on all the Heavy Rescue reports. The attendance at 'the incident' almost never named individual squad members, but he finally found a record of Frank Gatling's citation, published in the *London Gazette* along with many others at the end of the war.

Member of the Order of the British Empire. Frank Gatling (Kensington and Chelsea). Gatling took part in ARP Heavy Rescue operations from 1940 until 1945 during which time he repeatedly exposed himself to the danger from collapsing buildings while he searched in the debris for buried residents who had survived the initial bomb blast. Over a long period Gatling displayed a complete disregard for his own safety and was responsible for recovering alive a substantial number of bomb victims.

A single clipping from the local newspaper revealed that Frank Gatling had received his MBE from the hands of the Mayor at the old town hall in Kensington High Street.

Chapter Twelve

'Well, Gunner may have been beastly to horses but we now know he wasn't all bad,' Gervase reported that evening. 'Must have taken guts to turn yourself into a human mole. People like him used to burrow into the rubble when it was still on fire, for Christ's sake, and sometimes even when there was an unexploded parachute mine dangling from the telegraph wires above their heads. I don't know how they could have kept it up year after year. I'd have gone loco.'

'You didn't need a world war to make you loco,' said Nelly. 'You got there all by yourself. Just keep digging. Percy Start was trying to tell you something and I don't think you've found it yet.'

In eight days, Gervase had listed the names of twenty-seven men who had been in Heavy Rescue in Kensington and Chelsea during the blitz but not one could be identified as having worked alongside Gunner Gatling.

'Right. It's my turn,' said Nelly Tripp, taking the list from him. 'I'll launch a computer search of electoral rolls, starting with the inner London boroughs and working outwards. Don't expect too much. Most of 'em will be dead.'

In the event, Nelly scored three possibles. One was same spelling, wrong man. The second, according to his daughter on the telephone, was in the early stages of Alzheimer's disease. The third said, 'Gunner Gatling? Now there's a name from the past. What a rogue!'

Nelly's computer had spread its electronic net wide to snare Jim Goldsworthy. He was eighty-seven, a bit arthritic, and lived in St Leonard's Road, Hove, on the south coast.

'Let's both go,' said Gervase. 'We'll see the old boy and spend the rest of the day in Brighton. I need some fresh air. I don't think I was cut out for life down among the dusty archives.'

'Then you'd better reconcile yourself to spending the rest of your miserable existence choosing the ten most fanciable men for the likes of Tabitha Gatling,' said Nelly.

'You sound just like my mother.' Gervase gazed fondly at the little dynamo and experienced an odd emotion in his stomach and throat. He had only the flimsiest data to go on but suspected he was falling in love. Nelly, he mused, would look good in a tin helmet set at a rakish angle, gas-mask container slung over one tiny shoulder. He took her in his arms and gave her a cuddle.

'What was that for?'

'No reason,' said Gervase.

Jim Goldsworthy had been a clerk in the borough housing department when war broke out. After the fall of France, when the British were under no illusions about what was to happen next, he was charged with organizing a Heavy Rescue unit to be based in central Kensington. His men and women drilled and awaited the onslaught.

Like his contemporary Percy Start, Jim was a widower. His semi-detached house needed a lick of paint but was clean enough inside. He had home-help visits twice a week and meals-on-wheels. A lifetime in municipal government had left him with a keen awareness of his rights as a pensioner.

Gervase was relieved to see that his bodily infirmities had not touched his mind. He got out the coffee-pot and biscuits, and Nelly made a fuss of being mum under his appreciative eye for a pretty girl.

He told them, 'I was glad to have Gunner. He was a powerfully built brute, which was useful when it came to shifting the heavy stuff. Most of my blokes were either medically unfit for military service or were over the then call-up age – which, before he got hurt, was the case with Gunner.'

Gervase said, 'I've no record of him being hurt.'

'Oh, yes, it was ironic, really. He took all the most hare-brained risks you could imagine in the blitz. Then, during the lull before the arrival of the V1 doodlebugs and the V2 rockets, he was searching a bomb-blasted house in Kensington Square when, quite without warning, a wooden crossbeam broke loose and crushed his left shoulder. Put him out of action for six weeks. There wasn't even an air-raid alert at the time. Hadn't been one for weeks.'

'Then what was he looking for? Bodies?'

'That's what he said.'

Gervase and Nelly watched the portly old boy slowly pick up his cup and take a sip of coffee. His eyes were lowered.

Nelly said, 'Correct me if I'm wrong, Mr Goldsworthy, but did I detect a note of, well, scepticism in your voice?'

Jim Goldsworthy sighed heavily. 'It was a long time ago and the man performed many courageous acts. But I have to say I ultimately formed some decidedly ungenerous thoughts about Gunner Gatling.'

'Such as?'

'He came to us as a volunteer from south of the river – from one of London's poorest boroughs to one of London's richest. I gave this fact no significance at all at the time. He was an enormous asset. After a raid, we'd have what we called "live" debris. That is, rubble newly created by the Luftwaffe under which there might be people. In the total collapse of a building you could reckon that eight out of ten people underneath would be recovered dead. Bomb blast and crushing injuries were the two biggest killers. A surprising thirty per cent would die of asphyxiation – unless you dug them out fast. And that's where Gunner came in. He tackled live debris like a demon, frantically burrowing in like a hound trying to follow a rabbit down its hole. He always had with him a pile of short timbers, rather like a coal-miner's pit props, and in he would go, shoring up as he progressed during the inevitable delay while we brought up the cranes and other heavy equipment.'

'He sounds as if he earned that MBE,' said Nelly.

'Oh, please, don't misunderstand me. I wouldn't deny him that, but I came to learn that there was another side to Gunner. A much less acceptable side.'

They waited for him to continue but, tantalizingly, he fell silent and took several swallows of coffee. He was plainly sorting out inside the shiny dome of his hairless head the best form of words for what was coming next.

'You hinted that there was eventually a significance in his switching from Bermondsey to Kensington,' prompted Nelly.

'Yes,' said Jim Goldsworthy. 'It's a sad business, really. The times were so . . . I suppose *selfless* is the word, that one hesitates to direct attention to the cracks in the monument. But the truth is that for some people the war was a business opportunity rather than a noble cause. Gunner, I reluctantly came to believe, was such a person. What I thought was his reasonable belief that he was less likely to get a German high-explosive bomb down his chimney in Kensington than if he remained living near the docks in Bermondsey was totally in error. He came to us for a much more predatory reason.'

The old man's quavery voice suddenly took on a firmer timbre, like a judge passing sentence. 'I believe Gunner Gatling was a looter. There was little to steal from the poor of Bermondsey but in Kensington the homes of the rich were being ripped open almost daily, with their owners either dead, injured or evacuated. The area represented ripe pickings. When Gunner went diving in he was as greedy for buried cash and jewellery as he was anxious to save someone's life.'

'Christ! That's a terrible charge,' said Gervase. 'Was he ever caught?'

The old town hall bureaucrat shook his head. 'Of course not. There'd have been no MBE for him if he had.'

'Then how do you know this?'

'It is perhaps difficult for the young now, who seem to speak with such appalling candour about everything under the sun and hide nothing, to understand that in the war the truth could not always be told because it was sometimes too demoralizing. The Germans weren't the only ones to exaggerate their successes in battle or to conceal shameful acts. By the end of 1940, the looting of bombed buildings in Britain was becoming a scandal – a fact that the authorities discreetly concealed from the population at large. Newspapers and radio broadcasts were censored. For propaganda reasons, the civilian population could be portrayed only as steadfast and brave as they stood alone against the might of the German air force. And in general that was a true picture. But at the same time Scotland Yard was quietly setting up a special anti-looting squad and severe penalties for offenders were slipped through Parliament. You could get five years' hard labour for stealing from a bomb site.'

'So how did you come to suspect Gunner?' asked Nelly.

'We'd been tackling a particularly bad incident in the Gloucester Road. A gas main under the debris had fractured and ignited and the National Fire Service had been pumping water on the flames for two days. The Heavy Rescue team, Gunner among them, had been plunging into the rubble at every opportunity. Everyone was exhausted. I happened to be in the Incident Post phoning a situation report when Gunner came stumbling through the door, rushed over to me and emptied the contents of his dirt-encrusted overall pockets on to the district map that I'd spread on the bench. He didn't even wait until I'd finished my call.

'I looked down in amazement. Among the filth and dust a small fortune in diamond rings, bracelets and brooches glittered up at me. Oh, yes, and there was also a broken tiara, worth God knows what. I put down the phone. Gunner was positively babbling. "Came across this stuff in the cellar, guv'nor. Thought you'd better have it for safe-keeping – daren't leave it where it was." That sort of thing. I was impressed with his honesty – for precisely one minute.'

'What happened?' asked Gervase, hooked on the old man's recollections.

'The police happened,' he said. 'Two plain-clothes detectives – part of the new squad, it turned out – followed Gunner through the door. Unknown to all of us involved in the rescue operation, they'd been keeping observation on the site because it covered the homes of at least two wealthy families. Their valuables under the rubble represented an ideal temptation for looters.'

'I get it,' said Nelly. 'Gunner spotted the cops before they could waylay him and catch him with the goods hidden in his clothes. To screw them, he rushed to you and pretended to do his duty and hand the stuff in.'

'Exactly right,' said Jim Goldsworthy. 'I would have given him the benefit of the doubt except for his unseemly rush in dumping the stuff on me while I was still in the middle of a telephone conversation. If nothing underhand had been going on, common courtesy alone would have obliged him to wait until I'd finished speaking. He was fast-thinking in divesting himself of the loot. That's how he foiled them and embarrassed me. For a while I'm sure the police even harboured a suspicion that I was in league with him.'

'He had a narrow escape,' said Gervase. 'Were there any more?'

'If there were, no one ever again caught him at it. The war was coming to an end and I think he must have already made his pile. He used to wear a long topcoat and I took the liberty one day, when he'd left it hanging in the Incident Post, to take it down and examine it. He had poacher's pockets sewn on the inside. I held my counsel but from then on I took every opportunity to examine those pockets. After his close shave, there was never anything in them except tools, sandwiches and a flask of tea. Gunner emerged from the war with a medal, a wonky shoulder – and whatever treasure he had been squirrelling away for five years. The next I heard, he was buying up job lots of our old equipment. Now where did he get the cash for that? It certainly didn't come from wartime wages. Like Britain itself, we were all on our uppers.'

Nelly said to Gervase, 'I've had a nice idea. Mr Goldsworthy's been so kind and helpful. Why don't we take him to lunch?'

'Absolutely,' said Gervase. He turned to the old man. 'Do you like fish? We were thinking of going to English's in the Brighton Lanes.'

'I'm a bit stiff, but if you can get me into your car I'd love to come. I don't get into Brighton too often, these days.'

Over the sea-food platters, Nelly had a thought. 'How come Gunner Gatling got an MBE and you didn't?'

'Because I got an OBE,' laughed the old boy. 'My wife used to make me blush, reminding everybody. She was very proud of that gong. When she died, I placed it in her hands. Just before they closed the coffin.'

'How sweet!' said Nelly. She placed a hand over his. 'I can't imagine anyone ever doing anything as wonderful for me.'

'Oh, I dunno,' said Gervase, from across the table.

They were drinking their coffee and Jim Goldsworthy was savouring a large Hine that Gervase had pressed on him when he said suddenly, 'I suppose the first book must have been published only in America. I asked for it several times here but the public library said they had no record of it on their computer.'

Gervase and Nelly said together, 'What book?'

'The one that American chap was writing. Yours will be the second history of the Gatlings, won't it? I thought you'd already know. I've been through most of this Gunner Gatling stuff before with the American,' said the old man. 'We went over much of the same ground. He said he was writing a biography. Have I got it wrong?'

'When was this?'

'Three or four years ago. Was he misleading me?'

'No, Mr Goldsworthy. I think you must mean Gus Meldrum.'

'Yes, that's the fellow. Very amiable – though he wasn't as gracious as you two. I wasn't treated to lunch.'

'There was no book,' said Gervase. He decided not to risk upsetting the old man with the news of the American's death.

'I'm not surprised,' said Jim Goldsworthy. 'Meldrum was depressed. He'd been to interview old Gunner and he told me his son, Vernon, had found out and blown a fuse. He wanted nothing to do with a biography. Hated publicity, he said.'

The two young writers stared at their guest as if he had just revealed the secret of the universe. 'Did you say he *interviewed* Gunner?' said Nelly. 'But surely Gunner's long dead.'

'You've not been doing your homework,' said Goldsworthy.

Gervase slapped his own forehead. 'Oh, God! We just assumed . . . We hadn't got round to collecting his death certificate.'

'Well, I don't think you'll find it,' said Goldsworthy. 'Unless he's died recently, the old rascal's well into his nineties. The devil looks after his own. Your American tracked him down to a nursing home in Bournemouth.'

Chapter Thirteen

Gervase and Nelly reviewed Jim Goldsworthy's testimony.

'At least we now know how the Gatlings went from dog-shit to the big-time,' said Gervase. 'If the father's still alive we're going to have trouble with the libel laws. Robbing the dead and dying! What an arsehole!'

'You'll still have to check Gunner's story of winning on Vernon's Pools,' said Nelly.

'It'll turn out to be bullshit,' predicted Gervase.

In the event, the inquiry was inconclusive.

'A post-war winner? You're asking a lot,' said the company's female records manager, on the telephone from Liverpool. 'We keep archives going back twenty years at most in this office. When we went from paper to computer we didn't input data from earlier years. Anyway, if he was a genuine winner and requested no publicity, we're forbidden to give out any information.'

'I understand that,' said Gervase. 'But I was hoping you'd be able to confirm that Vernon's Pools never did have a big winner of the name of Frank Gatling. Your ideal response from our point of view would be to say, "No one named Frank Gatling ever won a penny from us."'

'I can only sort through the old paper files,' she said. 'There's also a collection of photographs of long-ago winners. Give me a few days. I'll get back to you.'

She did. 'As far as I can ascertain, what you suspect is true. There was no big winner named Gatling just after the war,' said the records manager. 'But I couldn't swear on the Bible. It may well be that the paperwork was pulped in the seventies. It's about sixty–forty that your suspicions are correct. Over the years, there's been many a villain who's explained away his sudden good fortune to a non-existent pools win. There's not much we can do about it.'

'We have a problem,' said Nelly. 'We've more or less brought the story of the Gatling family up to the present generation.

Gus Meldrum's clash with Vernon Gatling proves that our instinct in staying away from the family was the right one. But we're gonna have to face it soon.'

'Where's the best place to kick off? What about the Beverly Hills SkyCity story that Gus Meldrum was piecing together?'

Nelly shook her head. 'Negative. Most of it's already in the public domain. What did he truly expect to dig up – that Vernon had crossed a few public officials' palms with silver? Big deal! Is there a major developer who hasn't? No. I think Meldrum merely fancied a few days in sunny California to cheer himself up. Remember, he already wanted to hand back his advance. I think that by the time he checked into the Chateau Marmont he was merely going through the motions. I'd say he was sitting alone by the pool each day brooding. Something had happened to discourage him.'

'Do you think he was going to take a pay-off from Vernon – and then saved Vernon the money by slipping in the bathroom?'

'You refused to be bought by Vernon so why should you think Meldrum would?' said Nelly sharply. 'His record as a journalist suggests he was an upstanding guy so don't be so quick to speak ill of the dead.'

'Rebuke acknowledged,' said an abashed Gervase. 'So where do we go from here?'

'Vernon Gatling's construction empire was founded in Britain. Let's go for past and present employees, and Vernon's women. If he has any of Gertie the Murderer's genes or Gunner the Looter's *cojones*, there should be plenty of tittle-tattle to be unearthed.'

'What about old Gatling?'

'For Christ's sake, Gervase, didn't you listen to what Jim Goldsworthy had to say? If we make the approach too soon we'll have Vernon on our necks at the head of an army of lawyers.'

A week later a paragraph in the gossip column of the *Financial Times* acutely focused the would-be biographers' attention. It read:

We hear Vernon Gatling, the multi-millionaire tower builder, has ruffled the feathers of the City fathers. They have quietly investigated his complaint that Corporation officials improperly frustrated Vernon's plans to redevelop Abura House in Bishopsgate, seriously damaged in the Baltic Exchange IRA bomb blast.

Vernon (pictured left, with the Countess Zoë di Sola at Newmarket) was given an unaccustomed rap over the knuckles for his allegations.

'Totally unfounded,' we are told by our man in the Mansion House. 'We all know Gatling is a colourful character but he overstepped the mark this time. He finally apologized to the Corporation, admitting he had been overly incensed at losing the reconstruction contract. It seems he put up the post-war monstrosity on the site of the old Fletcher Hall when he was only just out of his teens and he is still sentimentally attached to it. Goodness knows why. The Taj Mahal it ain't.'

Gervase Meredith telephoned Percy Start. 'Mr Start, would you mind if I asked you a couple more questions?'

'What else have I got to do, sonny? Fire away.'

'Who were the Gatlings' associates in the fifties when the construction company was expanding?'

'You can count me out. I was of no use to them once they got big. They needed proper firms of accountants for their book-keeping. The building workers were mostly casuals. They kept only a tiny core staff. Everyone else was hired for a particular project. They were too mean to maintain a labour force between contracts.'

'Can you remember any names of the few regulars?'

'Their clerk of works was a chap named Collins. I know for sure he's dead. I went to his funeral. There was also a jolly Irishman called Fling. It was hard to forget his name. He was known to everyone as Denny Fling, the Bullshit King. He'd been a sergeant-major in the war and they wouldn't let him forget it. He was their site foreman for many early projects.'

'Is he still alive?'

'I haven't heard anything to the contrary. He was living up Kilburn way. The Gatlings used him for years. He was good with the men.'

149

'Mr Start, when we spoke originally, you failed to mention that Gunner Gatling was still alive.'

'Did I? Perhaps you didn't ask me.'

The shaft hit home. 'You're quite right, Mr Start. I've never written a biography before. I've a lot to learn.'

'If you say so,' said Percy Start indulgently. 'Frank Gatling's tucked away very comfortably, thank you, in a nursing home down on the coast. Vernon actually sends me the fare once in a while to go and visit him. He says the old man likes to see a familiar face from the old days. But the visits are very hit and miss.'

'How do you mean?'

'Sometimes Frank's way out of it, just rambling. I can sit there like a lemon for more than an hour before I get a glimmer of recognition from him. The nurses say he has terrible nightmares and they leave him weak the next day. The wicked strokes he's pulled in his time, I should think they do.'

'So he's totally ga-ga then?'

'Not entirely. You can catch him on a good day when he's more like his old self. He sits crying over Fred Astaire.'

'The dancer?'

'Who else? He's never lost his love for ballroom dancing. In old age he still worships Fred Astaire. Vernon had video-tapes made of every dance number Fred Astaire ever filmed and ran them together. They go on for ever. I'm not much of a cinema-goer myself but they're quite magical to watch. When Frank gets a bit too difficult to handle, the nurses shove a tape in the machine and the sight of Fred Astaire in his top hat and tails somehow calms him down. He sits watching for hours with tears in his eyes. It's better than giving him the liquid cosh those damned doctors think they can use on anyone over seventy-five.'

The old man's voice had risen to a screech that was a blend of indignation and personal panic. 'Vernon has forbidden the medical staff to prescribe any of that muck. Whatever else you might say about Frank and Vernon Gatling, they hail from generations that came up the hard way. They faced the world as it was, not through a cosy drug haze. Vernon isn't going to let his father be turned into a zombie at the end of his life just for their convenience.'

Gervase said, 'Grey Power, yeah!' And he added, 'For my book, if I wanted to visit Gunner Gatling, would you come with me?'

'If you've got the price of the fare, I don't see why not. But there's no guarantee Frank will be in any condition to answer your questions.'

'It'll be worth a try. I'll let you know when.'

Chapter Fourteen

Nelly Tripp's computer search of the United Kingdom telephone directory failed to turn up Denny Fling, the Bullshit King. They put the problem aside while they concentrated on more easily contacted people whose own lives had touched Vernon's in his climb to vast riches.

They discovered that those who had been bested by him in business, or women ill-used by him more intimately, were happy to talk; those who still hoped for future Gatling favours were more cautious. Still, the book was beginning to take shape and Nelly was kept busy duplicating every written note and taped interview.

She was transcribing one interview, which Gervase had conducted at the Athenaeum Hotel in London, when her fingers came to an abrupt halt above the keyboard. She rewound the section and replayed the dialogue.

The subject was a minor Hollywood actress named Anna Scopes who, a few years previously, had been extensively photographed in magazines and had appeared in gossip columns as a regular companion of Vernon Gatling. The affair had lasted for more than a year and, towards the end, the columns were speculating that the couple planned to marry.

To get the interview, Gervase had run the usual tiresome gauntlet of the film company public-relations people, who had flown her to London to publicize her latest movie. He pretended he was writing a profile for *Vanity Bazaar*.

Nelly listened to him going through the motions of questioning her about her far from remarkable upbringing in the empty wastes of South Dakota, and of her escape from 'abusive' parents – an obligatory revelation for Hollywood stars of the nineties – to head for Los Angeles 'where I could chase my dreams'.

So far so predictable in the life of little Anna.

Then Gervase got to the nitty-gritty. 'I'm surprised a lovely-looking girl like you isn't married. I know at one time some of us expected you to seal Anglo-American relations, so to speak, by becoming the wife of Vernon Gatling.'

There was an audible intake of breath on the tape, followed by a long sigh. 'Yes,' said Anna, 'so did I.'

'What happened?'

'Look Gervase – may I call you Gervase?' ('No, you bloody-well may not,' muttered Nelly.) 'I won't hear a word said against Vernon.'

'No, no, of course not. Quite understood,' said Gervase hurriedly. 'From all I hear he's a thoroughly decent chap.'

'Vernon and I had a wonderful relationship. I'll be frank with you, it was my agent's idea in the first place for me to see him. He arranged for Vernon to escort me to the Oscars. I was nominated in the best supporting performance category for *Broken Wings*, you know.'

'Yes, I know,' lied Gervase. 'And awfully good you were, too.' (Smarmy sod, thought Nelly. He's in the shit if she asks what he liked best about her performance.)

But Gervase's hypocrisy was saved from exposure. Anna, deep into her memories of a busted romance, went on, 'My agent said I'd get good publicity with Vernon on my arm. He was already famous in his own field. That was the first time we met and I thought that would be the beginning and end of it. But next day Vernon sent me the most wonderful flowers and a limo to fetch me to lunch at Spago's. He was so gentlemanly and attentive that I was seriously flattered. And I loved his funny accent. So British! The next weekend he flew me in his private jet to Las Vegas and we stayed at the tower he'd built on the Strip. He and his staff treated me like a queen, which isn't the way young actresses normally get treated in Tinseltown before they become marquee names. It's usually a case of wham-bam-what-did-you-say-your-name-was-ma'am?

'I'm not ashamed to say we began a really lovely affair. I was with him all through that fight he had to get his skyscraper built in Beverly Hills. And he wasn't a sore loser, either. He laughed at the uproar he was causing to the old guard of Beverly Hills. He wasn't handsome in the movie-leading-man sense but he was enormously dynamic and attractive. A great many women tried to put their branding iron on him.'

'Did another woman come along?'

Nelly listened to the tape hissing in the silence while Anna Scopes mulled over her reply. Finally, she said, 'Why don't we just say there was family opposition to our marriage?'

'I thought you were estranged from your family?'

'The black spot came from his family, not mine. His daughter, Tabby, didn't approve of me.'

'How did it end?'

'Oh, dear. I'm not sure I should say any more. Vernon wouldn't like it.'

'I know, let's go off the record,' said Gervase brightly. 'Then you can decide what, if anything, is attributed to you and be able to deny everything if you so wish.'

The tape clicked off. 'Here comes the old two-tape trick,' sang Nelly. She plugged into the mini-recorder that Gervase habitually kept concealed in an inner pocket, with a tiny microphone clipped under his tie.

On the second tape, the actress continued, 'That's cool. But none of this comes from my mouth. Okay?'

'Not a word.'

Anna continued, 'Back in England, that daughter of his must have been reading the gossip columns speculating about a wedding because unannounced she flew out to California. There were some very unfortunate scenes.'

'Between Vernon and Tabitha?'

'Yes. And finally between her and me.'

'It must have been a painful parting?'

'More painful than you can possibly imagine.'

'Oh?'

There was another silence on the tape. Then Nelly could hear a rustling sound. Anna was shifting uncomfortably on her couch. She said, 'Be a good guy. Treat this carefully. I really mean it. Some of what happened definitely shames Tabitha. I don't want trouble with the Gatling lawyers.'

'Here it comes. Here comes the dirt,' thought Nelly.

'I was living in an apartment in Brentwood. One evening my doorbell went while I was studying a script. I thought it must be my laundry service. But there stood Tabby. I don't know how she charmed her way past the front desk. She stalked in, her face set in stone. I already knew from Vernon that she was trying to break us up. Sure, there was an age gap. I had truly fallen for her father but she refused to accept it. She was furious with me, called me the most awful names, of which gold-digger was the mildest. I attempted to reason with her, calm her down. I told her how the romance had started, how nothing had been further from my mind. I described how her father had wooed me like a gentleman, how we – she and I – could become good friends, be like sisters rather than stepmother and daughter. I tried to get her to sit down but she refused. She's slightly taller than me and she stood facing me in the middle of my living room, her fists clenched and her face contorted. The word stepmother seemed to trigger some kind of fit. I swear she had foam on her lips. She screamed, "He's mine and he'll always be mine! You'll never have my daddy, you slut!"'

'Gosh,' said Gervase. 'That must have been horrible.'

'Shut up, you idiot. Don't break her train of thought,' murmured Nelly, pressing the earphone tighter against her skull.

'I was thoroughly alarmed. She seemed to be crashing out of control. I thought I'd been more than civil to her. I asked her to leave. That did it.'

'Did what?'

'Vernon Gatling's daughter half killed me. Without any

warning, she whirled round like one of those kung-fu guys from a chop-socky movie and lashed out with her foot. She caught me on the side of the head and I went down, stunned. I staggered back to my feet screaming but she put an immediate stop to that by whirling once again and smashing me in the ribs. All the breath was knocked out of me. I simply could not believe what was happening. I work out but I know nothing of martial arts. Against this spinning madwoman I had no defence at all. I tried to run for the door but she could move with remarkable speed. She then proceeded to beat up on me quite mercilessly until I was black and blue and begging for my life.'

'My God!' said Gervase.

'What was even more frightening was that she handed out my punishment in complete silence. Then she said, "You promise me now that you'll never see my father again or I'm going to smash your face." I was lying on the carpet in my own blood. I had no doubt that was exactly what she would do and my career would be over. At that point I would have said anything to stop her permanently crippling me. I gave her the undertaking.'

'Surely you didn't leave it there?'

'Of course not. I was hospitalized with three cracked ribs, mild concussion from the head kick and multiple bruising. For a while it looked as if she had damaged my kidneys. My first call was to Vernon and my second call to my lawyer. Vernon was horrified. When he appeared at my bedside he actually wept although, looking back, I'm not sure whether he was weeping for my hurt or for his daughter's madness.'

'Were the police involved?'

'They would have been, except that Vernon instantly made himself responsible for all my medical bills and came to a generous settlement with my lawyer. To forestall a call to the police, Vernon actually handed him a blank cheque in my hospital room. I said I would only accept the compensation without dragging his deranged daughter through the courts if he undertook to get psychiatric treatment for her. Vernon agreed but I see from recent newspaper stories that she still has a wild side that they haven't curbed.'

'And that beating ended the romance?'

'I'm afraid so. Nothing could be normal after an episode like that. Our love affair quickly soured. Tabitha Gatling had her way, after all. She brought Vernon to heel as if she were his wife rather than his daughter.'

The tape ended and Nelly Tripp sat back. 'Wow!' Anna Scopes's testimony slotted in so well with Gervase's account of Tabitha's vengeful slugging of the recalcitrant viscount. The psychopathy, the calculation, coldness and violence of both acts were all of a piece.

'Great stuff, huh?' said a smug Gervase, who'd been standing by, watching her reactions as the tape unreeled.

But Nelly wasn't listening. She'd just spotted something curious. She took from the cabinet Gervase's account of his visit to Gus Meldrum's widow. After a few moments she said, 'Now that's a funny thing. Gus Meldrum died in Los Angeles during the same week that Tabitha Gatling was in town beating the bejesus out of Anna Scopes.'

'So?'

'Remember Gus's injury was a blow to the side of the head? And what was the first blow Tabitha landed on Anna? A blow to the side of the head with that fancy footwork at which she is so skilled.'

'Aw, come on! Tabitha's Gus's killer? Get away!'

'Why not? She's crazy enough. She's proved that. What's to say she wasn't the woman sent by her father to the Chateau Marmont to ask if he'd finally decided to stop rooting around among the family scandals, found that Gus Meldrum was still dithering, got overwrought and "punished" him the way she "punished" Anna? Only that time she went too far and killed him.'

'Tabitha is a blonde. The LAPD description of Meldrum's visitor was of a woman wearing a beret over black hair.'

'A wig,' said Nelly. 'With the beret to hold it in place. Who the fuck wears berets these days except those guys who follow the Spanish bullfights and women in French Resistance movies?'

'We're gonna have enough trouble getting Anna Scopes's stuff past the lawyers without throwing in speculation that

Tabitha might have bumped off our distinguished predecessor,' said Gervase. 'It'll be tears before bedtime if we go down that road.'

'All the same, you watch yourself with that girl,' said Nelly. 'I agree with Millie Moses. She's definitely, positively *nuts*!'

BOOK FOUR

Chapter One

Police Constable Ken Young, on foot patrol in busy lunch-time Bishopsgate, was trying to keep his mind on the serious business of suspiciously parked vehicles and unexplained packages left on pavements. But, by jiminy, it was difficult when the world swarmed with girls in their summer dresses. Look at that one in the skimpy turquoise number. He could see the dark roundels of her nipples showing right through the material. Her mother would have a fit. And that little tottie in the smart business suit. How did she sit down without showing her lot?

PC Young, pacing in approved dignified manner, skirted a clangorous building site, checked that his boots' had not picked up any filth from the dust-covered pavement, and moved on – only to have his pleasant reverie rudely invaded by a shout of 'Oi, you, Officer!'

His first inclination was to turn and say frostily, 'Are you talking to me?' But the public's propensity for complaining about police discourtesy being what it was, PC Young decided otherwise. He turned and said, 'Yes, sir?'

A man in a cheap two-piece suit with a yellow safety helmet perched on his long, greasy hair had emerged from the building site. He looked solemn. He said, 'Officer, I think you'd better come and have a look at this.'

PC Young stepped gingerly back into the filth. The man said, 'I'm the clerk of works. Here, you'll need this,' and handed him another yellow safety helmet.

The constable could see that as the helmet looked silly enough on the clerk, it would look bloody ridiculous on himself, standing six foot three as he did. The girls in their summer dresses would not be impressed.

With a heavy heart, PC Young removed his handsome helmet, a symbol of the Law's dignity, celebrated the world over, and donned the awful headgear that would allow him access to the site.

'Just follow me and mind your step,' said the clerk of works. The site was a tip, a wasteland of broken concrete, dangerously protruding and contorted steel reinforcing rods, and girders mown down to stumps by oxyacetylene cutters. Demolition of the original building had reached the ground and basement and the men had laid in an impacted earth slope to give easier access to machinery.

PC Young followed the clerk down into the depths and became suddenly aware that all noise had ceased and that the workforce on all levels was silently watching his progress. He looked up, almost losing his helmet, to note the stilled crane and dangling chain above his head, and the operator leaning from his cabin, following his progress.

They were all waiting upon PC Young.

He followed in the man's wake across the clay and concrete that had been broken into manageable segments by a mechanical pneumatic drill known as a pecker. His boots, he realized with dismay, were going to be well and truly fucked up.

They reached the far corner. Over the shoulder of his cheap suit, the clerk was saying, 'For the past few days we've been taking the reinforced concrete floor up. It had been laid on aggregate in the usual way. But when the pecker reached this corner it came up against a second, lower, layer of crudely laid concrete – which was a bit surprising.'

'Why surprising?'

'Perhaps unnecessary would be a better word.' With his wellington boot, the clerk nudged aside several sizeable pieces. 'This is the stuff. It was covering this hole.'

PC Young advanced carefully to the edge of a circular rim, formed of thin old bricks. The hole had a diameter of approximately five feet. 'What is it? An old well?'

'Either that or one of those medieval refuse pits you occasionally find on sites where ancient buildings have stood.'

PC Young peered over the edge. A cut block of stone had fallen into the pit and was wedged at a depth of about fifteen feet. 'Did your blokes do that?'

'No, it was already there when we removed the concrete cap. But I want to show you something. Just come round to the other side.'

The constable half circled the rim and the clerk handed him a powerful directional lamp. 'Just take a gander down the left-hand side of the stone.'

PC Young switched on, leaned forward and directed the beam, so that it penetrated the darkness below the trapped block.

They were all watching him closely and got what they hoped to get. PC Young flinched minutely, but not minutely enough, and drew back his head. Everyone grinned.

PC Young, unaware of his entertainment value, once again cautiously leaned forward to check his first impression. There was no mistake. Grinning up at him, even more broadly than the demolition men standing around him, was a human skull.

He stepped back. He knew what he had to do. 'I'm afraid I'll have to ask you to stop work in this vicinity,' he said.

'I hope this isn't going to take long. We're behind schedule as it is,' said the clerk, agitated. 'I mean, we've done our duty in reporting it. We could have just filled it in, you know.'

'And you would have been in big trouble,' said PC Young.

'It's most probably hundreds of years old. Nothing to get excited about.'

'Most probably,' said PC Young, reaching for his lapel radio. 'But we have to go through the motions.'

Ten minutes later a uniformed woman inspector was on the site. And ten minutes after that, the magic words 'human remains' were interrupting Detective Superintendent Herbert Dalton's daily tussle with *The Times* crossword. To the woman inspector he said, 'Is the SSU on the way?'

'Yes, sir. And I've sealed off the area.'

'Good girl,' said Bert Dalton, an impenitently unreconstructed male. 'I'll be right along.'

The detective superintendent did not need his car to get him to the site of the old Fletcher Hall. His office was in

Bishopsgate, a short stroll along the road. He put on his top coat and set out.

Like PC Young, he muttered, 'Fuck', to himself, when he saw the state of the place. He took out his pocket radio and said, 'Send along my car.' His wellingtons were in the boot.

Preliminaries finally completed, Bert Dalton ventured on to the site and took a look. 'It's human right enough,' he confirmed. 'But there's bugger-all we can do until the SSU get here. Who first spotted our severely dieted friend?'

The Scientific Support Unit arrived while Detective Superintendent Dalton was questioning the clerk of works. The team kitted up and began exploring the surface scene and the first few accessible feet of the well. One officer's sole task was to video every stage of the forensic examination.

The SSU boss, a detective sergeant, left his team to erect some arc-lights and strolled across to the clerk of works' hut to report to Bert Dalton. 'We'll need to have that jammed block hauled out to take this thing further, sir.'

Dalton turned to the clerk. 'Could your chaps manage that without causing too much damage?'

'We'd have to use the crane. Lower someone in a bosun's chair to rig a makeshift sling round the block. The edges'll get rasped a bit but lifting it shouldn't be too much bother.'

By now the uniformed branch had been reduced to guarding the demolition site. The woman inspector had withdrawn, PC Young had been sent off to write up his report, which included a short interview with the gateman, and the City's criminal investigation department was in full charge of proceedings.

Bert Dalton's deputy, Detective Chief Inspector Tim Armstrong, arrived from the Guildhall magistrates' court, where he had been giving evidence in a fraud committal case.

'Tim, would you give Professor Dart a tinkle at Guy's Hospital and get him over here? And that egghead from the Museum of London Archaeology Service at Walker House who helped us with those bones found in Cripplegate. What was his name?'

'Stevens, sir. Bruce Stevens.'

'Fine. This might be more his kind of thing. Pound to a

164

pinch of shit, this is going to turn out to be just another 1665 plague victim. He'll love it.'

Professor Franklyn Dart, Professor of Forensic Medicine and Home Office Pathologist, and Dr Bruce Stevens, Science Supervisor (Archaeology) MoLAS, were both in attendance by the time a volunteer workman had been lowered into the well and, with much effing and blinding, had succeeded in encircling the stuck block with two hawser lines and a canvas sling.

Dr Stevens had already pooh-poohed a hopeful suggestion from the detective superintendent that the concrete cap on the well was of ancient origin. 'Wrong consistency altogether,' he said, rubbing a chunk with his bare hand. This stuff was laid this century. Depend on it.'

'So whoever laid the concrete must have seen the skull?'

'If they could see beyond the block. Yes. Also, please note there are fragments of rotted timber resting on the block. Wooden planks must originally have formed the crude base on which the concrete was poured.'

The volunteer workman had attached a larger hook to the now bound block and Dr Stevens signalled for it to be lifted out.

One of the arc-lights was moved to the edge of the well and the SSU cameraman began filming as the crane took the strain of the heavy block of masonry. There were a few moments of suspense when nothing seemed to be happening. Then, abruptly, the block jerked free, scarring the sides of the well and sending a shower of dust and small debris tumbling into the depths. The block swung lazily and was slowly hoisted aloft.

Dr Stevens said to the clerk of works, 'Get your crane man to lower it gently. I'd like to have a close look at that stone.'

The attention of Detective Superintendent Dalton, DCI Armstrong and Professor Dart was elsewhere. They lined the edge of the well and peered downwards.

Professor Dart said, 'Aha!'

DS Dalton said, 'I'll be buggered.'

DCI Armstrong said, 'Now that *is* a surprise.'

The trio had each recognized the signs.

The grinning skull was part of an almost completely preserved skeleton, which ruled out plague victim or any leftover from antiquity. There was no sign of any shred of clothing. When the corpse had landed on its back on a bed of dried mud and ancient refuse, it had been naked. Unless the corpse had been taking a bath at the moment the bomb fell, this most probably ruled out wartime blitz victim, although blast had been known to strip victims to the buff. The possibility could not be dismissed just yet.

But these factors the three experts in death absorbed almost subconsciously. What they were staring at in the glare of the arc-light was the yellow tinge on the bones and a similar discolouring of the surrounding area.

'Slaked lime,' said DS Dalton.

'Indubitably,' said Professor Dart.

'Murder,' said DCI Armstrong.

It has occasionally been of great assistance to detectives in murder inquiries that the guilty party will shovel slaked lime on to their victim in the belief that this will destroy the body. What it actually does, most obligingly, is delay decomposition by keeping the maggots and beetles at bay and thus preserve evidence.

'Someone has been most considerate,' said Professor Dart. 'Do you think you could get this crane chap to lower me into the well?'

Bert Dalton eyed him dubiously. The Prof was not a young man. 'Are you sure you can manage?'

'We'll find out, won't we?' said the Prof, a trifle sharply. 'There may well be some advantage in looking at the remains *in situ*.'

Professor Dart went down, holding on with one gloved hand while he held a small tape-recorder in the other and made note of his observations. He stretched down at one point and touched the ground alongside the skeleton. His safety helmet rolled off and he did not attempt to retrieve it.

Back on the surface and red-faced from his exertions, he said, 'The bones still have a degree of articulation. There is a total absence of soft tissue. Death was not recent but I'd say it took place certainly in the second half of the century. There is hair. Short-cut and dark brownish. The pelvic characteristics indicate that the subject was male. A cursory examination of the dentition suggests you are dealing with a youngish person. There are only a couple of molar cavities and little in the way of wear and tear on the crowns.'

'What about the grave itself?'

'I'm sure Dr Stevens will confirm that what we have here is a dried-out medieval well, later used as a refuse pit – there are some fragments of domestic animal bones in the floor. I've seen several wells like it in the past.'

The archaeologist nodded his agreement.

DCI Armstrong was writing furiously in his notebook.

Detective Superintendent Dalton said, 'Any indication of cause of death?'

The pathologist shook his helmetless head. 'Too soon. We'll know more when your chaps get everything over to my laboratory. Oh, by the way, this attracted my attention. It was lying alongside the remains.'

He held up a medal, dangling on the few remaining threads of a ribbon. The SSU boss held open a transparent plastic bag and the professor dropped it.

'Looks like a war decoration,' said Bert Dalton.

'Depends which war you mean,' said Dr Stevens. Wordlessly, the SSU boss handed him the pouch. 'The ribbon may be modern but the medal is not a medal at all. It's a coin. Roman, I'd say. Best part of two millennia old. And someone in modern times has perpetrated an act of vandalism by soldering a ribbon holder to it.'

Dr Stevens held it up to the light, examining obverse and reverse through the clear plastic. 'Good gracious,' he said. 'I can confirm Roman. This coin is worth at least five thousand pounds.'

'So if we link this to Mr Bones, robbery isn't likely to be the motive for murder, then?' said Dalton. 'Unless this was part of a stolen collection – the one the thief dropped as he did a runner?'

'I doubt a genuine coin collector would have tolerated this

ribbon attachment,' said Dr Stevens. 'This is much more likely to be somebody's one-off prized possession being worn as adornment.'

'Pity. Robbery as motive would make life a lot simpler,' sighed Dalton. 'Anyway, you'd better give DCI Armstrong a full description.'

'Most certainly. Apart from the modern addition of the ribbon holder, this coin has been carefully looked after. It is in excellent condition and belongs in a museum. If you look closely at the obverse you will see three of what are called jugate busts, the stamped profiles of no fewer than three Roman emperors side by side where you would normally expect to see only one. They are most rare and date from the short reign of a British usurper named Carausius who is believed to have set up his own mint and coined these multi-heads to curry favour with Rome. End of third century AD, if memory serves.'

'Interesting,' said DS Dalton. 'Let's hope there's a new owner whose name isn't in Latin.' He turned to the SSU boss. 'Right, Sergeant, get everything up from the well logged and then set up a tent over the site. Get everything human bagged and taken over to Guy's Hospital for Professor Dart. We'll nose through what's left under cover here on the site.'

He turned to the archaeologist. 'You want to examine the stone block? Go ahead.'

Chapter Two

Nelly Tripp, clutching a bunch of daffs and a bag of deep purple grapes, sat in the back seat to keep Percy Start company on the way to Bournemouth. Gervase was driving. Neither had yet felt it proper to address this upright old man by his first name.

Gervase said, 'Mr Start, when we arrive at the nursing home

it'll probably save some nosy-parker questions if you say Nelly and I are a younger generation of the Gatling family.'

'I'm not doing anything underhand,' he said firmly. 'I don't mind escorting you past the staff but I insist you tell Frank Gatling who you are and exactly why you wish to talk to him. If he says no, you'll have to wait for me outside.'

'That'll be absolutely no problem,' said Gervase. 'It's just that we don't want to get involved with any pettifogging rules about who may or may not visit the old man. You know how officious some people can be.' As he let loose the words he remembered the three old 'uns in the pub shouting, 'Put that bloody light out!'

'Hmmph,' said Percy Start.

The Aitkin-Adams Home was perched high on the cliffs, a handsome Victorian mansion in well-tended grounds. Gunner Gatling had been put out to grass in green pastures. In the event, the only formality required before gaining access to the nonagenarian was that all three sign the visitors' book. The receptionist had instantly recognized Percy Start and greeted him with professional warmth.

A nurse, in the kind of reassuring starched uniform now largely abandoned in modern hospitals, led them down a spotless corridor. Gunner had a ground-floor suite overlooking a stone terrace and a croquet lawn.

'He's had a pretty rotten night so go gently with him,' whispered the girl. Then to her patient, she said loudly, 'Look what I've brought, Frank – visitors! Be nice to them now!'

Gunner turned his head towards the open door. His gaze was unfocused. He was seated in a high-backed chair with his left arm resting on a cushion. His pyjamas and dark blue dressing-gown were made of silk and freshly laundered. The spacious sitting room boasted a wide-screen television that was turned off, a video-cassette recorder and a superb music centre. Vernon had not let his father want for anything.

Gunner had apparently been watching through the french windows a decrepit pair of croquet players feebly swinging their mallets. The three visitors advanced over the thick carpet. Percy Start said, 'It's me, Frank – Percy Start.'

The old man's face slowly gained some expression. He said,

'Yes,' and allowed his hand to be lifted from his lap for a shake. Gervase, remembering the description they had recorded of a man who could punch a horse and make it stagger, found it difficult to reconcile this with the man they now faced. Gunner Gatling's once powerful body had shrunk. He had only a few wisps of white hair remaining on his deeply wrinkled head. The fists that had punched horses were now fragile bundles of mottled twigs.

As he had warned, Percy Start scrupulously introduced the pair of them and outlined their purpose. Gunner Gatling looked bemused. 'Book?' he said.

'Yes, Mr Gatling. We're writing a history of your family's wonderful rise to fame and fortune,' said Gervase, jumping in eagerly.

If he asks now if Vernon knows, we're banjaxed, thought Nelly.

But Gunner said, bewildered, 'I never made a book. Street betting was illegal in them days. I was in demolition and building.'

'That's right, Frank. They know that,' said Percy.

The three pulled up chairs in a semi-circle in front of him. Nelly, searching for a vase for the daffodils, noticed that Gunner's framed MBE rested dead centre on the marble mantelpiece.

Percy Start sat quietly while Gervase corrected Gunner's misapprehension about the book and painstakingly attempted to talk the old man through his life. 'Hard times. Percy knows,' he mumbled.

It was a dogged business getting this old man with his wandering mind to say anything meaningful for the benefit of the tape-recorder. Gervase said, 'You were very brave in the war. I see you have your medal over the fireplace. Did any money come with it?'

Gunner looked puzzled. 'Money? What money?'

'Did the authorities give you a gratuity at the end of the war so that you could start up in the demolition business?'

Percy broke into the questioning for the first time. 'I think you'll find, Mr Meredith, that gratuities were given only to returning servicemen.'

Gervase knew this perfectly well but the query had been his ploy to broach a delicate subject. He persisted, 'Before the war had ended, you were already buying up surplus Heavy Rescue machinery so that you could get started in demolition.'

'Auctions,' said Gunner shortly. 'Cash on the nail.'

Gervase took the plunge. 'Didn't some people accuse you of having made your fortune on the black market?'

'Fuck 'em,' said Gunner. For the first time he showed agitation.

'Yes, but that doesn't tell us where the money came from, does it, Mr Gatling?'

'Pools. Won it on the pools. They couldn't prove anything different.'

'Was that Vernon's Pools?'

'Yes, won it on Vernon's.'

'How much?'

'A lot.'

'How much is a lot?'

'Enough to get started.'

He clamped his mouth tightly shut. For a while, the old man drifted. He eyed them all curiously, as if becoming aware of his visitors for the first time. Nelly washed his grapes under the bathroom tap and returned to pop one into his mouth. He had his lower set in but not the upper. She gave Gervase a significant look that said, 'Lay off for a while,' and began to flirt mildly with him.

She drew her chair up until she was almost knee to knee. She said, 'Mr Gatling, you must be so proud of Vernon.'

His empty gaze alighted on her, travelled down to her shapely legs in black stockings and up again to her pert face.

'Stupid bastard,' he said.

Nelly professed shock. 'Oh, Mr Gatling, I'm sure you don't mean that.' She popped another grape into his willing maw.

'Don't I?' he said. 'Gave him his first building to put up and what was the thanks I got?'

'What?'

'That'd be telling.' A sly expression slid across his features and was gone.

'Oh, go on. You're teasing me.' She stroked his cheek. The

171

nurse had not yet given him his morning shave and Nelly's palm prickled.

'Ask Vernon,' he said, and then surprised them all by breaking into a high-pitched cackle. 'Yes, ask Vernon,' he repeated. 'Then you'll have your book. Ask him about that dance we both missed.'

The three exchanged puzzled glances. Percy shrugged. Nelly said, 'Dance? Is it something to do with Fred Astaire?'

This triggered another unsettling cackle that ended abruptly in a bout of coughing. The spasm racked his sunken chest and he expectorated into a tissue that he twisted and tossed on to the floor.

Winded, the old man turned to Percy, 'Can I have my tape now?'

'Of course you can, Frank,' he said, rising and going over to the video shelf before either Gervase or Nelly could divert him. He ran a finger along the titles and pushed one into the machine. Almost instantly the great Hollywood hoofer flashed on to the screen, performing a remarkable sequence in which he appeared to be dancing up the walls of a room and across the ceiling.

Gervase looked at Gunner. He was already lost in the movie magic. His gaze was rapt. The interview was torpedoed. 'Shit!' muttered the would-be biographer.

The nurse poked her head round the door. 'Is he being a good boy? He's due in physiotherapy in ten minutes' for that left shoulder of his.'

'What's wrong with it?' asked Nelly.

'It's an old injury. Gives him a lot of gyp. Especially when it rains.'

He's actually been quite talkative,' said Nelly. 'Could we wait for more?'

'Not a chance,' said the nurse, glancing at the screen. 'Once he takes off with the immortal Fred there's no bringing him back.'

She stopped suddenly. 'Uh-oh!' she said. 'Not that one!'

'Dancing In The Dark' was now playing and Fred Astaire was wafting Cyd Charisse across a giant set of Central Park. The nurse swiftly crossed the room and pressed the eject button. Gunner Gatling instantly began to scream obscenities and attempt to struggle up from his chair.

The abrupt transformation was shocking. The three visitors flinched and exchanged helpless glances. The nurse hastily plucked another cassette from the shelf and the screen burst to life with an Astaire–Ginger Rogers sequence. The effect on the old man was instantaneous. He fell back into his seat, a beatific, gummy smile once again in place. The nurse strolled to his side. She stroked his brow and said, 'Sorry, Frank. You didn't really want that nasty bit, did you?'

He grunted and tried to move his hand to take hers. But his eyes never left the screen.

The nurse said to Nelly, 'There's a bit that comes after "Dancing In The Dark" that drives him potty. Don't ask me why. It's just another dance number. The tune must hold some sad memories for him. I'm afraid you've had the best of Frank Gatling for today. Actually, I'm surprised he's been so chatty. After one of his nightmares he's usually a basket case. It's as well he has his own rooms. We could never have him in a shared ward. His screams are dreadful. You've caught him at his best. He'll be giving us hell in a few minutes when we drag him away from Fred. But he must have his physio. Doctor's orders.'

'What bugs old Frank in his sleep?' said Nelly.

'What bugs most old people. Fear of imminent death, I suppose. It's sad. He also seems to have taken against his son, who does everything for him. No one could be more generous. Yet in the night Frank rants and curses poor Vernon and someone named Lionel, who I think must be a dead son. I wonder if when they were younger father and sons were always fighting each other.'

'What makes you think that?'

'Frank has a recurring nightmare in which Vernon, in particular, figures. Frank screams, "That's enough, Vernon, that's enough!" as if the son is giving his father a good pasting and he can't take any more. Then, "Don't do it! Don't do it!" The language is appalling. I hear they were both tough characters once upon a time. Still, they aren't the first father and son to spend their lives head-butting each other.'

Gervase said, 'I can explain one thing for you. Vernon and Lionel are one and the same. Lionel changed his name.'

Gervase and Nelly both shook Gunner Gatling's limp hand to say goodbye. He did not notice. Fred was now partnering Judy Garland.

They waited outside while Percy tried to get through to Gunner to say his farewells.

Nelly said, 'I'm sorry, kiddo. I fucked up proceedings by mentioning Fred Astaire. Did you see his face? It was like throwing a switch. In an instant, he was off, flying down to Rio. We were blown right out. What do you make of it all?'

'Pools win, my arse. The old bugger definitely got his start through looting.'

'I agree. I was surprised that he seems to have fallen out with Vernon.'

'Yeah, that's a turn-up for the books. What was that dance bullshit all about?'

'I suppose the only way to find out will be to ask Vernon.'

'I'm not looking forward to that,' said Gervase, with feeling.

Chapter Three

The crane raised the stone block slowly in its secure canvas hammock and lowered it on to a forklift pallet. Then it was trundled into the police marquee that had been swiftly erected to screen off the well and surrounding area. Dr Bruce Stevens, having made a brief return to Walker House to pick up some necessary equipment, was now fussing around the block with a magnifying glass and a soft brush.

'I say,' he kept repeating in surprise. 'I say.'

Finally, Detective Superintendent Bert Dalton, irritated, turned from his other exhibits and noted the archaeologist using the magnifying glass. 'It's a bit late for fingerprints, Dr Stevens.'

'Of course, of course,' said the boffin, nodding vigorously. 'But just look at this, Superintendent.'

The policeman stepped gingerly across the broken ground and followed his gloved finger. 'Letters,' said the archaeologist, triumphantly.

'Latin, isn't it?' said the detective. And drily: 'But I think we can safely eliminate the stonemason from our inquiries, don't you?'

'It's not that,' said Dr Stevens, straightening up and looking distressed. 'I think a terrible outrage has taken place on this spot.'

'You mean, in addition to the outrage perpetrated on Mr Bones?'

'Yes, indeed.' The archaeologist was almost snorting in indignation. 'The carving on this block tells me that this was the altar stone in a temple of Mercury and dedicated to the Emperor Vespasian. See, here, this stone even carries the name of the Roman trader in London who paid for the dedication.'

The gloved finger ran along a row of the inscription: MARCUS LICINIUS RUFUS.

'So where's the outrage?'

Dr Stevens took Detective Superintendent Dalton's elbow, led him to the open flap of the marquee and embraced the whole of the demolition site with a wide sweep of the hand. 'Where is the temple? Do you see any remains to go with this wonderful find?'

'They must have been swept away.'

'Exactly! Almost certainly swept away by the barbarians who tossed the altar stone into the well. They're as bad as the army of Charles the Fifth who sacked Rome.'

'Diabolical,' said the DS, who had no idea what the archaeologist was talking about, history not having been his strongest suit at school.

'This outrage must have happened after your body was thrown in the well, otherwise the positions of altar block and body would have been reversed. Therefore, these two events could only have happened between the date the original Fletcher Hall was bombed in the war and the date at which a new building was raised on this site a few years later.'

'Yes, I see that,' said DS Dalton. 'But why destroy the Roman remains?'

'Greed,' said the archaeologist promptly. 'Many builders regard the finding of historic remains as a confounded nuisance. They want to get on and meet their contract dates. They don't want delays caused by eggheads like me swarming over their sites and perhaps obtaining injunctions to compel them to cease building work while archaeological surveys are carried out. If you look into the history of post-war rebuilding in the City of London, there were many rumours of such things happening.'

The detective superintendent was now paying full attention. 'So if a dodgy builder found ancient stoneworks what would he do?'

'Quietly bulldoze 'em up with the rest of the site rubble before anyone like me got to hear about it. At that time a great deal of debris was carted out to dumps in Essex. God knows how many unknown temples and other artefacts from the medieval and classical worlds are lying in fragments in the Essex infills.'

'So how do we tie this particular act of vandalism to Mr Bones?'

'For a start, the people who hauled that block to the well-head must have spotted the corpse, even if they were not responsible for putting Mr Bones there.'

'But doesn't the existing evidence suggest they were responsible for both acts and that the block was meant to crush and conceal the victim?'

'Precisely. The only thing that went wrong for them was that the block wedged itself during the drop and failed to hit the mark. More than one pair of hands must have been involved. The altar is far too heavy for one man to manage.'

'Thank you, Dr Stevens. I believe you have made an important contribution to this inquiry. It seems to me we have two courses of action to pursue. Identify Mr Bones and find out who cleared the site and rebuilt Fletcher Hall after the war.'

'Yes, I agree that is what the evidence so far dictates,' said the archaeologist, flattered that his analysis had been so readily accepted by the towering detective.

*

Yellow-tinted Mr Bones was laid out on a stainless-steel slab in Professor Franklyn Dart's mortuary. He was complete, apart from a couple of toe and finger joints. The two detectives were gowned and the eminent pathologist said, 'Better put your masks up for a moment.'

Dalton and Armstrong hastily complied as Dart took a drill and bored a small hole in the skull. Smoke and a fine white dust were violently ejected. The grey cloud briefly floated before dispersing in the air-conditioning current and the bone dust settled back on to the table. The two onlookers winced in unison.

'See?' said Dart. 'Completely dried out. No marrow. This chap has been nearer to God than thee for a long time. Fifty years or so, I should say. Radiocarbon-dating may give us a more precise date. He was approximately five foot nine tall, quite lightly framed. Look here.' The two detectives moved for a better view as Professor Dart pointed with a probe at the bone plates that knitted the skull together. The lines he traced with his steel probe were as tortuous as the course of the Irrawaddy river. 'Ossification takes place as you grow older. Eventually the lines disappear altogether. Bony union in this instance is in the early stages. From that, the absence of bone disease, and from the good condition of his teeth I'd place him between the ages of eighteen and thirty.'

'Are you able to give us a cause of death, Professor?'

'No trouble at all.' Professor Dart lifted the skull, leaving the mandible on the table, and turned it round so that the detectives could get a complete view of the back.

'Poor Mr Bones suffered a single blow to the back of the skull on the right side. He was struck most violently. The X-rays show bone splinters within the vault of the skull. The supra-occipital bone is crushed up to and beyond the lamedoidal suture.' Professor Dart placed a finger on these features so that the detectives could fully understand. 'Unconsciousness would have been immediate, and death would have followed soon afterwards.'

Professor Dart turned his hand sideways to the indentation and demonstrated, with a sharp hacking motion, how the indentation must have occurred.

'Could he have sustained that injury in the fall to the bottom of the well?'

'Absolutely not. This is a wound of intention. And when I went down the well I satisfied myself that there was nothing there – a large stone, for instance – that could explain an indentation of this severity.'

'Anything on the weapon?'

With a solemn flourish, Professor Dart restored Mr Bones's head to its rightful place, rather in the manner of an archbishop placing a crown on a monarch's, and picked up a pair of tweezers clamped around a five-centimetre splinter of wood. 'This was embedded in the area of damage. He was struck with such force that this fragment was driven straight through the soft tissue into the bone.'

'A wooden club of some sort?'

'Now that's a bit of a puzzle. The striking area was long, up to twelve centimetres, and blunt, perhaps three centimetres thick. It was also L-shaped. I've never seen an injury quite like this. The slant of the wound suggests the victim was standing slightly to the right of his assailant.'

Using DCI Armstrong as a stand-in victim and with himself as the murderer, Professor Dart acted out his theory, with his own laboratory assistant and Dalton as his audience of two. He froze the tableau alongside the mortuary table and said, 'The dead man must have been standing sideways to the assailant or actually passing in front of him or her.'

'Unaware of danger or moving away from it?'

'Yes. I'd subscribe to that.'

'So, if I understand you correctly, Professor, the murderer, if we ever catch up with him or her, is going to have a hard time pleading self-defence.'

'That would be possible only if the murderer claims he or she was wounded by the victim prior to the fatal blow and was lashing out blindly in fear for his or her life. It won't be much of a defence if the accused has no serious scar tissue to display or medical record of a serious injury having been treated at the relevant time.'

Detective Superintendent Dalton placed a hand on the edge of the table and gazed sadly at the remains. He was silent for a few moments, then he said, 'It was a long time ago, old son, but we'll do our best for you. I promise.'

Chapter Four

The discovery of the skeleton on the site of Abura House made only three paragraphs in London's sole surviving evening newspaper the *Standard* and, only because the site was within the City square mile, was noted briefly in the 'heavies' – *The Times*, *Telegraph* and *Financial Times*.

At Detective Superintendent Dalton's request, the City of London Police spokesman did not use the word murder. Dalton wanted some peace and quiet while he nosed into an ancient mystery.

'The remains are of a male and are old. Various possibilities, including undiscovered 1939–45 bomb casualty and seventeenth-century plague victim, are being investigated. There'll be a full report to the coroner in due course,' said the sergeant.

The crime reporters weren't inclined to waste time on the subject. The bones would probably turn out to belong to some long-forgotten meths drinker.

The police spokesman did not mention the slaked lime. That would have raised considerably their level of interest.

Nelly Tripp read the item in the *Standard* twice. Something niggled at her.

That was it. Abura House! She went to her files and dug out the clipping from the *Financial Times* that had recorded Vernon Gatling's interest. Abura House had been Fletcher Hall – and that had been Vernon's first post-war building.

'Look at this,' said Nelly, laying the two clippings side by side under Gervase's nose. 'The police have found a body under the building.'

Gervase read the two items. 'Well, we can't pin that on Tabitha. She wasn't alive to swing a lethal leg when this bloke died.'

'No, but if that *Financial Times* report is correct, her dear daddy was very anxious to get his hands on that particular site once again – to the point at which he seems to have made a bloody fool of himself in front of the City planning-committee panjandrums. Do you think he knew there was a body to be found?'

'For Christ's sake, Nelly, we've already convinced ourselves his daughter bumped off Gus Meldrum. Now you want to award Vernon a corpse of his very own. Don't you think you're letting your imagination run away with you?'

'If you want the Woolworth's psychoanalysis based on our own research to date, I'd say the Gatlings have a criminal streak as wide as the Mall. They come from dog-shit and they remain dog-shit. I wouldn't put any dirty deed past them. Vernon isn't a lord of creation because of his sweet nature. The meek may inherit the earth – but not Vernon's leaseholds. If you don't want to do anything about this, I want to hand the facts over to my news desk. The *Guardian* crime man will love it.'

Gervase jumped up, furious. 'Nelly, that's a rotten thing to threaten me with. When I asked for your help with the book I didn't think I'd also have to ask you for an oath of secrecy. I trusted you.'

'Then you have to trust my judgement now,' said Nelly, jutting the little jaw he was finding ever more cute. 'We have to push on with our own inquiries. You want a book that's going to hit people between the eyes, don't you? What was the name of that site foreman who worked for the young Vernon and his old man?'

'Denny Fling, known as the Bullshit King. Lived in Kilburn. We drew a blank.'

'Right, my boy. Off you go to the borough council offices to comb the old electoral rolls. Find his former address, talk to the present occupants, the neighbours and anyone who knew him at the neighbourhood pubs. He sounds the sort of colourful character who would be well remembered. Someone must know where he is today – if he's still alive.'

'Nelly, this could take days.'

'Weeks,' Nelly Tripp corrected cheerfully. 'I'll make a researcher of you yet.'

In the event, at the Westminster City Hall, Gervase took four tedious days to find Denny Fling in a 1982 register, living in Kilburn Park, with an Eileen Fling, presumably his wife.

The address turned out to be a Victorian house in multiple occupation. An old lady living in the basement with four cats remembered the Flings. They'd moved . . . now where had they gone?

A tired Gervase held his breath.

'Streatham . . . that was it, to be near their daughter. Eileen and Denny, really lovely couple, were getting on a bit . . .'

Not only was there no Streatham Fling in the London telephone book, there was no Fling in the book at all. Gervase wearily reported back to an unrelenting Nelly. 'Streatham comes under Lambeth. Get over to Lambeth Town Hall. At least the recent electoral rolls will be computerized.'

They were, but they offered Gervase no satisfaction. 'There's only one Fling family and it's not them. They must be dead,' he wailed into the telephone.

'*Nil desperandum*,' said Nelly. 'A lot of people dropped out of the electoral rolls to avoid paying Mrs Thatcher's poll tax. Go and see the Flings listed. I bet they know.'

Nelly Tripp, who had done two turns in Bosnia and one in Afghanistan, was apt to put Gervase in his place when he put on airs by accusing him of luxuriating at the *chaise-longue* end of journalism while she represented the inky commandos who had a bloodhound's instinct and obsession for the truth. He'd yet to fault her. And certainly not on this occasion.

The middle-aged woman who answered the door of the pleasant villa in Tangmere Avenue, Streatham, was wary. Gervase said hastily, 'I'm not on official business. I'm just a writer researching a history of some people Mr Fling once worked for. I thought he might be able to help.'

Still holding the front door half-open, she shouted over her shoulder, 'D-a-a-d!' Back came a muffled response from upstairs. ''Ullo?'

'There's a gentleman to see you.'

Relief flooded Gervase. Thank Gawd. No more of those fucking electoral rolls. Even if the Bullshit King merely told him to bugger off.

At last, the woman – Denny Fling's daughter – let go of the door and he watched a tall old man with clipped iron-grey hair ease himself down the stairs, one step at a time.

'Arthritis in the feet,' he explained, even before the introductions.

Gervase explained his mission as a biographer. 'The Gatlings, eh?' said Denny. 'I gave 'em my best years, the bastards.'

Gervase said, 'I'd have rung before calling, but I couldn't find you in the book.'

'It's in a company name for my son-in-law. Bloody nuisance sometimes.'

The daughter said, 'You'd better take the gentleman into the front room. Would you like some tea?'

'We'd like some whiskey,' said Denny bluntly.

'Well, you can't have any. Mum's orders. Not before six o'clock.'

'Focking women!' said Denny. 'It's worse than being confined to barracks.'

'You're not the sergeant-major now. I'll get the tea,' said his daughter equably. 'And watch your language in front of the gentleman.'

Denny Fling rolled his eyes and Gervase grinned. 'Don't worry, Mr Fling. My girlfriend's just the same. They're saving us from our wicked selves.'

'I don't see why a nice glass of Paddy's would recruit us for the devil,' the old man grumbled.

Denny Fling was around seventy-five. His feet might be letting him down but not his head. He remembered almost everything. And, more importantly, he was manifestly happy to welcome Gervase's visit to break the monotony of his suburban posting. His *last* posting, as he put it.

He permitted Gervase to turn on his tape-recorder as he rambled on about life as a construction worker in the post-war years.

Denny was another who scoffed at Gunner Gatling's pools

win. 'He got that money by looting blitzed houses. Or from the bodies he found under the debris. I've known men accuse him of it to his face. He'd go crazy. He was a big focker and he'd jump in swinging punches like Joe Louis. We all laughed like hyenas when Lionel changed his name to Vernon to back his dear old dad's lies. But Gunner had covered his tracks well. No one ever proved a thing.'

'Were you foreman when the Gatlings rebuilt Fletcher Hall in the fifties?'

For the first time Denny Fling stopped his stream of memories to ponder for a moment. 'There were so many projects in the City once the building materials became available. The Gatlings grabbed all the work they could. You really earned your wages with them. They copped bonuses for completion on time and penalties if they ran over. With the men, the Gatlings were like focking Nazis. I always had my work cut out to stop the lads downing tools. To keep the workforce happy, I turned a blind eye to the little extra they made from the historic bits and pieces they dug up – pots, coins, jewellery, that sort of thing. We had regular visits from dealers. Hovered like bloody sharks around raw meat. Looking back, I'm willing to bet we were all cheated. What did we know about the true value of a Roman pot? If a dealer offered you a couple of quid, you took it. That was two days' pay in the fifties. The Gatlings were like the rest of the contractors; they didn't care a fook so long as you didn't find any historic remains that were too big to flog to the dealers. They wanted no trouble from the museum people who often came snooping around. I had standing orders to refuse them access to the Gatling sites.'

Denny Fling's daughter brought in the tea on a tray covered in a crocheted doily. He watched her set it down and leave, then said suddenly, 'Fletcher Hall was in Bishopsgate. Yes, I was the foreman on that job.'

Gervase handed him the *Financial Times* and *Evening Standard* clippings. Denny read them carefully. Gervase noted that he seemed puzzled and then ill-at-ease. Gervase started to speak, but the old man said abruptly, 'Pipe down for a minute, son. I'm thinking.'

The silence was disturbed only by the ticking of a ponderous marble clock on the mantelpiece above the imitation coal fire.

Finally, he looked up. His face was strained. 'God help me, I think I know who this poor man must be.'

Gervase spilled tea into his saucer. '*What?*'

'These remains. They're not the victim of the focking plague. I'd lay money that when the coppers identify him, it turns out to be a little lad I once knew.'

Gervase was trembling. He wished he'd brought Nelly with him. 'Who are we talking about?'

'His name was Larry something, a nice kid. He worked for one of the antique dealers I was telling you about. I've done a little business with him myself. He gave better prices than any of the others. He was a wiry little bugger. The police used to chase him all over the bomb sites at one time but nothing seemed to get him down. We were all sorry when he went missing.'

'He went missing?'

'As far as I know, never seen again. I well remember this happened during the clearing of the ruins of the old Fletcher Hall. We searched our site at the request of the police – just like all the other contractors working in the Square Mile. The theory was that a wall had fallen on him or that he was lying injured in a hole. He took an awful lot of chances, did Larry. But neither hide nor hair of him was ever found.'

'But if you searched your site, how can you say that these remains are those of this Larry chap? Surely you would have found him back in the mid-fifties?'

Denny Fling clasped his big hands under his chin. It seemed to be a gesture of anxiety. He said, 'I didn't suspect a thing. I just went along with Gunner and Vernon.'

'What happened?' Gervase felt the sweat trickling from under his armpits. He prayed that the old man did not clam up now.

'The day comes back very clearly. It was a Monday. We'd been having some lovely early-spring weather. I turned up at the site at seven a.m. as per usual. The men were still out on the pavement with Gunner and his son barring the way. I wondered what the hell was going on. They drew me inside and Vernon said, "Send the men home on full pay. Just for today." It was so out of character I gazed at him as if he had gone mad. Vernon saw the look on my face and he added, "Tell them we've hit a town-planning snag. Don't argue. Do it!"

'So I went back outside and did as he ordered. There was no trouble once I explained their wages would be paid. Back inside, Vernon said, "Over the weekend we've found some focking Roman temple. We've been bulldozing it up before the pricks from the museum find out."'

'*Had* the Gatlings found a temple?'

'Sure. Or something similar. By the time I clocked on, the temple, or whatever it had been, was just a heap of piled masonry. The only admissions to the site that day were the regular dumper lorries. We had our earthmovers, and behind closed gates I helped the Gatlings load the debris. By evening you'd never have known anything historic had been there. The site was clean. They gave me some money – ten quid, if I remember – to keep my mouth shut.'

'But if the site was clean, how can this Larry person have been overlooked?'

Denny Fling picked up the *Standard* clipping. 'This one says the remains were found in a well. And I do remember a small section of concrete they'd laid during the weekend when they had the place to themselves. I distinctly remember asking, "What the fock is that?" And old Gunner said, "The temple had a well. It was a giveaway. So we've plugged it."'

'In that case, they must have known your Larry character was in it.'

The former foreman slowly nodded his head. 'That's what I'm thinking. Little Larry must have fallen in and broken his neck. Those miserable buggers must have been shit-scared of being sued for negligence and decided to make him disappear.'

'But if Larry whatsisname was trespassing on an enclosed site, how could they have been liable in law? They had no need to hide the body.'

'If they called the police they'd also have to reveal the existence of the well and the Roman temple. That would have played hell with their rebuilding schedule.'

'The mean bastards,' swore Gervase. 'The dead man's relatives must have been frantic.'

'They were,' said Denny. 'I remember all too well.'

'Have you remembered his full name?'

'I remember he was nicknamed Vanishing Larry – for his exploits on the sites, not for what happened to him.'

The daughter re-entered the room. Denny's rheumy eyes brightened. She was carrying a tray covered with another finely crocheted doily. On it rested a bottle of Paddy's Irish whiskey, two tumblers and a small jug of water. 'You two must be thirsty talking over old times for so long,' she announced.

'A miracle,' said Denny, falling back in his armchair in surprise. 'It's not six yet.'

'The Empress Eileen upstairs decreed that there should be an act combining mercy with hospitality.' She swished from the room once again.

Denny poured two enthusiastic tots. 'Sorry the missus can't come down to say hello. She's had a bit of a fall,' he said, raising his glass in a toast towards the ceiling.

On his second tot, Denny Fling, the Bullshit King, remembered the name.

'Larry Varnish,' he said. 'That's who the poor little devil was. Vanishing Larry Varnish.'

Over his glass, Denny captured Gervase's gaze and added, 'I want to make one thing clear. If I had known the lad was down that well, I would never have gone along with the Gatlings. Even if it meant the sack, I would have insisted on the poor lad being raised for a Christian burial.'

Gervase nodded. 'Yes, I believe you, Denny. The Gatlings have their own peculiar brand of nastiness that, thankfully, is not shared by many other people.'

'I suppose you have to go to the police now?'

'I was wondering about that,' said Gervase, who had been thinking of little else for the past half-hour.

'Can you keep me out of it?'

'It'll be difficult.'

'You go to them as you came to me – as the Gatlings' biographer. I'll dig out the dates and you get the newspaper reports of Larry's disappearance. You take the reports to the

186

police, which you say you came by in the course of routine investigation into the Gatlings' business lives. No need for my name to come into it. To tell the truth, I'm feeling bloody ashamed.'

'I'll see what I can do,' promised Gervase.

When he left, the tape-recorder seemed to be emitting heat in his jacket pocket. 'Christ, it's dynamite stuff,' he whispered to himself. He was quite looking forward to presenting his day's work to Nelly.

Now who was just a *chaise-longue* journalist?

Chapter Five

In his tidy office at the Bishopsgate police station Detective Superintendent Bert Dalton had his murder team gathered around him. Instead of the more usual thirty or so officers, he had, as ever, DCI Armstrong, plus a sergeant and two detective constables. There was no flamboyance. No one was calling the location an incident room.

The City of London Police commissioner had decreed, and Bert Dalton could not but agree, that so ancient a crime was unlikely to yield a rapid explanation or a culprit still living. There was no point, therefore, in a lavish expenditure of manpower on the task. Still, murder was murder, and the City police had to be seen to be taking its solution with due seriousness. Therefore, the investigation called for a commanding officer of Dalton's rank even if his team was of the Potemkin variety.

In truth, Dalton was happy with the arrangement. Unlike most police officers, he enjoyed puzzles. The smallness of the team meant he would be able to keep every facet of the inquiry firmly in his own hands. He would not be frustrated by the incompetence of others lower in the pecking order.

One of the DCs had just returned from the Imperial War

Museum and Crick's, the West End coin dealers where the experts had studied the recovered medal and tattered ribbon. Now he placed the plastic evidence bag in front of Dalton. 'The War Museum bods definitely identify the ribbon as originally being pale buff, with three vertical coloured stripes, dark blue, red, light blue, running from left to right. Hanging from it rightfully should be a five-point bronze-gilt medal known as the Africa Star, awarded to those who fought in North Africa during the Second World War. They hadn't a clue about the attached coin. But Crick's confirm Dr Stevens's identification. It is a coin from the period of the Emperor Marcus Aurelius Carausius and has no business being linked with the Africa Star ribbon. Crick's say that at auction, even though it has been tampered with, it would most likely fetch in excess of four thousand pounds.'

'Do any of 'em have any theory as to how the two disparate parts became married up?'

'The Crick's man says it had to be the work of a rank amateur, guv'nor. He says no collector worthy of the name would dream of committing such an act of vandalism.'

'Right,' said Dalton. 'But let's bear in mind that this may have no connection at all with the dead man. What's next?'

Detective Chief Inspector Tim Armstrong said, 'Guv'nor, I now have the relevant information concerning Abura House. The building, which was then known as Fletcher Hall, was bombed in an air-raid on the night of the sixteenth of October 1940. It was damaged beyond repair. It was classed as dangerous and the bulk of it was cleared away by Italian prisoners-of-war. The Guildhall archives give only the vaguest dates for this work, but their people stress that the clearance work would not have gone below ground level. There would have been two or three metres of rubble filling the basement, so that seems to rule out the Eyeties as suspects.'

'What about post-war?'

'Nothing happened until the mid-fifties.'

'The basements remained rubble-filled until then?'

'Yes, guv.'

'So who did the clearance?'

'The contractors who built the post-war block that took the

IRA blast in 1992. It was a firm called Gatling Construction. They began work in March 1955.'

Detective Superintendent Dalton studied his desk-top for a moment. He looked round at his men and said, 'In every building I've ever seen go up, the concrete for the foundations was poured first. So whoever dumped Mr Bones in the well must have done the deed during the short period when the bare earth was exposed and the disused well made accessible – but before the new Fletcher Hall started to rise from the war rubble. It is the people who had access to the well we must find.'

'Jesus, that'll be the entire labour force, guv'nor,' said the detective sergeant. 'Most of 'em will be with Mr Bones by now.'

'Whoever said life was just a bowl of cherries ought to have had his collar felt for false pretences,' said Dalton. He turned to Armstrong. 'Tim, you see what you can do to track 'em down. I'll concentrate on the identity of the victim. God knows, that's going to be bad enough after all this time. How many people go permanently missing in Britain each year? About fourteen thousand, isn't it?'

He looked at his notes. 'And there's one other line of inquiry worth a punt. The gateman on the site told the young PC first on the scene that he'd noticed a powerfully built man taking more than a passing interest in the progress of the demolition work. He was hanging around on the morning the bones were found but disappeared in a hurry soon after the first police vehicle arrived.'

Dalton looked up at one of his two available detective constables. 'Morgan, Bishopsgate has more closed-circuit TV cameras trained on it than Dartmoor Prison – our own as part of the anti-IRA precautions and there are any number on commercial premises. Collect the tapes and see if you can get a fix on this character. He may be the sort of chap who just enjoys watching other people work. But you never know . . .'

Chapter Five

Nelly listened to the Denny Fling tape and was gratifyingly impressed. 'Those Gatlings really are the most awful shits,' she pronounced, as she ran off a copy of the tape for her own file.

'I've a rotten feeling we should be handing this stuff over to the police,' said Gervase.

'You're right there,' said Nelly. 'But we're not going to. We're going to find out all we can about Larry Varnish. Gervase, this is a great coup for the book. I'll spit in your eye if I'm not promoted to co-author.'

'I promise,' said Gervase. Now he knew he was in love.

'Good,' said Nelly, putting on her new Jigsaw jacket and giving him a full body-contact kiss. 'I'll spare you a trip to Colindale. I'm off to the *Guardian* cuttings library to ask for anything on Larry Varnish.'

She returned with just one photocopy of a small item from the *Evening Standard* dated Tuesday 26 April, 1955. It was the one reporting the twenty-two-year-old Cockney's disappearance. Better yet, it supplied his wife's name, Lorraine, and address, Douglas Buildings, Marshalsea Road, in the Borough.

'May I just hope for once that the Widow Varnish is in the London telephone directory,' moaned Gervase.

'It is more than forty years on,' pointed out Nelly. 'She'll either be dead or remarried.'

As ever, Gervase's hopes were not fulfilled. Why did Nelly always have to be right? Lorraine Varnish was not in the book.

Nelly said, 'As it's a woman, we'd better go together over to the Borough.'

Gervase complained, 'The Borough? It's an odd name. I've only the vaguest idea where that is.'

'South of London Bridge and north of Elephant and Castle,' said Nelly. 'A tough area. If you'd ever been a crime reporter you wouldn't need to ask.'

'Are we back to *chaise-longue* journalism again?' grumbled Gervase.

At least Douglas Buildings still stood, a massively built tenement with an inner courtyard, accessed through an archway. Gervase and Nelly located the caretaker's flat and found his wife at home. To Gervase's relief, this did not prove to be the starting point for an exhausting hunt that would drag him to the outer reaches of the Metropolitan area.

'Third floor,' said the woman. 'She has Big Fran's old flat. Big Fran was her mum. Passed away six years ago. Lorraine is Mrs Sims now. Has been for years. Got grown-up children. Shocking business about her first husband, wasn't it? I'd almost forgotten his name.'

The woman was understandably curious at the young couple resurrecting a name from long ago and did her best to keep them talking, but Nelly cut in to thank her for her help. 'Third floor, you say?'

They plodded up the stone staircase. The door was answered by a small, plump woman with lemon-tinted hair in a petal cut that suited her. She wore a modish tweed skirt with a tobacco-coloured cardigan over a pale green blouse. The former Lorraine Varnish was still a pretty woman, even if she was drawing her pension.

Nelly made a mental note: stay plump in old age and keep your looks. It sure as hell had worked for Elizabeth Taylor.

Gervase introduced himself and Nelly and said, 'Mrs Sims, we are writers working on a book and we wondered if we might talk to you about your first husband, Laurence?'

Seeing the uncertain look on her face, Nelly fished her National Union of Journalists' press card from her bag and held it up so that Lorraine Sims could compare the photograph with the face of her caller.

Lorraine Sims looked inquiringly at Gervase. 'I'm afraid I'm not a member,' he said lamely. 'But I have a visiting card – though it doesn't have my photograph.'

Lorraine turned back to Nelly. The wariness had disappeared. She was smiling. 'Bit of a scab, is he?' she said. 'Just like my Larry. He was a real lone wolf.'

Nelly knew an ice-breaker when she saw one. Nodding at Gervase, she said, 'He's too bloody mean to pay the union subs.'

The woman laughed again and ushered them into a surprisingly large flat, heavily furnished with mahogany and tapestry furniture from a previous era. She sat them at a square table and said, 'Can I get you anything?' Aromatic smells were issuing from the kitchen.

Nelly said, 'May we call you Lorraine? Fine. Well, look, Lorraine, I think you had better sit down. Don't worry about us. We've eaten.'

Lorraine seated herself, neatly smoothing her skirt over her agreeable knees. She said, 'So how does my Larry figure in your book?'

Gervase said, 'The book will be a history of the Gatling family.'

Lorraine looked blank. 'I've never heard of them.'

Nelly took over. 'Where is Mr Sims?'

'He's a long-distance lorry driver. He's on a run to Bruges. He won't be back until the day after tomorrow.'

'We know about your first husband's disappearance in 1955. So you must have remarried some years later?'

'That's right. I had to wait seven years before he could be legally declared dead and marry Ronnie – Mr Sims. Our first two kiddies were at our wedding.'

'So you had become quite reconciled to the belief that your Larry was dead?'

'Oh, yes,' said Lorraine. She was quieter now. 'If you're going to tell me he's still alive I think I shall faint.'

'No, no,' said Nelly, hurriedly. She moved round the table and hugged Lorraine. 'But we believe there may be evidence at last to confirm what you've had to assume all these years.'

They showed her the newspaper clippings. 'What makes you think it's Larry? It doesn't say that here.'

They gave her a brief outline of Gervase's interview with Denny Fling, omitting the Gatling clandestine site-clearing activities and their theory of the Gatlings' heartless disposal of the body.

Gervase said, 'Mr Fling and his workmen occasionally did business with your Larry. They sold him trinkets and coins they'd dug up. Mr Fling confirms that he worked on the site where the remains of a man have now been uncovered. It all adds up. Larry must have been looking for more stuff and had an accident.'

A tear coursed down each of Lorraine Sims's unlined cheeks. 'Excuse me,' she said, sniffing and searching for her handkerchief. 'I thought I'd done all my crying over Larry. He was such a lovely boy. Not at all rough, like so many of 'em round here. He had his dreams.'

Gervase and Nelly carefully talked her through her lost sweetheart's life to their final Saturday. 'He was beside himself. If Millwall had been promoted to the First Division he couldn't have been happier. He said he was going to be famous. He said he'd discovered a blinking Roman temple, no less, and was going back that night to dig out a statue that had been worshipped by the Romans. He reckoned Mr McKintock would give him more than twenty quid for it.'

'McKintock?'

'Yes. Over in Pimlico. Larry started out selling stuff to him but ended up as his agent touring the bomb sites.'

'This was all . . . unauthorized, I should think?' said Gervase.

Lorraine waved away his delicacy. 'There's no need to mince words after all this time. Stealing was what it was, even if it wasn't doing harm to anyone. I couldn't wait for the City to be rebuilt so that Larry couldn't take any further chances on those ruins.'

'Did he tell you any more about the statue?'

'Only that, from what he could see with his torch, it was so high' – she held a hand about eighteen inches above the table-top – 'made of bronze and that when he got it home I wasn't to clean it because that's how collectors like it, with the surface something-or-other untouched.'

'Patina?' said Nelly.

'That's the word,' said Lorraine. 'He also said the figure was wearing a funny little hat. I remember asking him since when did the gods wear dopey hats. He had no answer to that.'

She added suddenly, 'Larry was in the movies, you know.'

They both stared at her and she grinned. 'I can show you.'

She left the room and returned with a quilted envelope

containing a video cassette. 'I taped this off the telly years ago.'

They watched *Hue and Cry* until Lorraine hit the Pause button on her remote control and jiggled the tape back and forth until the screen was crowded with the faces of a group of urchins running pell-mell along a pavement. She froze the moment, crossed to the set and pressed her finger against one. 'That was Larry. He was only a kid when they made that. For a time he fancied himself as a regular little Errol Flynn.'

Gervase and Nelly studied the soft face of the boy with the open mouth. His character had yet to imprint itself. There was little of the past and no future foretold in that guileless face. And that, they acknowledged to themselves, was merciful. Lorraine was now crying openly. 'I still light candles for the daft little sod,' she wept.

Nelly hugged her again and said, 'Gervase, if Lorraine doesn't mind, I want you to go and make us all a nice cup of tea.'

Later, Lorraine found Larry's tracings wrapped in a bin-liner on top of a highly polished wardrobe. 'I've not looked at these for years,' she said. 'He brought them home the day before he disappeared. Larry said he took them off the temple altar but I've never been able to make head nor tail of them. Me and my mum wondered if we should show the police when they were searching for him. But we couldn't see how these bits of paper would help. All they'd do would be to get him into trouble for being somewhere where he shouldn't be.'

The tracing paper had yellowed and dried out. The creases cracked as they slowly prised open the sheets. The co-biographers immediately recognized the Latin but neither had persevered with the dead language at university.

Gervase said, 'These have certainly been traced off old inscriptions. But I can't see they have any market value today. Still, better keep them safe for now. You never know.'

Lorraine said, 'I'd like to see Larry get a proper burial after all this time. Should I apply to the police for the body?'

Gervase said, 'Sit tight, Lorraine. There has to be identification beyond a doubt and that means scientific identification. It's upsetting, but you have to accept that there won't be enough left for you to do the job yourself. We'll telephone and keep you up to date with progress.'

Gervase and Nelly were silent as they walked back to Gervase's car. When they had got in, she said, 'That rather settles it. Vanishing Larry Varnish found Roman remains on the Fletcher Hall site, fell in the stupid well, and the Gatlings, *père et fils*, concealed the death. That's a crime. It's time to tell the cops what we know.'

Gervase nodded. 'Yup. No question. We'll get a hammering from them if we hold out. But there's just one thing more I'd like to do for the sake of the book.'

'What?'

'Go back and see old Gunner. I want to try a little experiment.'

'What are you cooking up in your addled brain?' said Nelly.

'It was Gunner's nurse who set me thinking. He loves Fred Astaire. Right? So what is so nightmarish in one sequence on one tape that sends him round the twist?'

'Do you expect me to be able to answer that?'

'From my *chaise-longue*,' said Gervase, ignoring her question, 'I rang the British Film Institute library and asked about the sequence where Astaire dances in Central Park to the tune of "Dancing In The Dark". They said it comes from a movie called *The Band Wagon*.'

'So?'

'So shortly after that comes the bit that gets Gunner screaming at the horror of existence. There's definitely some shock moment that summons up demons from his past. And I think I know what that shock moment is. *The Band Wagon* is an MGM classic. I have the tape and I'm going to play it for Gunner. I'm curious to see what reaction we get.'

'I reserve judgement,' said Nelly. 'If you give him a heart-attack you won't see my arse for fuel being dumped in my slipstream.'

'Co-author, remember?' said Gervase. 'Each for all and all for each.'

'Very funny,' said his beloved. 'Are you going to share the advance, then?'

195

Chapter Six

Gervase cruised slowly along Walham Grove seeking a residents' parking space. Nelly, in the nearside passenger seat, said suddenly, 'What do I spy with my little eye?'

'A space? Where?'

'No. Something beginning with T.'

'Trouble?'

'Not a bad guess. Tabitha Gatling is sitting in her pretty XK8 convertible not a hundred yards from your front door. If she's wearing her bovver boots you can introduce me as the cleaning lady.'

In fact, Tabitha was wearing a subdued pair of leather low-heeled Prada shoes and the crisply dry-cleaned overalls of the Williams racing team – a souvenir, Gervase judged, of her short fling with the Formula One driver in Monte Carlo.

The heiress saw them coming and bounded on to the pavement to greet them. She was smiling. 'Think barracuda,' muttered Nelly, out of the side of her mouth.

'So,' said Tabitha, 'this is the beauty who has lured you from my side!'

The two women eyed each other neutrally. Gervase mumbled the introductions as he fumbled for his door keys. There seemed no alternative but to invite her in.

Tabitha said, 'I must say Nelly here is a vast improvement on that greasy Moses woman. I congratulate you.'

'They are two entirely different relationships. One's professional, the other's personal,' said Gervase shortly.

'Oh, aren't you and Nelly a working partnership?' Tabitha's tone was one of innocent surprise but her eyes were roaming everywhere around the untidy living room. 'Charming,' she said, in a voice that meant 'Godawful'.

Nelly said, 'Gervase and I help each other out occasionally when his workload becomes too heavy.'

'Ah,' said Tabitha. 'Does that mean I've had the privilege of my name being appended to a piece of your ghost-writing?'

'No. That's strictly Gervase's work. He wouldn't hand the

job to me without getting your permission. He's a man of principle.' Nelly headed for the kitchen. 'I think we have some gin.' The door to the bedroom containing the files was ajar. On the way, Nelly pulled it shut.

Tabitha cleared away yesterday's newspapers and stretched her lithe body along the sofa, twisting and flexing to exercise her muscles. 'I'm as stiff as your greeting. I've waited ages for you,' she drawled. 'Aren't we friends any more?'

Gervase was alarmed. Tabitha did not have the patience to wait overlong for anybody, much less a man who was an employee in all but name. Something was wrong.

He said, 'Stiff? I was just surprised to see you, that's all. You've never asked before to see my digs.'

Nelly returned with the drinks. She said, 'Sorry there's no ice. Gervase isn't the most organized of men on the domestic front.'

'I know what you mean,' said Tabitha. 'If only they'd take our advice, their lives would be trouble-free. But they will insist on going their own sweet way. Then they wonder why they end up in deepest doo-doo.'

Tabitha eyed Gervase meaningfully. She was definitely driving at something.

'Gervase isn't so bad,' said Nelly. 'He's been known to listen to the feminine voice. He doesn't see women as sex objects.'

'Yes, I can certainly vouch for that. You never treated me as a sex object, did you, Gervase?'

'I'm your amanuensis, Tabitha. Sex is not part of the deal,' said Gervase. 'In any case, I can't see any man treating you as a mere object, sexual or otherwise. Though I daresay there's many a man who is *your* abject object.'

'But not you, Gervase,' Tabitha murmured thoughtfully, rolling her gin glass in her hand. 'But not you.'

Gervase said finally, 'Is there some special reason for your visit?'

'I almost forgot,' she said, swinging her feet on to the floor. 'I'm being given a screen test as a late-night glamour-puss on the *Women In Yer Face* talk-show. I'll need a scriptwriter. Interested?'

Gervase shook his head. 'You'll need someone with experience of that world. I'm a dead-tree newsprint journalist.'

'There's good money in it.'

'Sorry, Tabitha, I have to pass. For another thing, I simply don't have the time.'

Gervase could not be sure whether the glint in her eyes was merely mischievous or positively dangerous. 'Now what could you be doing that's more important than getting your first break in television?'

She turned to Nelly. 'What about you, Miss Tripp? Do you hanker after the life of a successful scriptwriter?'

Gervase could see that Nelly was having thoughts similar to his own: that Tabitha was toying with them.

Nelly said, 'Sorry, Miss Gatling. I'm tied to the *Guardian*.'

'Yet you have time to collaborate with Gervase?'

'Out of friendship, Miss Gatling. I'm just a helpmeet.'

Tabitha finished her gin and tonic. They watched her silently. The eyes were now hooded and the ravishing face was giving nothing away. Then she perked up, smiled brightly and said, 'I wonder if I might use your bathroom?'

They did not have to look at each other to sense their joint dismay. The bathroom was *en suite* with the bedroom – and the Gatling files.

Nelly reacted first. There was no alternative. 'This way. I'll show you,' she said.

Apprehensively, Gervase watched them go. Through the open door, he watched Tabitha halt boldly at the foot of his bed and survey the room, noting in her unhurried glance the filing cabinet, the paper-strewn trestle desk, the bookcase and the personal computer as well as the more conventional furnishings of a bedroom.

She stepped into the bathroom and closed the door. From a distance, Nelly silently signalled her helplessness and swiftly turned all the desk documents on their face. She sat at the foot of the bed until Tabitha re-appeared. She gave a short laugh when she saw Nelly on guard.

'It's all right, darling. I know my way back,' she said.

To get her to depart, Gervase finally undertook to give her television proposition some consideration.

As Gervase shut the door behind her, Nelly said, in a voice that brooked no argument, 'The cow knows something.'

'Christ! That was my feeling,' said Gervase. 'But what?'

Chapter Seven

They had to wait three days before Nelly had a day off. Then she bought grapes and a bunch of flowers and they headed for Bournemouth. They had not brought Percy Start with them on this second visit to Gunner Gatling.

Gervase said, 'From what I saw last time, old Gunner evinced a certain interest in you. Or, at least, an interest in your mini-skirt. When I pop the cassette in, could you try to be giving him a cuddle? It might keep him calm enough to make sense. We don't want him going completely ga-ga on us.'

'I didn't know you listed pimping among your many talents.'

'Oh, yes. I'm BA (Hons), University of Soho.'

At Aitkin-Adams they were relieved to see the same receptionist on duty. 'Hi!' they both said, with false *bonhomie*.

The girl remembered their faces but not the patient they'd visited previously. They signed the visitors' book and she called the nursing station. 'Could you take a seat for a while?'

'Is something wrong?' asked Gervase, suppressing his alarm. 'Has poor Mr Gatling had a turn?'

'No, nothing like that,' said the receptionist. 'The girls are cleaning him up a bit. Won't be long. I'm sure he'll be very pleased to see you. He doesn't get all that many visitors.'

Nelly said idly, 'Does Tabitha ever come to see him?'

The girl looked uncertain. 'I don't believe I know that name.'

'His granddaughter. Very blonde, very beautiful, always in the newspapers.'

The girl laughed. 'Is that the granddaughter? I never made the connection. She's incredibly glamorous, isn't she?'

The girl pulled the visitor's book towards herself and ran a finger down the signatures. 'Yes, here she is. Tabitha. She visited a week ago.'

Gunner's regular nurse came busy-stepping into the hallway. She brightened when she saw Gervase and Nelly. 'Oh, it's you two. I'm sure Frank'll be happy to see you. We've told him he's got visitors and he has to be on his best behaviour. It's poor Vernon who gets him worked up.'

She bustled them down the corridor. She apologized for the delay. Frank had had an accident with his breakfast. 'Well, actually, he threw it all over the room,' she confided in a low voice. 'And he's also started wandering. We've had to tag him. He's furious but better that than find him in the middle of the road. His son will have to give his consent for the daily administration of a hundred milligrams of Melleril or whatever else the doctor recommends. It can't be long delayed. It'll stop him having these terrible outbursts. His screaming in the night is heartrending. It's as if he's looking into the fiery furnace.'

Gunner Gatling was glowering as they walked into his living room. 'Now, Frank,' said his nurse firmly, 'you can wipe that look off your face. You promised me you'd be a good boy.'

She spoke to him as if he were an eight-year-old. God, thought Gervase, I hope someone puts me down before I regress this far into infancy. He shook himself back to the task at hand. Nelly was already performing. Gunner, in clean clothes, was seated in the same chair as before and she was planting a kiss on his temple.

She said, 'Lovely to see you again, Mr Gatling. Sorry we couldn't bring Percy Start with us.'

'Where's Percy?' said the old man doggedly.

'I don't think he's very well,' extemporized Nelly.

'Take me to Percy.'

'I don't think that's a very good idea. Aren't I good enough for you?' Nelly twinkled, pouted and wriggled shamelessly as she removed her topcoat.

Gunner gazed thoughtfully at her emerging torso, with its hand-span waist and small, high breasts captured tightly under a maroon sweater. At least the glower was fading from his face. He waggled his left foot, raising his pyjama leg. An electronic tag was locked around his ankle. 'They must think I'm a fucking dog,' he grumbled to her.

Given the family history, rather appropriate, thought Gervase, while Nelly had resumed her former game of popping grapes into his mouth. He had in his full set today and began to enjoy himself. She started to address him as Frank.

By now Nelly was perched on the arm of his chair and showing a great deal of leg. From the moment Gervase had entered the room, the old man had ignored him. He had eyes only for the coquettish Nelly.

Gervase was thinking, She'll be in his bloody lap in a minute, when she said calmly, 'Gervase, why don't you let Frank see one of his dance tapes?' And to Gunner Gatling, as if she were pleasing a baby, she purred, 'Frank would just love that, wouldn't you, Frank?'

'Hmmm,' said the old boy, as she brushed back his few remaining wisps of hair with her hand.

Gervase kept his back to Gunner Gatling, made a pretence of selecting a tape from the rack and slipped his own copy of *The Band Wagon* into the machine. He'd wound the film on beyond the 'Dancing In The Dark' sequence. Nelly stopped fussing and moved aside so that Gunner could get a clear view of the screen. Gervase backed away until he was out of Gunner's line of sight. Then he moved up close behind his chair and switched on his tape-recorder.

Almost immediately Fred Astaire flashed on to the screen. He looked very snappy in a pale suit with a fedora pulled down over one eye. He seemed gangsterish but was intended apparently to be a New York dick. While he kept up a Sam Spade-ish commentary, mayhem broke out in the background: a team of male dancers gave a dazzling, athletic display of hoods taking part in a shoot-out. Soon the stage was strewn with bodies.

Nelly glanced at Gunner. He was engrossed and his knuckles were clearly visible through the transparent skin. He held on tightly to the padded arms of his chair. He had finished chewing Nelly's last grape but his mouth was still working furiously and there was a dribble at one corner. From his throat came a rising sound as if a rusty manhole was being opened.

The sound rose and rose and, on the screen in a crescendo of screeching jazz, the scene shifted to the exterior of the Dem Bones Café. Its sign was in eyeball-searing neon strip. Moulded in the shape of a human skeleton.

The sound of an other-worldly shriek merged with the wail from the twin speakers. It raced up Gunner's throat and out of his mouth as Gervase pressed the Pause button on the remote control and froze the skeleton on the screen.

The old man screamed, 'Take it away! Take it away!'

Nelly took his head and pressed it between her breasts, muffling his cries for fear of bringing the nursing staff on the run.

Gervase ruthlessly left the image of the skeleton – gleaming, mocking – where it was.

Nelly said, 'What's wrong, Frank? Does it remind you of something you and Vernon did?'

'It was him. He ruined everything.'

'It was him what, Frank?' Nelly eased her hold on his head to make his answers more distinct but Gunner Gatling remained resolutely a child at her breast.

'It has to be secret,' he mumbled. 'Vernon says.'

'I think I know the secret, too, Frank. You dropped that boy Larry Varnish in a hole, didn't you, Frank? In a hole where he'd become just like that skeleton in the movie?'

Gunner began howling again and Nelly pressed his mouth into her chest to quieten him. She stroked his head and cooed soothing noises while Gervase made furious don't-mention-skeletons gestures at her.

She nodded silently in acknowledgement and eased Gunner's face off her body. 'You hid little Larry because you didn't want anyone to know he'd found some Roman treasures. Isn't that right, Frank?'

'Don't tell Vernon I told you,' he wept. He turned an eye towards the television screen and added, 'Is it still there?' It was, and once again he hurriedly buried his face. For comfort, he now had both arms around Nelly's slender frame.

'We'll chase the nasty thing away in a minute,' she said. 'Was the lad already dead when you looked down the hole?'

'Vernon said he was.'

'Aren't you sure? Shouldn't you have called an ambulance?'

'Vernon said we'd both end up dancing at the end of a rope.'

'But hanging was for murder in those days, Frank. You didn't kill little Larry, did you?'

Gunner Gatling was attempting to burrow with his forehead into Nelly's sternum. He could not bear to look at the screen. 'The horrible picture won't go away until you tell Nelly the truth, Frank,' she said firmly.

He twisted his head and looked up at her with watery eyes. 'Vernon hit him, not me, and took away his little statue. He wasn't content just giving the little devil a good hiding. Had to clout him with a hod, didn't he?'

'Larry was unhurt until Vernon hit him with a bricklayer's hod?'

'The little bugger tried to run away but Vernon swung the hod and got him.'

Behind the chair, Gervase was holding his breath and the tape-recorder as close to Gunner's head as he dared.

Nelly said, 'If Vernon hit him, why should you have nightmares? You didn't do it.'

'Vernon said it didn't matter. They'd hang both of us just the same. He said if I squealed he'd say I hit the kid as well. He'd lie and swear he was still alive when we mixed a batch of concrete and sealed the well.'

'That wasn't very nice of your son, Frank.'

'The bastard. I've held it against him all his life. We've all pulled some dodgy strokes in our time, that's business, but murder is something else. If they want to hang me now, they can. Fuck everybody. Anything's better than being treated like a dog in this place.'

Nelly marvelled. The Dem Bones Café scene had acted like electric shock therapy. Gunner was talking with complete, if tremulous, lucidity.

She said, 'You wouldn't have buried Larry Varnish alive, would you, Frank?'

'That's what I've never stopped asking myself,' he croaked. 'Vernon swore he was a goner and we could do nothing for him. We burned his clothes. We had to think of ourselves. But I still wonder . . .'

Nelly nodded at Gervase and he wiped the luminous skeleton from the screen. 'You can look now, Frank,' said Nelly gently. 'It's all over.'

The nonagenarian relaxed his hold on her and glanced fearfully at the screen to check. He was like a child who'd been told that Mummy had chased the bogeyman from the room.

Gervase leaned over the high back of Gunner's chair and spoke for the first time. He asked, 'What happened to the little statue, Frank?'

Gunner seemed surprised to be reminded of his presence. He said, 'What statue?'

'The one Larry Varnish had. The one you just mentioned to Nelly.'

'Dunno. I haven't got it. Just a piece of junk.'

'Did Vernon take it away?'

'Probably dumped it in the well with the kid. Still there.'

They realized simultaneously that Gunner Gatling no longer bothered with the news. There were neither newspapers nor magazines in his sitting room. He did not know about the grisly discovery at Abura House.

They stayed with him for another hour. Gervase, still in shock from the confession of murder, recovered his Fred Astaire tape and did little more than sit out the time. Nelly, torn between her disgust at the grotesque Gunner Gatling of yesteryear and her gentler feelings for Gunner's present-day hellish existence, waiting out his time in death's vegetable patch, finished feeding him the grapes as he slowly relapsed into forgetfulness.

When he said, 'Who are you?' she knew it was time to go. Gervase walked out into the corridor without saying a word. Nelly took her handkerchief and wiped the old man's eyes and mouth. 'There, there . . . We have to go now, Frank. Just try to remember, we all come to judgement in the end. If Vernon did something terrible all those years ago, God will know. He'll not be fooled.'

But the shutters had descended. Frank Gatling turned a blank gaze upon her. 'Where's Percy?' he said.

Chapter Eight

'My God! We have a bestseller,' gasped Gervase. 'This is going to be a publishing sensation. From dog-shit collector to unimaginable fortune . . . A Gatling murderess – perhaps two . . . a looter and robber of dead bodies . . . and now a Gatling murderer with Gatling accomplice. Chantry's will go apeshit when we hand them a synopsis.'

'Chill out,' said Nelly, who had taken the wheel for the drive back to London. 'You're forgetting a certain six-letter word.'

'What?'

'P-O-L-I-C-E. We have to tell them what we know right away.'

'Bollocks to that!' Gervase removed his feet sharply from the dashboard where he'd been performing an Astaire-like triumphalist tap-dance of his own and turned to her profile. 'Let's get our manuscript ready for the printers. It'll take only four or five months. The mystery of Vanishing Larry Varnish has remained unsolved for more than forty years. A while longer won't make any difference.'

Nelly shook her cropped head. 'Obviously *chaise-longue* journalism doesn't include a course in the legal implications of publication. Withholding the sort of dynamite information we have constitutes obstruction of the police in their investigation. I'm not so sure we haven't already overstepped the mark. Strictly speaking, we should have gone to them after we interviewed Larry Varnish's widow. For another thing, how do you expect to get all that juicy stuff about Vernon into the book unless he cops a guilty verdict in a court of law? We'll be able to incorporate every word of the trial proceedings.'

'And so will every bloody newspaper in Christendom,'

wailed Gervase. 'Our exclusivity will go sailing down the Swanee. What'll be our edge after all the bloody digging we've done?'

'It'll be in the manner of the telling,' said Nelly, calmly keeping her eyes on the unreeling M3 motorway. 'It'll be our *Washington Behind Closed Doors* – two journalists setting out, blow by blow, how they cracked a great criminal conspiracy and brought one of the world's richest men to a belated justice. We'll have the kind of glory that Woodward and Bernstein enjoyed.'

'With Denny Fling as Deep Throat? Do me a favour.' Gervase, who in his earlier euphoria had failed to buckle on his safety-belt, half turned from her. He gazed moodily at the passing scenery.

'Why not? If that's what'll make you happy. Gerv, I don't believe you've yet grasped the enormity of what we have uncovered here. We'll be stars in our own right.'

'We'll be stars anyway – if we save everything for the book.'

Nelly sighed. 'No, my sweet. We're off to the police. They can do the remainder of the donkey-work. The moment the judge sends Vernon off into durance vile our book will hit the streets – here and in America. Can't you just see us on the cover of *Time* magazine? If only Alfred Hitchcock were still alive to direct the movie.'

'Can I be played by Hugh Grant? I've got to get some satisfaction out of this.'

'I was thinking of someone more on the lines of Danny DeVito.'

Gervase Meredith grumbled all the way into central London, but in his head, if not his heart, he knew Nelly had outlined their only realistic course of action.

The English libel laws formed a straitjacket from which there was no escape. Vernon must be convicted or their Gatling family saga would be an emaciated thing, *sans* guts, *sans* balls, *sans* teeth. And Vanishing Larry Varnish, who had dared to dream and forget his place, would remain unavenged.

Gervase slid across to take the wheel of his jalopy so that Nelly could be dropped off at the King Street shops, near the flat in St Peter's Villas, Chiswick, that she shared with another freelance journalist named Melanie Lamb.

She stood on the pavement and said, 'Give me the Gunner tape. I'll run off the copy for my file. Meanwhile, you assemble everything that the police will need to see. Tomorrow morning we'll dump it all on that bloke Dalton, who seems to be running the case. Let's hope he's properly grateful and not snide the way some coppers get when Fleet Street does their legwork for them.'

Nelly watched him vroom off, much too fast for the car's maturity. She shook her head in old-maid fashion. When they were married she would need to snip the flares from that lad's mental trousers. Her beloved still had not put on his seat belt.

She dived into the supermarket and tossed into the wire basket some vacuum-packed croissants, milk, unsalted butter and a tube of the toothpaste her flatmate complained she had failed to buy on her last turn.

The furnished flat consisted of the upper half of a semi-detached cottage. It had been handed down through a long line of cash-challenged freelancers from the halcyon times when newspaper offices and printing presses were still huddled around Fleet Street.

Nelly let herself in and took the stairs two at a time. Her downstairs neighbour's parlour door was ajar. 'Afternoon, Mrs

Keen,' she sang out, over the mahogany handrail. Esther Keen was a dour sixty-six-year-old widow, who always got invited to the girls' parties. That way there were no complaints about the bouncing ceiling and the din.

Mrs Keen failed to respond. Nelly shrugged and pressed on up the flight to her own front door. She stepped inside. There was none of the usual Melanie noise pollution: no radio blasting the roses off the wallpaper, no tape, no clatter. Nelly assumed immediately that her flatmate, a health 'n' beauty writer for various publications, was out – until she spotted the back of Melanie's head. She was sitting on the sagging Victorian sofa facing the fireplace.

'Hello, love. You're bloody quiet for a change. Tongue on a diet, is it? What've you been doing to your hair?'

Melanie was wearing some kind of plastic shower-cap.

Nelly plonked her shopping, shoulder-bag and keys on the breakfast bar. She reached for the kettle to fill it for a much-needed cuppa but stopped with it held in mid-air. The silence was as oppressive as if the room had been lined with acoustic tiling in her absence.

'Mel?' Nelly's voice rose in anxious query. 'Melanie, are you all right?'

Melanie neither moved nor spoke.

Nelly rounded the breakfast bar in a rush and reached the sofa in four strides – when she screamed then whimpered and dropped the kettle.

Melanie was still in the peach-silk wrap that had been a freebie on a press trip to Paris with Lancôme. Her mouth was open wide and her eyes hooded and dreamy. Her lips were dark blue and small blood vessels had burst on the cheeks she so conscientiously moisturized every night.

Nelly could see all this through the greyish veil of the shower-cap which wasn't a shower-cap at all but a transparent plastic bag that had been drawn over Melanie's head and held tightly around her elegant neck until her lungs exhausted the last of the available oxygen supply and she had expired.

Nelly virtually fell down the staircase and tumbled into Mrs Keen's parlour. On assignment Nelly had seen dead bodies and had always conducted herself with fortitude, even when the victims had been children. She had found that rage helped keep despair and nausea at bay. But in this little house her professional guard was down so that she fell to her knees and puked into the hearth when she saw Mrs Keen, composed as anything, hands folded in the lap of her flannel dressing-gown from British Home Stores, sitting with a plastic bag over her head. Just like Melanie upstairs.

Nelly found herself shaking so hard that her two bangles rattled. 'Deep breaths! Deep breaths!' she told herself. After a while – seconds? minutes? later, she was unable to recall exactly – she regained her senses and cuffed the copious spittle from around her trembling mouth.

Still on her knees, she scrambled across the carpet to the ugly olivewood side-table where Mrs Keen kept her telephone. She remembered finger-prints and gingerly held the handset in one of Mrs Keen's tissues. No dialling tone. In something close to despair, Nelly's eye followed the white cord to the wall. The killer had yanked out the plug. Bastard! She scrambled across to thrust it back into the slot and at last was able to dial 999.

Some time later, when two stern-faced detectives had escorted her to Mrs Keen's pine-panelled kitchen in the rear of the house to isolate her from the pandemonium, she remembered her files and she remembered Gervase.

They didn't want to let her return upstairs yet but she pleaded and said that if they allowed her to peek into her bedroom she might be able to throw some light on this terrible thing that had happened.

'Oh?' they said in unison. And their expressions changed subtly from those of two men cherishing a valued witness to suspicion. So they took her up, past the uniforms and the men in white overalls photographing, dusting with zinc powder, brushing, magnifying, and lifting samples on sticky tape.

At the landing, a third detective started to object but one of her guardians said, 'She can't contaminate the scene. She lives here.'

So they let her peek into the bedroom where there should have been two cardboard wine cartons, bottle compartments removed, containing the duplicate Gatling files stacked one on the other in the far corner. They were gone. As was her laptop computer.

Nelly, drained of emotion, said, 'Would you please ring this man and tell him what has happened?' She handed them Gervase's name and number. They asked if she had an address to go with it.

They didn't ring. Instead, they sent two detective constables to pick him up.

The two detectives double-parked behind a white patrol car that was already double-parked outside the Walham Grove address that Nelly Tripp had supplied. They stared at each other and pursed their lips.

'Funny,' said one.

'Funny,' said the other.

The door was answered by one of the two uniforms inside, a fetching policewoman with lustrous chestnut hair piled into her cap and green eyes to dive into and die for.

They flashed their cards and one said, 'We're looking for a Mr Gervase Meredith.'

'You've found him,' said the doll in blue. 'Better come in, but don't touch anything. We caught the call. He's reporting a break-in but we haven't found any sign of it so far.'

They found Gervase, slumped in a chair holding his head in his hands.

'Mr Meredith? We're detectives from the Hammersmith police station. What's happened here?'

Gervase looked up bleakly. 'The fuckers have cleaned out everything. Eight months' hard graft. I must have been mad not to see it coming. Murder's never stopped them so why should they balk at a little housebreaking?'

The two detectives exchanged the purse-lipped look a second time. Murder? This guy knew nothing yet – or so they had been instructed by their superiors – of the day's gruesome events in Chiswick.

Just then the doll's male sidekick re-entered the living room. 'I can certainly confirm, Mr Meredith, that the contents of your filing cabinet are nowhere on or around the premises.

Neither is your computer hard disk. I've looked in the back garden and in the area. All gone, I'm afraid.'

One of the DCs said, 'What was in the files?'

Gervase had again buried his head. In reply he groaned anew. The woodentop said, 'All the research material for a book he was writing – documents, taped interviews, that sort of thing.'

'How'd they gain entry?'

'No sign at all. He's gonna have trouble with his insurance.'

Gervase, listening through his self-flagellating thoughts, mumbled, 'It must have taken at least two of them to get my stuff out of here.' He straightened up from his slump. 'I suppose I ought to look on the bright side. The shits have wasted their time because my girlfriend has kept a duplicate of everything.'

'What would her name be, sir?' said one of the detective constables.

'Miss Nelly Tripp,' said Gervase.

Without a further word, the detectives shepherded the two uniforms out into the hallway. The doll was saying, 'It's a bit of a Mickey Mouse job. I can't see SOCO bothering.'

'Darling,' corrected the DC, who fancied her beyond all reason, 'before the moon rises over Fulham power station, SOCO is going to be swarming all over this crib like bimbos over an eighty-year-old zillionaire.'

Chapter Ten

Within thirty minutes Nelly Tripp and Gervase Meredith had been isolated in separate interview rooms at the nearby Hammersmith police station. Asked whom she thought was responsible for the murders at St Peter's Villas, Miss Tripp had replied, 'That monster Vernon Gatling and his evil daughter Tabitha. Who else?'

Asked if that was the same Vernon Gatling who was the multi-millionaire and builder of skyscrapers, Miss Tripp replied bitterly, 'It is, unless he's paid to have himself cloned.'

Asked whom he thought was responsible for the thefts from his home, Gervase Meredith, who still had not been told of Miss Tripp's terrible discoveries, had replied, 'That bitch Tabitha Gatling – helped, no doubt, by that murdering father of hers.'

Asked if the father in question was the immensely rich construction tycoon of the same name, Mr Meredith replied, 'Yes, there's only one Vernon Gatling, thank God.'

The detective chief inspector who, until this moment, had been nominally in charge of the double-murder case, heard the unmistakable shrill sound of alarm bells dinning in his head. You didn't take liberties with the ultra-rich, not if you wanted a thirty-year career to continue in upwardly mobile fashion.

He went to his office, closed the door on his subordinates in the outer room and rang Area who rang the Yard who rang the assistant commissioner (crime) who rang the commissioner of the Metropolitan Police who said, 'Astounding. Can it possibly be true?'

'The two witnesses are both pretty shaken, sir – especially the woman who found the bodies. But I'm also informed they both appear to be balanced people. They say they've been collaborating on a biography of Vernon Gatling and his family.'

'Isn't Gatling a big financial supporter of the government?'

'I fear so, sir. His companies contribute annually. He obviously has a K in mind and all the signs are they have a K in mind for him. The usual window-dressing is being put in place to make it look right for the vetting committee. They've wished him on to a government advisory board on public building policy, arranged a few charity board memberships and so forth.'

'Christ! He'll most certainly be disappointed if any of this stuff sticks. Not to mention the Party treasurer.'

The AC (crime) propped the direct line to his ear while the commissioner navigated his customary torments, which involved the enhancement of his own personal standing as much as the fight against crime.

Finally, the commissioner said, 'We obviously can't keep a double murder under wraps but I want you to take the major incident team and the Press Bureau by the balls and squeeze. If the name of Gatling leaks I'll expect to see the scrotum of the guilty party on my desk dripping blood and minus the owner.'

'There is a major problem, sir. The female witness is a freelance journalist working for the *Guardian*.'

'God Almighty!'

'Suggestions, sir? Ringrose and Firth, perhaps?

'Yes. This has to be one for our resident wizards. You'd better get them out of the pub and on the road. Ringrose can be an awkward bugger but the prime minister has loved him like a brother ever since our man saved his arse over those beauty-queen kidnappings. If this business really does have Vernon Gatling's fingerprints on it, at least we'll have a friend at court.

'Oh, and tell the DCI down at St Peter's Villas that everything is freeze-framed until Ringrose assumes command. Ringrose can take over the nearest permanent major incident suite. At Kensington, isn't it?'

'Yes, sir.'

'I don't want our maestro moaning to me that when he arrived the orchestra was playing Handel's firework music when they should have been into "Silent Night".'

Chapter Eleven

The commissioner was doing Commander Thomas Ringrose and his assistant, Lionel Firth, an injustice. The pair were not in the pub. They were at the American embassy in Grosvenor

Square where, in a secure room, Ringrose and the CIA station chief in London, Jake Bishop, had just conducted a joint seminar for the benefit of a handful of CIA and FBI officers and Special Branch senior ranks. The subject: Anglo-American policing and co-operation in the new millennium.

In the convivial aftermath, they were all toasting – in a surprisingly acceptable Californian champagne – the formidable long-time partnership of Ringrose and Firth, solvers of some of Britain's greatest crimes of the late twentieth century.

The mutual-admiration fest came to an abrupt close with the assistant commissioner's call and his order for Ringrose and Firth to shake the Yankee dust from their shoes and get to a telephone that did not go through the wily Americans' switchboard.

For once Ringrose allowed the driver to use the howler. Screaming down the Cromwell Road, headed for Kensington police station, he said above the racket, 'The first question I always ask myself when I know the AC and the commissioner have been sharing little boys' secrets is, "Why us?"'

Detective Inspector Firth knew his cue. The two men sang out in harmony. 'There may be troubles ahead . . .'

That was the last laugh to come their way for a long time.

The Kensington nick in busy Earls Court Road was agog. Ringrose was coming. The big cars of One Area brass already filled the station yard. They formed a reception committee fit for a plenipotentiary.

Ringrose and Firth sped through the handshakes and comradely greetings of brother officers, hardly breaking step as they headed directly for the interview room where the woman, recently transferred from the Hammersmith station, which lacked facilities for a major investigation, was being held incommunicado.

'Must see her right away. First priority,' muttered the fast-moving commander.

They found Nelly Tripp much recovered. In fact, she was shouting so loudly that the policewoman watching over her had her back to the door. She was relieved when Ringrose and Firth barged in.

Nelly abruptly ceased hostilities. In recent years a cult of personality – futilely resisted by the commissioner – had grown up around the two detectives. Whatever their own preferences for discretion and anonymity, the long, lean Ringrose with his silver forelock, and nipper Firth with his marmoset eyes, were a familiar duo in the papers and on the television screen.

Nelly, who had been standing and leaning across the deal table, all the better to yell at the hapless policewoman, sat down with a bump. 'Well,' she said, 'I was certainly expecting the big guns for a crime of this calibre but I wasn't expecting the Royal Artillery.'

Nelly waved aside their introductions. 'For Christ's sake,' she said, 'I didn't mistake you two for Batman and Robin.'

'We usually get mistaken for Sexton Blake and Tinker,' said Lionel Firth. 'We didn't want you to be in error.'

'So what was all the shouting about?' said Ringrose.

Nelly made an exasperated gesture and glanced at her wristwatch. 'It is now six twenty p.m. and I take it that you two stars already know that I'm a journalist working for the *Guardian*. In five hours from now the presses will begin to roll and the editor will expect my account of these murders to be prominently displayed on his front page. I've been trying to get these knuckleheads to give me the use of a phone but for the past ninety minutes I've been denied everything except a cup of coffee and a doughnut, which I did not ask for in the first place on account of the distressing condition of my stomach since I found the bodies. So just answer me one question: am I a suspect or am I free to go?'

'That's two questions,' said Ringrose. 'To answer the former, I don't know enough about the case yet, but it seems unlikely. As for the latter, no, you are not free to go. If we have any suspicions at all about your involvement we may detain you for questioning – for up to ninety-six hours if a magistrate gives us the nod.'

'Oh, fuck,' said Nelly.

The two men drew up their chairs and Ringrose said, 'Don't despair. Here's the deal, Nelly. We'll let you write the story of what happened today and phone it to your paper – on one condition.'

'Uh-oh,' said Nelly.

'There's no catch. You just leave out any mention of the Gatling family. You may report your discovery of the bodies and that your laptop was stolen but you make no mention of your missing research material or that the biography you and Mr Meredith are working on involves the Gatlings.'

Nelly went ballistic again. 'My God! Has the cover-up started even before the bodies are cold? I can't believe men of your reputation would do that.'

'Don't be silly,' said Ringrose. 'You're a woman with a good brain. Use it! These murders are lurid enough. They'll make big headlines without the Gatlings spicing up the story. How the hell do you think Lionel and I are going to be able to conduct an adequate investigation and bring the killers to book if we have to operate in the centre of a three-ring circus? The Gatlings are powerful people with access to unlimited funds and the finest legal advisers. If your allegations are true, they'll be throwing obstacles in our path at every turn. We need to work without a constant spotlight on us. We can't hold you here for ever. You choose: be a big help or a big hindrance. What's it to be?'

Nelly held up her hands, palms outward in surrender. 'Okay, I hear what you're saying. And I have to assume you know your business. You've proved it enough times.' Nelly looked fiercely at the two detectives. 'But if I ever find that you're covering up for Vernon Gatling – and, take my word, he thinks he can buy his way out of any situation – then I swear I'll find a way of making what I know public.'

Ringrose held out his hand. 'So it's a done deal?'

Nelly took and shook it. Firth went off to find a typewriter and copy paper. Nelly eyed Ringrose. He was fiftyish and quite handsome in a hungry, gaunt way. She said, 'I'm curious. What would you have done if I'd said no?'

A grin split that bony face. He said cheerfully, 'I'd have kept you banged up without access to a telephone for the legal limit and given all your rivals a four-day beat on the *Guardian*. After twenty-four hours you would've been crying for mercy.'

'Bastard!' said Nelly.

'That's right,' said Ringrose, the grin spreading even further.

They did not tell her about the theft of Gervase Meredith's entire file until she had finished composing her vetted first-person story and had faxed it to the *Guardian*'s editorial offices.

Nelly screamed, 'My bag! Where's my bag?' She had a sudden recollection of dumping her shoulder-bag on the breakfast bar moments before the finding of Mel's body drove all thought of it from her head. She said, 'It's still in our flat.'

Firth said, 'Do you need it right away?'

'They may have cleaned out all our source material but they've missed the jewel. In my bag is a tape of Frank "Gunner" Gatling confessing that his son Vernon murdered some relic-hunter back in the fifties and the pair of them buried the body. Gervase and I took the confession only this morning at the old boy's south-coast nursing home.'

Chapter Twelve

By the time the two detectives had listened to Gunner Gatling's taped confession and the two seriously depressed biographers had individually related their stories – conducting Ringrose and Firth back through nigh on two centuries of scholarly and journalistic research in their quest for the true story of the Gatlings, the clock was showing one a.m.

Ringrose and Firth went to the room that the station chief superintendent had set aside for them. It boasted a stocked fridge, a coffee-making machine and a selection of freshly cut sandwiches, thoughtfully arranged under a clear plastic cover on a side-table.

The plastic reminded Ringrose that they had yet to visit the murder scene. He was content to let SOCO get on with the scientific examinations and for Professor Franklyn Dart to have the victims. Above-the-title television detectives who arrive at a murder scene and instantly spot the vital clue that a posse of scientific officers had missed was bullshit.

Even as Ringrose and Firth munched their sandwiches and meticulously combed the two transcribed statements for discrepancies, Professor Dart had Nelly's flatmate on the same slab that a few days earlier had accommodated the sad remains of Vanishing Larry Varnish.

'Meredith and Tripp match chapter and verse in every detail, guv'nor,' said Firth. 'If it weren't all hearsay, these two statements represent a complete argument for the prosecution of Vernon Gatling for the murder of this Varnish kid. No one has a stronger motive than Gatling for destroying the evidence that our two scribes have gathered.'

'Which means he also has to silence the people who've given our scribes that evidence,' mused Ringrose. 'Do you realize, while we're sitting here with our version directly from the lips of Meredith and Tripp, the people who lifted their files and killed those two women are combing the stolen research material for those names? We need to know, and fast, who is at risk.'

Ringrose and Firth went back to the beginning of the statement sheets and began sifting out the names. An hour later they had the list. It was headed by Gervase Meredith and Nelly Tripp themselves.

'I think there's not much doubt that the unfortunate girl she shared the flat with was mistaken for her. Better not mention that to our Nelly. I think she's had enough shocks for one day,' grunted Ringrose.

The next name on their presumed hit list was Denny Fling. 'He's by far the most credible witness,' said Ringrose. 'If what our scribes say is true, he has a good memory and is the only non-relative who can directly link Vernon and Gunner Gatling to the death of this boy Varnish.'

'What about old Gunner, guv'nor? Eye-witness or co-conspirator in murder?'

218

Ringrose waggled his hand in a maybe gesture. 'Either or both. Do you see him grassing up his own son? And if he did, can't you just see Vernon's clever counsel producing a quack to prove that in his dotage Gunner was prone to hallucinations?'

'What about the taped interview with him?'

'The judge wouldn't wear it. You saw for yourself what a tasty little minx our Nelly is. On that tape you can hear her slithering all over old Gunner. Vernon's brief would have her for breakfast. "Now, Miss Tripp, isn't it true that for much of the time during this so-called interview you were embracing Mr Gatling? In fact, did you not encourage him to place his head between your breasts? Am I correct in thinking that you do not normally wear a brassière? I put it to you that far from comforting Mr Gatling you were granting this poor, deluded old man sexual favours in return for his giving you the answers that you wanted rather than the innocent truth that would have destroyed your absurd suspicions concerning this man's only son. Even at this late stage, I ask you to release Vernon Gatling from jeopardy. Admit it! Your and Gervase Meredith's real – and profoundly wicked – purpose is to invent a murder that will help get your biography of the Gatling family on to the bestseller list. Your motive is not to see justice done but to make large amounts of money for yourselves."'

'Yeah,' said Firth. 'I can just see the jury swivelling round to Nelly stewing in the box and twelve pairs of eyes straining to see if she's come to court wearing her Wonderbra.'

Ringrose said, 'Lionel, I want you to send a patrol car to sit outside this chap Fling's house in Streatham. No need to wake the family at this hour but tomorrow they get a round-the-clock guard. As do our crestfallen scribes. I'm certain the pair of them are only still with us because they fancied a day by the sea. If they'd been at home, old Franklyn Dart would be poking around in their innards right now. Meantime, let's see if Kensington has a couple of camp beds as soft as their sandwiches. A few hours' kip won't go amiss.'

Chapter Thirteen

The day that dawned just five hours later became progressively action-filled as Ringrose and Firth cranked up the investigation that was ostensibly of a double murder committed only yesterday.

The incident room manager and admin officers were nominated and the computerized HOLMES (Home Office Large Major Enquiry System) permanently installed at Kensington was initiated.

Nelly Tripp's scoop story in all editions of the *Guardian*, and ruthlessly plundered by the trailing rival morning newspapers for their own late editions, omitted mention of the Gatlings, made no connection with a minor housebreaking at the home of a magazine writer in Walham Grove, and had nothing to say about a current investigation into the discovery of human remains on a City of London construction site. Nelly had played the game.

Ringrose was on the phone to Detective Superintendent Bert Dalton of the City of London Police at eight-thirty a.m. Dalton took the call in his apartment with its spectacular views from the fifteenth floor of the Barbican, a modern complex within the City walls.

Ringrose said, 'That skeleton in your cupboard, Bert.'

'What about it, Tom?'

'Bet I can put a name to it, Bert.'

'Can you, by Jove?'

'I take it you know it's an unlawful killing?'

'I do, but we've stayed schtum about that. Goes back a long time.'

'Bert, if you care to climb into your chariot and get yourself to Kensington nick, I'm holding a couple of characters who seem to have saved you the legwork.'

By early afternoon, Bert Dalton had given both a hangdog Gervase Meredith and a chastened Nelly Tripp a severe bollocking for having withheld vital information, knowing that a police inquiry was in progress.

'You'll be fucking lucky if I don't have you up before the beak before this business is over,' he roared.

Gervase tried to protest they'd not known about the slaked lime that made it murder. He and Nelly had thought they were dealing with an ancient accident.

Dalton had thrust his great face so close that Gervase could smell his breakfast. 'Doesn't matter,' bellowed the detective superintendent, who had been comprehensively upstaged and humiliated by the Met with the connivance of a couple of bloody hacks. 'It was an unexplained death. It wasn't for you to decide when you would or wouldn't grace us with your testimony, you wally.'

Ringrose and Firth stood in the corridor outside, gazing innocently at the ceiling.

When Dalton emerged, puce-faced and breathing heavily, Ringrose said in an infuriatingly tolerant tone, 'That's telling 'em, Bert. Best to get it off your chest. Now, on with the show . . .'

Bert Dalton stomped off to play his part. Lorraine Sims, formerly Varnish, was collected from the Borough and delivered to Bishopsgate. Bert showed her the Carausius coin and she instantly burst into floods of tears. 'That was my Larry's. He found it in the ruins. He was as proud of it as anything. I'd recognize it anywhere.'

Dalton watched with pity her cuddly little frame racked by sobs for her long-ago lost love. He decided she should not be told that there was a small, terrible possibility that Larry Varnish had not been dead when his murderers sealed him into his tomb.

'We don't understand the attachment on the coin,' said Bert Dalton, handing her another tissue.

'He borrowed the ribbon off one of his dad's war medals. Daft little bugger wanted to wear it on his coat like a medal of his own.' She suddenly held up the transparent evidence bag and emotionally kissed the homemade medal through the material.

'Was he wearing it the day he disappeared?'

'Oh, yes. You couldn't part him from it.'

'I'm informed by those writers who came to interview you that Larry left behind something on tracing paper – on the day you last saw him alive, which would have been Saturday, the twenty-third of April, St George's Day.'

Through renewed tears, Lorraine instructed Dalton where it could be found.

By nightfall Detective Superintendent Bert Dalton had assembled enough circumstantial evidence to satisfy any of Her Majesty's coroners that the skeleton was indeed that of one Lawrence Varnish, last seen alive in April of 1955 when he was twenty-two years old but immature for his age.

The altar block that had wedged above Larry in the ancient well had been too unwieldy to be hauled to the evidence store. Instead it had been placed under seal in a police garage. Dr Bruce Stevens, the City archaeologist, was summoned once again from Walker House in Queen Victoria Street to confront the stone and examine Larry's inexpert tracings.

'Absolutely no question,' said Stevens. 'The dead man definitely took these rubbings from this stone.'

'So the rubbings give us solid evidence that the bomb site Varnish mentioned to his wife was the same one where he was conducting his search for relics and where he told her he had discovered a Roman temple? The same site that he intended returning to on the night of his disappearance?'

'Absolutely no question,' repeated Dr Stevens. 'Unless some superman was carting the altar block from site to site, which doesn't seem the remotest bit likely.'

Next, Detective Superintendent Dalton telephoned Professor Dart at Guy's where he was mid-way through his postmortem on Nelly Tripp's landlady. The pathologist took the call on the no-hands squawk box.

'Mr Bones,' said Dalton.

'Yes?'

'That head injury.'

'Yes?'

'The weapon was unusual?'

'That appears to be the case.'

'Suppose I said bricklayer's hod?'

'Which end?'

'The business end where the bricks are stacked.'

The pathologist paused for a mental visualization of the homicidal scene that this suggested. 'The aggressor would have to be a muscular person of decent stature to swing the hod at the height required and to achieve the momentum to cause such a catastrophic wound. The action would take both hands and all the killer's strength. But that L-shape ledge on the brick carrier would fit the bill – and the wound. Absolutely. Well done.'

'Thanks, Professor. We may have such a man with such a weapon in the frame. I'll be in touch.'

Chapter Fourteen

Ringrose and Firth at last had time to visit the scenes of crime. At both places, small armies of officers were 'on the knocker', combing neighbourhood residents for potential witnesses.

The duo were accompanied to St Peter's Villas by an apprehensive Nelly Tripp. Neither the front door nor those of the two murdered women had been forced. Ringrose took Nelly's hand to reassure her.

'The killers were admitted either by your flatmate or Mrs Keen. Professor Dart tells me neither woman had a chance to struggle. At least two persons must have been involved. Bruising on each woman's arms in particular shows that each was held in an iron bear-hug while a second party placed the bags over their heads. It must have been over very quickly.'

Nelly sat on the stairs and stared emptily at the black and white Edwardian floor tiles that Mrs Keen had kept polished.

At Walham Grove, Ringrose told Gervase Meredith, 'The malefactors went in and out of here in broad daylight, carrying your files. Forget the garden – too much risk of being spotted. It has to be the front door. They either had a key or they picked the lock.'

Malefactors? Gervase had never heard a policeman use that word before. 'Couldn't they have simply slipped the lock with a plastic credit card?'

Ringrose looked pained. 'Have you got a credit card? Good. Go on, try to slip the tongue.'

Ringrose and Firth watched indulgently as Gervase attempted to push his MasterCard round the jamb and into the crack.

'Won't go,' he said sheepishly.

'Of course it won't go. Your flexible friend isn't flexible enough, is it? The next time you see some actor doing it in the movies blow a raspberry at the screen. It only works if there isn't a deadlock and a wooden lip on the door jamb – and how often do you see that in real life? No, your lock was picked by a pro and it takes a long time to become a pro at picking security locks. You've been turned over by the A-team. If it really is Vernon Gatling who's out to get you, he's hired the best.'

'The malefactoring élite?' said Gervase who, in the middle of the cyclone, was trying hard to recover his sense of humour.

After the two writers had been taken back to the Kensington nick, Ringrose let them meet for the first time since Gervase had dropped Nelly off at her local supermarket.

They fell on each other's necks wailing. The two detectives left them to it – to keen over the deaths of two women who would still be alive but for Gervase and Nelly's insatiable curiosity, and failure to go to Detective Superintendent Bert Dalton the moment they had spoken to Denny Fling.

They sat rocking each other, and also mourning the loss of more than half a year's work. 'We'll put most of it back together again from memory,' swore Nelly.

They railed impotently at their own ineptitude in not fore-seeing the lengths to which Tabitha Gatling and her father would go. They cursed their own inefficiency in not making a third copy of their damning material. 'We should have lodged a set in my agent's safe,' said Gervase.

They were inconsolable.

Later, sitting in limp-limbed despair while extra locks were being fitted on Gervase's doors and windows, Nelly suddenly said, 'Stupid bastards!'

'Who?'

'Me and you. We thought we'd been so bloody clever staying well clear of the Gatling family while we snooped around. I've just realized how they got on to us.'

'How?'

'Percy Start. Remember, Vernon used to give him the money to visit Gunner. I'd wager that if you rang Percy now he'd tell you that Vernon had been on. You can imagine the conversation. "Thanks all the same, Vernon, but I've just been down to Bournemouth to see your dad. Two nice young people who're writing your family history took me in their car. Names, Vernon? Just a minute, I have them here somewhere . . ."'

Gervase said, 'That accounts for the sudden visit of Tabitha to the flat here. The sight of my filing cabinet looming like a bloody great tombstone in the corner of the bedroom and you nervously escorting her to the loo must have confirmed her darkest suspicions. When she left us, her next call must have been to the nursing home. The girl on the desk as good as told you Tabitha had never bothered before.'

'Yes, and I'd also wager that cutesy Tabitha managed to have a good look at the visitors' book, with our signatures telling her that she wasn't just being paranoid. Telling her that treacherous Meredith the amanuensis and his tiny tottie, the evil Nelly Tripp, were out to get dear Daddy.'

'At least we now know where we fucked up,' said Nelly. 'I just hope those Scotland Yard sunshine boys can do better.'

Chapter Fifteen

Lionel Firth, who had been tasking the forty-strong murder team, took a verbal report from a sergeant who'd been briefed to check the medical status of Frank 'Gunner' Gatling.

Extracting information from a member of the medical profession is always a delicate and often frustrating business for a policeman. Doctors live in dread of writs and litigation. But on his telephone call to the medical superintendent of the Aitkin-Adams Home, the response to the sergeant had been unequivocal. 'I'm afraid I'm in no position to help. Miss Tabitha Gatling arrived – rather dramatically, I must say – on our back lawn this morning in a helicopter air ambulance and we discharged Mr Gatling into the care of the nursing team and the qualified medical practitioner accompanying her.'

'You let him go on her say-so?'

'Certainly not. She had written authorization from her father, Mr Vernon Gatling, who has been the administrator of his father's affairs for some years.'

'Who was the quack?'

'I beg your pardon!'

'You said a qualified medical practitioner was with them.'

'He was no quack. He was Dr Hector Crumley-Smith of Wimpole Street, a respected specialist in diseases of the aged.'

'All right, Doctor. Did he say where they were taking the old boy?'

'I understand that Mr Gatling is to take a cruise on his son's yacht and later will be returned here to undergo a new treatment, supervised by Dr Crumley-Smith, in an attempt to arrest his growing memory loss and to improve the condition of his heart.'

'How ga-ga was he as of yesterday?'

'Please do not use that expression. It is most offensive. Mr Gatling was having considerable difficulty with his short-term memory but was capable, especially after a restful night, of great clarity. He could recall a great deal about his early life and the hardships he endured.'

'Is it true his son Vernon would not allow you to use drugs to sedate him when he became difficult?'

'I'm not sure I have the family's permission to give details of his treatment.'

'Lemme put it another way. You could always get old Frank Gatling to behave by putting on a Fred Astaire tape?'

'I wouldn't quarrel with that. Mr Gatling adored ballroom dancing – a glamorous contrast, I suppose, with what he told us of the grimness of his upbringing.'

'But there was one dance number that was on the nurses' no-no list?'

'If you mean they preferred that he did not play it, yes, there was.'

'Involved a skeleton in flashing neon lights?'

'I believe so. Would you mind telling me where you obtained all this information and why it is needed now by the police? Aitkin-Adams has a reputation for discretion. We have members of the peerage and people prominent in public life among our patients.'

'Can't do that, Doctor. The Metropolitan Police also have a reputation for discretion.'

The detective sergeant had a final question. 'Could you confirm from your visitors' book that a couple named Gervase Meredith and Nelly Tripp made two recent visits to the Aitkin-Adams and also Tabitha Gatling, at least once prior to her latest drop-in?'

'Funny you should mention the visitors' book. The blessed thing has gone missing.'

Ringrose and Firth sat with the Yard's psychological profiler, Constance Armitage.

They'd all stood silently in the rooms where the two women had been asphyxiated – a cause of death now confirmed by Professor Dart – and they had carefully studied the SOCO videos and still photographs.

Now they were seated in Ringrose's office in Kensington. Constance, a prematurely grey forty-year-old who affected red-framed spectacles on a chain, said, 'Let's try a little experiment.' She handed the two men sheets ripped from her note-pad. 'Let's each write what we feel are the main characteristics of the perpetrators.'

They were like three adults playing a parlour game. Firth even cupped his hand over his scrawl and made Constance grin. She took a mental bet that he was back doing a school exam with the invigilators prowling the aisles between the desks.

They read his contribution first. It went: 'Two persons. One possibly female. One powerfully built. A contract killing.'

Ringrose had written. 'Both professional killings. First-class operators. At least one female involved.'

Constance showed her lengthier contribution.

Both murders are professional hits by the same people. Two men and one woman. The men did the actual killing. One held the victims still for the quietus while the other used the bags. The woman was the 'introducer'. She was the one with the reassuring persona who gained non-violent entry to the house and was subsequently able to admit the other two to the premises. The 'introducer' will be a person who is accustomed to having her own way, can be charming and persuasive. She probably gained admittance by asking if she could wait for Miss Tripp's return. She would have appeared on the front doorstep alone. The landlady let her in. Mrs Keen was a cautious woman by the accounts I've been shown. She would not have been so accommodating if the 'introducer' had had two other strangers standing at her shoulder. It was her bad luck. If Melanie Lamb had answered the front door and Mrs Keen had remained unseen and unseeing, she'd probably be alive today.

It is odds-on that the 'introducer' is the hirer of the other two. She is squeamish in as much as the use of guns is alien to her. I would say that the killers gave her a choice of death scenarios — gunshot, stabbing, bludgeoning, poison, strangulation, among others — because they needed her to accompany them and they would have been anxious that she should not fall apart at the critical moment. She fell upon asphyxiation as the least messy method.

If you ever catch her and she confesses her role, I believe she will tell you she stepped outside the rooms while the wicked deed was done or, at least, stood behind the poor women as they met their end. She would not have wanted to see their faces as they turned blue and their tongues filled their mouths behind the plastic sheeting.

The 'introducer' is used to nice things. She will have a mother who is house-proud to the point of obsession. Note how neatly the victims are arranged in their seats. The killers are truly at the top of their game. They understood their client. They went out of their way to keep the whole business clinical – swift, orderly, no struggle, no overturned furniture, nothing smashed, as little as possible to degrade in the memory and cause nightmares for their employer.

The killer who held the victims in the death hug will probably have bruises on his shins where the victims kicked out, their legs being their only movable parts once he had enfolded them in his arms.

Firth pushed Constance's profile aside and said, 'I take it we work on the assumption that Tabitha Gatling was the "introducer". But what we have learned of her so far is that she is a most untidy person. A pain in the arse to the servants.'

Constance said, 'That'll be her personal rebellion against her mother's boring orthodoxy. But we are no longer talking about a disco-mad teenage girl dropping her dirty knickers on the bedroom floor. This is a double murder, a matter of great magnitude and gravity. In these circumstances the girl reverts to – and is reassured by – what Mummy tried to drum into her, tidiness, fastidiousness, ladylike behaviour.

'In her heart, she's always known that Mummy was right but there's no satisfaction in rebelling unless Mummy *is* right. If Mummy is wrong you're not rebelling but correcting. And that's no fun. No, the killers read your Tabitha with great skill and gift-wrapped the whole disgusting business for her as if she were buying a frock in Harvey Nichols. She or her father went shopping for two housebreakings and two murders, the intended victims being your two journalists, but as far as the murders were concerned darling Tabitha took delivery of the wrong package.'

Ringrose said, 'Lionel, did our intrepid hacks ever interview Tabitha's mother?'

Firth glanced at his notebook. 'They couldn't. But they had begun to collect some newspaper clippings. Alice Gatling, a trainee cashier, married Vernon when she was eighteen and he was twenty. Courting couples got hitched early in those days. But Vernon didn't want to be held back by children while he was on the upward path to fame and fortune. So Alice was in her late thirties before she had Tabitha. The birth nearly killed her. By then the Gatlings had a large house at St George's Hill, Weybridge in Surrey, and yes' – Firth glanced at Constance Armitage – 'she ran a very spick 'n' span establishment. In later years, Vernon did a 180-degree flip about children. He adored Tabitha, couldn't get enough of her. Which may have a bearing on what's happened. Our scribe Meredith has painted for me a very unsettling picture of their closeness that borders on incest. There's no question that she is fiercely protective of him and he of her.'

Ringrose said, 'How does the mother take this?'

'She doesn't. She threw herself out of an upstairs window at Weybridge and broke her neck when Tabitha was fifteen years old and already a beauty. Did she discover Vernon in a compromising situation with their wayward daughter? Who knows? If she left a note, Vernon had whisked it away before the local talent in blue arrived on the scene.

'The coroner was told that Alice had been depressed because she couldn't have more children and because growing success took Vernon away from home for most of the time. The coroner recorded a verdict of suicide. The case made the papers, of course, and Vernon demonstrated his grief and, at the same time, his flair for publicity for his business by bulldozing the £1.2 million family house in front of the television cameras.

'It's the only time the media were able to penetrate the shield behind which he herds his family. These days he doesn't go near any woman who doesn't have a fortune of her own – presumably on the theory that she could never be bought by the tabloids even after they'd finished with each other.

'You want to interview him about those bloody great Sky-

Cities of his, and he'll be delighted. Ask him about Alice or kindred matters and you get shown the oblong in the wall.'

Chapter Sixteen

Tabitha Gatling was with her grandfather and his doctor aboard the *Black Glove*. Present position: south of San Remo and heading into the Gulf of Genoa at the beginning of a Mediterranean cruise of a duration as yet undecided.

Vernon Gatling was with his executive team – and had been for the past week – in San José, Costa Rica, from where they were directing the construction of a new hotel-resort in the balmy highlands and testing the local prospects for a spot of venality to ease the path.

Tom Ringrose put this information aside and said to Firth, 'Lionel, I want everyone at the Aitkin-Adams home questioned. Let's see if any of them ever extracted a word from old Gunner about Vernon and Larry Varnish.'

Firth said, 'Guv'nor, we ought to put our heads together about these hitmen. Where the fuck did Tabitha Gatling find them?'

'Exactly the thought I've been shuffling around,' said Ringrose. 'Almost everything Constance Armitage posited gelled with my own thinking. But when you read her stuff and listened to her afterwards, didn't you get the feeling that there was something . . . well . . . *foreign* about the business? There was something terribly *unBritish*?'

'More Mario Puzo than Agatha Christie?'

'Exactly. Since when have we had contract killers of the St Peter's Villas level of prissiness in this country? The British state has the SAS rope-swingers, the IRA do it with bomb and bullet, those hitmen-for-hire that you can reach through Dublin wouldn't know the meaning of finesse if you flushed it down their throats with a pint of Guinness, and our home-grown psychopath's weapon of choice is the sawn-off shotgun plus he'll set fire to your house if he's feeling particularly narked at you.'

'Dear Tabitha picked up her diamanté telephone, rang some foreign shore and ordered two five-star killers from the Hit Boutique?' suggested Firth.

Ringrose swung his legs off his desk. 'Lionel, let's put our bundle on it. I simply can't believe she or Vernon would put themselves in hock by hiring a couple of South London thick-ears who'd come back for more when the original wage had been pissed away. I'd lay money that the Gatlings dealt with people who know their business – and stay in business because they take pains, and work to the recommendations of satisfied clients. They do the job as specified, take their pay and don't return for second helpings.'

Firth said, 'The Gatlings must have set the whole thing up in one hell of a hurry after Vernon sent Tabitha round to Gervase Meredith's flat to confirm their suspicions. Real pros wouldn't normally have taken an amateur like Tabitha Gatling along for the kill. They'd have carefully surveyed the scene, taken their time, made their plan and done the business alone. But these weren't normal times. The Gatlings must have pressed hard to have the job done fast. For imported pros, the ground would have been unfamiliar. They would have been strangers to local custom and practice, so they needed some-one like Tabitha to guide them swiftly through the shoals, be the "introducer", just as Connie said. The Gatlings must have done a heap of panic-stricken transatlantic conferring to agree such a drastic response to enemy action. We need the list of her telephone calls for the past week and I think you'll need to contact the Shadows of Vauxhall Cross to see what they can do about Vernon's calls from Costa Rica.'

Chapter Seventeen

The part-time MI6 man in San José was the usual expat who got the job because there wasn't much sound, cricket-loving, monarchy-respecting, public-school talent of British stock to choose from in this turkey-neck of isthmus sandwiched between the more volatile Panama and the faction-torn Nicaragua.

If the trouble-making Americans weren't interested in stirring up the dozy, bug-infested hole that didn't even possess an army to buy British weapons, then the Foreign Office had no interest either. And, if the FO had zero concern, then likewise Britain's Secret Intelligence Service.

Consequently, Our Man, one Gordon Abbotsbury, coffee exporter and bridge player, was surprised to be required for once to earn his retainer.

A sniffy commercial attaché phoned to say His Excellency would be joyful of his company. Abbotsbury acknowledged the coded summons from the ambassador and plunged out into the steamy heat of Costa Rica's capital to grab a taxi to reach the western edge of town.

At the Edificio Centro Colón, a glassy cube of offices, restaurants, cinemas and commercial enterprises on the Paseo Colón where the British embassy dozed away the day, Our Man played a mental game of Eeny, Meeny, Miney, Mo with the three lifts. They were notorious for stopping between floors and trapping the occupants for interminable, sweltering lengths of time before the engineers could be roused from their torpor.

He came down in favour of the middle lift and took it to the eleventh floor, which the British embassy shared warily with the Israeli Mission. Our Man arrived without hitch and was left alone in a swept room to take the call from London on the little-used secure line, the telephone being housed in a padlocked, battered metal box.

'There's a Brit named Vernon Gatling in town. Big-time builder,' said his liaison at Vauxhall Cross, who went by the name of Sinker, which was not his name at all. 'He's planning a holiday complex or some such for Costa Rica. Our masters don't care what he's up to. However, we do need a list of his telephone calls for the past seven days. And pronto. See what you can do.'

Gordon Abbotsbury, vaguely remembering his indoctrination into the trade mysteries, knew better than to ask why. In the event, Our Man, despite his long years of neglect by the motherland, performed immaculately. He established that Vernon Gatling was even now occupying the Bartholomew Columbus suite of the Pacific-Coronado Hotel in San José.

Abbotsbury scurried through the morning heat, anxious to be indoors before the noonday rains began making their infernal din on the red corrugated-iron rooftops, called at the *banco* for some readies, then took up station in the hotel's Galleon bar and waited for the under-manager to heave into view.

The bar presented its usual unnerving sight, which was why Our Man would normally not be seen dead there. The dark leather banquettes were thronged with people who appeared to be survivors of a nasty train crash. Nose splints, chin and head bandages abounded. This was the low self-esteem crowd sitting out their vacations while their bruises healed. He watched with distaste as they sucked up their drinks through straws.

San José was the (cheap) cosmetic-surgery capital of the world.

Gordon Abbotsbury was two gin slings down before the under-manager glided into the gloom created by the plantation shutters. This functionary spoke beautiful American-English and – praise be to God – was a sometime bridge partner of Our Man.

Abbotsbury wasted few words on softening him up. He said, 'Miguel, this chap Gatling you have in the presidential suite upstairs is a threat to every hotelier in the territory. If he succeeds here, you'll all end up with occupancy rates in single figures. He'll steal your business the way he has everywhere he's thrown up one of his giant holiday hotels. He's a bigger threat than the Arenal volcano.'

Miguel said, 'I've never heard that.'

Our Man said, 'Believe me, I know whereof I speak.' At the same time, as advised in his dimly remembered training lectures – 'Nothing works like a glimpse of the green stuff' – he extracted a thousand American dollars in C-notes from his wallet and laid them on the bar with his hand over them.

Miguel's eyes flickered downward and up again to Gordon Abbotsbury's schoolboy-pink face, which was charged with unspoken meaning. 'What's that for, Gordy?'

'For you, Mig.'

'If . . .?'

'If you get me a list of all the telephone calls Vernon Gatling has made from your hotel during the past week. For the sake of our little paradise, Gatling has to be stopped. I know people who are prepared to take on the task.'

Miguel placed his olive palm over Gordon's puffed and vein-crossed hand, which Our Man then withdrew. The dollar wad slid unseen to the bar's edge and disappeared into Miguel's striped trouser pocket. The doorman at the Ritz could not have made a tip disappear with greater fluidity of movement.

Adding a final polish to the day's trade, Our Man, who, unlike Vernon Gatling, already had a veteran's grasp of local venality levels, said, 'A month after delivery, there'll be another thou – if I'm satisfied you haven't spoken to another living soul of our little transaction.'

In the recent past Ringrose had not been MI6's most favoured copper. His investigation into the Conrad Niven assassination had brought the service to the edge of disaster. But, sitting with a list of Vernon Gatling's Central American telephone calls in his hands, he recognized the prompt response to his request for what it was – a peace-offering. The spooks wanted to be chums once again.

Which did not, of course, mean to say that Vauxhall Cross's interest ended with delivery of the telephone printout. Sinker's report of a gig neatly accomplished travelled upward, being initialled on its journey by ever more senior officers.

In most circumstances the report would have found its way into a registry folder before reaching the director-general. After all, this was an operation of the most minor kind.

However, anything with Commander Thomas Ringrose's name attached cried out for attention. What was that sly bastard up to? Had he not once had the service by the knackers? Brought them to their creaking knees? Saved only by the prime minister's plea on their behalf for mercy and understanding?

The DG studied Sinker's self-congratulatory report with interest. But it was the other name on which he focused. Like the assistant commissioner (crime) at Scotland Yard, the DG was well up on the warm glow of approval that shone on Vernon Gatling from within government circles.

In a very British fashion, inquiries were put in hand.

The DG met the Foreign Secretary for a snort at Boodles. 'Why's that bluebottle Ringrose taking an interest in Vernon Gatling?' the chief spook asked.

'According to the papers, he's in the outer conurbations investigating a couple of murders,' said the Foreign Secretary.

'What? Murders in Costa Rica?'

'Chiswick, I think. Where does Costa Rica come in?'

The DG told him.

The Foreign Secretary said, 'What the deuce do murders in Chiswick have to do with Vernon Gatling's phone calls?'

'You wouldn't expect Ringrose to tell me, would you? We're hardly best friends since the Niven thing.'

'Christ! Don't even utter the name.'

The Foreign Secretary finished the drink he had come near to spilling and left the DG to the mercy of sundry approaching bores.

Within the hour, the Foreign Secretary had telephoned the Prime Minister who had telephoned the Home Secretary who telephoned the Commissioner at Scotland Yard.

'Is Vernon Gatling, the construction chap, in some kind of trouble?' the Home Secretary wanted to know.

The commissioner placed a hand to his temple and attempted to rub away the sudden throbbing. 'I don't know where you heard that, Home Secretary,' he murmured, as one might to avoid rousing a man with a carving knife. 'True, his name has arisen in connection with an operational matter. But these are early days.'

'Ringrose is on the case, isn't he? And I'm told he's already got Six cloak-'n'-daggering for him in Costa Rica. I appreciate this is not your concern, but *entre nous* the gentleman at Number Ten, not to mention the Party chairman, is a mite jumpy at the news. Vernon Gatling has been a prominent financial backer of the Party for a long time. We'd hate to pick up the tabloids one fine morning and find we've been caught with tainted money in our back pockets. Remember the Major administration and Asil Nadir? I'd appreciate some early warning if Ringrose is about to swing into his usual collar-feeling mode.'

'Of course, Home Secretary,' said the commissioner, in a tone that suggested he would never have contemplated any other course of action. He held the receiver between thumb and forefinger and dropped it back into the cradle as if it were diseased. 'Conniving bastards!' he muttered. The heat he could feel was not emanating from the radiators.

He buzzed the AC (crime). 'Tell Ringrose to watch his step. Those shits at Six have been earning Whitehall Brownie points. Vernon Gatling's friends in high places are on red alert.'

Ringrose and Firth set aside all Vernon Gatling's telephone calls made internally in Costa Rica and the workaday calls made to his Mayfair offices. From the Pacific-Coronado there had been a flurry of calls to his London home in Cheyne Walk, Chelsea, all bunched around the time his daughter had dropped in casually on Gervase Meredith's flat. And a corresponding flurry from Cheyne Walk to him. There was one call to Antibes in the South of France when Vernon, presumably, had given instructions for the *Black Glove* to be provisioned in preparation for a rapid getaway on the Mediterranean cruise.

The two detectives finally isolated three calls to a 718 number in the United States. The 718 code covers the New York borough of Brooklyn.

Not only did the Federal Bureau of Investigation supply, with commendable promptitude, the identity of the subscriber, the Trapani Athletic Club of Brownsville, but considerable further enlightenment.

'It's a Family-run joint,' said Marty Groot, the Bureau's London liaison.

'Whose family?' said Ringrose.

'Family with a capital F, *comandante*, if you take my meaning.'

'As in *The Godfather*?' said Ringrose, remembering his deputy's 'More Mario Puzo than Agatha Christie'. Score one for Lionel.

Marty Groot was saying, 'Tom, these are heavy-duty people, members of one of New York's Five Families. We've had the Trapani wired for a long time and we had Vernon Gatling tagged by the time he made the second call. He's well known to us. How d'you think he gets so many of his SkyCities built? He crosses palms with mucho silver to get his plans approved by zoning commissions and mucho more *denaro* wings its way to the Mob to keep his construction sites trouble-free. He's not alone. They all do it.'

'What about the calls?'

'On the first, a male voice said, "It's Vern. I have to talk to Albert." The guy who answered the phone said, "Albert's not here. Try later," and cut Vernon off. Our trace to Costa Rica immediately identified the hotel and Vernon Gatling as the caller. No sweat.

'Vernon made his second call an hour later and got the same reply from the same man. But before the meathead could cut the line, Vernon screamed at him, "Do you know who I am, you fuck? Albert is a dear friend of mine. I have urgent business with him." Vernon sounded a liddle *distrait*. The guy on the phone said, "Ring again at eight. Albert's watching his ponies run at Aqueduct."'

'Do you have Albert's identity?' said Ringrose.

'Who hasn't? Albert is one Albert Penn, still known to his momma as Alberto Cesare Pennelli. He controls large-scale laundry, catering and garbage-disposal businesses on behalf of the Family. The Gatling hotel empire is tied to him by a number of these legitimate contracts. Albert is nicknamed the Pen Man. In certain morally deficient circles it is considered

238

extremely unlucky to have Albert write your name and draw a circle round it.'

'Did Vernon finally get Albert?'

'He did. And Albert was as brusque as the lug who answers his phone. Vernon said, "Albert, I need a favour." But before Vernon could tell us what that favour might be, Albert said, "For fuck sake, Vern, you know better than this. This line has a bigger audience than Channel Thirteen. Gimme your number. I'll be in touch."'

Ringrose was disappointed. 'That was it?'

'Not quite, *comandante*.' Marty was enjoying himself. 'Do you know why Albert is named Albert?'

'Of course not.'

'The Pen Man is named in honour of a distant uncle, the late Albert Anastasia, who was lord high executioner for the Mafia until he went for a haircut at the Park Sheraton Hotel, off Central Park South, one fine day and got his in the finest tradition of Warner Brothers' movies. Two masked guys strolled into the barber's shop and pumped Albert senior full of lead. There's long been a belief in the Bureau that Albert junior inherited his forebear's line of work. The wise guys call it the Bash and Bury Syndicate.'

Ringrose gave his excitement free rein. 'Listen, Marty, this is terrific news. This fits exactly into the theory that Lionel Firth and I have been batting back and forth. We have a couple of homicides here and we think Vernon Gatling booked a couple of really top-hole hitmen to come to England and help his daughter cover up an old crime that could put Vernon behind bars. Could you check the manifests to see if this Albert Pennelli and a companion flew to London at any time in the past ten days?'

'Whoa there, *comandante*! Albert draws the circle round the name, other hands see that it ends up carved on a tombstone. What was the method of execution?'

Ringrose told him.

'That helps because Albert can call on many craftsmen. And they don't all work the same way. Our nerds will need computer-time to run the possibilities and flight manifests. The search may take a while.'

'Do it, Marty – and thanks. Whenever I catch anyone again saying what a gruesome old bastard Edgar Hoover was, I'll tell them to shut their lying mouths.'

'I'm touched,' said Marty, and rang off.

Chapter Eighteen

The polling of the residents of St Peter's Villas and neighbouring streets had produced nothing of any worth. But the Metropolitan Police incident board appealing for witnesses, and placed on the pavement outside the murder house, produced Mrs Nancy Leith, aged seventy-six.

Good citizen that she was, she noted on the back of her shopping list the estimated time of the crime and the date, went home, conscientiously checked her World Wildlife Fund calendar, and realized that that was the same time and the same day on which she collected her pension at the post office, a journey that necessitated a walk via St Peter's Villas.

More to the point, Mrs Leith, with her little birdy eyes peeping out from two lizardy folds of flesh, distinctly remembered seeing two men sitting in a car. One in the front passenger seat, one in the rear. She gave them what she called 'an old-fashioned look' because it was the middle of the morning, the local menfolk should all have been at work, and you didn't expect to see two males simply sitting, not moving, in a large parked car in that quiet street. Suspicious, she called it.

'Weren't they doing anything at all?' asked the bobby who first talked to her.

'Well, they might have been a couple of dirty old men, I suppose – not that they were that old.'

'How's that?'

'They were ogling a very attractive young lady who was

ringing the bell at a house a few yards up the road. I'm sure it was the house where there's been trouble.'

Swiftly transported into the presence of Detective Inspector Lionel Firth, the old lady had further snippets to impart.

No, she couldn't give the make of car, colour or registration number. They all looked alike to her. Who did they think she was – Miss Marple? But the two men had worn dark suits. The one in front was pale and looked as if he could do with a few meat puddings to fatten him up. The other was a hefty individual with a tiny nose that seemed not to suit his broad face. He reminded her of her late hubby who'd been a fish wholesaler – apart from the little boy's nose, that is. The men saw she'd caught them leering at the girl and they guiltily turned their heads away so that she couldn't see them blush for shame.

'What about the lovely young lady they were making eyes at?' said Lionel gently. 'Do you remember much about her?'

'She was like all these girls today – they seem to be ashamed of the looks God gave them.'

'How do you mean?'

'She was one of those gungy people but she couldn't hide her looks entirely.'

'Do you mean grunge people? They dress rather drably.'

'Yes, that's right. I'm an old fool. Grunge! Horrible word. I can't think where they get words like that.'

'The girl . . .' prompted Firth.

'She had black hair with an ugly woolly beret – dark blue, I think – pulled down over her fringe. No style at all. But Lady Hamilton herself would have been proud to have those eyes, nose and lips. Why on earth would the silly girl want to dress like that?'

'They think it's fun being contrary, Mrs Leith. Like to wind up their elders.'

'What nonsense!' she spluttered. 'We made our undergarments from parachute silk during the war just so that we could feel nice. Now they have everything their hearts desire they dress like nothing.'

'What about her dress?'

'She didn't have a dress. She wore one of those dark brown

Australian cattlemen's cloak things that covered a pair of overalls – I could see the gather at the ankles. Oh, yes, and she had those frightful white plimsoll shoes.'

'Trainers?'

'Yes, trainers. What are all these young people today training to *do*? I'd like to know.'

'Would you recognize her or the two men again?'

Mrs Leith sipped her police canteen tea, nibbled her chocolate biscuit and evinced uncertainty. 'If they all wore the same clothes I might. As for the girl, I saw only a few square inches of her face. Lovely as she was, there are lots of girls like her in London – models, actresses, singers. I wouldn't like to take a chance and get some poor innocent girl into trouble.'

'Which one would give you the best chance of identification?'

'The skinny one in the car, I'd say. His face was quite close up to the glass. He's the one I gave the look. But I suppose the other man's nose was what you might call a distinguishing mark . . .'

Within the hour her descriptions were in the hands of Marty Groot. Firth said to Ringrose, 'I think we should have our scribes in for another chat. It's been a dormant line of inquiry so far, but what about that tale Gervase Meredith told about a woman in a beret visiting that American writer, Gus Meldrum, in Hollywood before he was found dead? Everything we have learned about Tabitha Gatling adds to the picture of her as a woman capable of great violence. I'd say she's the son Vernon Gatling never had. Let's throw Marty the baton and see how far he can run with it.'

'That's fine by me,' said Ringrose. 'But first I think we need a search warrant for the Gatlings' Chelsea base. Mrs Leith's description of the clothes sounds so positive that I feel willing to risk stirring Vernon and his Whitehall friends for the chance of getting inside Tabitha's wardrobe.

The ground-floor windows were shuttered but the housekeeper, Mrs Burroughs, answered the door. She put up token resistance to the warrant flourished in her homely face and the platoon of coppers in its wake. But Ringrose took her firmly by the elbow and said, 'In the absence of the Gatling family, I want you to accompany my officers while they conduct a search of the premises.'

'What's wrong?' said the uncertain woman, holding her fluttering throat. 'Mr Gatling should rightly be here.'

'I wouldn't argue with that,' said Ringrose. 'But he's not so let's get going.'

The platoon had been briefed and they produced fourteen pairs of trainers, mostly with white panels, from Tabitha's walk-in wardrobes and a dozen sets of designer overalls or dungarees, including those she'd brought back from Monte Carlo. There was no Australian cattle-rancher's coat but on an airing line in the fully equipped laundry room at the rear of the premises hung a woollen beret that was a strange, smeared mud colour.

Mrs Burroughs saw Ringrose and Firth gazing wordlessly up at it. 'The stupid girl tossed it into the machine without saying a word to me. It went in with my whites and the colour ran. Just look at my pillow cases.'

From a cross-hatched plastic basket she produced one specimen from a selection of bedding that looked as if it had been used to wipe the pavement. 'I'll never get it out,' the housekeeper wailed. 'That girl has no consideration.'

'What was the original colour?'

'Navy blue, by the looks of it. Though I can't say I've ever seen her wearing it.'

A scientific officer carefully unpegged the offending garment and bagged it. He then dismantled the washing-machine and removed the water filter. He also collected the contents of the air filter from the tumble-dryer.

Ringrose was about to steer Mrs Burroughs from the room when he stopped and pointed at a huge hanging cupboard. 'What's that?'

'An airing cupboard. It has only my duvet covers.' She pulled back the door. The slatted shelves were stacked with folded satin duvets of high quality. Ringrose began to run his fingers up the folds, trying to separate and count the items. 'There are just three,' said the housekeeper.

'Didn't you tell me when we arrived that only Miss Gatling had been in residence recently?'

243

'Yes. The other two duvets come from the beds of her two weekend guests.'

'Last weekend?'

'Yes.'

'What were their names?'

Mrs Burroughs shrugged and signalled disapproval with a pursing of the lips. 'She didn't tell me and I didn't ask. She has a great many friends who come and go without a by-your-leave. Miss Tabitha is a young lady not much concerned with etiquette.'

'What did they look like – the weekend guests?'

'I've no idea. I couldn't even say whether they were male or female, although there was no perfume on the duvet covers so they were probably male.' The housekeeper's lowered voice hinted at rampant troilism.

'Strange, isn't it? You're the housekeeper. I assume that means you have the run of the place.'

'True. But when the young mistress orders me and the rest of the staff to take the entire weekend off, one does not ask questions. She's young. One assumes she'll be doing things that she would not want to reach her father's ears. Mr Gatling has always been very . . . concerned . . . for his only child.'

Ringrose noted her hesitation while she sought an uncontroversial adjective to describe their relationship. Mrs Burroughs must have witnessed a great deal in the bonding of father and daughter.

She conducted him up the broad staircase to the two thirties-style Syrie Maugham bedrooms that the two mystery guests had occupied. The mattresses stood bare of the bedding that Ringrose had already seen downstairs. He said, 'Have you vacuumed and dusted these rooms yet?'

'No. That was to be today's chore – before you people arrived.'

It took thirty minutes for SOCO to report. 'The rooms and bathrooms have been wiped clean, sir. Either that, or the occupants wore gloves throughout.'

'What about the dustbins? Any remains of food? Empty cigarette packets?'

''Fraid not, sir. Emptied on Monday.'

Ringrose turned to the housekeeper. 'Miss Tabitha's guests seem to have been hygiene-minded to the point of obsession, Mrs Burroughs.'

Her throat was fluttering again. 'I don't understand. I give you my word, my staff have not cleaned these rooms since Miss Gatling spent the weekend in the house before going off to collect her grandfather for his cruise.'

'Don't worry, Mrs Burroughs. I believe you. We shall have to ask Miss Gatling about it, shan't we?'

In the car on the return drive to Kensington, Lionel Firth said, 'Our Tabitha is not just a pretty face. She knew enough about police procedure to prevent the Mob guys from checking into an hotel and leaving their spoor marks by way of the register and on the credit-card transaction.'

'If Marty Groot is right about their likely professionalism, I'd say it was they who handed her their list of dos and don'ts,' grunted Ringrose.

It took a whole day to organize a special kind of identity parade for the benefit of old Nancy Leith. From the manufacturers, Lionel Firth borrowed ten fibre-glass models of the type used to display the latest fashions in the windows of the big stores.

At the back end of the CID office a policewoman who had gone begging to Harrods dressed the haughty mannequins in Tabitha's trainers, designer overalls, and borrowed Aussie topcoats. She placed Tabitha's beret on the sixth mannequin and berets of differing designs and colours on the remaining nine.

Ringrose and Firth kept well back while a uniformed inspector ushered the old lady forward. She surveyed the frozen tableau with her sharp little eyes and said, 'Well, you've certainly gone to a great deal of trouble. The clothes are very good.'

'Take your time,' said the inspector. 'Concentrate on the trainers and the berets.'

Mrs Leith did the trainers first. After due consideration, she said, 'It has to be number one or number eight. All the rest have coloured bits. Hers were all white.'

'G-oooo-d,' said the inspector. 'Now, what about the berets?'

Mrs Leith snorted. 'You can take out those puffy ones for a start – and that crocheted thing with the glitter.'

She moved slowly along the row, head forward like an elderly tortoise. 'That's out!' she said, as brutally as the fashion editor of *Vogue* and pointing at an offending creation trimmed with a discreet single feather.

She ended up having eliminated all but number four, in beige, and Tabitha's number six. The inspector said, 'Sure?'

Mrs Leith said, 'No, I'm not sure. It could be either one of those hats or neither. The style is right but somehow I haven't got these colours in my mind's eye. What's happened to number six? It looks as if it's had a nasty accident.'

'Good girl,' breathed Ringrose. 'She's bright as a button. Lionel, see she gets home safely. Her name and address are to be kept under lock and key. Don't frighten her, but you must impress on her the need to say nothing to anyone about what she saw. I want a female CID officer to call on her every day to check she hasn't received any funny phone-calls or noticed any strangers hovering. Area cars to do regular run-bys. Get Technical Branch. She's to have panic buttons installed in every room.'

BOOK FIVE

Chapter One

Oscar Ruttmann and Kazuo Iwasaki had been in successful partnership for seven years. Not that more than a handful of people knew this.

Oscar was known as Oz the Schnozz – but not to his fleshy face. Oscar was a six-foot-four-inch mastodon of a man, the end of whose nose had been bitten off by a crazed Mexican in a bar-room brawl in Vera Cruz when Oscar was in the oil business. The missing portion had been reconstructed with bone, skin and gristle transferred from elsewhere on his person.

The result was puny, laughable even, a small baby-pink triangle set above the mouth of a stormtrooper. Although he did his best to minimize his fearsome appearance, no one outside his nearest and dearest had ever had the nerve to introduce it as a subject of conversation. His torso was so muscular that his arms could hang only in curves from his sides.

Incongruously, Oscar now owned a large toy emporium in Hoboken, New Jersey, whose clients usually came no higher than his kneecaps, plus a gabled Victorian mansion at Cape May, where Mrs Ruttmann had blessed him with three sons and two daughters.

Oz had big overheads. Yet, somehow, he seemed to manage even though the store was rarely bustling outside Thanksgiving and Christmas. Oz occasionally left the management of this establishment to underlings and went away on his own for what he called 'toy conventions'. Mrs Ruttmann, who loved her house and her children, had learned not to ask questions.

A toy convention in Fairbanks, Alaska? Tonopah, Nevada? West Palm Beach, Florida? Puh-lease!

Kazuo Iwasaki was known as Kaz because most Americans could not be bothered to get their tongues around Kazuo. Strictly speaking, his surname was Parsons. His father was American, his mother Japanese.

Kaz was a slender five foot eight, whose cast of features was only subtly Oriental. Nevertheless, his interests ran to martial arts and meditation. Kaz was an unshowy homosexual. He was also a beautiful, sinuous dancer and earned a spasmodic living as a Broadway gypsy – in other words, a chorus boy.

For the theatre he had taken his mother's family name as being more exotic than Parsons and more likely to lead to regular employment. When a show like *Miss Saigon*, or revivals of *Teahouse of the August Moon* or *Kismet* came to town, Kaz invariably got the call. With make-up, he could become as Oriental or Middle Eastern as you liked. Kaz, too, seemed to manage handsomely despite the fitful nature of his stage work from which he was sometimes obliged to absent himself – but always with a doctor's certificate. Kaz was a meticulous person about small courtesies and details.

Kaz and Oscar. Physically they represented polarity in the human frame.

The dancer had become a welcome visitor to the Ruttmann home after an incident at a picnic ground on the Jersey shore. Kaz had been on a Sunday jaunt with a party of the kids from *Miss Saigon*. Nearby, the Ruttmann family was enjoying its own summer afternoon recreations. Oscar and his children were at the water's edge. Mrs Ruttmann, sitting on a blanket on the grass above the sandy strip, gazed blissfully at her brood and placed her purse at her side.

She was quite unaware that a motorcycle carrying two Hispanic youths was approaching at speed.

Thirty yards away, in one smooth motion, Kaz rose and shifted a plastic ice box so that it was squarely one pace in front of his feet. He could see what was about to happen.

In the act of speeding past Mrs Ruttmann's blanket, the youth on the pillion stooped low and scooped up Mrs Ruttmann's bag. Kaz waited calmly. To reach the exit from the picnic ground, the young thieves had to pass close by. They had to run the gauntlet of Kaz.

He timed his action perfectly. Mrs Ruttmann had just begun to scream for her husband as the belching dirtbike drew level with Kaz. He took a sharp step up on to the box, drew a huge breath and twisted his torso into the air so that he was momentarily horizontal to the ground. At the optimum height of his leap he lashed out with both feet. It was the action of a superb athlete and he was rewarded with a most satisfactory sound of a double thud as the soles of his loafers connected with two bikers' helmets.

Their machine went roaring on; they went sailing off.

Kaz broke his fall with a forearm, nimbly sprang to his feet and was upon the youths before they knew what had happened. One tried to rise groggily to his feet and Kaz gave him a painful tap on the spine with his knuckles. 'Stay down or I'll kill you,' he said pleasantly.

Oscar, making the ground shake as he lumbered up to the scene, was all for beating the shit out of the pair of them. But Kaz, demonstrating to Oscar for the first of many times to come his sagacity and calming influence, said, 'Don't do that, sir. There are witnesses. The police will charge you with assault and put you in the next cell to these lowlives.'

'Police?' yelled Oscar. 'I'm not bothering with the police. These sleazebags will be on bail in twenty-four hours with a snake of a lawyer convincing the judge they were just collecting for charity.'

'I'm sure you're right,' soothed Kaz. He pondered for a moment. He eyed their gathering audience of fellow picnickers and noted the existence of a leafy copse up the slope. 'May I suggest we take the pair of them up into the trees for a private talk?'

Oscar was about to scorn this suggestion when he caught the steel glint in Kaz's flat, tawny eyes. Beyond doubt, they were sending him a message. 'Sure,' he said, intrigued.

While Oscar's indignant children gathered up their mother's scattered belongings, their father took the dazed thieves by the collars of their studded leather jackets and dragged them without ceremony in the wake of this mysterious little guy who was as cool as a Budweiser straight out of the Frigidaire. The other picnickers clapped and cheered knowingly as they went. 'Break their fucking thieving fingers,' shouted one man.

'No, no,' said Kaz severely, when they were screened by the trees. 'We must do this without getting ourselves into trouble.'

Oscar had hauled the pair upright and was clasping them close to himself. He had also managed to corral their legs with his own massive stems. Inside their helmets they had recovered sufficiently from their shock propulsion through the air to begin mouthing obscenities.

Kaz unstrapped the helmet of the pillion rider and tossed it on to the ground. The boy immediately spat at Kaz. 'Sir, would you clamp your hand over his mouth?' said the dancer mildly.

Oscar moved one paddle-sized hand upward and sealed off all sound from his prisoner.

What happened next worried the bejabers out of Oscar. Hey, hey, where the hell was this going? he thought.

Kaz unbuckled the youth's belt, unzipped his 501s and reached inside his underpants. The youth immediately began to buck and twist but Oscar held him firmly while Kaz stood, impassive, appearing to be doing nothing more than keeping his right hand inside the youth's pants.

But under his palm, Oscar could feel the boy screaming in his throat. Abruptly, he stopped struggling and Oscar felt him slump and become a dead weight.

Kaz said quietly, 'Sir, you may let go of him now.'

Oscar removed his hand and leg and the youth fell to the ground. He had fainted clean away.

Because Oscar had been clasping the thieves one on either side of himself, the motorcycle driver had not been able to observe his companion's fate.

Kaz moved round to Oscar's flank, removed the helmet, unzipped the other boy's jeans and repeated his previous actions. Soon two unconscious thieves lay side by side on the bare earth.

Kaz stooped to restore their disarranged clothing. 'Jesus, what the hell did you do?' said Oscar.

The dancer turned to him and said simply, 'I've administered appropriate punishment. There'll be no need for further steps. I've crushed their left balls beyond hope of recovery. The pain is unendurable. You are avenged.'

Oscar stared at him, transfixed. 'Jesus!' he said again.

The two men returned to the other picnickers. On the way, Oscar asked, 'Where the hell did you pick up that ball-busting idea? I thought only women did that – in a manner of speaking.'

Kaz said, seriously, 'The idea came from movie gossip when I was a small boy, sir. I read that when the director wanted Lassie to growl, his trainer off-camera would sneak a hand between the dog's hind legs and squeeze Lassie's testicles. When I read that, I wondered what he did to make Lassie howl. I have always been curious about such things.'

Oscar's bulk heaved and quivered with mirth. He placed a mighty arm around the dancer's slender shoulders and said, 'Louis – or whatever your name is – I think this is the beginning of a beautiful friendship.'

Kaz permitted himself a small smile and said, 'It was my pleasure to help. But may I suggest, sir, that you drive your family away from this spot? The two thieves will soon recover sufficiently to begin acting like victims rather than the scum that they are. And I'm sure you and your charming family would rather avoid any further unpleasantness. Perhaps you would also give me a lift to the nearest railway station. I'd rather not implicate my friends in any future inquiry.'

That's how the partnership had begun.

A few weeks later the Ruttmanns' hero was weekending with them at Cape May. After Sunday lunch, Oscar took him aside. He had absorbed the lessons of the picnic-ground incident well. Could Kaz help him with a business difficulty? A distributor had sold him 250 microchip-operated mini-robots. The demonstration toy had performed excellently but the microchips in the 250 had proven faulty. The robots acted in a deranged manner and frightened the youngest kids. 'I'm in the hole for more than six thousand bucks and the bastard is refusing to take back his shitty goods. I'd take it out of his greasy hide but that won't get me my money.'

Over the next month, Kaz studied the problem meticulously, then said, 'We have to take him somewhere quiet when the banks are open and when we may be certain he has his checkbook with him.'

The wholesaler of defective toys, carrying his executive briefcase, stepped into his Cadillac in the darkness of his garage one morning, operated the automatic door and headed for another day's work. On a quiet stretch of road before he hit the New Jersey turnpike a black-clad Kaz rose up from the footwell of the back seats and placed a scalpel to the terrified driver's throat. Kaz ran the blade up and down the stretched skin so that the man could feel its sharpness. He did not draw blood.

The wholesaler was obliged to drive to a derelict riding stables. When he saw Oscar Ruttmann waiting he began to curse and threaten him with the law. Oscar's normal reaction would have been to punch him in the mouth but Kaz had rehearsed his new partner sternly in the virtues of self-discipline. They tied the man to a wooden gate, leaving his writing arm free.

Oscar rummaged in the man's briefcase and his hand emerged triumphantly with the checkbook in his fist – plus two thousand dollars in hundred-dollar bills. He pocketed the money. Oscar said, 'You will write me a check for four thousand two hundred and fifty dollars. You'll then telephone your bank on your mobile to authorize immediate payment. Tell them I'll be in within the hour.'

'Go fuck yourself,' said the wholesaler.

'He's all yours,' Oscar said to Kaz.

The wholesaler gazed apprehensively at the slender partner who was unrolling a cloth holdall to display a set of surgical instruments that twinkled at him in the early-morning sunshine.

Kaz remained silent. He made no plea for the man to change his mind, gave him no second chance. He selected several instruments, one of which had a scoop-like attachment.

'Wait a minute,' said the man. But Kaz did not wait a minute.

As he approached his sweating victim, he nodded at Oscar

and the big man clamped their victim's head between his hands.

Kaz took the man's left eyelid and prised it upward with his forefinger while the thumb pushed down the flesh below. The eyeball, fully revealed, swivelled in terror.

'If you struggle you'll blind yourself,' murmured Kaz, as he concentrated on inserting the scoop over the ball.

Kaz made a small movement with his wrist and the man shrieked, 'What are you doing to me?'

Kaz stood back, admiring his handiwork. 'There, that was really quite simple.'

He selected a small steel mirror from among his instruments and held it up for the wholesaler to see. The man howled. His right eyeball had been extracted from its socket and was hanging by its muscle and optic nerve over the cheek.

'You really are a foolish man,' said Kaz conversationally. 'Mr Ruttmann is not trying to rob you. He merely wishes for you to put right a wrong that you have done him.'

He selected a pair of scissors and held them up for the shaking man to see. Kaz opened and shut them and said mischievously, 'Snip, snip.' He added, 'That's all it will take to send your eyeball rolling down your chest and landing between your feet. Isn't it worth six thousand two hundred and fifty dollars to avoid such a terrible tragedy?'

He took the man's own briefcase to use as a table and watched him write the check. Kaz punched in the bank's telephone number for him and let him hold the mobile while he cleared the check.

Only then did Kaz take a gauze pad, return the eye to its socket and clean up the twitching face.

While they waited for Oscar to return with his money, Kaz said, 'Of course, you are already thinking that when this is over you'll go straight to the police and have Oscar arrested.'

'No, I'm not,' whimpered the man.

'Of course you are. You'd be less than human if you were thinking of anything else. Right this minute you are clinging to the picture of Oscar being dragged away in handcuffs as your sole comfort. Revenge can taste so sweet. But, if that fate befalls him, I promise that one member of your family will be dead within a week. It could be your wife, one of your two children, a brother, a sister, or your elderly mother in Newark. Oh, yes, I know about your mother in Newark. I know a great deal about you and the rest of your family. The police will become tired of protecting them all. And, of course, you must understand that you will also die most painfully at the earliest opportunity given to me.'

The wholesaler looked into the cold face and saw the truth. 'Oscar'll have his dough,' he mumbled. 'Let's draw a line under the whole fucking business. You don't hex me. I don't hex you.'

'Congratulations,' said Kaz. 'You see how simple life can be when men deal honourably with each other?'

Oscar returned, a happy man, with his money. They untied the wholesaler and dusted him down. Apart from a bloodshot eye, he did not have a mark on him. Oscar and Kaz stood back and the wholesaler headed hastily for his Cadillac.

Oscar said, 'Aren't you forgetting something, schmuck?'

The man turned, alarmed. 'What?'

Oscar opened the trunk of his own car. 'You just bought back two hundred and fifty psychotic robots. Take 'em and find another sucker.'

'No, no. That's all right. Keep 'em,' said the man hastily.

'Take 'em!' repeated Oscar.

'Please do as Mr Ruttmann says,' added Kaz. 'Until you do, the transaction will not be legitimate.'

When the wholesaler had departed with his defective goods, Oscar shook Kaz's elegant hand. 'You're an artist, man. A real fucking artist!'

It was the frightened wholesaler who might be said to have cemented the business partnership between Oscar and his mysterious friend. The wholesaler did not complain to the police but he did, from time to time, whine to intimates at the method used to terrorize him out of his money. The story was so unusual that it assumed a long afterlife and spread outward from Hoboken and Cape May. Soon Oscar was being asked by other aggrieved businessmen if he could assist – for a percentage of the recovered money – in similar situations. After consulting Kaz, he said he could.

Kaz drew up the ground rules. All contracts would be fronted by Oscar. Kaz would remain the anonymous partner. They would do all they could to achieve their purpose without spilling blood. They would extract no more than was due to their hirer. They would no longer maintain their original, open friendship and would never travel together to the same appointment. They would never use the knowledge gained to blackmail their clients. They would never inform on each other.

For two years, in this near-prissy fashion, they prospered, progressing from shortchanged businessmen to alimony welchers and woman-beaters who had to be discouraged – for a fee.

Oscar grew to have limitless admiration for Kaz's patience in the planning of their outings to the 'toy conventions' and in Kaz's understanding of where the mark's greatest fear lay hidden, waiting to be teased out into daylight, and played on. They were making sizeable sums. To avoid awkward questions from the Internal Revenue they opened European bank accounts in a secretive place called Liechtenstein.

Then Albert Penn happened to them.

One morning a blue Oldsmobile drew up outside Oscar's toy emporium and a handsome young man in an Armani topcoat strolled through to the back. He smiled at the secretary and while she was still dazzled walked past her and knocked politely on Oscar's door.

'What can I do for you?' growled Oscar, wondering where the hell was his secretary.

'Mr Albert Penn presents his compliments and would like to have urgent words with you,' said the young man, without preamble.

Oscar felt a chill in the gut. 'Is this the Albert Penn I think it is?' said Oscar.

'Mr Albert Penn is the well-known sportsman and public benefactor,' said his visitor agreeably.

'That's the one,' said Oscar. 'When would Mr Penn like this meeting?'

'If you'll come with me now, Mr Ruttmann . . . And please wrap up warm. Mr Penn would not like you to catch a cold on his account.'

'That's good to know,' said Oscar.

An hour later they were through the tunnel in the young emissary's car and nosing up to Central Park.

Albert Penn wore a black lambswool hat over his razor-cut hairdo and was huddled in a thick, mohair coat with a blue silk scarf that covered the lower portion of his fleshy, clean-shaven face. He was watching the skaters on the rink, especially the girls in their minuscule flared skirts. He reached out a gloved hand and shook Oscar's cold mitt.

'Bobby, go fetch Mr Ruttmann a hot chocolate,' he said. Turning to examine Oscar's face, Albert Penn lingered on the nose where most men would not have dared. He said bluntly, 'That's the worst fucking nose job since Michael Jackson.'

Oscar grinned. 'You're the first person on this earth to have the guts to say to me what I say to myself every morning when I shave.'

'Wanna change it? I can get you the best cosmetic guy in Beverly Hills. You'll come out looking like Mel Gibson.'

'Nah,' said Oscar. 'I've got used to it.'

'Isn't it a bit noticeable in your line of work?'

'What? Selling toys?'

Penn laughed. 'Yeah.'

Bobby returned with the hot chocolate. Gratefully, Oscar wrapped his hands round the cup.

Penn said, 'Oscar, I hear the most remarkable things about you and your spooky other half. Excellent things. You do clean work. No fuss. No hassle. No repercussions. You don't take advantage of what you know. You don't squeeze the clients. You don't take the creeps for more than they owe. My guys say you have no criminal record. Is that true?'

'Yes. I'm clean.'

'Your partner?'

'He's clean too.'

'Do I get to know his name?'

'No. I'm frontman.'

258

'Okay. No *problema*. How'd you two characters like to make eighty thousand bucks?'

'Sounds interesting.'

'It means promotion.'

'How's that?'

'My guys say that, as far as they've been able to check, you two haven't actually put anyone in the ground yet. This job I'm contracting out requires a woman to be offed. It has to be within the next six weeks and has to look like an accident. The cops will know it isn't because she's a witness in an upcoming trial. An accident would be too much of a coincidence. However you go about it, they'll treat it as murder but won't have the proof – if it's done right.'

'Is she guarded?'

'They keep a casual eye on her but she doesn't have round-the-clock protection because they don't know we're even aware of her existence.'

'I have to confer with my partner. This is a big step for us.'

Albert Penn fixed Oscar with his pale blue stare. 'You tell your boy he has a big admirer in Albert Penn. The pair of you have a style that's lacking, these days. Do this thing for me and I'll make you rich. There is much highly paid work that has to be done at a distance from the Family. Bobby here will give you his telephone number and be our link.'

He turned to his aide who was stamping his feet and blowing steam. 'Bobby, take Mr Ruttmann back to his place of business – and take it easy on the icy roads. We must take especially good care of Mr Ruttmann. His nose may not be much but his balls are big.'

Oscar had to laugh.

The woman lived with her husband in a duplex in a leafy street in an old section of Charleston, South Carolina. Kaz did the preliminary work, staying in motels and moving on each day.

He observed that the woman, a book-keeper who had inadvertently seen books best left unseen, took the family pooch for its early-morning walk at weekends while her husband slept on. The pooch invariably cocked a leg against the same trees.

Like the dog, his mistress was a creature of habit. She stood on the same spots patiently holding the extended lead while the schnauzer did his business.

One live oak in a neighbouring road, where the large houses were usefully set well back, stood at the sidewalk's edge outside a derelict mansion protected from the public gaze by an ancient red-brick wall with three inset gateways. The section nearest the live oak was ten feet long and eight feet high from the damp course to the capstone. The sidewalk was only seven feet wide and the spot where the woman stood while her pooch pungently marked out his territory was only four feet from the wall.

Kaz summoned Oscar to a toy convention. He decided that a quiet Sunday morning represented their best opportunity to complete their assignment without interruption.

Shortly after midnight on Saturday, Oscar lumbered silently down the street on rubber heels and plunged a sharp chisel into the wall's damp course. Using all his strength, he raked the steel point along for ten feet, dislodging old, powdery mortar that fell to the sidewalk. He then sleeved the chisel and kept moving until he turned the corner and disappeared from view.

Kaz watched from a distance to make sure Oscar's action had not raised a neighbourhood alarm. When he was satisfied, he called his partner on his mobile telephone and Oscar returned to repeat the action, raking in the opposite direction.

Three more times during the hours of darkness Oscar raked out crumbling mortar. Then he slipped inside the garden and tentatively rocked the undermined wall. When he was satisfied he was getting movement Kaz drove up with brooms and pans and the pair of them swiftly swept up the sidewalk mess and drove away.

The woman appeared just after seven-thirty a.m. with the pooch who positioned his mistress nicely. She was fumbling for a cigarette when Oscar on the garden side placed both meaty hands against the brickwork and pushed.

The pooch abruptly ceased peeing, gave a screech and bounded into the road, jerking his mistress's leash hand so that she dropped her Lucky Strike pack.

The photograph on the inside page of the *New York Post* next day was accompanied by the headline 'Freak Accident'. The shot showed a woman's hand protruding from under a toppled wall. The dog lead was still coiled round her wrist while the pooch who'd killed his mistress was sitting on its haunches playing innocent.

Albert Penn was studying the picture and caption when Oscar arrived at the rendezvous at Battery Park to collect his wages. 'It says here, "High winds may have been the cause." Did you two geniuses fix the weather, too?' Albert couldn't stop laughing. He really liked these guys. 'Bobby, give Mr Ruttmann the green.'

Albert Penn was as good as his word. He paid well for class and artistry.

He sent them next to Coral Gables in Florida where a local politician's hurricane-wrecked tropical garden was being replanted. The target went for his usual morning swim and was later found drowned, pinned to the bottom of the pool by a palm tree that had unaccountably toppled into the water.

Over the next five years Albert Penn created the most successful team of contract killers in the United States. And, unknown to the duo, they had evolved into the greatest single weapon in his armoury, earning him great respect from the Mafia oligarchy to whom Oscar and Kaz were often despatched on loan-out as a goodwill gesture.

Great-great-uncle Albert would have been proud of Albert Penn.

Chapter Two

Oscar Ruttmann and Kazuo Iwasaki, or Charles Ganz and Lon Beamish as their stolen passports proclaimed, hung over the immaculate mahogany aft rail of the *Black Glove*, well away from earshot of the crew, and watched the churning wake. Neither had seen the Mediterranean Sea before.

'Some fucking situation,' grunted Oscar finally.

As always, they had travelled separately. From London, Oscar had flown to Genoa where the rich bitch sailed into the harbour and picked him up. Kaz had got himself to Paris via the Channel Tunnel and had then flown to Bastia on the island of Corsica where he'd had a longer wait for the Good Ship Lollipop to come in. He did not complain. Infinite care had kept them alive and made them rich. He intended keeping it that way.

Kaz was still chiding himself for breaching their own ground rules in London. The assignment had not been properly scouted.

As Oscar had told it to him, Albert Penn had practically gone on his knees. He respected their professionalism, he knew they didn't like to rush things, but here was a Limey friend in deepest trouble who needed fast action to save his ass. At least go to London and talk to his daughter. Money no object.

If they couldn't see a way to help, then he'd respect their judgement. But from what the Limey had said, the hit would be a doozey. Two nosy reporters who weren't expecting trouble . . . and the Limey also wanted the targets' files lifted.

'You won't have to worry about having the Feds on your ass,' said Albert Penn. 'And those Limey cops, what do they know?'

So Kaz had flown Concorde from Kennedy to Heathrow and Oscar had travelled more humbly Newark–Gatwick. Chauffeured limousines had waited to convey them individually to a grand house near the river Thames in Chelsea.

They'd both enjoyed that part. They'd only ever seen London in the movies.

The rich bitch was an eyeful but neither of them was happy at her current mental state. She was jumpy and talked too much. She had said, 'Do you have guns?'

Kaz told her, 'Of course not. We could not carry firearms aboard our planes.'

This response seemed to give her great satisfaction. Almost

preening, she said, 'Don't worry. I anticipated something like that. I have friends. They've sold me these.'

She unwrapped a soft cloth containing an old Webley revolver and a Czech 9mm automatic, a spare magazine and a handful of ammo for the Webley.

Oscar remembered how they had both stared at her, stunned. Finally, Kaz said, 'Miss, did you tell your friends why you needed these guns – and who it was intended should use them?'

She had pouted as if Kaz was treating her like a child and that this little performance would get her off the hook.

'Cut the Julie Andrews crap,' Oscar had said. 'Just tell us the plain truth.'

'Do you think I'm crazy? I told the boy who's my contact I wanted them for personal protection – one to keep here and one to keep at our house in the country.'

'Is this "boy" a criminal?' Kaz had asked quietly.

She'd shuffled her feet and Oscar had taken a threatening step towards her. 'Well?' he bellowed.

'I don't think he's actually an angel,' she finally conceded. 'Everyone says he robs banks.'

'Jesus H. Christ!' said Oscar.

She appeared to start crying but given her obvious flair for manipulation neither man could be sure that this wasn't just another feminine wile.

'Why are you being so beastly to me?' she snivelled. 'I'm only trying to help.'

'If we need your help, we'll ask,' said Kaz. 'We don't like using guns. They're noisy.'

He drew on his gloves, took the cloth and wiped down the two weapons, the magazines and each individual bullet. He rewrapped the bundle and said, 'I want you to get into your car right now and return these things to your friend. You will thank him for his consideration and tell him you've changed your mind about keeping illegal firearms in the house. Let him keep half the money as a mark of your appreciation for his discretion. Have you got that?'

Tabitha Gatling nodded dumbly. From a first-floor window they watched her drive away. Oscar had said, 'My gut tells me we should go see Buckingham Palace and then get the fuck outta here.'

'It's too soon to call,' said Kaz. 'Your Mr Penn will lose face with his Limey friend. And that could pose more difficulties for you than me. Remember, Oz, he knows where you live.'

She was gone for almost two hours. She was still agitated when she returned but nodded her assent when Kaz asked, 'Did all go as I asked?'

She said, 'He laughed and said I was going soft. I didn't give him an argument.'

Kaz got to work on her, calming, soothing, giving her the your-troubles-are-over balm even though, at that stage, they had only the vaguest idea of what those troubles were. Kaz sat her in a chair in her huge, empty house and massaged her temples while she outlined her worries in staccato snatches.

Oscar summed up her tale as she sat, elegant knees together, eyes closed, while Kaz's fine hands moved into her shining hair and began gently massaging her scalp.

Oscar reflected that, as she already knew their line of work, she was either extremely brave to have Kaz's hands laid upon her or too agitated to fear her visitors. He decided on the latter.

'So these two hacks have been sifting the sewage on your daddy's life. We need to stop them but that's no good if we leave their records behind. Have we got that right?'

Kaz went out and, armed with Tabitha Gatling's cash, bought a black Toyota Corolla off a second-hand dealer's forecourt in Brentford. In it, Tabitha drove them to the separate premises where Gervase Meredith and Nelly Tripp lived.

The deal Tabitha agreed was three hundred thousand US dollars for the elimination of Gervase and Nelly, plus fifty thousand for the seizure of the files. There would be a 'fee' for Albert Penn, but that was okay, too.

Tabitha paled when Kaz had murmured, 'Normally, we would not expect to carry out an assignment of this importance in under three weeks. We shall be breaking our own rules working so fast. Our strictest rule is that Mr Ganz and I always work alone. But if this matter is as urgent as you say, you will have to be our guide. Show us the way. Be pointwoman. We are in a strange land where we are not sure of the difference between the uniforms of a policeman and a car hop.'

Kaz stopped massaging and stepped round the chair to stare into her eyes. 'Can you do it? Can we rely absolutely on you? Please do not answer without thinking.'

Tabitha Gatling had thought and nodded eagerly. 'You'll see. I'm my daddy's daughter. No one messes with him and gets away with it.'

They had hit Gervase's semi-basement flat first. Oscar, his knowledge of the complexity of modern electronic toys matched by his knowledge of the construction of modern locks, gained them swift access.

'He must be round at his tart's place,' said Tabitha, turning in a helpless circle in the living room. 'But at least we get the files.'

While she and Kaz emptied the contents of the filing-cabinet drawers into bin liners, Oscar dismantled Gervase's tabletop computer and removed the hard disk. Ten minutes later Kaz closed the front door behind them and they headed for Nelly's place.

The two killers stayed in the Corolla and watched the rich bitch talking to a woman at the front door. Then she beckoned them to come on in.

Later, Oscar and Kaz agreed that this was the moment when the whole fucking operation blew up in their faces. What the bitch should have done, on learning from the landlady that neither of their targets was at home, was to thank her and politely withdraw.

Instead, the landlady and the flatmate got to see their faces. After that snafu there was no going back. The only consolation was that the bitch got the rest of the files and disks.

'There'll be no second chance of a hit,' Oscar told her harshly when they were back in the haven of Cheyne Walk. 'You might be your daddy's daughter but you fucked up.'

Despite her boast, Tabitha was still trembling. She had abruptly left Nelly's room while Mr Beamish so coolly placed the hood over Melanie Lamb's struggling head, and had stood on the landing, knuckles pressed so tightly into her mouth that her teeth drew blood, as she watched Mr Ganz and Mr Beamish tiptoe downstairs and slip into Mrs Keen's quarters.

'A million dollars,' said Tabitha recklessly. 'Stay with me for a million dollars. I've got to get my grandfather out of the country. The people you should have found today have been attempting to get him to tell lies about my father. I need time to examine their research – see who's been talking to them. See who needs taking care of.'

For a million bucks – and telephonic permission from Albert Penn, relayed to them by his aide Bobby because Albert never talked business on the wire – Oscar and Kaz agreed to a Mediterranean vacation aboard the *Black Glove* while Tabitha Gatling studied the extent to which Gervase Meredith and Nelly Tripp had burrowed into the Gatling family's most closely guarded secrets.

The two hitmen prowled the decks. Despite their arresting physical disparity the crew spared them barely a glance. Vernon Gatling entertained aboard his vessel many people who were not obviously from the top echelons of society.

Oscar, in particular, was having difficulty in finding his sealegs. He eyed the waves malevolently. 'I used to see pictures in the magazines about the rich on their Mediterranean cruises in their fancy yachts and wish I was there. Old man Onassis. Jackie. Winston Churchill. The Duke and Duchess of Windsor. Now I'm here, I wish I was home,' he grumbled. 'All this fucking water can really bring you down.'

They saw Tabitha only at dinner. She spent her first two days locked in her father's stateroom, working her way with increasing unease through the material that the treacherous Gervase and his little whore had assembled. She quailed when she reached the notes Gervase had made concerning the mysterious death of Gus Meldrum in Los Angeles and his nocturnal woman visitor in the beret. He had pencilled 'Tabitha?' in the margin. She cursed. He *knew*!

She dined alone with her two hired killers. She had arranged for her grandfather, his doctor and female nurse to occupy a separate suite of rooms in the stern of the boat that gave main-deck access for Gunner's wheelchair.

After evacuating him from the Aitkin-Adams Home and escorting him to Antibes and the waiting boat, she had not been near him.

Kaz noticed.

'Do you love your grandfather?' he asked at the end of the meal when the whitecoated stewards had withdrawn leaving them with drinks, cigars and sweetmeats. She had not dressed for dinner. She wore white jeans and an old seadog sweater. Her makeup was not fresh. The bloom was temporarily off the golden girl.

'I hate the old bastard,' she said bluntly. 'If he wasn't my father's father, I'd as soon kick the dirty old sod over the side.'

'That seems somewhat extreme,' said Kaz mildly, while Oscar shook his head at this evidence of family dysfunction.

'When I was a kid I hated going anywhere near him. Always patting me and breathing hard. When he started to go off his trolley and my daddy put him in the home I was delighted. I thought I'd never have to see the old git again. And here I am stuck with him on the boat while Daddy decides what's best for the future.'

Kaz said gently, 'I hope you're not communicating with your father from this boat, Tabitha. Satellite links are monitored by all sorts of government agencies, you know.'

Tabitha kicked off her deck slippers and moodily put her feet up. 'I'm not communicating with anyone until I've finished going through the papers we lifted. Behind my back those bastards have been doing a thorough hatchet job on me and my family.'

'A hatchet job on you, Tabitha? Surely not . . .' said Kaz, still fishing.

'Fuck 'em,' she said. 'They think they can stick me with the death of the first guy who tried nosing into my family's business. Well, let 'em try.'

'Ah, so there have been other seekers after the family secrets?'

'Not really. He was just a guy from the *Wall Street Journal* who got above himself.'

'He died?'

'Yes. At the Chateau Marmont in Hollywood. Slipped in the bathroom.'

267

Oscar began chuckling in a knowing manner.

Kaz said, 'Were you a naughty girl, Tabitha?'

She tossed her magnificent mane which, after seven days at sea, was now in need of a hairdresser's ministrations. 'You don't expect me to answer that, do you?' she retorted.

Then all three began to laugh. Deep and conspiratorial.

Chapter Three

Tabitha Gatling's work on the Meredith-Tripp archive was done. She finally knew all there was to know about the short, eventful life of the Cockney boy known as Vanishing Larry Varnish into whose disappearance Gus Meldrum had begun to inquire before she bought the cheap black wig as a disguise and went to confront him at his hotel. She hadn't meant to kill Meldrum but, in a moment of rage when the reporter treated her so contemptuously and was attempting to show her the door as if she was some no-account bimbo, she had swung her leg and fetched him such a blow on the head that he dropped like a lead weight – not in the bathroom but in the living room.

While he recovered his senses she grasped the opportunity to ransack his papers and extract all his Gatling family material. Only afterwards did she notice that he wasn't recovering as a healthy fiftyish man should. His face was sallow and he had stopped breathing.

'Oh, shit!' muttered Tabitha. His eyes were wide open, staring at her in terminal shock.

But she was barely moved by the sight of a man who was either dead or dying. 'You don't look so bloody clever now, do you, Mr Bigshot?' she said, as she stripped him, dragged him into the bathroom and sprinkled water on the floor to indicate an accidental slip.

She surprised herself at her gratifying lack of remorse. No

one, but no one, was going to ruin her daddy. No price was too high to pay to prevent that happening.

Coolly, she tidied the dead man's papers that did not concern her, then took a towel and wiped every surface she could remember touching. She left behind the rock of crack cocaine she'd bought with the idea of framing him if he had failed to co-operate with her.

She surveyed the room for the last time. They wouldn't find the body until the maid knocked next morning.

'So long, you prick,' she said, as she slipped into the empty corridor and closed Gus Meldrum's door.

Tabitha, an arresting sight in a silver leotard and black leggings, was working off her tensions of the past few days in the ship's gymnasium. Oscar and Kaz, who had travelled light from the United States wore borrowed jogging pants and singlets.

Oscar's shins still showed traces of the bruises earned when his recent victims had kicked out before he had brought their legs under control. As he punished a heavyweight punchbag he watched appreciatively as Tabitha went through her routines. Her exercises with an imaginary opponent were an effective amalgam of Thai boxing and *tae kwon do*. She was good.

Kaz watched with folded arms for a few minutes then joined her on the mat. They wove around each other, lithe and graceful, like lead dancers of the *corps de ballet*. 'Yesss!' she cried, delighted at some particularly fluent movement on Kaz's part.

Oscar could see them bonding before his eyes. If he had not known Kaz's preference, he would have predicted a sexual ending to the encounter. As it was, in the intimacy of her quarters, she told Kaz what she had discovered and asked his advice. 'When my daddy was young he got involved in a quarrel and a young man died. His body has just been discovered in London. The police and the two journalists we hired you to kill will try to say it was murder and send him to prison for life. I swear I'd do anything to block them.'

Kaz said he could offer no advice without seeing the

269

material, and she showed him everything. Finally, Kaz said, 'There is a great deal of circumstantial stuff that I'm sure your father's lawyers can neutralize. There's a whole heap of hearsay that is not admissible in court. You don't really need to bother with the two journalists as witnesses. Smart lawyers would get most of their stuff withheld from a jury. But your father's defence would be impregnable if just two people were not available as witnesses.'

'Who?'

'The first is the man who was your father's foreman – Denny Fling – who is still alive and living in a place called Streatham, which I take is somewhere in London.' Kaz pronounced it Street-ham. 'He was on the scene the day after the death of this Larry Varnish character and, although he didn't know it, assisted in concealment of the body. He would be a powerful witness for the prosecution.'

'What about the other?' asked Tabitha, holding her breath but already knowing the answer.

'Your grandfather, of course. He was there. Whatever happened he saw and, perhaps, took part in. The ravings of an old man could damn your father.'

They sat silently facing each other.

Finally, she said, 'My daddy would never sanction killing him. There has been too much living between them. Even when the old bastard's raving, Daddy won't let the doctors reduce his quality of life by quietening him down with drugs.'

'That could prove the most costly indulgence of your daddy's life unless . . .'

He let the sentence hang.

Tabitha said, 'Unless he has an accident?'

'No, no, absolutely not!' said Kaz instantly. 'A natural death, yes. An accident, no. Your father would be bound to suspect and there would be complaints to friends in America that would have serious consequences for Mr Ganz and myself.'

'So what do we do?'

'We? Are you sanctioning your grandfather's death, then?'

'I told you before that I'd cheerfully push his wheelchair off the boat. I wasn't kidding. I'd shed no tears for him. In London I promised you a million dollars. Help me. Both give me your bank numbers and the funds will be electronically transferred from my personal holdings before nightfall.'

Kaz smiled and shook his head. 'Believe me, you are better off without such knowledge. Our rule is to deal only in cash.'

'Okay,' said Tabitha. 'I'll order the skipper to start heading west. When we reach Monaco I'll go ashore and return with the money. I have convertible holdings there.'

'Very good,' said Kaz. 'In the meantime I want you to start being nicer to Dr Crumley-Smith and the nurse. Have dinner with them. Visit with your grandfather. Find out where they keep their medical supplies.'

'The ship has its own drug cupboard but the captain keeps the key.'

'Let him keep it. We will use only what Dr Crumley-Smith brought aboard. Everything must appear normal.'

The sleek Dr Crumley-Smith had been hurt by the beautiful granddaughter's shunning of the convalescent quarters and his difficult patient. But now she came swanning down the companionway, a vision in tight cream pants and a mauve top that bared her midriff. She was smiling warmly and was profuse with her apologies.

'Doctor, I am so sorry to have neglected you. I have had a family crisis that has simply eaten up my time but now I am all yours. We must have dinner this evening.'

She had inspected the medical quarters, given Gunner Gatling a brief, perfumed hug while he rambled and grumbled about the lack of video tapes, and sat chatting to the Irish nurse until she had brought Gunner's eyedrops.

The drug supply was housed in a portable block-shaped leather case that opened out to reveal tiered shelves of medicaments. The case was kept in the nurse's bedside cabinet. Kaz took a full inventory while both nurse and doctor were coping with one of Gunner's tantrums. The old man was grievously missing Fred Astaire.

Over dinner, thoughtfully set up within hailing distance of Gunner's room, Tabitha had sympathized with their difficulties. Three times during the meal, the nurse had been obliged to attend to the old curmudgeon.

'I won't tell tales if you slip Grandaddy a sleeping potion,' Tabitha twinkled. 'You two look as if you could do with a decent night's sleep yourselves.'

After that, a nightly sedative for Gunner became routine and both doctor and nurse found more time to enjoy the cruise and the company of their charming hostess.

Tabitha and the *Black Glove* had not sailed into the Monte Carlo harbour since the Grand Prix. This time, there was a choice of moorings under the Hôtel de Paris. They tied up alongside a quay for a day while Tabitha went ashore to conduct business. She returned with a brand new polished alligator-skin case containing the money.

Kaz and Oscar checked the count and then the two men went ashore briefly to make their own secret deposits in their own numbered accounts.

Watching Mr Beamish and Mr Ganz go, Tabitha wondered if they would return. When they did, she knew they were committed. A great feeling of relief and confidence washed over her. The *Black Glove* continued to head west.

For some nights now, the old man had not interrupted dinner at all and the medical team were showing the benefits of sea air, sunshine and a regular eight hours of sound sleep.

Over dinner that night, when Tabitha had persuaded even the nurse that a single glass of a fine Nuits St George would not breach her duty of care, Tabitha said, 'I think we can risk a little soft music.'

Oscar and Kaz could hear the distant strains of a Johnny Mathis ballad as they slipped into Gunner's cabin. The wall lamps were dimmed. Close up, they could see that the old geezer was lying on his back, mouth open, making small gargling noises in the back of his throat. He was dead to the world.

The bedclothes were loose around him, but they took the two canvas straps used to hold the invalid in place during rough seas and threaded the buckles across his body.

Oscar took hold of the two ends while Kaz unpeeled the gauze from a large sticking plaster. At his nod, Oscar jerked the buckles tight while Kaz placed a hand under Gunner's chin, unceremoniously snapped his mouth closed and sealed it with the surgical plaster. He then placed a flannel mask over Gunner's face that left only his nostrils exposed.

Even in his drugged state, Gunner sensed that something was wrong and began to struggle feebly against the restraints. His breath rasped in and out of his nostrils. They could see his white nasal hairs fluttering like plant tendrils in an underwater current.

Both men pulled surgical masks over their noses. Oscar placed himself over Gunner's shrunken frame and held him still.

Kas took a small box of amyl nitrate 'pearls' from his pocket and broke one under Gunner's nose. Their victim had no option but to inhale the fumes. As they hit his brain, his arteries widened as if a dam-keeper had opened a spill channel. Blood coursed through his ancient arteries. The heart jerked. If Gunner had been an angina sufferer a single amyl nitrate 'pearl' would have brought instant relief from pain. But Kaz broke ampoule after ampoule, keeping the blood racing and the heart leaping. Gunner's frail heart would not take the appalling strain for long.

Finally, Oscar sensed the body beneath him give a long shudder. Under the sheet, the heels attempted to drum and then Gunner was still. 'I think that's hit the spot,' Oscar said, and climbed off the bed.

Kaz removed the facial mask that was now stained yellow from the chemical fallout. He peeled off the plaster and the mouth fell open. While he took a neck pulse – 'None,' he reported – Oscar turned up the air-conditioning to dispel the penetrating odour of the amyl nitrate.

They shone a small torch on the dead man's cooling face and used cotton buds soaked in surgical alcohol to remove evidence of the sticking plaster and minute traces of amyl nitrate from around the nostrils.

Finally, they unbuckled the retaining straps and returned the air-con to normal. Both men removed their own masks and sniffed. There was still a faint strangeness about the air quality but it was disappearing rapidly.

As they slipped away to the main deck to drop the detritus

of murder overboard, they could hear Johnny Mathis distantly singing 'Everything Is Beautiful'.

Chapter Four

The doctor was puzzled and the nurse crying. 'I'm so very sorry,' he told Tabitha. 'I really was not expecting anything like this. Mr Gatling was showing no prior symptom of cardiac distress. It was entirely unexpected, although with a man of his age . . .'

Tabitha did not even pretend to cry.

They watched as a shrouded Gunner was removed to the ship's bowels to be laid out in a bath packed with ice. Dr Crumley-Smith thought that a post mortem would be in order once Gunner's corpse was put ashore.

Tabitha rounded on him with a vehemence that made him jump. 'Don't be a bloody fool,' she hissed. 'You sign the death certificate. If there's a post-mortem they'll find traces of the sleeping pills and my daddy will go ballistic. He'll be furious at you for going against his orders and me for giving you permission. He'll create hell for both of us.'

'Well . . .' said Dr Crumley-Smith hesitantly. His pot belly was beginning to ache as it did whenever emotional levels rose around him.

'Well, nothing!' snapped Tabitha. 'You've been in the Gatling employ for years. Have we ever questioned your huge fees?'

'No, but—'

'I know my daddy. He'll find ways to ruin you if he finds out you've been administering drugs to his father. What's the problem? He was an old man. You as good as said he could have gone at any time.'

Dr Crumley-Smith sighed and signed the certificate, if only

to stop his belly aching. He entered the cause of death as an infarction.

Vernon Gatling and his entourage had moved on from Costa Rica. Tabitha reached him by satellite link at his Manhattan penthouse. Now she managed to cry as she broke the tragic news. 'I'm so sorry, Daddy. Grandaddy was such a sweet old man. It was all over so quickly. He didn't know anything. He passed away in his sleep,' she said, with a certain amount of accuracy.

She heard her father utter a single sob of pain and for a few seconds there were snuffling noises at the other end while he composed himself. Tabitha held her breath and waited.

Vernon came back and said gruffly, 'Stay out at sea but send in the tender to pick me up at Toulon the day after tomorrow.'

The intercept from GCHQ Cheltenham landed on Tom Ringrose's desk twenty hours after Tabitha Gatling made the call.

'Shit,' he told Lionel Firth, tossing the flimsy across to him. 'Old man Gatling's popped his clogs on the boat. Vernon's daughter has told him it was a heart attack. That quack who snatched Gunner from Bournemouth has signed the certificate.'

'There goes the only person who could positively finger Vernon for murder,' said Firth. 'A very convenient death, I'd say.'

'Yeah. Vernon's flying from New York to pick up the boat in the South of France. Lionel, let's keep the *Black Glove*'s position monitored. Wherever they bring Gunner's body ashore, we'll try to persuade the locals to perform a post-mortem and perhaps get them to invite old Dart to be in attendance. Give him a call and put him on stand-by with his nightie packed.'

Vernon Gatling turned away grimly from his father's remains, glimpsed in refracted form beneath the layer of kitchen ice that the crew members dutifully replenished twice a day. In death, Gunner's face had turned a greyish-yellow.

In the privacy of the stateroom, Vernon, still wearing the

Huntsman vested suit in charcoal wool in which he'd travelled without entourage in his personal jet, confronted his daughter and said, 'Are you sure those two characters Beamish and Ganz had nothing to do with this?' He held her by both arms and peered into her eyes.

Tabitha kept them wide and unflinching. 'Daddy, that's absurd. They're here to help us. All right, they screwed up in London but that was mostly my fault for giving them wrong information. At least they got all the files. And they've promised me to go back and do one final task for us.'

She led him through the stolen Meredith-Tripp archive and, like his daughter before him, Vernon kept muttering, 'Shit!' and 'Fuck!' and 'Christ!'

He asked Tabitha to pour him a neat Scotch when he came to Gervase's one-word annotation alongside the Chateau Marmont–Gus Meldrum material.

Drained by the revelation of the extent of the journalists' knowledge, Vernon said, 'This lot has to go into the shredder and Beamish and Ganz have to get my old foreman, Denny Fling. I can't believe the bastard would try to cut me off at the knees like this. I gave him work for fifteen years. I hope they throw him alive into a furnace.'

Tabitha hugged him. 'I know they're an odd-looking couple, Daddy, but they are not in the least bit crude. They'll find a way. You'll see.'

Tabitha had washed her hair and made up her face exquisitely in preparation for her father's arrival. She gazed up at him from under lowered silver-mauve lids, and added, 'I know this isn't a very tactful thing to say, but Grandaddy timed his own death when it was of most use to you, his only son. It was almost as if he planned his own passing as a last gift to you. Perhaps, somewhere in his fuddled old brain, he realized we couldn't have kept him aboard the *Black Glove* for ever and out of reach of the police. God knows what he might have said to them on a lucid day. If you look at your daddy's death like that, I think you'll gain some comfort.'

Vernon nodded but said no more. While she was still coaxing him, Tabitha unlaced and removed his shoes, slipped off his jacket and unbuttoned his waistcoat. 'There,' she said, loosening his tie, 'isn't that better?' Then she slid on to his lap and pulled his head down to press it into her bosom.

He rocked her for a while. Then, in a little-girl tone of reproach, she murmured into his ear, 'You never told me about that death on the building site. I thought we had no secrets from each other, Daddy. I thought you hired Mr Beamish and Mr Ganz only to protect me from my accident in Los Angeles. What really happened with you and Grandaddy?'

Vernon grunted and shifted her weight. 'It happened a long time ago and I'd almost forgotten. I would have totally forgotten if the fucking IRA hadn't blown up half the City of London. I never dreamed Fletcher Hall would be demolished in my lifetime. If I could have grabbed the contract for the rebuilding I could have cleaned up the site and squared everything. But I acted when it was too late. Instead, the police and that fucking hack friend of yours I should never have allowed on this boat are sniffing around and I've had to give my marker to some very dangerous people in America to acquire the services of Ganz and Beamish – if those really are their names.'

'Poor Daddy,' she crooned. 'I'm going to give you lots of hugs and kisses and tender, loving care. It's just horrible about Grandaddy. I'll make it up to you. I promise.'

She nuzzled his hair. 'What will you do about Grandaddy's body?'

'Fly him back to London and bury him alongside your grandmother,' came Vernon's muffled answer.

Tabitha was statue-still for a moment. 'Won't that lead to difficulties because he died at sea? They'll want a post-mortem. I can't bear the thought of Grandaddy being cut open. Can't you have him cremated at our next port-of-call? Then we can take his ashes home and have a nice funeral service for his friends. It'll be a lot less complicated than transferring his body from one country to another. A lot less red tape . . .'

She undid two buttons on her silk blouse. Vernon was eventually persuaded.

*

Vernon had a fully equipped office aboard the *Black Glove*. He and his daughter did the shredding and dragged the sacks to the stern where a bemused crew watched the paper spaghetti stream of the Meredith-Tripp research material reach out into the wind. The hard and floppy disks were mutilated and followed the paper into the water.

A day later, the *Black Glove* made an unannounced call at Málaga in Southern Spain then radioed ahead for a berth at the Costa del Sol holiday resort of Puerto Banus.

The Spanish Garda armed with papers from the Ministerio de Justicia e Interior – papers requested by Scotland Yard via Interpol – were waiting.

The Garda greeted the vessel as it made fast alongside King Fahd's yacht. The police were first up the gangway and served the captain with an authorization to remove the body of one Frank Gatling, a British subject known as Gunner, for a post-mortem examination.

But Vernon Gatling's wealth had worked its usual wonders. The captain produced legitimate papers issued in Málaga plus Dr Crumley-Smith's death certificate. Alas, the body was no longer available to forensic science. The late Mr Frank Gatling had been taken ashore at Málaga and the proper formalities completed' by the undertaker. Mr Gatling had been conveyed directly to the modern crematorium along the coast . . .

'I intend returning his ashes to England where they will be scattered on his wife's – my mother's grave,' Vernon Gatling explained, to the frustrated police captain.

The Garda immediately got through on the telephone only to be informed that the Englishman, who had had no flowers and no mourners, had gone up the steel chimney that very afternoon. A police car had gone howling along the twisting country lane that led to the crematorium behind the sprawling town of Fuengirola. The uniforms were promptly shown a still-warm bronze urn encased in a tasteful purple velvet zip-up cover.

Gunner Gatling now weighed some seven pounds of ash and crushed bone. It was an irony that, despite the span of more than forty years between the two deaths, he was now in a worse state of preservation than Larry Varnish, the amateur archaeologist he had helped to murder.

Chapter Five

On the telephone, Ringrose imparted the bad news to Detective Superintendent Dalton.

'Bert, that wily bastard Vernon Gatling has shafted us. He had his old man cremated in Spain before Franklyn Dart could get his hands on the body. The whole thing cries foul play, but Gatling's money has been busy removing the smell. He has a kosher death certificate from that Wimpole Street quack and proper authorization papers for what the Spaniards tell me was an *incineración*.' Ringrose even managed the slight lisp in the pronunciation. He sighed heavily into the mouthpiece. 'Consequently, the audio-tape our two scribes made with the old boy will never be anything but hearsay evidence. I'm sitting here grinding my teeth. How's the Varnish inquiry shaping up at your end?'

Bert Dalton sounded no more chipper than Ringrose. 'The circumstantial evidence is fairly solid – provided you don't let the people who bumped off those two women in Chiswick get to Fling the foreman. He's the only one who can positively place Vernon and Gunner at the Varnish death scene in 1955. If Fling goes, such case as I have goes.'

'Don't fret yourself,' said Ringrose. 'I've got the erstwhile Bullshit King and his family tucked away in a safe-house.'

'Keep 'em there,' said Bert Dalton. 'At my end there's been one further development that underlines Vernon Gatling's obsessive interest in the Fletcher Hall site. On the day Varnish's bones were discovered, one of our brighter young constables took a statement from the site gateman. He said he'd noticed that for some weeks a big guy had been taking more than a passing pedestrian's interest in the demolition work.

Hanging about and so forth – and making himself scarce on the day the remains were discovered. The statement didn't seem to add up to much but, for want of something better to do, I put one of my chaps on to it. He started by collecting all the available CCTV tapes from the umpteen cameras along Bishopsgate and, sure enough, there was the big guy large as life. We ended up with a couple of dozen prints taken from different angles and different cameras and all identified by the gateman. Then, when Vernon Gatling's name came into the frame, my smart little bugger, who no doubt is already eyeing my chair, had a brainwave. He did a day's observations outside Vernon Gatling's Mayfair offices and eyeballed the staff in and out. He came up with one Archie Kenny, former Wasps prop forward. He's supposed to be a Gatling Construction costing clerk but looks more like a nightclub bouncer to me. I'm going to give him a tug as he leaves home for work in the morning. See what he has to say for himself. Put the frighteners on him. Want to watch?'

Bert Dalton placed Archibald Kenny of Richmond, Surrey, in the interview room and let him stew. From the other side of the mirror, Dalton and Tom Ringrose watched him fidgeting and shifting his backside on the wooden chair that was too small for his buttocks.

Kenny was wearing a Big Man navy-blue two-piece business suit. The trousers needed letting out. He was starting to grow a paunch now that his rugby-playing days were over and only the after-game beer-swilling was left. 'What's this all about? I don't understand. I'm going to be late for work,' he complained to the uniformed constable posted in the room to mind him.

The constable said, 'You didn't hear this from me, son. You're being kept on ice for the big boys.' Which is precisely what the constable had been instructed to say when asked.

Kenny jumped visibly. 'Big boys? What big boys?'

The constable put a finger to his lips. 'For fuck's sake, keep your voice down. Just because you're in the shit doesn't mean you have to drag me in, too.'

'Shit? I'm not in any shit. What's going on?'

'I'm sure Detective Superintendent Dalton will explain everything when he gets here. Take it easy.'

'A detective superintendent? What the fuck does a detective superintendent want with me?'

Bert Dalton said to Tom Ringrose, 'Let's go in and enlighten him.'

The two detectives filed in and the uniformed constable withdrew. Archie Kenny began to rise but Dalton said, 'That's all right, Mr Kenny. Stay seated, if you please.'

The pair seated themselves facing him. Archie said, 'Which of you is the detective superintendent?'

'Me,' said Bert. 'My name's Dalton. My colleague here is Commander Thomas Ringrose of the Metropolitan Police.'

'*What*?' It was as if alarm bells had sounded. As usual, Ringrose's fame – or notoriety – had preceded him. 'What can you gentlemen possibly want with me?' croaked Kenny.

Bert Dalton placed his elbows on the table. 'Before we begin, Archie, let me ask you something. We can do this in one of two ways – very officially, with a tape-recorder taking down every word to go into the record, or we three can simply have a little chat about certain matters that are bothering us.'

Kenny looked at them, bewildered.

Bert Dalton added, 'If we have the little chat we will most likely be able to keep matters on an informal level. But if you become an official part of our inquiry, well, who knows where it will end?'

Ringrose said, 'If Archie is frank with us, Bert, and holds nothing back, I'm sure you can find a car to get him to his office before his boss notices that he's a trifle late this morning. No one need know he's even been here.'

Archie said hastily, 'Let's just have the chat. But about what?'

'About Vernon Gatling.' said Dalton. 'Tell us how you come to know him. You do know him, don't you?'

'Oh, yes – although not too well. I'm merely an underling, an employee. I can't help you with his financial affairs.'

'That's okay. We know he's richer than God. That's enough.'

'Look here, I don't think Mr Gatling would like me talking

about him behind his back. Some of our work is confidential.'
Archie Kenny was recovering his balance.

'That's why we're having a chat just between ourselves rather than formally cautioning you and taping an interview,' said Dalton. 'I'm sure you've already deduced that Mr Ringrose and I are too senior in rank to be engaged in anything other than a most serious business. We don't want to throw our weight at you, Archie, and I promise you we won't – if you answer everything truthfully. I'm afraid an excess of loyalty to Vernon Gatling could land you in deep trouble.'

'I still don't understand.'

'Just tell us about Mr Gatling,' encouraged Dalton. 'In your own words. Take your time.'

Kenny nodded assent. 'All right. If you say it'll help. I've been with Gatling Construction for seven years, for the past two as senior costing clerk. I first had contact with the boss man at the topping-out of a new building in Milton Keynes. The tradition is that after the last skip of concrete has been poured and spread with souvenir shovels by the new owners, the guv'nor throws a party for the builders. It's usually a bit rough-and-ready. Not exactly teatime with the Queen. At these meet-the-workers piss-ups we always serve the drinks in plastic beakers and the food on cardboard plates. On this occasion, as usual, everyone got thoroughly rat-arsed and one of the blokes started to give Vernon Gatling bother. The bloke had some sort of grievance about overtime rates. As if the big boss would know anything about such piffling stuff. Anyway, the idiot kept prodding Mr Gatling in the chest while that bunch of fruits he calls his personal staff stood around like statues doing nothing to stop it. The guv'nor had to keep taking backwards steps. You only have to take one look at Mr Gatling to know he isn't likely to put up with that sort of crap for long. Things were about to get out of hand so I stepped in, wrapped my arms around the piss artist and dumped him back among his mates on the other side of the beer kegs. I wasn't looking for a medal but the guv'nor later came over and thanked me. He said, "I was about to chin him." I replied, a bit cheeky, like, "Oh, that would have been very clever, I don't think.

You'd then have to pay out a wedge as big as this building to stop him suing you for assault." Mr Gatling asked my name. I thought I'd gone too far but, on the following Friday, one of his secretaries appeared at my desk with a hundred quid in an envelope for me and a bunch of flowers to take home for my missus. He may have the reputation of having a jet of blue flame coming out of his arse but at least he's got a bit of style.'

'Did that incident lead to a job as his bodyguard?' asked Dalton.

'No, not at all. Although, after watching his personal brown-noses perform, I'd say he could have used one. No, it was months later before I heard from him again. Out of the blue I got a summons to the great man's office. It had never happened before. There'd been redundancies during the building slump and I thought, uh-oh, I was about to join the queue. Instead, he shut the door and greeted me as if we'd been in the trenches together. He said he had a personal favour to ask. Would I shlepp down to Bishopsgate on every working day each week and give him a written report, without keeping duplicate copies, on the progress of the demolition work on a building, Abura House, that had been damaged by the IRA? I was to put the reports in envelopes marked Strictly Personal and hand them to his principal secretary, Miss Cannon. It was hardly a job for his senior costing clerk but I wasn't about to get on my high horse. I said, "Certainly – anything for Mr Gatling, sir, Your Excellency, Your Wonderfulness." Never tell me brown-nosing doesn't pay. A couple of days later I received a note from Personnel that my salary had been increased by three thousand a year. I was staggered. We'd all heard about his run-in with the City Corporation over the rebuilding of Abura House but, I mean, the job he'd asked me to do was a doddle. The office boy would have done it for a bus fare and a packet of fags. All the guv'nor wanted was for me to stand on the pavement in Bishopsgate, make notes and report back.

'For weeks I was embarrassed to be taking his money. The site was boarded up and nothing was happening. He'd put a spanner in the works with his complaints to the City

Corporation and demolition had been delayed, which, I suppose, was exactly what he was aiming at. My reports usually consisted of one line: "There is no activity on the site."

'Then the heavy equipment began to arrive and the scaffolding and the rubble chutes were rigged. I made my reports accordingly. It doesn't take long for a building to be dismantled these days. He rang me and said, "Archie, I want you there full-time. Telephone me when they reach ground level." He gave me a special number. I thought he was planning some master stroke to take over the reconstruction and I was his spy on the ground. Of course, I didn't spend the entire day on the pavement. I would have been bored out of my mind. But I made regular walk-bys. I went down to the City one Tuesday morning, mooched past the site and rang his private number on my mobile. He answered immediately and I said. "The peckers are just breaking through into the sub-basement, sir. They'll be ready for the pile-drivers in a fortnight." There was a silence then he said, "Keep reporting daily, Archie. I may be moving about for a bit but you'll always get me through Miss Cannon." He sounded very subdued, not at all his usual ball-busting self.

'Four days later I stood eating a bacon roll and watched the drills breaking up the sub-floor. They were well advanced and I thought that if Vernon Gatling was in some way going to pirate the contract he'd have to be sharp about it. I couldn't imagine how he was going to pull it off. There'd been an office rumour that he'd even ordered a feasibility study to see if Gatling Construction could make a takeover bid for the rivals but that his bankers had told him they were just too big to swallow. It was real lateral thinking but I couldn't believe he'd go to those lengths for one shitty contract. It wasn't exactly winning the right to rebuild the Bank of England, was it?'

'How did your arrangement with him resolve itself?' asked Dalton.

'A couple of days later I was on pavement patrol when I spotted a sudden flurry of activity in and out of the site office. A number of management suits arrived, were handed hard hats and disappeared below pavement level. When they re-appeared there was some earnest discussion on the pavement between a tight little group. I then realized all work on the site had come to a standstill. I was intrigued so I hung on and thirty minutes later a police car arrived and a uniformed inspector joined the suits. They all disappeared once again into the sub-basement.' Archie Kenny stared at Bert Dalton. 'Come to think of it, it was you who came strolling along later as if you didn't have a care in the world.'

'Well observed, Mr Kenny,' said Bert Dalton. 'Indeed, I didn't have a care in the world until Vernon Gatling came into my life. What did you do after I arrived?'

'I made my report to Miss Cannon. She said she'd pass it on right away. By then Mr Gatling was somewhere in Central America. I had to wait for next day's paper to learn that human remains had been found on the site.'

The uniformed constable had brought in tepid mugs of tea. All the talking had parched Archie Kenny's throat and he stopped to take a gulp.

Dalton said, 'Was that the end of your personal association with Mr Gatling as opposed to your routine daily work as one of his costing clerks?'

'Not quite. He had his daughter contact me at home.'

Ringrose forced himself not to show any heightening of his interest.

'Do you mean Tabitha Gatling?' asked Dalton.

'Yeah. Jesus, that is some looker.'

'You are a friend?'

'God, I wish! We'd never met. The only stuff I knew about her was what I've read in the papers. Did you see the photos of her tits in the *Sun*? A knockout!' Archie Kenny swallowed the rest of the cold tea as if to cool himself down.

Ringrose said, 'Tell us about Tabitha.'

'Right. She rang me at Richmond on a Friday evening three weeks ago. I thought it was a wind-up. You know, some mates getting one of their tarts to impersonate her posh drawl. She soon put me right! She can be very Lady Muck when she wants. Anyway, she said her father had asked her to telephone because he trusted me. He had two associates coming to London for a crucial business negotiation that was so secret he couldn't even trust the details to his immediate advisers. Of course I was flattered, but then a bit deflated when she told me what Vernon Gatling wanted me to do.'

'Which was what?'

'Spend Saturday as a bloody chauffeur.'

'The next day?'

'Yes. It meant missing the Harlequins' game.' Dalton and Ringrose glanced briefly at each other. This had been two days before the Chiswick murders.

Kenny, oblivious, went on, a note of complaint rising in his voice. 'Truthfully, I wanted to tell her to get someone else as I was otherwise engaged. But her father had been more than generous with me so what could I do? I was in a bind. I never miss the home match.'

'But this time you did,' prompted Ringrose.

'Yes, dammit. Tabitha Gatling waved her father's name at me like a bludgeon. It told me clearly on which side my bread was buttered. She gave me specific instructions. I was to use my own car and go to London Airport and meet the morning British Airways Concorde flight from New York. She told me to get a large piece of cardboard and write VERN on it. The passenger would find me. He was to be shown into the back seat and I was not to talk to him. I was then to drive him to the Gatling home in Chelsea.'

'Did everything work out as instructed?'

'Like clockwork. I stood among all those other drivers holding up their bloody cards. I felt a right fool. Up came this guy carrying a two-suit shoulder-bag. He never said a word. Just nodded as if to say, "Let's get on with it." Rude bastard. We didn't exchange a single syllable all the way to Cheyne Walk. I held the car door when he climbed out. I thought I'd take the piss. I said, "Have a nice day, sir," in that creepy singsong way that the Americans have of saying it.'

'How d'you know he was American if he didn't speak?' said Ringrose.

'It was just an assumption. His clothes were definitely American. I've taken Florida holidays enough times – pale green polyester suit, Florsheim shoes with the thick soles.'

'Who let him into the house?' said Ringrose.

'The lovely Tabitha, of course. She opened the front door, took him in and gave me a brief wave as she closed it again.'

'What then?'

'I was off to Gatwick, wasn't I, for the second pick-up of the day. The same rules applied. Hold up the board. He'll find you. No talking. This time it was a Virgin budget flight, which surprised me because all the big brains surrounding Vernon Gatling usually travel in the company jets or first class on scheduled flights. But, as Tabitha had impressed on me, discretion was paramount.'

'At no stage did you learn your passengers' names?'

'No. I delivered the second geezer – a really big geezer at that. Fuck knows how he squeezed himself into those Virgin seats – and this time Tabitha came out to the car.

'She said, "Archie, my daddy was right. You're a star." She handed me an envelope and added, "Remember, today didn't happen." Then she hurried back into the house and closed the door.'

'What was in the envelope?'

'A thousand quid. I mean, excessive or what? But that's the way Vernon Gatling likes to spread his money if you please him.'

Ringrose said, 'Where's the money now?'

'In the building society.'

'Had Miss Gatling written on the envelope? Your name, perhaps?'

'No, it was blank.'

'So perhaps you saved it to use again?'

'Yeah, matter of fact I believe I did. It's a nice big cream envelope. It'll come in handy some time.'

'Where would it be now?'

'In my desk drawer.'

'Has anyone but you and Miss Gatling handled it – your wife perhaps?'

'No, I handed my missus the dosh – it was in used notes – and she put it in her handbag with our building-society passbook. She deposited the entire grand at our local branch after I'd gone to work on Monday morning.'

Bert Dalton handed him a telephone. 'Archie, you'll not be getting to work, after all. Ring your office and tell them you have flu. And then ring your wife and tell her not to go anywhere near your desk.'

Archie Kenny looked hurt. 'You promised. What did I say wrong?'

'Archie,' said Tom Ringrose fervently, 'you didn't say anything wrong. You've just talked your way out of a conspiracy-to-murder charge.'

'I don't understand,' said the bewildered witness. 'That guy they found in Bishopsgate died before I was born, for Christ's sake.'

'You're talking about the wrong murder,' said Ringrose.

The costing clerk spent a mentally exhausting day. Two detective constables accompanied him to his home, where he was allowed to open his desk drawer and identify a 27 x 21.5 cm envelope large enough to contain a thousand pounds in assorted banknotes. One DC produced a pair of tweezers, lifted out the envelope and dropped it into an evidence pouch.

Kenny was requested to pack an overnight bag. He was then returned to Bishopsgate police station where he was obliged to repeat everything he had told Dalton and Ringrose. Only this time the tape-recorder was on.

The testimony secured, Kenny was then transferred to an altogether nicer room where an artist waited to assist him in making E-fit pictures of his two passengers.

By midnight his head was swimming and he was permitted to get seven hours' sleep in a cell with the door left open. Then, just to show he was in no way in detention, a couple of jovial coppers took him to the canteen for a Big British Breakfast before he was delivered once again to the police artist.

Archie Kenny had flu for a second day and could not get to his office. But by eleven a.m. the police had a fair likeness of Oscar Ruttmann, including a fair depiction of his unfortunate nose.

However, the E-fit of Kazuo Iwasaki was much too vague to be of realistic use. Archie had accurately captured his slenderness, his height and the shape of his head but he had missed the hint of the Orient in Kaz's eyes. The killer had sat well back in Archie's car.

Chapter Six

Tom Ringrose and Lionel Firth were driven up to the City of London for a summit meeting with Bert Dalton. Because of the vaster resources possessed by the Metropolitan Police it was already tacitly understood that the three-murder investigation had to be headed by Ringrose.

The motive in each case led inexorably back to a Saturday night in 1955 and the killing of an uneducated Cockney, who had acquired an unlikely reverence for the world of antiquity.

The death of Gus Meldrum in Los Angeles, so far listed as an accident by the LAPD, could also be said to lead back to the same dismal scene. But the British police wanted first bite at the Gatlings.

Ringrose opened with a tactful tribute to the City's tiny force. 'Bert, you and your boys have done a first-class job. Thanks to your team digging Archie Kenny out of the woodwork, for the first time we have some leverage. The good news is that the prints on the envelope have been compared with latents lifted from Tabitha Gatling's bathroom at Cheyne Walk. Take away Kenny's dabs. The rest are all hers. That homicidal young lady has a great deal of explaining to do when she returns to England.

'The other advantage we have is that, almost certainly, Vernon and his daughter do not realize that our two journalists got to old Gunner a second time and taped his confession before his ever-loving granddaughter could whip the old boy abroad and out of our reach. Thanks to Gunner telling the truth for once in his squalid life, we know exactly what happened on the night Larry Varnish was murdered, who did it and the unusual weapon used.'

Bert Dalton said, 'Do we all agree that the two characters picked up by Archie Kenny and delivered to Tabitha must be hitmen hired from Vernon's Mob connections?'

'Absolutely,' confirmed Ringrose. 'We've given the FBI the names of all the male passengers who were on the Concorde and Virgin flights that Archie Kenny says he was sent to meet. We've questioned without result the cabin crews of both planes which, unfortunately, were both packed to the doors. The crews were busy.'

Ringrose shrugged and stretched his long legs under the conference table. 'Still, I thought one of them might have remembered the guy with the odd nose. So far no luck. The FBI are working on the identities but they're coming up empty. These two jokers do not appear to be known members of the criminal fraternity. It is looking increasingly likely that they do not have criminal records. That being the case, I've asked the Bureau to concentrate on that damn nose. It must have required hospital treatment at some time. Was it a souvenir from the Vietcong?' He smiled. 'Marty Groot asked, while I'm about it, if I'd like the name of every American male who crooks his pinkie while he drinks his tea.'

The three detectives laughed. Lionel Firth said, 'The awesome thing is, if you'd said yes, some computer crazy at Quantico would come up with the answer.'

Ringrose said, 'Our two journalists are busy reconstructing from memory their missing Gatling archive. They're still convinced they'll have their bestseller book one day. I intend to keep the pair under protection although the death of Gunner Gatling really makes it unnecessary for Vernon Gatling to take out a second contract on them. Meredith and Tripp could do little damage to either Vernon or Tabitha in the witness box now that they have only hearsay stuff to peddle.

'What we have to keep at the forefront of our thinking is that, by now, Vernon has had time to study every word they wrote or recorded – with the exception of that final damning tape from his father. He'll know the one person he simply has to shut up is the one person who places him and Gunner on the scene of the murder back in 1955. Denny Fling.'

'You think he'll have those two Mob guys return to take a pop at Fling?' asked Bert Dalton. 'It'd be an open declaration of war on the British judicial system. You wouldn't need to be Einstein to guess who was bankrolling hostilities.'

'He can't do anything else, can he? He may not send in the same guys but I'm sure the people he deals with in New York have a taxi line of killers for hire. I'm told contract killing is a growth industry in the Land of the Free.'

'So what's the plan?' said Dalton.

'I've had Denny, his invalid wife and his daughter moved out of their house in Streatham. Two policewomen and a police sergeant, who with a bit of makeup and a grey wig has a resemblance to Denny, have moved in. They're all weapons-proficient officers and they are at the centre of my web. Now we wait.'

Ringrose was gathering up his papers when he stopped and turned to Dalton. 'By the way, Bert, I almost forgot. It's time to put your tin helmet on. The shit from above is starting to fall. I was called to see my commissioner yesterday. Sir Marcus Coombes, legal adviser to the gentry, was with him. Very chummy. He'd been sent over to the Yard by his friend, the attorney-general, for what he termed a private chat. Sir Marcus, you should know, also handles all Vernon Gatling's personal legal affairs. Among other things, he's Tabitha's trustee.'

'What was that old crocodile after?' said Dalton.

'He was on a fishing expedition,' said Ringrose. 'His client had been distressed to learn that I'd obtained a search warrant for his London home. What possible motive could I have had for this invasion of his privacy? Sir Marcus was well aware I was investigating two horrible murders. How on earth could his illustrious client be linked to such an appalling business?' Ringrose smiled thinly. 'My commissioner, of course, stepped in to pronounce this meeting highly irregular and ejected Sir Marcus from his office.'

'Yeah, I'll bet,' said Dalton.

'I couldn't believe it,' said Ringrose. 'My slippery leader pulled the oldest dodge in the book. He had his secretary call him out to take a vital call in the next room.'

'So you were left alone with old Coombes? Did the subject arise of just how generous Vernon can be with large sums of money?'

'I think the withering look I directed at the commissioner's back as he fled informed the old boy that he'd better not try his luck with me. But there was plenty about Vernon's huge donations to charity, friendship with half the cabinet, reputation for probity to maintain as a business leader. I listened to all this verbal massage and kept my mouth shut. Finally, he was forced to ask: had I reason to believe Vernon Gatling was involved in the crimes I was investigating? I was sweetness personified. I said if Sir Marcus would produce his client and his client's daughter I'd be happy to set out my reasons for taking an interest in their activities. When might that be? I asked politely.

'He then gave me a further line of bullshit about the pair being in mourning for the death of Gatling senior. They were recovering from their loss in the Mediterranean. Coombes is too wily a bird to get angry, but the way those yellowing old eyes stopped blinking and simply bored into my face tells me I've made a powerful enemy. He's an Establishment Mr Fixit who is nothing if he loses the power to fix.'

Chapter Seven

The two killers had gone ashore at Málaga soon after Gunner's body was removed from the *Black Glove*.

Tabitha had run them the taped interview with Denny Fling before committing it to the sea, and Oscar and Kaz were careful to note the extraneous information that emerged from the daughter's background interruptions and Denny's wandering remarks. There were three people in the suburban household. The wife had stayed upstairs.

As best he could remember, Vernon described Denny's physical look as a young man.

'You can't give us anything more recent than that?' Oscar wasn't happy.

'It's years since he was in my employ. There's no one from the old days I can give you to finger him,' said Vernon. All the famed bounce and strut by which the world recognized the developer of SkyCities was absent. Vernon was shaken.

'You want us to go in blind?' said Oscar. 'On our own? In a foreign country? Where our clothes and our accents will make us stand out like zits on Chelsea Clinton's face?'

'At least we can do something about the clothes,' said Vernon.

Kaz said quietly, 'Tabitha, we were hasty. We should have let you hang on to those two firearms we made you return. Mr Ganz and I hate using guns but I can foresee that we may have no choice on this occasion. Please give us the name and address of your supplier. We may need this person.'

She jumped. 'Absolutely not, Mr Beamish! He's a friend. I swore I'd never get him into trouble. Surely, in your line of work, you must have British contacts who can find weapons for you?'

Edgy silence fell on the stateroom. Kaz turned to Vernon. 'I regret to have to say this, sir, but I fear we shall have to inform your friend in New York that we could not obtain from you sufficient back-up to proceed. This is a highly hazardous contract you expect us to accept. We cannot go in naked. Your daughter isn't placing her priorities in the correct order.'

Vernon wheeled on his daughter. 'Give them what they want,' he said harshly. 'Mr Beamish is right. This is no time to be worrying about the hurt feelings of some lowlife.'

'Oh, Daddy!' Tabitha wailed. 'He'll hate me.'

'Do it!' he yelled.

Oscar picked up the Corolla from the long-term car-park at Heathrow where he had left it. Kaz flew Gibraltar–Gatwick. Each booked separately into small hotels in Bayswater and went shopping for off-the-peg clothes. They used cash everywhere, never credit cards. They studied street maps and made a number of long drives to acclimatize themselves with unfamiliar surroundings.

Tabitha's friend Wes – full name Wesley Terence Lake – had his regular pubs and clubs on his nightly pleasure round. Tabitha had given the killers all the names and addresses.

Wes was a South London boy who often drank in a pub in the Old Kent Road with friends in the same line of work. They were blaggers. They raided building societies, post offices and, on one occasion that had earned them underworld status, an armoured truck. The living was easy.

Wes had bought a magnificent riverside flat in Rotherhithe, with views of the Canary Wharf tower and the City skyline and was considered a colourful, entertaining character by well-bred girls looking for a touch of louche excitement in their lives.

The security door on the apartment block, a converted tea warehouse, presented no problem to Oscar.

After a night's pub crawl with his mucker, Waxy, Wes returned to his bachelor heaven shortly after midnight. He'd taken a taxi because he'd been drinking. He knew the filth would just love to catch him at the wheel and over the limit. Apart from the police, Wes hadn't an enemy in the world. He was humming to himself as he inserted his key in his classy, panelled front door.

He had no time to be amazed. A voice behind him said, 'Hey, you, dickhead.'

Wes wheeled round. He was no midget but the guy with the moonface whose fist was already travelling through the air at supersonic speed was towering over him like Guy the Gorilla – Wes's mum had taken him to see Guy at the zoo when he was a kid.

When Wes came round, he was naked and had been dumped on one of the matching silk sofas he'd had made at Heal's. His hands and feet were tied. Through uncertain vision, he immediately saw the two characters – Moonface and some sort of Chink or Nip. They were sitting on the other sofa watching him.

Moonface said, 'Hiya, Wes.'

Fuck. This wasn't a mistake. They knew his name.

'What's going on? Who're you guys?'

Moonface said, 'Stay cool, Wes. You have a coupla guns we need.'

'What guns? I don't have any fucking guns. Who told you that?'

'Tabitha Gatling told us that, Wes.'

'Who the fuck is Tabitha Gatling? I don't know anyone of that name.'

Oscar turned to Kaz, who so far had said nothing. 'I wonder if you would refresh his memory?'

Kaz rose and advanced. Wes struggled against his bonds and spewed obscenities until Kaz calmly slapped a plaster over the tirade. He then squeezed Wes's left testicle until he fainted.

Once again Wes came round. The pain in his groin was excruciating. His torturers were seated as before – silently watching him. They'd removed the plaster. 'Why are you doing this to me? Tabitha is a friend of mine.'

Oscar said, 'Rich bitches don't have friends. They only have worshippers.'

Kaz said, 'Now, Wes, let's start again. You have a Webley pistol and a 9mm automatic. We want them.'

'I swear I haven't got them. I've sold them on.' Kaz remained impassive but he saw Oscar sigh in disbelief. 'No, wait a minute. It's the God's honest truth. But I can let you have an Uzi with two spare mags and an under-and-over sawn-off shotgun.'

'Are they here?'

'No, in my lock-up round the corner. I'll show you.' Suddenly Wes was eager to please and anxious to get these frighteners out of his crib.

'Just give us the keys and tell us how to find this lock-up.'

During the twenty minutes that Kaz was gone Oscar sat watching Wes.

'There was no need for the heavy stuff,' said Wes sullenly. 'My goolies are killing me. And my jaw doesn't feel much better.'

'We haven't time to be jerked around, kid,' said Oscar.

Kaz returned empty-handed. An instantly alarmed Wes said, 'Where's the gear?'

Kaz ignored him and turned to Oscar. 'It's okay. I've put it in the car. The stuff's just as he said – a used Uzi and a new shotgun, plus mags and shells. Everything seems to be in working order.'

'See?' said Wes. 'I wasn't shitting you, guys. American, aren't you? What's going down? Maybe I can help.'

They did not reply. Instead, Oscar took hold of Wes's ankles, dragged him off the sofa, turned him on his face and sat on him.

Wes gave a yelp and said, 'Whaaaa!' before his head was tugged upward by his hair.

Kaz said, 'You've seen those movies where they say, "It's nothing personal. Just business," haven't you, Wes?' His tone was heavy with regret. Just think of it like that and it won't hurt so much,' he added, as he slipped the plastic bag over the young blagger's head.

Gervase Meredith dropped his glass on the table with such force that his whisky spilled and made a puddle. Nelly jumped. 'Idiot! Don't do that!'

'Christ! Sorry, Nell. Look at this.' Gervase held up the *Evening Standard* front page. Wesley Lake's photograph ran across three columns.

'So?'

'It's Tabitha's friend, Wes. He's been found dead. Remember Millie Moses and me spending a weekend at the Gatling country pile? Wes was there with his friend Waxy. I think they're a couple of villains.'

'Does the *Standard* say it's murder?'

'Doesn't say for certain. Could be a kinky sex thing that went wrong. Wes was naked.'

Ringrose had moved the two journalists to a small furnished house in Tottenham, north London, where they had forgotten their drear surroundings and were applying themselves furiously to the task of re-creating their stolen work.

They occupied the upstairs rooms. Downstairs was strictly for their protection officers.

Gervase, brandishing the paper, stepped out on to the landing and shouted down.

Lionel Firth burst into Ringrose's office with the two journalists. 'Looks like the hitmen are back in town,' he announced.

Gervase and Nelly sat in front of Ringrose's desk grimly holding hands as if to let go would send them tumbling into the abyss.

Ringrose listened without interruption to Gervase's account of the weekend at Spear's End. Firth slipped out of the room.

At the end of Gervase's gabbled recital, Ringrose said, 'This Wes and Waxy seem odd company for Tabitha Gatling to keep?'

'You have to know her,' said Gervase. 'She gets her jollies from doing outlandish things – look at that bosom-baring business in W. O. Wilkie's department store, and beating up that titled poofter. She keeps strange company. She likes a bit of rough. Shopping and lunching with the girls isn't enough for her.'

Firth re-entered. Ringrose raised an eyebrow. 'Do the local nick confirm it's murder?'

'I've instructed them to get Professor Dart for the post-mortem, but it looks like death from asphyxiation. There's a bag over his head. It's getting to be a trademark.'

'Oh, Christ!' said Gervase, devastated. 'That could have been us. I wish I'd never heard of the Gatling family.' Nelly stood and held him tight.

Waxy wasn't his real name but he'd been called that for as long as anyone around the Old Kent Road could remember. He was really Wallace Bates, aged thirty-three, with a long record of teenage offences and one eighteen-month sentence of youth custody on his sheet.

Looking at him now, muscles rippling under his shirt, you'd never think he had once been a sickly child with a waxen complexion, thanks to an upbringing in the mildewed flat of a Victorian tenement where the tin bath hung on a nail on the open balcony and the sun penetrated, at best, for no more than an hour a day.

The correctional institution had been Waxy's university. Tougher young criminals had bullied him into shape and shown him how to pump iron and build the kind of body that had the chicks creaming their knickers. Smarter young criminals taught him how to 'box clever'. He graduated with honours.

Consequently, in his adulthood Waxy had been hauled into police stations many times on suspicion of involvement in serious crime but he'd only ever once gone to trial.

He had been acquitted by a jury from which his canny lawyers had contrived to exclude anyone who looked like a *Daily Telegraph* reader. In lawyer-speak, to come under suspicion of being a *Telegraph* reader is to be a likely purveyor of guilty verdicts, especially when the accused is of the 'undeserving' lower orders.

The two coppers who called to feel Waxy's collar for the umpteenth time were disconcerted to find the serial miscreant red-eyed from weeping. 'Wes was me best mate, wasn't he?' sniffed Waxy, shaking the hand of the law off his Dougie Hayward suit. 'If I'm nicked, I want my brief. I'm not saying a fucking thing.'

'Shut it,' said the senior detective constable. 'No one's nicking you, Waxy. You're in the big-time now. Ringrose wants a word.'

Waxy's moist eyes widened. 'Wot, that geezer they call the Ringer? What the fuck does he want with me? Do you think I'd top my bestest pal – the pal I went to school with?'

'I didn't know you'd been to school, Waxy,' said the other DC.

'Very bloody funny. Have you tried the Palladium?' Waxy expected a little more sympathy in his grief.

They flanked him on the way out of his splendid Georgian house near New Cross. 'Can't we go in my car?' he said, as he eyed with condescension their two-year-old Rover saloon.

The two coppers enviously noted the Bentley gleaming on the hardstand in front of the garage. 'Waxy, we'd only get jealous and be driven into a life of crime,' said one.

'Definitely the fucking Palladium,' said Waxy.

*

298

Waxy Bates was not afraid of Ringrose. In a perverted way, he was enjoying the encounter. As the cheeky DC who'd brought him to the Kensington nick had pointed out, you didn't get to meet a copper of Ringrose's calibre unless you were in the big-time. If pride comes before a fall, this cautionary thought was not uppermost in Waxy's mind.

'Lemme get one thing straight, Mr Ringrose. Am I under arrest or am I suspected of murdering Wes Lake? Do I need my brief?' Waxy said, thrusting his beautifully barbered suede head aggressively forward.

'Three times no,' said Ringrose. 'Would you like something to drink, Mr Bates?'

'Vodka, ice, twist of lemon,' said Waxy promptly.

'Perhaps I could persuade you to settle for a coffee?' smiled Ringrose.

'Don't hit me with your truncheon, guv'nor. I'll take it.'

Waxy put his elbows on the table and both Ringrose and Firth matched him so that their heads were only inches apart. Ringrose got down to serious business.

'Now, look here, Mr Bates, I wager you want to get the bastards who did this to Wes Lake as much as we do. We need your help.'

'You've got it,' said Waxy. 'When I leave here, the word goes out: Waxy Bates wants the fuckers who did his best friend. I'll even put up money for the grasses.'

'Off the record, that's okay by us. But, if you get a whisper, you come to us. We want live bodies to bring to trial. We don't want floaters in the river.' Ringrose caught Waxy's look of cynicism. 'I mean it, Mr Bates. I'll be down on you like a ton of hot manure if there's a nasty accident.'

'Yeah, yeah!' said Waxy.

'In any case, we don't think you have much chance of getting a result. The two men we wish to question we believe to be foreign nationals brought to Britain to carry out the murder of your friend. They won't be among your usual crowd.'

Surprise sent Waxy shooting back so hard that his chair almost toppled. 'Hitmen? To kill Wes? Do me a favour. That's for the movies.'

'Nevertheless, we believe it to be true. We believe the same killers have already committed two other murders in the London area.'

'But where does Wes come in? He's not – wasn't – mixed up in anything international. He had no dealings with those maniacs in the drugs trade. If he had, I'd know. And I'd tell you.'

'Tell us about your friendship with Tabitha Gatling,' encouraged Ringrose suddenly.

Waxy looked from him to Firth and back again. 'Have I missed something? What the fuck's this got to do with her?'

'Just tell us about Tabitha,' said Lionel Firth. 'We'll get to the reasons later.'

'She's just a high-class bint who sort of took me and Wes up and introduced us to high society. She comes to the Ministry of Sound and the other South London raves. We've introduced her to a few faces, if you know what I mean. We've taken her to the races and she's entertained us at her father's place on the other side of the river and at his estate out in the boonies. Gorgeous bit of crumpet but she's a lot tougher than she looks. She's a bit wicked with the Bruce Lee stuff. She's got all his old movies on video. She goes to some martial arts academy when she's in town. I partnered her once. I lost a stone keeping out of harm's way.'

'Were you and Wes her lovers?'

'Leave it out. Tabby likes to flash the flesh and I won't say we didn't give it a go. But she's a bit of a prick-teaser. I think she's saving it for the richest man in the universe. What she does is get you worked up and then pass you on to one of those other rich cunts she usually has hanging round her. Wes and me have shagged half the minge in that big red form book. What's it called? Shagging themselves silly with us proles is what they do to pass the time. Then they marry geezers out of the book and settle down in houses like Tabitha's old man's place and start collecting dogs and children.'

'The book's called *Debrett's*,' said Ringrose. 'It may interest you to know Tabitha is not actually in it. When was the last time you saw her?'

'Three months ago – when we had a weekend at the Gatlings' country home, Spear's End. She's been travelling ever since, otherwise I might have thought I'd been given the elbow.'

'And Wes?'

'I know he saw her less than a month ago.'

'How do you know?'

'He told me.'

'They had a date?'

'Nah. She called at his flat.'

'Why?'

'A bit of business, I should imagine.'

Ringrose and Firth both thrust their faces at him. Ringrose said, 'Don't mess us about, Waxy. Your best friend told you what the bit of business was.'

Waxy squirmed. 'I had nothing to do with it, right? So anything I tell you isn't down to me, right?'

'I thought we'd already agreed that,' said Ringrose. 'There's no recording so let's get on with it.'

'I just want to be sure I'm not being stitched up here,' Waxy whined. 'Wes happened to have two guns and she bought them off him.'

'Ready for the next blagging?' asked Firth.

'Leave it out. You don't expect me to answer that, do you?'

'What kind of guns?' said Ringrose.

'A couple of small pieces. I know one was a 9mm job.'

'Why did she want them?'

'Wes said she wouldn't tell him. He was a bit nervous about selling them to her. I mean, she can go a bit doo-lally when she doesn't get it all her own way. He didn't want her doing anything crazy and dragging him into the frame. He was very relieved when it worked out fine. She even let him keep the money.'

'How do you mean?'

'Only kept them three days, didn't she? And then gave 'em back unused.'

'What did Wes make of that?'

'He said she was a bit down. She said she was trying to do

some geezers a good turn but they'd told her to stick her guns up her jacksey. Tabby wasn't used to being treated like that. Wes said she was well pissed off.'

'The Rotherhithe CID found no firearms in Wes's flat this morning,' said Firth.

'They wouldn't, would they? I suppose you'll find it sooner or later so I might as well tell you. Wes kept his Bentley in the garage under his building but he had a lock-up two streets away. That's where he kept anything a bit iffy. Most likely, you'll find the shooters there. If Tabitha Gatling's involved in this, I hope you find her fucking dabs all over them.'

Ringrose's men did not find the weapons but they did find the garage unlocked and evidence that someone had been searching among Wes Lake's more chancy possessions. There were no fingerprints worth a damn.

Ringrose said, 'Lionel, I want you to impress upon that team who've taken over Denny Fling's house that they must wear body armour at all times. We have to assume that our killers are now armed with more than plastic bags.'

Chapter Eight

Oscar Ruttmann and Kazuo Iwasaki were beginning to get the feel of London and were becoming more comfortable with the stick-shift on the Corolla. Back home they drove automatics like everyone else.

They arranged to meet in the Kyoto Garden, deep inside Holland Park in West London. 'So serene,' murmured Kaz, taking in the waterfall, the stone lanterns, the ducks, and the peacock strutting alongside their bench on a grassy knoll.

'Sure is,' said Oscar, hardly noticing. 'Are we ready to finish this fucking job and get out of here? I'm homesick for a decent pot roast and the sight of my kids.'

Kaz spread his sketches and Polaroids between them. One showed a street plan of Denny Fling's neighbourhood, with Denny's house inked in. 'The hit has to be at the house. There's this guy Fling, a son-in-law who's away a lot on business, plus two women. Fling answers the front door when his daughter goes out to work. His wife stays upstairs. Sometimes he frigs around in his front garden but I've yet to see him step further than the gate.'

'For fuck's sake, we're not going to off the women, are we? They're not in the contract. We've already given those rich arseholes a couple of freebies.'

'No, Oscar. This is a very busy area, two hundred yards from a main shopping centre. We hit him early and we hit him fast. Then we're outta there. It has to be a crude Panzer strike. If we take over the house to do it coolly, the wife sees us and we have to kill her.'

Oscar relaxed. 'That's okay, then.'

Kaz's finger traced their getaway route. 'The far end of Fling's road ends in a big open space – commonland. There's a road runs across it a short distance to the subway, what the Brits call the Tube, at a place called Tooting Bec. From the time I do the hit to the time we dump the car and disappear underground should take no more than eight minutes.'

'You do the hit?'

'It has to be me. The local mailman is more my size. I'll need his uniform.'

Dubiously Oscar studied the paperwork, photographs of the road and Denny Fling's frontage. 'How's the police activity?'

'Very little. Just an occasional patrol car. They hassle the whores who operate down at the commonland end.'

'Isn't that suspicious – the lack of cop interest? Those fucking reporters we missed must have told Scotland Yard about the little talk they had with Fling. We wouldn't be sitting here planning to nix him if he wasn't a mega-embarrassment to Vernon Gatling. Why isn't the big mouth getting witness protection?'

'I guess because no one's been charged with any crime yet – and maybe no one ever will be. You heard that tape. Fling didn't actually see Vernon and his old man commit murder.

This guy is just what you say – an embarrassment. Who says British cops are all as smart as Sherlock Holmes? After our recent efforts, they know Vernon isn't just going to hold out his hands for the iron bracelets. They know now he'll go a long way to preserve his lily-white reputation. But has it occurred to them that he would consider this guy Fling significant enough to have a contract out on him? I don't think so. We know something they don't know. You can bet your bundle that Vernon ain't going to set foot again on these shores until we've cleaned house for him.'

The peacock was displaying his iridescent plumage. Oscar shot out his boot and the bird drew back sharply. He transferred his stare to his meaty hands. He felt racked by conflicting thoughts.

He said, slowly, 'I must be getting old. I don't feel so great about this one, Kaz. What say that when we get back home I tell Albert Penn we're retiring from the fray? We've made our pile. We've had a better run than Johnny Carson.'

Kaz shook his neat head, smiling wryly. 'Don't fool yourself, Oscar. We're in until our teeth fall out. From all I've learned about your friend Albert, I don't think he's very nice to quitters. We'd have the money and the oceanside estates in Florida but sooner or later Albert would want yet another favour. We'd stretch out in our hammocks, sip our martinis and say no to his goons. From that moment you might just as well kiss your sorry ass goodbye.'

Kaz moved the sketches and, with difficulty, slid an arm around Oscar's wide, hunched shoulder. 'It'll be a sweet job, Oscar. You'll see. I'll take the sawn-off, deliver the fucker's letters, and when he opens the front door I'll push him back down the passage and let him have a barrel-load square in the chest. I'll immediately close the front door to shut myself off from the women of the house. They're certain to scream the plaster off the ceiling. While they're doing it, I'll be out the gate and into the car. It'll take five seconds from the moment I let him have it. We'll be in the subway before it's even occurred to Fling's wife and daughter to get off their knees and dial nine one one.'

'Here it's nine nine nine,' said Oscar, gruffly. 'For fuck's sake, Kaz, don't screw up on the details. If anything goes wrong, this time we won't have the rich bitch to blame.'

They bought an old Ford transit van for cash and, for three mornings between the hours of eight and ten a.m., parked it in Hilly Place, a short thoroughfare running at right angles to Denny Fling's road. Then they waited. Oscar was rather taken with the sturdy houses and the well-tended front gardens. 'The Brits may be a bunch of losers but they sure know their flowers,' he said.

The mailman's regular route took him along Hilly Place before he turned right to continue his deliveries in Tangmere Avenue.

Conditions, Kaz repeated almost obsessively, had to be perfect – which meant that when Oscar jumped him there must be no witnesses.

For the first two days their unwitting target came into view at nearer ten a.m. and there were other pedestrians in sight. On the third day, the mailman was in fact a mail*woman*. The regular guy must have been having a day off.

Oscar, happy for something to relieve the tedium, mused that Kaz could possibly squeeze into her uniform but he wasn't so sure that his partner's muscular calves would not be a giveaway.

The killers were not fazed by the delays. They'd endured much longer stake-outs on past contracts.

On the fourth morning, the usual mailman was back. The time was eight-ten a.m. and the sidewalk was otherwise empty.

'It's showtime,' said Oscar. He wore grey chinos, a black windcheater and a Malcolm X baseball cap. Later the cap would be tossed and the windcheater reversed. The inner lining was red. He slipped from the van and crossed to the far side of the road. He trudged along the pavement, walked to the corner and recrossed so that he was at the mailman's rear. The rest depended upon an uncertain timing.

The killers could have no prior knowledge of the houses on which their target was calling to make his deliveries. Oscar had to strike as the man, in his late thirties, drew parallel with the van and just as Kaz was opening the rear doors. If a pedestrian appeared ahead, the attempt was off. Oscar had to rely on Kaz to intercept him with a request for a match if eye-witnesses suddenly turned into the road behind him.

Oscar watched the mailman's progress. Lift the gate latch, five strides along the short path, stuff the mail through the letter-box, return to the pavement, examine the number on the next batch and move forward, pushing his trolley ahead of him.

Oscar waited until the guy was three houses' distant from the van. The road ahead, beyond the van, beyond the mailman, remained clear. Oscar began his walk on rubber soles. He watched with approval as Kaz slipped from the front seat and begin to move towards the van's rear doors. Oscar quickened his pace. The mailman had given one house a complete miss and was now only thirty yards from the blind spot between the van and a garden wall where he had to be hit.

The guy made a delivery and pushed on. Now Kaz had the van doors open. Oscar, coming up rapidly, looked at him for the okay. Kaz lifted his eyes briefly beyond Oscar's broad frame, scanned the road, and gave an imperceptible nod.

The mailman actually obliged Oscar. He halted alongside the van to fish out more mail from the trolley. Instead, the manila wad in his hand fell back as Oscar's fist slammed into the side of his skull. He did not hit the pavement. Oscar caught him as he slumped, rushed him round to the van's rear and threw him in like a sack of potatoes. Kaz followed with the trolley.

They leaped in, pulled the doors together and sat listening for sounds of alarm. The assault and the man's disappearance from view had taken nine seconds.

There were no sounds of alarm or outrage from outside. In the van's dim interior light they hurriedly stripped off the poleaxed man's shoes and uniform and swiftly bound him in tape. A piece went over his eyes and another over his mouth.

Kaz shed his one-piece overall and transformed himself into an English postman while Oscar tied the original – who, bound in shiny tape, now looked like the chrysalis of some giant butterfly – to the van's metal wall. He then slid the shotgun down the inside of the trolley's leather pouch, the dull metal barrel pushing aside the letters, postcards and parcels.

Everything had been rehearsed. Neither man had uttered a word throughout.

The uniform fit was tight but passable. Oscar looked Kaz up and down and made the A-okay sign with circled thumb and finger.

Oscar opened the door a few inches, peered round cautiously and then climbed out into the pale sunlight. There was still no one in view. He poked his huge head round the side of the van. There was only one distant pedestrian exercising a dog. Oscar tapped the door. 'Go!' he said.

Kaz swung his legs on to the roadway and lifted down his newly acquired trolley. He ignored the remainder of the Hilly Place deliveries on the top of the mail pile and reached in to bring up the Tangmere Avenue stuff. Oscar patted Kaz's tightly jacketed shoulder and his partner headed for the hit.

Oscar watched for a moment as the man to whom fate had yoked him swung briskly along the sidewalk. Oscar gave their first victim of the day a final inspection. His head was moving and muffled sounds of groaning emerged from behind the gag.

He placed a hand under the sap's nostrils and felt the powerful jets of air hit his palm. If you gag a guy you'd better be sure a cold isn't blocking his schnoz. Oscar and Kaz didn't off anyone they weren't paid to off. No freebies. Pity that rich bitch had forced their hand with her dumb attempts to help. That was the only time they'd breached a proud working rule. Satisfied that the mailman would live, Oscar closed the van doors.

The Corolla was parked in Tangmere Avenue three hundred yards from Denny Fling's house and facing towards the common. Oscar strolled round to the vehicle, unlocked all four doors, settled himself in the driving seat and turned on the ignition. While he waited and watched Kaz's progress – his partner was making a few deliveries so that things would look right – he tugged a bag from under the passenger seat and extracted the Uzi. Oscar locked in the magazine and waited.

As Kaz would say, so far so sweet.

Chapter Nine

Sergeant Alan Passingham of Ringrose's special detail was attempting to prove to his two female colleagues, Policewomen Jill Crombie and Maya Considine, that he wasn't the complete macho pig they frequently alleged, but was every inch a New Man.

He was cooking breakfast for three in Denny Fling's spruce kitchen. 'I'll even wash up afterwards,' he promised to ironic cheers. There was a reason for his largesse: he had not yet shown his hand but he had definite designs on the delectable Maya – once this fucking boring watch had been called off.

The girls – he had to remember to stop calling them girls, it pissed them off – had just finished renewing the grey tint in his hair and painting ageing lines into his face. They said they were giving him the face they judged he would have in thirty years' time. He would, they agreed, undoubtedly become an ugly old bastard.

Alongside the badinage, they were all fretting at the lack of action, the confinement of Denny's small house and the inconvenience of the body armour.

They dared not disobey orders. The guv'nors were wont to slip into the house unannounced via the back garden. They'd all been caught out once. After the bollockings, never again!

The two women wore belt holsters containing snub-nose .38 revolvers while Passingham favoured an underarm holster and a .9mm Browning automatic. WPC Crombie was 'wife' and wore a cardigan to conceal her deadly waistline. WPC Considine was 'daughter', more comfortable in blue jeans and loose blouse.

They were relaxed. They could not be taken by surprise. The house was monitored back and front from concealed observation points. The OP in front was situated in the first-floor bedroom of the house directly opposite.

As the trio ate the eggs and bacon Passingham had cooked quite ably, their ears were cocked to the monotony of the police radio commentary informing them of every vehicle and passer-by in Tangmere Avenue.

A dog-walker had gone past, heading for the common, several cars, a removal van, a Thames Water lorry . . .

The radio crackled and the voice from across the road said, 'Hello, the postman's calling . . . He's at your gate . . . Now he's on your path, sorting out your stuff . . . There's a parcel. Ooooh, wonder if it's a nice pressie for someone? The postman is about to ring your bell . . .'

Almost as soon as the observer finished speaking, the sound of the doorbell shrilled along the passageway.

'Shit,' said Sergeant Passingham, and put down his fork. He reached for his jacket to conceal his holster. The two police-women continued eating.

As he turned out of the kitchen into the narrow passage alongside the stairs, he could see the shape of the postman's head distorted by the coloured sections in the stained glass panel that formed the top third of the door.

The bell shrilled a second time. 'Okay, okay. Coming,' said Passingham. He turned the key in the five-lever mortice, twisted the worn brass knob of the Yale and pulled the green-painted door towards him.

Oscar had already edged out from the line of parked cars and was slowly moving the Corolla forward.

From his rear, Sergeant Passingham heard a sudden burst of radio chatter from the blabbermouth in the house opposite. The words that reached him at the front end of the house were so much distorted cackle.

What blabbermouth was screaming into his set was. 'Abort! Abort! The postman has a gun!' He'd just observed Kaz lift the sawn-off out of the trolley and let it dangle down his right leg.

Several things happened simultaneously. Oscar pressed the metal to the floor, Policewomen Crombie and Considine sent their breakfast flying and tugged free their firearms. And Passingham completed opening the door and said, 'Good morning.'

The sergeant's hand went out to take the parcel that the postman was proffering with his left hand.

At the same moment, the urgency, if not the sense, of the frantic radio messages emanating from the kitchen began to register in Sergeant Passingham's brain.

Too late. Kaz turned slightly and launched a powerful kick with the flat of his foot into his chest. The police officer's lungs instantly ejected all air in one great gout via his astonished open mouth and he staggered.

Kaz dropped the parcel, took one step across the threshold, brought up the sawn-off and gave him a blast in the chest at close quarters that no man could withstand.

Passingham was hurled backwards to the foot of Denny Fling's staircase. He was still flying as Kaz, satisfied, stepped back outside on to the tiny porch and pulled the front door shut behind him, sealing in the chaos.

He kicked aside the trolley, scattering letters on a bed of crocuses, and lunged for the gate as Oscar came roaring up in the Corolla.

Inside the house, the two policewomen, aghast, came storming into the passageway and were confronted by the appalling sight of Sergeant Passingham's sprawled body. They heard the Yale lock click shut and glimpsed the tip of the assailant's retreating head through the stained glass.

'Get him!' screamed Maya Considine. 'Get the bastard!'

She jumped over Passingham, landed four-square facing the door and began pumping rounds through the woodwork. Screaming like a banshee, Jill Crombie threw herself full length alongside her and began to empty her magazine in the same direction.

Denny Fling's front door all but disintegrated in a shower of splinters and glass fragments as the rounds hit home and bored through.

Oscar had the passenger door open. His face was a study in desperation. 'Kaz,' he bellowed. 'It's a set-up. Get in here!'

The spring-hinged gate had swung shut, barring the killer's flight. Kazuo Iwasaki had a hand on the galvanized drop-catch when a round, spinning in a trajectory distorted by its passage through the front door's wood panelling, struck him in the spine and careered around the lower cavities of his body doing fatal damage to his internal organs.

It did not matter. The next round took him in the heart and he fell across the gate, already dying. He raised his head to look, puzzled, into Oscar's frantic face and then the blood gushed crimson from his mouth and the narrow, neat head dropped.

'Jesus!' Oscar could see that the bastards who'd hit Kaz were trying to drag open the shattered door. They were being hampered by the debris they themselves had created. He grabbed the Uzi, leaned across the empty seat where Kaz should now be sitting, if everything had remained sweet, and fired a burst at the house front to discourage pursuit.

He dropped the weapon, yanked the car into gear and took off. From the corner of his right eye, he saw movement for the first time in the garden of a house on the other side of the road. He glanced over and cursed. It came from a cop wearing a checkered blue cap and armed with a heavy piece.

'Holy Christ!' said Oscar, crouching low and uncertain as to whether he should get out of there fast or stay and shoot it out with this asshole. He decided to go. They'd walked into a trap. There could be more of them on the ground at any second.

The cop who had been the radio chatterer hurled himself into the lee of a garden wall, and raised his Heckler and Koch. In an instant, he took in the situation. Fuck the required shouted warning. A fellow officer was down. He'd worry later about the board of inquiry. The fucking Toyota was getting away.

He stood up and began to pump rounds at the retreating vehicle. Then he leaped the wall and ran down the road, awkwardly changing magazines and screaming, 'Police officer! Get back! Get back!' The sound of mayhem was bringing residents out into their front gardens.

Three hundred yards along the road, when he'd almost reached the common, Oscar took his first hit. The car swerved as his hands involuntarily jerked upward and he lost control of the wheel. The car veered and struck the kerb with such force that it turned on its side and skidded, with a shriek of tortured metal, across the pavement and into a garden, uprooting bushes and plants before it was stopped by a lime tree.

The windscreen fragmented into a million diamonds and

Oscar landed in a heap with his lacerated cheek pressed through the driver's open window and into the earth. He felt something clatter on to his crumpled frame. The Uzi.

The sight of it gave him fresh power, and with a supreme effort he rolled his bulky frame out through the windscreen, dragging the weapon with him. The sudden searing lance of pain told him the location of his wound. He'd been hit below the left shoulder.

There was a sound. He looked upward. A woman drying her hands on a towel had appeared at her front door. She had come out to help an injured motorist. Then she saw the Uzi, gave a short scream and ran back inside. Oscar could hear her putting on the security chain.

He shook his head like a wet dog to clear the fog. The blood was already seeping through the windcheater. Red on both sides, he thought dumbly.

Oscar tore his mind back to imminent danger. He clawed at the tree and hauled himself to his feet. The wrecked Toyota's offside wheels were still turning slowly. He looked over the vehicle. The bastard who'd plugged him was advancing warily down the road. A dame in jeans, holding a piece pointed skywards, was also coming up fast on foot. Distantly, Oscar could hear the wail of police sirens.

He had to get outta there – *fast*!

The cop in the road saw him bring up the Uzi and, to Oscar's satisfaction, dived for the nearest wall. Oscar gave him a brief burst just to demonstrate he still had killer rounds in the magazine. He surveyed his situation. He was just three houses from the open common where there were trees and bushes and perhaps sanctuary.

He cursed the garden layouts. Back home, the neighbours shared unobstructed front lawns. The insular Brits sealed themselves in with dividing fences, shrubbery and walls.

Oscar waded into the lattice fencing and flattened it. He charged on groggily, blundering through plants and a hedge-row and painfully clambering over a four-foot wall of mellow old bricks. He was like a mad hurdler with demons in pursuit.

Suddenly he was there. Only the roadway separated him from the green expanse of the common.

A brick pillar with a pyramid capping stone marked the street corner. He flattened himself against it and peered back into Tangmere Avenue. Both the cop and the dame were moving up again. They had to be discouraged long enough to give him time to get across the road and into the trees.

Oscar Ruttmann blinked to clear his eyes, thrust the Uzi round the pillar and squeezed the trigger.

Nathaniel Marley was about to become a hero of sorts. Nathaniel, aged thirty-six, was a water-softener salesman and a married man with two children. Later, the official version of his story was that, when things began to happen, he was on the way to see a prospective buyer in nearby Thornton Heath. And so he was – although the appointment was for ten-thirty a.m. But that was a mere detail that no one thought to query.

Right now the time was nine and Nat was cruising alongside the common in his Mercedes 190 looking for his morning pick-me-up, a prostitute who called herself Kimberley. This was a weekly encounter because Nat's wife had turned funny about sex ever since the difficult birth of their second child.

Kimberley grumbled about getting up early, but Nat was a reliable regular and he sometimes gave her a little present in addition to the money. Which is more than you could say for most of her punters.

He'd just spotted her in the distance in her black thigh boots – yummy! his favourites – when an apparition burst out of a roadway to his left. The bloke, as Nat told it later, was like a half-mad Conan the Barbarian – massive and frightening.

'At first I thought, He's been at the hard stuff early. He was lurching and swaying and looked half-cut. I almost shit myself when I saw the gun and the blood on his chest. When he pointed the thing down the road and let fly, I *did* shit myself. In complete panic I braked hard, which was a mistake because he heard the scream of my tyres, saw me and ran into the road pointing the gun at my windscreen.

'You should have seen his face. It was twisted – the face of someone from the loony-bin. If you want the God's honest truth, I totally lost it. I thought, He's going to shoot me and take my car.

'Almost without thinking, I ducked and pressed the accelerator. I felt the car jerk forward. Immediately there was an almighty thump and I felt the wheels go over something. I knew straight away I'd hit him. Bang went my no-claims bonus.

'I scrambled out, and I'm not ashamed to say I was shaking. It didn't help that I almost trod on his face. The front wheel had gone over him and his body was directly under my Merc with his head poking out and facing upwards. He was staring at me. Even lying there helpless, he was so scary.

'Despite my nerves, I had the presence of mind to kick his gun into the gutter. He was still alive at that point, a few moments before the police officers came running up. But it was obvious to me that his huge chest had been stoved in by the underside of my car. Blood was spreading everywhere like spilt paint and I thought he was a goner. Then I saw his lips move. He was trying to say something to me. There was nothing I could do on my own to help him but I knelt down nervously to listen. This was difficult because his mouth was bubbling spit and blood. He managed to say, "My real name is Rat Man. Don't let them put me in Potter's Field." Then he began to dribble and his eyes closed. I guess I actually witnessed his death.

'Well, he was Rat Man, all right, and I assumed he'd seen too many Hollywood movies because, in America, Potter's Field is where the down-and-outs get dumped. Of course, I didn't know until much later he actually *was* American and that I'd misheard his name. They're a gun-crazy bunch, aren't they? They never learn.'

Tangmere Avenue and a short section of Garrad's Road on the edge of the common resembled a battle-zone. The police barriers were up, the entire front garden and shattered façade of Denny Fling's house screened from the public gaze by tarpaulins and a tent placed over Nathaniel Marley's Mercedes.

A long line of officers in dungarees was moving laboriously down Tangmere Avenue chalk-marking and taping the sites of mayhem and locating the expended bullet casings of both the police shooters and the killer.

The media were being kept at a distance. Ringrose and Firth could hear their angry cries of protest floating down the road. The detectives had ordered a total news blackout while they concocted a convincing scenario.

Denny's houseminders had already been whisked away to a sealed ward of St Thomas's Hospital, across the Thames from the Houses of Parliament. Ringrose and Firth followed on.

They found everyone still shaking like aspen leaves now that the tension was gone and the adrenaline had drained away, leaving the quartet feeling as if their veins had been pumped full of fast-moving cold air.

They'd all handed in their weapons for examination and bagging as evidence, but they were still on duty. Ringrose said immediately, 'Send someone for a bottle of brandy, for God's sake.'

The two policewomen flanked Sergeant Passingham's bed like on-duty caryatids. He smiled weakly and raised a bandaged hand in greeting as the two senior officers entered the guarded room. The chattering constable who had made the final pursuit of Oscar Ruttmann was slumped in a chair. He was unhurt.

Passingham's clothes and body armour had been stripped off and he had been put into a pair of pyjama bottoms. His naked upper torso looked as if someone had worked him over with a wooden club.

The deepening bruises stretched in a ragged circle from a point just below his shoulders down to his navel. The blast from the would-be assassin's shotgun had been blocked impressively by the body armour but the chest beneath had taken an overall sledge-hammer impact from the lead shot.

A police doctor was going as delicately as he could over his ribs, seeking underlying injury. Sergeant Passingham winced but the doctor said finally, 'I don't think the damage is any more serious than you can see although Sergeant Passingham is going to be a very sore man for a couple of weeks. We'll do some X-rays to make sure. We've put a dozen stitches into his right hand which he was holding out in front of him to accept the parcel when the flesh was ripped by peripheral pellets but the scarring should be minimal.' The doctor smiled at his patient. 'Sergeant Passingham has been fortunate. If the gunman had waited for him to stagger back just one more pace, the shot would have had a greater spread and would certainly have resulted in damage to his unprotected face and possibly caused death or blindness.'

He patted Passingham's head. 'Your assailant was just too eager to bump you off. Perhaps he had a train to catch.'

When the doctor had left the room, Ringrose and Firth congratulated and thanked the four officers. WPC Considine said, 'We should be thanking you, sir. I'll admit we thought you were being a bit fuddy-duddy when you sent the order for us to wear the armour full-time. Well, we know better now, don't we? Those guys were complete maniacs.'

Ringrose said, 'For reasons I cannot explain, all four of you are to be kept out of sight for the immediate future. There'll be no press interviews, no photographs. The inquest on the dead men will be opened and adjourned immediately. None of you will be required to give evidence at this stage. I'm afraid your bravery must wait a while before it is properly recognized.

'You'll not discuss any detail of this incident with fellow officers. Furthermore, you may see me quoted in the press and appearing on television saying things that you know to be downright lies. Don't be thrown. It is all part of a plan that

Detective Inspector Firth and I are about to put into operation to net some very dangerous people.'

Not a word of the Tangmere Avenue slaughter had reached Denny Fling and his family in their safe house in Croydon for the simple reason that Ringrose had telephoned ahead and told the senior protection officer to pull the TV plug and silence the radio.

Consequently, Ringrose and Firth found the Fling family restive. The dissatisfaction turned to horror when they gave the Flings an accurate account of the day's events. 'They were two hired killers and the person they were hired to kill was you, Mr Fling,' said Ringrose heavily.

The three Flings huddled on the same settee and clung to each other. 'Jasus,' said Denny. 'I wish I'd never set eyes on those focking reporters. I should never have opened my stupid mouth. What's to stop Vernon Gatling from hiring more and more of those fockers until one of them finally gets me? He has enough money to get the entire focking IRA to do his dirty work.'

'I don't think we need worry about the IRA for once,' said Firth. 'Our plan is to get Vernon and his mad daughter. Stop the paymasters and we stop the attempts on your life.'

'And how do you propose to do that?'

'Brace yourself, Mr Fling,' said Firth.

'We're going to announce that the killers got you,' said Ringrose.

Mrs Fling crossed herself. 'Holy Mother, what is the man saying?'

Denny clasped her hand. 'And what will that do, apart from upsetting my relatives and friends?'

'You give me a list of your nearest and dearest and we'll look after them for a few days – just as long as it takes for news of your death to lure Vernon and Tabitha Gatling back on to British soil where we can arrest them.

'They're on their boat in the Mediterranean and they won't come back until they believe they're safe. You are the main threat to Vernon's freedom because you can place him at the site of Lawrence Varnish's murder. The only other person who

317

could do that was his father, Gunner. Whether by luck or foul play, he is now dead. You're the bait on our hook to catch a man who has built a vast fortune on murder. Would you want him to get away with it?'

The press conference was the most unsatisfactory that Tom Ringrose had ever conducted. In the light of his previous triumphs in murder investigations, his status with journalists was little short of iconic. But Ringrose's pedestal was now undergoing a severe chipping.

'. . . the police had taken seriously a death threat on a Streatham householder . . . protection had been given but unfortunately his fears had been well founded and, despite a police presence, he had been shot and killed . . . However, the two perpetrators had been challenged by armed officers and gunfire had been exchanged during which the two perpetrators had been shot dead . . .'

No, at present he could supply no names. Delicate inquiries were continuing.

No, he could not confirm that the killings were connected with the murders in Chiswick nor the one in Rotherhithe.

Why, then, was he also leading the investigation of the assassination in Streatham? Didn't he already have enough corpses to keep him busy? (Cries of 'Yeah, what about that?' at this sarcastic thrust.)

'I can make no comment at this time,' said Ringrose, who was not usually a pompous man.

The crime reporters grilled him to a crisp but Ringrose doggedly blanked off every attempt to extract from him the crucial connection between the killings.

On the way out, a reporter known as the Prince of Darkness, because he favoured black cloaks in his daily attire, brushed shoulders with Ringrose and complained, 'That was a fucking waste of time, Tom.'

'Not entirely, Jimmy,' said Ringrose mildly. The name Gatling had not crossed anyone's lips. No hack had attempted to get him in a corner for a private word about rumours that had come his way concerning a very rich man and his lovely daughter.

Ringrose was satisfied there had been no leaks from his intricate investigation. There was nothing that Vernon would hear on the news bulletins or read in next day's papers to alarm him.

Ringrose bought a consoling pint for the Prince of Darkness and then went back to his office where he issued a ports alert and waited.

Chapter Eleven

They went ashore at St Tropez to pick up the English-language newspapers. They studied the zoom-lens photographs of the scene of the shoot-out and carefully analysed Ringrose's cautious words.

'Christ, it couldn't be better,' whispered Vernon Gatling. 'Those two gravediggers got Denny the Mouth and then the coppers got them. It's perfect. There's no one left to lay a glove on us.'

He stretched his arms high above his head. 'God! I can feel the weight lifting as I speak.'

For the first time in ages, his upturned face was pink and untroubled. She thought he looked no more than a man of forty. She wanted to sit on his knee and kiss him all over his dear head but they were in public. She compromised by holding his hand and pressing it to her cheek.

In the Byblos bar, they shared a bottle of Pol Roger. Tabitha said suddenly, 'Daddy, won't your friend in New York be upset – at the loss of two of his men, I mean?'

'I don't see why,' said her father. 'Those guys were professionals. They knew the score. I'll put some more money their way – for their families. Come to think of it, we don't even know if our late friends Ganz and Beamish *had* families.'

Father and daughter strolled arm-in-arm back along the harbour. Vernon was humming. He immediately gave his captain orders to set sail for the *Black Glove*'s permanent mooring at Antibes.

'We're going home,' said Vernon gleefully. 'We're in the clear.'

'Cabin six, bunks two and three,' said the mortuary attendant cheerfully. Each stainless-steel refrigerator contained three sliding shelves.

The attendant liked to regard his domain as a cruise liner in which the passengers were cosily tucked up three to a cabin.

They were always so well behaved, he liked to joke. They never complained. They demanded minimal room service, apart from the obese ones who tended to get wedged, and the rotters from the river.

Unidentified male number one was in bunk two. The attendant slid him out and tugged down the body-bag zipper. Archie Kenny nervously inclined his head and studied the cleaned-up face of Kazuo Iwasaki.

Never particularly expressive, in death the killer's face was bland to the point of featurelessness, apart from the slightly Oriental cast of his eyes and brow that Kenny had failed to observe in life.

'It could be,' said Kenny helplessly. 'But nothing about him exactly leaps out at you, does it?'

'I keep a hammer and pointed stake for that sort of emergency,' cackled the attendant.

'All right, zip him up and let's see the other one,' said Ringrose, ignoring the gallows humour.

Oscar Ruttmann was in bunk three. The moment the zip fastener divided, Kenny said, 'Now you're talking. That's the nose. That is definitely the guy I picked up at Gatwick and ferried to Tabitha Gatling.'

When Kenny had been escorted from the room, Ringrose turned to the mortuary attendant and said, 'Cool it, Sid. We're bringing in an old lady.'

With the decorum of an undertaker, Sid showed Mrs Nancy Leith his passengers. She looked down sadly at Kazuo Iwasaki and murmured, 'Such a pale little thing. How could that frail body have contained such wickedness?'

She gazed, unflinching, at Oscar and told Ringrose, 'Just as I said – a man with a child's nose.' She gave positive identification of both as being the men she'd seen waiting outside the Chiswick death house.

The widow turned to leave the long, spotless mortuary with its pitiless overhead lighting glinting off the serried ranks of Sid's cabin doors but stopped and, with those shrewd little eyes, took in the antiseptic scene. 'Given my rapidly advancing age, I suppose it's highly likely they'll be wheeling me in here before long. How depressing,' she said.

Sid the attendant was about to reply, 'Don't worry, darling. I'll see you get an upper berth on the first-class deck,' when he caught Ringrose's warning eye. 'Don't worry, darling,' he said, hastily rejigging his patter. 'You look good for a few knees-ups yet. Whatcha doing next Saturday night?'

Photographs of the dead killers' frozen features were taken and the pictures animated in a computer, with the eyes opened by an artist. Copies were sent to the FBI in Washington and also released to the newspapers. The response from the staff of the two Bayswater hotels where the killers had stayed so discreetly was immediate.

Despite rigorous scientific examination of the modest rooms and their clothing, the only solid result was the finding of both men's passports in the names of Charles Ganz and Lon Beamish. These were swiftly proved by the FBI to have been stolen from the original owners and doctored.

But the circumstantial evidence involving Tabitha Gatling was piling up. The men's false names were on the manifests of the aeroplanes that Archie Kenny had met at Gatwick and Heathrow. Kenny was now a direct link between known killers and Tabitha Gatling. Over his protests, he and his young wife were placed under immediate police protection and he was informed, to his immense distress, that he would almost certainly be unable to return to Gatling employment.

What worked for the British police also worked for the Americans. Photographs of the hitmen were published across the fifty states. As a result, a shocked Cape May woman came forward to claim 'Rat Man' as her husband, Oscar Ruttmann, and Greenwich Village friends of the absent dancer came forward to identify Kaz. The details of their grotesque friendship, and the toy conventions that always took place in towns where there had been an unsolved killing in the proximity, began to unfold.

With their usual machine thoroughness, the FBI referred back to their surveillance files on Albert Penn. Sure enough, they came up with two misty photographs of Oscar Ruttmann in Albert's company. 'Unfortunately, *comandante*, there's no audio-tape to go with them,' Marty Groot explained to Ringrose. 'Albert only ever met the guy in the open and briefly at that. Until now, the Bureau was never able to identify him.'

'Still, it's another nail in the Gatling coffin,' said Ringrose. 'The link now goes unbroken from Vernon in Costa Rica to Albert Penn in New York to Ruttmann and Iwasaki to our witness Archie Kenny to Tabitha Gatling and, once again, to the two killers.'

'Do you want us to lean on Albert Penn?' said Groot.

'Is there anything to be gained?'

'Not unless he's looking for a hundred-year vacation in the Federal pen at Marion,' said the FBI man. 'Truth is, we'd rather leave him *suspecting* the extent of our surveillance than actually *knowing*. We're not yet ready to get him under RICO but we will.'

'RICO?'

'Yeah, our Racketeer-influenced Corrupt Organizations programme,' said Groot.

'Then leave him in blissful ignorance,' said Ringrose. 'Let sleeping dons lie.'

Chapter Twelve

Ringrose had been damned underhand, complained Sir Marcus Coombes. During their previous meeting in the commissioner's office, why had he not informed the Gatling family solicitor that he proposed to arrest his clients?

'Would they have returned to Britain if I had?' Ringrose was as blunt as a battle tank. He was determined not to give quarter to this legal wheeler-dealer with his whispers, nudges, contacts and conduits to preferments delicately hinted at.

'My clients have nothing to fear in returning to the land of their birth,' snorted the old boy.

Clearly Vernon had kicked him in his august, pinstriped arse for leaving him unprepared for the police reception he and Tabitha had received when the Gatling jet touched down at Gatwick airport.

Ringrose and the solicitor faced each other in the custody suite at Kensington. Coombes said, 'Their absence from these shores, as I afforded you the courtesy of explaining, was in order to observe a period of family mourning. I shall vigorously challenge any implied guilt arising from their absence abroad. I have instructed both Mr Gatling and his daughter that they are to make no statements either to you or any of your officers unless I am present at the interview.'

'I wouldn't want it any other way,' said Ringrose mildly. 'We are investigating the gravest matters and I promise you everything will be done according to the Police and Criminal Evidence Act. I take it your clients will be willing to assist in this and will not be deliberately obstructive?'

For once the old crocodile's skin was penetrated. 'Commander Ringrose, my clients are not criminals. They are always ready to assist the Law in any way they can – although both of them have already expressed to me their bafflement. They have no idea why their London house was arbitrarily searched in their absence nor why they have been detained in this undignified way. Why could you not approach me to arrange an interview with them in a more civilized manner? I shall have something to say to your commissioner and the home secretary about this. Vernon Gatling is a great public benefactor. He deserves better.'

'Maybe,' said Ringrose. 'As the Bard said, "Use every man after his desert, and who should escape whipping?" Sir Marcus, if you will return at two p.m. we shall begin questioning Miss Gatling concerning a number of recent violent deaths.'

From the moment they'd escorted her off the plane she had not been allowed to see her father. She'd heard him shouting and protesting behind her but two policewomen had hurried her down the steps and into the police car that was waiting on the tarmac.

'How dare you!' she repeated, several times, as they shoved her unceremoniously along and silently manhandled her into the back seat. One read her the caution and her rights but, in her rage, she barely heard.

Now, somewhat dishevelled, she was seated alongside old Coombes and opposite that bastard Ringrose – she'd read all about him – and his monkey, Detective Inspector Lionel Firth, who carefully read her her rights once again and opened the questioning by trying to take the piss.

What scholastic qualifications did she have? *A handful of GCSEs.*

No university degree? *No.*

What was her occupation? *She didn't have one.*

What was the source of her income? *Everyone knew her father was rich. She also had a trust fund.*

What was her address? *She had a number of addresses. Which did he have in mind?*

London? *You mean the house in Cheyne Walk.*

The weekend before she took her grandfather on a Mediterranean cruise: where was she? *Here and there.*

Here and there where? *Mostly in London.*

Where did she sleep on Saturday and Sunday nights? *At Cheyne Walk.*

(At this point Ringrose and Firth observed Tabitha, who had been effecting a nonchalant slouch, stiffen a little.)

Could anyone vouch for that? *She'd slept alone, if that's what he was driving at.*

Anyone else in the house? *She'd given the staff a weekend off.*

That's not what he asked. Any guests? Any visitors? *No.*

Bit odd, wasn't it, for a popular girl-about-town? No Saturday night date? *No doubt the inspector could sing that oldie, 'Saturday Night Is The Loneliest Night Of The Week'. What could she say?*

Didn't she have callers during the day on Saturday? *Not that she remembered.*

Not even from one of her father's employees? *Nothing came to mind. She met so many of his workers.*

What about a chap named Archie Kenny?

Tabitha Gatling was now sitting upright with her manicured hands tightly intertwined on the table. She was silent for a beat of five, then she said, 'I need to talk to Sir Marcus.'

When they all returned to the table and the tape was again running, she said, 'I realize now you must be referring to the weekend when a couple of Americans who were involved in some confidential business negotiations with my father flew in. They were collected at the airport by Mr Kenny, one of my father's employees. I gave the Americans beds for a couple of nights as a matter of courtesy.'

'What were their names?' asked Firth.

'Oh dear. I've forgotten.'

'Describe them.'

'I really don't remember much about them. Business affairs bore me. I let them into the house, showed them their rooms and left them to it. It's a big house. I never saw them again. They left me a thank-you note on Monday morning and were gone by the time I got up. I'm not an early riser.'

'Do you have the note?'

'I think I must have binned it. Yes, I'm sure I did.'

Firth showed her photographs of the two contract killers. 'Are these the two men who came for the weekend?'

'No, I don't think so.'

'You don't seem at all surprised at being shown these particular photographs?'

'Why should I be?'

'Because these photographs have been all over the news-papers and on television as being those of two particularly vicious killers. If I'd been shown these photographs and was in your place, I'd have jumped and said Good God! I've most certainly not seen those two.'

'Really, Detective Inspector!' intervened Sir Marcus. 'You are trying to put words into my client's mouth. Is she to be criticized merely because she is a worldly woman who is not easily shocked?'

Unruffled, Firth went on, 'Archie Kenny has identified these two men as being the same two he delivered into your care on that Saturday.'

'He's seeing things.'

'How much was Mr Kenny paid for his services as chauffeur?'

'How should I know? I told you, he works for my father, not for me.'

'He says you handed him a thousand pounds in used bills.'

'That's ridiculous. If he has a thousand pounds, it certainly didn't come from me.'

'The thousand is in his building society account. But it was handed to him in an envelope. This one.' Firth produced the evidence bag like a conjuror and held it so that she could see the envelope through the plastic window.

'What are they trying to do to me?' cried Tabitha, turn-ing to Sir Marcus for help. 'I've never seen that envelope before.'

'Then perhaps you can explain how your fingerprints hap-pen to be on it and what Archie Kenny has to gain by concocting such a story?'

'How should I know? I don't know the man. He could be the one you're after,' she said wildly, and began to weep.

They didn't wait for the lawyer to ask for an adjournment. Ringrose said, 'Talk to her, Sir Marcus. Your client is being less than frank with us.'

The old crocodile corrugated his lips and nodded grimly without speaking. He knew when to bite and when to digest.

*

Vernon Gatling was allowed to stew in the cells at Bishopsgate, a long way from his daughter being held in Kensington. He and a visibly tiring Sir Marcus Coombes spent half an hour in private consultation before the solicitor would allow his client to be interviewed.

By the time they trooped into the interview room, Ringrose had no doubt that Tabitha's fraught session with Firth and himself had been relayed word for word to the doting father. Ringrose was satisfied. He wanted Vernon rattled from the outset.

Once again, Ringrose of the Metropolitan Police was present for the interview. But this time Detective Superintendent Bert Dalton of the City of London Police handled the questioning and came at Vernon from a different angle.

Vernon, the cut-to-the-chase businessman, did not make a pretence of not knowing who Larry Varnish was. 'I read the papers,' he grunted. 'Let's get on with it. His body was found on the site of the old Fletcher Hall. Right?'

'We'd like you to explain how it got there,' said Dalton.

'How the fuck would I know? If what I've read is true, the poor little sod died more than forty years ago.'

'You were the contractor. A layer of concrete was used to seal the body into an old well. How do you account for that?'

'I don't account for it. The City is riddled with old wells. Builders cover them all the time. It's no big deal.'

'It becomes a big deal when the body has been stripped of its clothing and builders' lime poured over it in an attempt to destroy it.'

'I wouldn't know about that. From what I've heard of that Varnish kid, he was an accident waiting to happen – a regular will-o'-the-wisp on those bomb sites. What's to say he didn't fall in without any help from the outside?'

'What, then danced around naked and covered himself in lime? Come on, Mr Gatling, you can do better than that.'

'I'm just giving you a likely solution. Suppose he had an accident, just like I said, and some of the men on piecework on the site found him dead? They could have been laid off for days without pay while your people sniffed around, looking for suspicious circumstances. The site workers couldn't do anything for the lad so they sealed off the well and avoided a nasty loss of wages. Stranger things have happened.'

'I can see you've been giving the matter a great deal of thought,' said Dalton. 'But what about this for a scenario. Varnish had discovered important Roman remains that would have held up rebuilding work for months and cost you a great deal of money. You'd already seen something like it happen up the road at the Mithras temple site. You and your father confronted Varnish, there was an argument and you killed him to shut him up and save your bank balance.'

Vernon leaped out of his seat and leaned across the table. He roared into Dalton's face. 'That is BULLSHIT!' He turned to Sir Marcus, who was clutching the arm of his client's silver-grey suit and attempting to pull him back into his chair. 'Can these bastards do this to me?'

'Please, Vernon. These are merely allegations, easily refuted.'

Dalton said, 'Tell me, Mr Gatling, do you know a man named Denny Fling?'

Vernon took a mouthful of water and rolled it round his tongue before swallowing. His mouth had become suddenly parched. He said, 'Denny used to be one of my foremen.'

'On the Fletcher Hall contract?'

'Could be. I wouldn't like to swear to it, after all this time.'

'He says he was. He gave us a statement.'

'There you go, then.'

'He said that on the Monday morning, the day after Larry Varnish went missing, you and your father sent the entire labour force home and he helped you bulldoze the remains of a Roman temple. He also remembers seeing an area of freshly laid concrete – laid by you during the weekend after the men had gone off at noon on the Saturday. He put it down to your eagerness to obliterate all signs of the Roman presence before the museum people got wind of it.'

'Denny Fling was telling you fairy-tales. There were no Roman remains and no such event ever took place. I hope he's burning in hell for saying that.'

'What makes you think he's dead?'

Vernon opened his mouth and shut it again. 'I just assumed . . .' he said. 'He must be getting on a bit.'

The tycoon found his nerve again and said defiantly, 'If he's still alive, you bring him here to this dump and I'll call him a bloody liar to his face.'

Neither detective responded. Dalton looked at him impassively, and asked, 'Why would he lie? What's in it for him?'

'Probably to save his own skin. If the kid was murdered, as you say, why couldn't Denny or one of his team be responsible? The little bugger was notorious for doing deals for artefacts dug up all over the City. They were perks of the job for all the contractors' men. Maybe Varnish had double-crossed one of them.'

'It's very plausible,' conceded Dalton. 'But I want you to listen to a tape-recording that offers an account of what really happened.'

They watched Vernon's eyes narrow as his father's shaky voice filled the room, with Nelly Tripp coaxing him along in an account of how his only son had battered Larry Varnish to death with a bricklayer's hod.

This time, the detectives were ready for Vernon when he hurtled from his chair screaming, 'This is a fit-up. That tape is a forgery. It's all lies.'

Sir Marcus was also on his feet shouting. 'This is monstrous. No judge would admit as evidence this shabby attempt to pit a mentally ill father against his only son. The man is dead. This can be nothing but hearsay of the most suspect kind. I must advise my client to decline to answer any further questions at this time.'

'Mr Gatling goes back to the cells. We've not done yet,' said Dalton grimly.

Chapter Thirteen

They'd come to the point that most coppers hate: the moment at which the Crown Prosecution Service thrusts itself uninvited into any investigation.

The stealthy hand of Sir Marcus Coombes was easy to detect and he was helped by the media. Thanks to the alertness of the news agency that covers Gatwick airport, the world now knew that the building tycoon Vernon Gatling and his luscious daughter – repeat publication of the breast-baring pictures – were, incredibly, being questioned over a number of violent deaths.

The assistant commissioner (crime) said to Ringrose, 'Sorry, Tom. Orders from on high. The Gatlings are to be handled as if they're made of sweating gelignite. The CPS is sending a bod along to ensure everything is done by the book titled *How To Keep Your Nose Clean*.'

The 'bod' turned out to be Ms Honor Pargeter, barrister-at-law, who affected a severely bobbed hairdo, a black two-piece suit, black sheer stockings and a white blouse that buttoned up to her throat. She was thirty-four and one senior judge had been heard to opine that Ms Pargeter would, *inter alia*, make a marvellous dominatrix.

Ringrose, Firth and Dalton fed her all the statements and transcripts and tried hard to stay in her good books. Finally, she took off her glasses with the mimsy oval wire frames and said crisply, 'You've just about got Miss Gatling for conspiracy to murder. But keep piling on the agony. Get the witness, Mrs Leith, to have a look at her in a dark wig and beret. Hammer her with motive – the elimination of witnesses and the stealing of the journalists' archive. And what does she have to say about the Rotherhithe chap with the guns?'

The three detectives, jointly mustering some eighty-five years of experience, contrived to look humbly grateful for these insights – as if Ms Pargeter were revealing new lines of inquiry that would never have occurred to them.

Oblivious, she cracked on, shaking her head over the case they'd so far built against Vernon. 'If his father were still alive, you'd have Vernon skewered for the murder of Varnish. That tape is quite damning although I'd have wanted the old man to repeat everything in the witness box.

'Vernon's connection to the contract killers is altogether more tenuous. He wasn't in the country when any of these murders was committed and I don't see the FBI blowing their long-term surveillance on this frightful chap Albert Penn just to give us a few snatches of recorded telephone conversation. They are indicative of Vernon's involvement but not conclusive. Who would give us expert testimony as to Penn's position in the Mafia hierarchy? According to FBI records, he has only ever been convicted for minor misdemeanours.'

She took in their sombre faces. 'Gentlemen, you need something more. Put up or let him go.'

A magistrate had granted Ringrose and Dalton extensions of the detention orders for up to ninety-six hours. Sir Marcus Coombes was reeling from the constant cross-town commuting between Vernon and Tabitha, even though he enjoyed a chauffeured Daimler and the help of two juniors to organize his papers.

There was more than one way of skinning a buzzard, thought Ringrose with relish.

For the resumed questioning of Tabitha, Ringrose took over the bowling. She'd asked for and been granted a complete change of clothes and these had been brought to the station by the housekeeper, Mrs Burroughs, whose mood was bitter.

She told the custody officer, 'I may lose my job because of you lot. Sir Marcus has given me an awful telling-off for letting you into the house and talking about Miss Tabitha. Thanks a bloody bundle!'

When a policewoman ushered Tabitha into the interview room, Ringrose saw she had changed from her casual travelling kit – jeans and T-shirt – and was now wearing a Vivienne Westwood two-piece suit in racing green. She had also renewed her makeup and was obviously making an attempt to reassert her vibrant personality in this alien environment.

Ringrose wasted no time. 'The two Americans to whom you acted as hostess for the weekend—' he began.

But her solicitor wasn't so weary that he'd let that pass. 'Commander, Miss Gatling previously told you she merely provided beds and a roof over their heads. The word "hostess" implies an intimacy that was entirely absent,' he complained.

'Very well. What business could they have with your father if he was in Costa Rica?'

Since the last session, Tabitha had been well primed by Sir Marcus. She assumed an apologetic air, which wasn't one that came easily to her. She gazed earnestly into Ringrose's unblinking eyes and said, 'I think I may have got the wrong end of the stick. I've had time to go back over events and I've remembered what my father told me in a phone call from Central America.'

'And what was that?' Coombes frowned at Ringrose's undisguised note of sarcasm .

'The two men were actually friends of American business friends. My father had never actually met them and certainly had no personal business with them. He was told that these people were passing through London and could he say hello – as a courtesy. He'd issued the invitation quite casually. That sort of thing happens all the time in business life – it's merely a goodwill gesture. Of course, my father wasn't here to meet these strangers. But he told me he'd already arranged for a car to pick them up – your Mr Kenny – and I said I'd show willing by offering them a bed. When they arrived, they appeared not to want to be sociable so I left them to their own devices.'

'So why clear the house of servants?'

'I didn't do it for the Americans' sake. I'd been expecting a boyfriend for the weekend but he let me down. I told you the truth when I said I slept alone.'

'What's this boyfriend's name?'

'I'm sorry, I don't see why he should be dragged into this mess.'

'You had another purpose in clearing out the servants, didn't you? You went shopping for firearms.'

Tabitha Gatling looked stunned. She turned hopelessly to

Sir Marcus, who had no idea what to advise because he had not known what was coming.

She said faintly, 'Guns? What are you saying?'

'Do you know two men known as Wes and Waxy?'

Over the next two hours, with just one break for refreshments, at Sir Marcus's insistence, Ringrose told her exactly what she had done that weekend and what she had done thereafter to assist in two killings and the stealing of all research material, relating to the Gatling family, that was the property of Gervase Meredith and Nelly Tripp.

By the end, she sat hunched and white-faced, still doggedly pleading ignorance of everything.

Ringrose summed up, 'So, you gave house room to two men, whose names you can't remember, who then, by the wildest of coincidences, went off and raided two sets of premises where copies of the Gatling archive were being stored and, while they were doing it, managed to murder two women who got in their way. These are the same two men who were killed later in a shoot-out with armed police officers at the home of another former Gatling employee, who might know something about your father's past activities.'

Ringrose turned to the solicitor. 'Does she seriously think Daddy's money is going to buy her way out of this?'

'That is a grossly improper remark,' snorted Sir Marcus.

'No doubt,' said Ringrose. 'But nowhere near as grossly improper as the killing of those poor women. I want her to take part in an identity parade and I want her to see the bodies of the hitmen. Let's see if the sight of them will refresh her memory.'

'Do I have to?' Tabitha wailed. 'That's just horrible.'

'No, you don't have to,' said Ringrose. 'But, these days, the fact of your refusal may be drawn to the attention of the jury, as I am sure Sir Marcus will tell you.'

Sid the mortuary man displayed his passengers from bunks two and three, but Tabitha Gatling turned swiftly away. 'I can't say I've ever set eyes on either of these men before,' she muttered.

A dozen berets and a dozen black wigs were distributed among the off-the-street participants but the identification parade was aborted because Sir Marcus Coombes strenuously objected to its composition.

'I do not wish to open myself to a charge of sexism,' said the old boy, 'but it is very clear that a number of these ladies are, shall we say, physiognomically challenged. A beauty of Miss Gatling's calibre will stand out like a beacon. This is totally unacceptable.'

Ringrose sighed. The solicitor had a point but the detective wasn't prepared to give up.

Ringrose took the conducting officer aside. 'For fuck's sake, get rid of this lot and go to the model agencies. They've all got to be lookers or the whole exercise is useless.'

The next day Tabitha took her place at number eight in a line-up of eleven models and drama students. Old Nancy Leith, a woman seemingly without nerves, subjected each to a basilisk stare and then asked to view their left profiles.

Ringrose couldn't believe his good fortune. From behind the glass, he watched the old girl trot back down the line and firmly tap Tabitha on the shoulder. An agitated Tabitha was led away.

Ringrose had not expected anything approaching such a positive result. Afterwards, he said to Nancy, 'I was surprised you were so sure. You were very doubtful before when I asked if you'd be able to identify the woman on the doorstep.'

'Aaaaah!' she said, giving Ringrose a knowing wink. 'The young aren't as clever as they like to think. Didn't you notice? All the women except number eight had made up very carefully. Well, they would, wouldn't they, knowing that they were coming to a place packed with handsome, healthy young men? They'd want to look their best. But number eight had deliberately played down her makeup as if she did not want to be noticed. So I paid special attention to her. And, of course, once I did that, there was no mistaking those lovely Lady Hamilton lips and eyes. Number eight was the girl on the doorstep, all right.'

Ringrose and Firth both sat down with a bump and began laughing. Finally, tears in his eyes, Ringrose said, 'Nancy, if you're not going out with Sid the mortuary man on Saturday night, how would you like to join the CID?'

Chapter Fourteen

Around the table in the conference room on the seventh floor at the headquarters of the Crown Prosecution Service on Ludgate Hill, in the shadow of St Paul's Cathedral, were arrayed a stony-faced Ms Honor Pargeter, barrister, Commander Thomas Ringrose, Detective Inspector Lionel Firth, and Detective Superintendent Herbert Dalton, who had his head thrust forward ready for battle.

Presiding – and here the detectives could detect the hidden influence of Sir Marcus Coombes and his Whitehall chums – was no less a personage than the CPS director of casework services, Hamish Gordon himself.

Disillusioned lawyers and policemen refer ironically to this floor as Seventh Heaven: it is here that so many potential prosecutions are blocked because the available evidence supposedly fails to achieve favourable odds on the likelihood of a win in court.

Ms Pargeter had been relegated to junior status. Under Gordon's guidance, the meeting had reviewed the evidence and he had decreed that there was insufficient to warrant the expenditure of public funds by charging Tabitha Gatling in connection with the murder by asphyxiation of Wes Lake in Rotherhithe. Neither could she be charged in connection with the attempted murder by shooting of a police officer in Streatham. Furthermore, she could not be charged, despite the strongest suspicions, in connection with the break-in at the home of Gervase Meredith in Walham Grove, Fulham.

'That brings us to the murders on the same day of Mrs Esther Keen and Miss Melanie Lamb, who were unfortunate enough to share the same house as the investigative journalist,

Miss Tripp,' said Gordon, steepling his fingers and trying to look sage.

Ringrose didn't like the way the cadaverous functionary was avoiding their gaze. He went on in a tone approaching a whine, 'Do we really have sufficient cause to charge her with conspiracy to murder?'

'Yes!' shouted Ringrose and Firth in unison.

The director of casework services shrugged. 'The only direct evidence putting her on the plot comes from a very old lady. You may imagine what a meal defence counsel would make of her.'

'She will make a fine impression on the jury,' said Ringrose. 'She has all her marbles. And we have Mr Kenny and an envelope with Tabitha Gatling's fingerprints linking her directly to the contract killers. No jury is going to believe for one moment her bullshit about having two strangers in the house for the weekend. Under all that glamour lurks a very violent young lady and we can bring a stream of witnesses to testify to her true nature.'

Gordon sighed deeply. 'Wouldn't it be simpler to encourage the FBI and the Justice Department to apply for her extradition? If they could stir the wretched Los Angeles police into action, they'd almost certainly be able to build a convincing case that she murdered that chap from the *Wall Street Journal*. Save us a great deal of bother.'

'If we let her walk,' said Ringrose evenly, 'her lawyers will just laugh at an extradition order. In America Vernon Gatling's money not only buys bent coppers, it buys judges, too. For the sake of the two dead women – and Gus Meldrum – we have to put her away on our home turf.'

Ringrose struggled to contain his temper in the face of this unfeeling bastard. 'I'm sure I speak for my colleagues when I tell you that anything less than a charge of conspiracy to murder is unacceptable to us. And I should warn you that if there is any suggestion of trimming you'll have our two journalists to contend with. They have been on the inside of this investigation from the start. Indeed, it could not have progressed so far without them. If I leave here without your blessing to go ahead and charge Tabitha Gatling, there'll be a public uproar guaranteed to wreck some distinguished careers.'

Gordon threw down his gold pen and snorted. 'That sounds like a threat to me.'

'No, it's not. It's a prediction. My arse will be as much on the line as yours. Regard what I say as self-interest.'

'Very well.' Gordon looked angrily across the table at Ms Pargeter in her funereal ensemble, her brunette hair held tightly in a bun. She had remained neutral throughout and had nothing to say now. 'Mark it for prosecution as conspiracy to murder,' snapped Gordon.

Bert Dalton said, 'Now that's decided, can we consider Vernon Gatling? He continues to play dumb about the friends of friends he said could stay at his place in Chelsea. He says he issues such invitations willy-nilly and can't remember this specific instance. I'm afraid there are juries just thick enough to believe him. That does not leave us with enough to collar him for the homicidal activities of the hitmen. We know he organized their trip to Britain and we know why, but the proof just isn't hard enough.'

Gordon looked relieved. Dalton gave him a look heavy with contempt, and added, 'Up to a point, it's the same situation with the Larry Varnish killing. We know Gatling did it – we have his father's testimony on a tape that, unfortunately, is no longer admissible in court. But, backed by strong circumstantial evidence and the testimony of his old foreman, Denny Fling, we have a case for a lesser charge – conspiracy to murder.'

Gordon shook his head. 'I was thinking more on the lines of conspiracy to pervert the course of justice by concealing a body, obstructing the coroner in carrying out an inquest, and so forth.' He had the grace to look apologetic. 'I realize the maximum penalty is likely to be little more than a slap on the wrist compared with a life sentence for murder, but given his public position it'll be a severe punishment – assuming the judge lays into him. He'll become a pariah in society.'

Dalton's sarcasm was undisguised. 'Oh, sure. Vernon Gatling will go down to Jermyn Street and buy himself two dozen hair shirts.' He glanced at his watch. 'We have to decide this morning because I have to release him six hours from now.'

Gordon said, 'Would it not be better just to release him but keep the investigation going – in the hope that something more jury-proof might turn up?'

'No!' said Bert Dalton, abruptly. 'That bastard deprived a harmless kid of his life. He has to make some payment for that. I know his brief will have him out on bail within twenty-four hours but we need to keep him agitated right up until his trial date. We're not going to give up on the murder charge. He's not going to buy his way out of this.'

Gordon brooded. He picked up his pen and began to tap the table. The three detectives and Ms Pargeter watched in silence. Gordon coughed. Ringrose raised an eyebrow. He knew this bureaucrat. Something was coming.

'What would you say,' said Gordon slowly, 'if Sir Marcus Coombes were to suggest a compromise – perhaps his client's admission that, influenced by his father, he hid the body? In return, there would be a prosecution application to the judge for the matter to be dealt with by way of a fine? And, at the same time, defence counsel would apologize in court to the widow and announce that Gatling had settled a substantial sum – say half a million pounds – on her?'

'Has that been proposed?' said Dalton glinting dangerously.

'It is just an idea that at this moment is floating in the wind,' said Gordon hastily.

'Look,' said Dalton. 'Tom Ringrose has already told you that we have two lively journalists dogging our every move. If you let Sir Marcus call in favours from his pals in the government to dilute the charges, the word will leak and the first thing swinging in the wind will be the director of the CPS, followed closely by you and me. Get this through your skull, Mr Gordon. If we get the evidence, Gatling goes down.'

'This is disgraceful, Superintendent Dalton.' They all noted that the DoCS could certainly bristle. He had had enough practice at it in this room in the face of cynical policemen. 'There is no hidden pressure being placed on the CPS. What I broached was one of a choice of possibilities.'

'Yeah, how dense of me not to appreciate that straight away,' said Dalton. 'So we go ahead with the body-concealment charge while we look for something weightier – murder or conspiracy to murder?' Dalton's dark eyes bored relentlessly into him.

'Yes,' said Gordon, reluctantly. 'With the sort of defence team Vernon Gatling can command, I only hope we can make it stick.' He swept up his papers and left in a huff.

The men had almost forgotten the presence of Ms Pargeter. Each was repacking his own box files when her voice broke into their thoughts. She was still seated, pale but quite composed, at the table.

Without change of her customary smell-under-the-nose expression, she said, 'Gentlemen, I apologize for my superior. I am outraged at what has been revealed to me here today.'

She looked at each of them in turn, like a headmistress attempting to sum up three recalcitrant pupils. 'I shall be severely disillusioned as to your talents as policemen if you don't go from here and nail that fucker Vernon Gatling for murder. To let him get away with it now would be unconscionable. That is all I have to say.' She rose and strode from the room on four-inch heels.

They were astonished. Lionel Firth said, 'If I asked her for a date, d'you think she'd say yes?'

'Leave your handcuffs at home,' said Bert Dalton.

'No, no, Bert. Take them along. Plus the leg irons,' said Firth. 'Phwoar!'

Chapter Fifteen

The media circus hit the road at 100 m.p.h. for Tabitha Gatling's formal remand at the magistrates' court. 'So the Mardi Gras begins,' sighed Ringrose. The charge would be bitterly fought but even the mighty Sir Marcus Coombes could not secure bail for his client when there were two murdered women to account for.

He had more luck twenty-four hours later when Vernon Gatling appeared at the Guildhall magistrates' court charged with illegally concealing the body of Lawrence Varnish, contrary to common law. Despite all Sir Marcus's persuasive eloquence, and an offer to surrender his client's passport, the magistrate remanded Vernon to Brixton prison.

He had just about time to count the bricks in one wall of his dank cell and test the thin mattress when he was in Sir Marcus's limousine being ferried down Brixton Hill to the comfort of his own bed in the infinitely more salubrious ambience of Cheyne Walk, Chelsea.

Anticipating the City magistrate's obduracy, Sir Marcus had had Queen's Counsel standing by to make bail application to a judge in chambers. This had been granted on a surety of £250,000 – also as immediately available as the QC.

But Vernon was in no mood to sit lauding Sir Marcus's legal skills. 'Where's my little girl? What have those bastards done with her?' he screamed at the solicitor. 'Why haven't you been to a judge for her?'

'Now, now, Vernon,' said the old boy, sliding shut the glass panel between the chauffeur and themselves, 'you must stay calm for both your sakes. Tabitha has been remanded to Holloway prison for a week and on such a grave charge there is nothing I can do about it. Indeed, if I did manage in some miraculous way to ease her lot, there would be a public outcry that the wealthy were receiving preferential treatment. And, remember, those same public will soon form the jury sitting in judgement upon her. It just wouldn't do.'

'So my daughter has to be banged up with whores and lesbians for the sake of public relations? Jesus!'

Sir Marcus put an arm round his shoulder. 'Vernon, I know how you feel. As her trustee, and knowing her as I do, I share your worry for her. But Tabitha is a strong girl. She knows how to take care of herself.' His heavy face fell into sombre folds. 'And, believe me, I share your worries about your own situation. It is not fitting that a man of your eminence should be entangled in this squalid business. But, be under no illusion, there is going to be some hard pounding before we reach the sunlit uplands once again.'

Vernon leaned back and closed his eyes, irritated by the *faux*-Churchillian rhetoric.

Sir Marcus lowered his voice, even though there was no possibility of their being overheard. 'I have learned through my own private channels that the police are being extremely devious. Since the gunplay in Streatham, they have given the impression that your one-time foreman, Mr Fling, was shot and killed by the two Americans. The little that Ringrose has said about the matter gives that impression without actually saying it in as many words. And during your interview with Dalton I detected a similar ambivalence.'

Vernon's eyes snapped open and he sat up again. 'Are you telling me Denny Fling is still alive?'

'Yes. Alive and unharmed. The person shot was a Metropolitan Police officer masquerading as Fling.'

'Shit!' said Vernon. Sir Marcus noted the Mediterranean tan turn sallow as the underlying skin drained of blood. A defending lawyer never risks troubling his own conscience by asking his client if he is guilty. For that relief, much thanks, thought Sir Marcus Coombes.

'So there's a dead copper to add to the charges against Tabby?'

'No,' said Coombes. 'He was wearing Kevlar protection. He is recovering. A conspiracy to murder will be left lying on the file pending the outcome of current proceedings against Tabitha. The immediate threat is not to her but to you. So far, you have been greatly shielded by the strict court rule excluding hearsay evidence but, because he is alive, he will be able to repeat in court that taped version of events Superintendent Dalton quoted at you.'

'My God! Can we buy Fling off?'

'Vernon, please do not embarrass me. I'm going to pretend I didn't hear that. And I'd strongly advise you not to do anything stupid. Fling is still being protected most efficiently by armed officers – as those two American thugs could testify if they were still alive to do so.'

*

From the day of the conversation with Vernon Gatling as they sped away from the dolour of Brixton Prison, Sir Marcus Coombes knew he would need the best. By the next morning he had Claud Collingwood QC on a huge retainer to be available to lead for the defence whenever the Gatlings' separate cases came to trial.

Both indictments were set down in the Old Bailey calendar, inking in Andrew Mission QC for the Crown Prosecution Service, with Ms Honor Pargeter as his junior.

Vernon Gatling emerged ahead of his daughter from the labyrinthine legal preliminaries of a showcase trial and was first to step into the dock in the crowded and infamous No. 1 Court. A not-guilty plea was entered.

Both sides sighed for the old days of jury selection to gain an advantage. Claud Collingwood preferred as many lower-middle-class women as possible – the type of female who read celebrity magazines and would be smitten by the sight of Vernon Gatling in all his manly glory.

Mission, on the other hand, wanted educated, no-nonsense males, who could see beyond the surface image. By the time the jury was completed Collingwood and Mission had each imagined small advantages – and effectively cancelled each other out.

Collingwood was not discommoded. He sprang to his feet immediately to demonstrate why he earned more than £1 million a year in fees and refreshers. He asked for the freshly empanelled jury to be withdrawn while he argued a point of law.

In their absence, the Bar Star, as Collingwood was known in vulgar press headlines, made a simple point: his distinguished client was charged with illegally concealing a body – and *not* with creating the corpse in the first place. Therefore it would be deeply prejudicial to his case if the prosecution were allowed to state, as a matter of fact, that Mr Varnish had been murdered.

Andrew Mission tried the withering-scorn approach. 'My lord, is the jury expected to believe that a healthy man of twenty-two years simply lay down on the accused's building site and died of nothing in particular? The jury will be thrown into utter confusion. The lacuna will create nothing but the suspicion that they are being denied evidence that should rightfully be theirs.'

Collingwood was back up in an instant. 'My lord, with respect, I can only assume my learned friend has failed to think this problem through to its inevitable conclusion. If his argument holds, this trial becomes, in effect, a murder trial. The defence would be obliged to challenge all evidence that the dead man was murdered – and, if he were, certainly not murdered by Mr Gatling. In the process, what jury could avoid the suspicion that Mr Gatling in some way had a hand in that death? And that, my lord, is not what my client is charged with. There is no mention of murder in the indictment and that is the way it should remain.'

Standing at the back of the court alongside Ringrose, Bert Dalton muttered, 'He wouldn't be looking so cocksure if we could get old Gunner's tape into evidence, more's the pity.'

Mr Justice Quarmby consulted his clerk *sotto voce* and pondered for five minutes before ruling, 'I'm afraid it's against you, Mr Mission. Mr Collingwood would be defending on two fronts. He would be placed in an impossible position.'

'Not to mention the impossible position Larry Varnish was placed in,' muttered Ms Pargeter under her breath, to the back of her leader's dusty wig.

The judge was saying, 'Any testimony from prosecution witnesses must eschew all reference to the manner of Mr Varnish's death. We have a body and Mr Gatling stands accused of disposing of it. That is the simple proposition we have to keep in mind. Let's not go off at any tangents.'

For the next three days, the prosecution meticulously built up Larry Varnish's eccentric history and the finding of the skeleton.

Because of the judge's ruling, Professor Franklyn Dart was permitted only to furnish an approximate age for the remains but not to give his expert opinion as to how Larry Varnish came to die.

Collingwood had a number of questions for him. 'Tell me, Professor, do you have any forensic proof that the remains are actually those of Lawrence Varnish?'

'The skeleton conforms in all physical respects to the details of Mr Varnish's physique supplied to me by the police.'

'What about identification by way of dental records? Did the police furnish you with those to make a comparison?'

'No. As I understand it, the police were unable to trace any surviving dental records.'

'So the answer to my original question is no, you cannot be certain that the body named on the charge sheet is, in fact, that of Mr Varnish.'

'That is correct.'

'The crafty old devil is just sowing as much doubt as he can in any direction that presents itself,' Andrew Mission whispered to Ms Pargeter.

'Tough,' said Ms Pargeter, who was not entirely enamoured of her learned leader's talents.

Collingwood continued to confirm Mission's observation after Larry Varnish's widow had told of her loss and tearfully recalled that final Saturday night when he had gone off on his final treasure hunt.

Collingwood was cool. He asked, 'Mrs Sims, do you have any direct evidence that the remains we have heard referred to here in this court are those of your late husband?' A murmur of surprise travelled round the court.

She looked perplexed, as if the thought had not occurred to her before. 'If you put it like that, I suppose not. The police told me there'd be no point in my seeing the . . .' she hesitated for a second ' . . . bones.'

Then she brightened. 'But they did show me Larry's special medal. He was really proud of that medal.'

'Yes, but we've already heard evidence that it was found near, but not actually on, the body. Everyone agrees he was a frequent visitor to the site among many other sites. He may have dropped his medal on any one of those visits. Finding it is hardly positive proof that Lawrence is the corpse.'

'I suppose not,' she said, doubtfully.

Collingwood assumed his most understanding expression. 'Now, forgive me, Mrs Sims, but I have to ask you this. Is it possible that your husband simply took off?'

'How do you mean?'

'You have testified that you had quarrelled on the day he disappeared and that his peculiar mode of life had caused friction between you. Perhaps he had become impatient of the shackles that married life place around a young man?'

Lorraine Sims thought about this for a moment and then realization dawned. Her voice rose shrilly into the vaulted ceiling, 'Are you trying to say my Larry is still alive?'

'Forgive me for being blunt, Mrs Sims. I do not wish to raise false hopes. But the possibility exists, does it not?'

Lorraine gazed wildly around the court, as if expecting someone to come forward to her aid. 'My Larry would never have walked out on me. It's all lies! We had a little row about going to a Saturday-night dance, that's all. We had a happy marriage.' She burst into tears.

Mission leaped to his feet. 'My lord, I really must object to this line of questioning. What purpose is served?'

Collingwood said doggedly, 'The charge specifies the body of Lawrence Varnish. No one has yet proved to my satisfaction that the body *is* that of Varnish. We are not here to prove or disprove that Mr Gatling disposed of the body of Adolf Hitler or Glenn Miller but one Lawrence Varnish and only Lawrence Varnish. I say, where's the proof of identity?'

Mission, back up again, could not disguise his irritation. 'My lord, this is an absurd argument. Who else disappeared in that vicinity on that April night in 1955? It certainly wasn't Adolf Hitler or the American bandleader. No, the only person to disappear at that time and in that place was Lawrence Varnish. Let's hear no more of this.'

'You've both made your points,' said the judge, neutrally. 'Do you have anything further for this witness, Mr Collingwood?'

Collingwood hadn't. But as Lorraine Sims was about to step down, he changed his mind. 'I apologize. One last matter, Mrs Sims. Did you ever hear your husband mention the name of a man named Denny Fling?'

'Oh, yes. Larry knew him. He worked on the ruins. I've never forgotten his name. It always sounded so funny to me.'

Collingwood smiled at her. 'I believe it was easy to remember because he had a rude nickname. Unless learned counsel wants to object to my putting words into your mouth, I'll save you the blushes and say it. He was known, was he not, as Denny King, the Bullshit King?'

A titter ran round the court and Lorraine managed to put a half-smile on her wet face. 'That's right,' she murmured.

'Mr Fling and your husband would perhaps do a little business occasionally?'

'Oh, yes. Mr Fling's jobs went from site to site. My Larry often saw him.'

'When your Larry was buying bits and pieces from Mr Fling and others – bits and pieces from the ancient world – I daresay a great deal of bargaining went on.'

'Oh, I'm sure it did,' said Lorraine. 'Larry couldn't afford to pay too much. The dealer he supplied wasn't very generous.'

'And in the course of what we might call tough trading, tempers might rise? Angry words might be exchanged?'

'Get up! Get up!' hissed Ms Pargeter into her leader's ear. 'The bastard is trying to plant the idea that Fling had something to do with the death.'

Mission sprang to his feet as if his junior had stabbed him in the backside. 'My lord, my learned friend is now putting more than rude nicknames into the witness's mouth.'

'Careful, Mr Collingwood,' snapped Mr Justice Quarmby.

'I'm so sorry, my lord. Perhaps I might ask Mrs Sims directly if her husband's negotiations for these excavated items ever led to violent dispute?'

Mission was up again. 'My lord, this is really too much! It was counsel for the defence who sought to place parameters on certain aspects of the available evidence. Let him abide by the consequences of his own manoeuvring.'

Collingwood went to speak again but Mr Justice Quarmby cut him off with an abrupt, 'Sit down, Mr Collingwood!'

The judge turned to the jury, 'Ladies and gentlemen, Mr Collingwood's last remarks make it necessary for me to explain something that may have been puzzling you. How did the dead man who is named in this charge come to die? Well, I have to tell you, as a matter of law, that is not your concern.

You have only to decide whether or not the defendant, Mr Gatling, for his own purposes, concealed the body. Therefore, I must ask you to cast entirely from your minds defending counsel's references to acts of violence. When you come to consider your verdict this aspect must play no part in your deliberations.'

'Too fucking late,' hissed Ms Pargeter. 'Collingwood has sown the seed that Fling bumped off Varnish. You should ask for a new trial.'

Mission twisted in his seat, an agonized look on his saturnine face. 'Think of the cost of a second trial. The director of the CPS would crucify me. Quarmby has read the jury the Riot Act. I don't see what else is to be done.'

While the legal squabbling went on around her, Lorraine stood bewildered. Her tears welled up once more when Collingwood rose again to resume his cross-examination. He ignored them. 'What about Mr Vernon Gatling and his father? Did your husband ever mention them in your presence?'

Lorraine shook her head. 'No, I'd never heard of them until all this trouble started.'

'Did you ever have any reason to think your husband had a difference of opinion with either of them? I put it no higher than that,' he added hastily, as he observed Mr Justice Quarmby begin to stir.

'How could I? As I say, their name never came up,' said the witness.

At last, Claud Collingwood QC was genuinely ready to let Lorraine Sims go. He sat down beaming with silky satisfaction. The ground was prepared. He could now save his fire for one final earth-scorching.

Vernon Gatling smiled across at him. His hired gun was doing well.

Vernon had dropped his Hugo Boss and Versace power suits and was appearing each day in a more understated suiting, superbly built for him by Poole's of Savile Row. He had also adopted a humble, wounded mien in the dock.

His image consultants had judged his luxuriant grey-blond locks too flamboyant for the occasion. They would not play well with the jury. There must be no distasteful displays of wealth or other ostentation, he had been lectured. Consequently, he now sported the kind of military trim more usually favoured by the stuffier male members of the Royal Family and his Rolex had been replaced by an altogether more discreet Cartier timepiece.

Denny Fling hobbled on his bad feet into the box on the eighth day of the trial and Mission took him competently enough through his dealings with the dead man and what happened the day he helped Gunner and Vernon Gatling to clear the site of the Roman remains.

Denny was nervous, repeating at every opportunity Mission gave him his oath that he'd had no idea there was a body under the newly laid concrete.

When Mission sat down, Collingwood went straight for Denny's jugular. 'You're a thief as well as a liar, aren't you, Mr Fling?'

'No, I am not, sir,' said Denny, affronted, shifting weight from one leg to the other.

'Well, let us see. You sold antique objects to young Varnish, did you not?'

'There were just bits of pottery and dirty old coins and stuff.'

'Where did you get the "stuff", as you call it?'

'From the site, sir. From the ground. There was no harm in it.'

'You also allowed the men in your charge to sell "stuff" that they'd found on the site?' Collingwood made 'stuff' sound like the contents of Tutankhamun's tomb.

'Yes, sir. For a few shillings.'

'But the truth is, the site belonged to the Gatlings, did it not? Together with everything on or in the earth, subject to a treasure trove hearing by Her Majesty's coroner? Is that not correct?'

'It wasn't treasure,' protested Denny Fling. 'It was just a lot of mouldy old stuff.'

'Answer the question, if you please!' thundered Collingwood. 'Were you and the men in your charge trading in stolen goods with Lawrence Varnish?'

Miserably, Denny Fling said, 'You're being a bit harsh. It was nothing as heavy as that.'

Collingwood had picked up a bundle of papers ready for this moment and now he threw them down on the desk in a gesture of theatrical exasperation.

He turned to the judge. 'My lord, might the witness be asked to answer the question?'

Mr Justice Quarmby peered down over his gold frames. 'Mr Fling, were you and your colleagues aware that the items you sold to Mr Varnish were not your property?'

Denny nodded miserably, 'I suppose so, sir. I can't deny it.'

Collingwood was happy. The judge had made an even-handed intervention but the jury, unaccustomed to court proceedings, would see this as the judge and defence counsel ganging up on a prevaricating prosecution witness.

Collingwood was far from finished with demolishing Denny. 'I put it to you that the story of the Roman remains and the site clearance is pure invention on your part. You, and perhaps some of your men, found him dead on that fateful weekend. You realized there would be a full police inquiry into that death and you were afraid the truth would emerge.'

'Truth?' said Denny Fling, perplexed.

'The truth that, thanks to your moral laxity and betrayal of your employers, the site had become a thieves' kitchen – what, in modern terms, might be described as the site for a chariot boot sale, where Roman and medieval objects plundered from the earth were available to the highest bidder.'

Denny was saying pathetically, 'No, no, no,' but Collingwood thundered on, 'Yes, yes, yes, Mr Fling. You knew your arrest and probable imprisonment were inevitable. So you came up with the callous idea of throwing the body into an old well and concealing your perfidy under a layer of concrete. The anguish for the dead man's family was terrible enough but then to implicate your totally innocent employers in your base scheme with the cock 'n' bull story of a Roman temple being swept away unnoticed in the heart of London in a single day was the act of a man without conscience or honour.'

'I swear on the life of my child, there's not a word of truth in any of that,' said Denny, desperately. 'Apart from the Roman temple,' he added lamely.

Ms Honor Pargeter groaned in her leader's ear. 'Just look at the jury. They're gazing at Fling as if he just crawled from under a stone. And Collingwood has already grabbed tomorrow's headline. "Chariot Boot Sale". It's not bad, dammit.'

The prosecution tried to regain some credibility for the story of the temple through the archaeological evidence of Dr Bruce Stevens of the Museum of London Archaeology Service, who had originally identified the masonry block lifted from the well as being an altar stone dedicated to the Roman god Mercury.

But when Collingwood got to him, Dr Stevens was forced to admit that there wasn't the smallest trace of any other Roman structure on the site.

Collingwood said, 'Is it not a melancholy fact, Dr Stevens, that over the centuries many fine buildings from the classical world have been lost for ever because they were dismantled and the stones used to create other, more convenient, buildings for a different age?'

'Yes, that is sadly true. Much has been lost in that way.'

'Is it at all unusual to come across, say, a Tudor structure that might have a foundation created from stone quarried in Roman times?'

'It has been known.'

'And those stones might have been transported to that site from the place where they originally formed part of another building altogether?'

'Yes.'

'So, what is to say that the altar block in the well was not transported in similar fashion to the site owned by Mr Vernon Gatling and his father?'

'I suppose one can never be one hundred per cent sure – failing the discovery of supporting evidence.'

'But in this instance there was no supporting evidence, was there?'

'No.'

'You have only Mr Fling's unsubstantiated word that the block was part of a temple on that site?'

The archaeologist hesitated and Collingwood barked suddenly, 'A straight yes or no will do, Dr Stevens.'

'Yes,' admitted Dr Stevens, recoiling from the unexpected onslaught. 'The evidence comes down to the word of one man.'

'Quite so. A man with no archaeological expertise whatsoever?'

'That seems to be the case.'

Collingwood was beaming warmly at him now. The archaeologist had come through with the right answers. 'Tell me, Dr Stevens, setting aside for a moment the existence of the altar block, which may or may not have originated on the site in question, do you have any reason to accept the word of the witness Fling over that of Mr Vernon Gatling?'

From the witness box, Bruce Stevens looked helplessly around and met the impassive eye of Detective Superintendent Bert Dalton. Collingwood caught the shift in focus and roared, 'Look at me, sir, and answer the question.'

Miserably, Stevens mumbled, 'No, not really.'

'Speak up, sir. Let his lordship and the members of the jury hear you. You cannot accept the witness Fling's word over that of Mr Gatling? Am I correct?'

'Yes, that is correct. If you separate the altar block from the site, I have no personal knowledge that would allow me to favour one version of events over another.'

When Andrew Mission had completed the prosecution case it was still only eleven-thirty – too early for a lunch adjournment. So the judge nodded at Claud Collingwood, who stood and gathered his black robe around his corpulent midriff as if to shield himself from malevolent spirits. The expression on his claret-red face was one of utter contempt.

After the jury had left the courtroom at his application, he said, 'If it please your lordship, having listened with growing amazement over so many days to a prosecution case that consists of rumour, wishful thinking and downright lies, my resolve on my way to court this morning was to submit to your lordship that there was no case to answer. But my client, Mr Vernon Gatling, would have none of it. He pointed out to me – understandably in the most forceful terms – that he was a man of considerable standing in the community and that he was determined to go into the witness box and face the jury like a man. I told him that, on my application, your lordship would most likely treat this indictment for what it is worth, and take a course that would not necessitate my client even having to give evidence. But Mr Gatling said, "How would it look if I did not take the stand? The jury would think I might have something to hide. I can't have that." Consequently, I call the only defence witness, Mr Vernon Gatling, to speak for himself.'

An excited murmur ran round the crowded court as Vernon, wearing a dark grey gabardine suit and a virtuous air, crossed to the witness box. The hacks on the press bench were jammed shoulder to shoulder, fighting for a flat surface for their shorthand notebooks.

Under Collingwood's gentle guidance, Vernon doggedly repeated his total bafflement at the plight in which he now found himself. 'Mr Fling's story is a total fabrication. Nothing remotely resembling what he described ever took place. I mean, if there had been a Roman temple uncovered on the site it would have been a matter for rejoicing not concealment. I've listened to the prosecution making great play with the financial loss they say my father and I would have incurred. Well, I'm not entirely without a reputation for making shrewd business decisions' – wry smile and appreciative laughter in court – 'and if there had been a temple I could quite see Gatling Construction setting up a viewing platform and charging admission!'

The court erupted in laughter and Vernon grinned boyishly. Ms Honor Pargeter whispered, 'Oh, shit! Half the jury are laughing with him.'

Collingwood said, 'Why should the witness Fling have taken against you in such a vicious fashion?'

'After four decades it is difficult to give a definite answer. I've attempted to trace the firm's old employment records but, unfortunately, they have long since been trashed. However, my recollection is that Gatling's employed Mr Fling as a site foreman well into the nineteen sixties when he was let go.'

'He was made redundant?'

'Either that or he had been sacked for some misbehaviour. I've racked my brains, but I can't remember.'

From the rear of the court, the unmistakable voice of Denny Fling bellowed, 'You got rid of me because I had a touch of arthritis.'

'Quiet!' shouted the clerk. The judge said to Andrew Mission, 'Another outburst like that from your witness, Mr Mission, and he'll be held in contempt.'

The hapless prosecuting counsel half rose and mumbled an apology.

Unperturbed, Collingwood went on, 'So he may have held a grudge all these years?'

'Apparently so. I'm mortified. Why didn't he come to me? If he was in financial difficulty I would have helped him for old times' sake.'

'You've heard evidence that you showed an unhealthy interest in the demolition of Abura House. The prosecution has alleged that this was because you knew there was a body under that building waiting to be discovered.'

'It is absolute nonsense. As I explained at the time to the City Corporation planning people, that building – Fletcher Hall, as it was then – was the foundation of my fortune. It held – and still holds – great sentimental value for me. If I had been allowed, I would have rebuilt it at a loss. I was really sorry that I was abroad when such an opportunity presented itself. I'm even sorrier that my attempts to take over the contract have been misinterpreted as something more sinister.'

Vernon Gatling's performance was perfect. He kept his voice low. He appeared sorrowful rather than indignant. In rehearsal, he had been instructed to show Denny Fling Christian charity for his treachery and he had managed it, even though his primal instinct was to charge across the courtroom and get his hands round the old bastard's throat.

In the cross-examination, deprived of Gunner Gatling's crucial taped version of events, Andrew Mission could only jab like a featherweight at the construction tycoon. Mission failed even to bruise except during one passing moment.

Mission said casually, 'When you first faced this charge, you answered in the name of Vernon Gatling?'

'Yes, of course.'

'Why "of course"? That wasn't the name you were born with, was it?'

'Oh, I see what you mean. No, my first name originally was Lionel. I changed it.'

'Why?'

'I didn't like Lionel.'

'Is that the truth, Mr Gatling? Didn't you change it at your father's behest as a gesture to celebrate his coming into a great deal of money at the end of the war? And, more importantly, to broadcast this fact to a post-war world that might have entertained suspicions about the source of his money?'

For a bulky man, Collingwood found his feet in an instant. 'My lord, what relevance has any of this to the charge?'

'If we give prosecuting counsel a moment, we might find out,' said Quarmby drily.

'It's no secret. My father had a win on Vernon's football pools,' said Vernon Gatling.

'Other men came back from the war with just their gratuity but your father who, I believe, had been in an ARP Heavy Rescue unit burrowing into wrecked houses, used this win on Vernon's to kick-start his new demolition and construction empire that you subsequently inherited and turned into a worldwide corporation?'

'That's right. I wanted a new name. I hated Lionel. So he said, "Take Vernon." It had a ring about it, so I did as he asked. I loved my dad,' added Vernon Gatling, oozing a well-rehearsed sincerity.

'So you became a walking advertisement for the fact that the first sizeable sum of money your father ever laid his hands on came from a win on Vernon's Pools?'

'Absolutely right,' said Vernon, robustly. But Collingwood was looking wary and casting beseeching looks at his client to tread carefully.

'It was a lie, wasn't it?' said Mission coolly. 'Your father never won any significant sum on Vernon's Pools, did he?'

'Of course he did.'

'No, sir!' said Mission. 'Wherever the money came from out of the war – the money that founded the Gatling fortune and made you one of the country's richest men – it never came from Vernon's Pools.'

'But I tell you it did. How can you be so dogmatic, Mr Mission?' Collingwood glanced unhappily at his junior. The damn fool was inviting trouble.

In reply, Andrew Mission reached behind and took a five-page document from Ms Pargeter's hand. 'My lord, I wonder if the witness might be asked to examine this.'

The foolscap sheets did the rounds – from clerk to judge to defending counsel, who saw immediately the problem that was about to arise. The jury was turfed out while Claud Collingwood challenged its authenticity and complained about lack of prior disclosure. But the judge said, 'Your client has been freely answering questions about the origins of his name. I see no objection to the matter being explored further.'

With the jury back in place, Vernon was handed the document and asked by Mission to read aloud its title. ' "A History of Vernon's Pools",' said Vernon.

'Thank you,' said prosecuting counsel. 'Now would you turn to page two and read the paragraphs under the heading "1940s"?'

Vernon read: ' "During the war years, government restriction (largely due to a shortage of paper) demanded that all pools operations were suspended, and buildings, staff and facilities were put at the disposal of the war effort. At a later date, it was considered that a re-start should be allowed in the interests of public morale and an organization called Unity Pools was launched by pools operators of the time, including Vernon's." '

Vernon completed the paragraph and looked up. Mission said quietly, 'And the next paragraph, if you please.'

Vernon began to read and stopped as the import of the words hit him. 'Don't stop. You're doing fine,' said Mission.

Vernon read reluctantly: ' "One year after the end of the war, in 1946, Unity Pools was disbanded and normal commercial competition was resumed." '

There was a silence. Into it, Andrew Mission said, 'So if there were no Vernon's Pools during the war, where did the Gatling money come from?'

The overhead lighting showed a film of perspiration forming on Vernon Gatling's upper lip. For the first time since the trial had begun, unease broke though the carapace that had been so carefully manufactured for him. He had to clear his throat of stress phlegm before he could speak. He croaked, 'The win must have been on Unity Pools.'

'In that case your first name would be Unity, would it not? Somehow it hardly seems appropriate, Mr Gatling,' sniffed Mission, thrusting home the shaft before a heated Collingwood could climb to his feet and bellow his objection.

The onlookers erupted in a gale of laughter. Collingwood shot up, dangerously puce and protesting, while Quarmby threatened to clear the court. But for the first time the jury looked at Vernon Gatling with less than total respect for his celebrity and achievements. A curtain had been drawn back. Something dark had been hinted at.

Chapter Sixteen

Mr Justice Quarmby took a whole day to sum up and the jury retired to their homes for the night. As is the custom, Vernon had to surrender to his bail and even Sir Marcus Coombes could not prevent him spending a night on remand back in Brixton.

In the prison interview room, Sir Marcus, Collingwood and his junior tried to calm their enraged client. 'How the fuck did that slimy bastard Mission get that stuff about Vernon's Pools?' He rounded on Collingwood. 'I knew I should never have got up on that stand. All that bullshit about wanting to face the jury like a man. Fuck 'em! A bunch of unemployed arseholes dragged off the street to sit in judgement on me and listening to me and my dad being rubbished by a prick who wouldn't have the faintest idea what it's like to drag yourself up by your bootlaces. What it takes out of you. What that first money represents. Who the fuck cares where my old man got the money? He did something great with it. That's what counts.'

Collingwood said soothingly, 'Vernon, you are getting exercised over nothing. What does it matter after all this time how your father acquired his original fortune? It is an irrelevance in this case. I'm sorry I was unable to block the questioning but once you had offered an explanation for your adopted name there was little I could do except let the matter run its course. The jury will see it as a small diversion and move on to more relevant matters. Of course, one does not like to second-guess juries, but I'd wager you will be sleeping in your own bed tomorrow night.'

'Hear, hear!' said Sir Marcus Coombes.

The deflated prosecution team watched on TV as the triumphant defenders escorted their famous charge from the Bailey. The jury had been so hammered by the words 'reasonable doubt' by both judge and defence counsel that they were unanimous after three hours of deliberation and two votes. Vernon Gatling was innocent.

In the ensuing uproar, after the judge had discharged him and left the bench, Vernon sprang across the well of the court and fervently wrung the hand of each of the twelve. Four asked for and got his autograph.

On the pavement, he nobly faced the cameras to say, 'Justice has been done. I have been the victim of a disgraceful character-blackening conspiracy but, thank God, I had a jury of fine people who saw right through this attempt to ruin me.'

'What about your daughter?' shouted a TV girl reporter. But Sir Marcus Coombes stepped in hurriedly to say, 'As much as he would like to, Mr Gatling cannot comment while the matter is *sub judice*.'

He took Vernon's arm and began steering him forcefully towards the open door of their waiting limousine. Ignoring his solicitor's caution, Vernon shouted defiantly over his shoulder, 'We'll get her out of it. My little girl is as innocent as me!'

Bert Dalton and Tom Ringrose watched grimly. 'That's the first truth he's uttered in weeks,' said Ringrose.

★

They were matched in gloom by Gervase Meredith and Nelly Tripp. Early on, the prosecution team had decided that, once the police had taken their own statement from Denny Fling, the two journalists would not be required as witnesses.

They were forbidden to attend the trial so they had followed the evidence in the morning papers and pressed on with feeding their publishers, Chantry's, with sample chapters of their proposed book.

They had each taken turns to recline on a squeaky leather couch and recall as best they could their stolen interviews while the other took notes. By this method Gervase Meredith and Nelly Tripp had already reconstructed 90 per cent of the Gatling archive that had ended up in a watery grave.

In reassembling the Lorraine Varnish material, it would have been easier to make a return visit to Lorraine and start again. But Detective Superintendent Bert Dalton had said, 'Not until the case is over. She's a witness.'

They had not dared to defy him. They still smarted from the verbal drubbing he had given them for their tardiness in coming forward. They had yet to worm their way back into his good books.

Like Ringrose and Dalton, they had watched Vernon walk away from the Old Bailey and were bitterly disappointed.

The pair drank too much Beaujolais that evening and went to bed grumpy. Nelly was particularly out of sorts.

They'd tossed and turned and made love very quietly so as not to embarrass the protection officers downstairs. Gervase fell asleep straight away – the pig! She lay wide awake, gazing up into the darkness. Something was niggling at her like a cranial termite.

Finally, she fell quiet. She was woken at eight by Gervase who was holding two steaming mugs of instant coffee. As sometimes happens when a problem is slept on, the answer came instantly to Nelly's tongue.

'No one mentioned Larry Varnish's figurine,' she said, stealing Gervase's pillow to prop herself up. 'There was no mention of it in the evidence.'

Gervase was still in his striped pyjamas. She said, 'Put down those mugs and get your notebook. Gervase obeyed. Nelly closed her eyes and said, 'Eighteen inches high. Bronze. Mustn't disturb the patina. Wearing what Lorraine called a funny hat. Larry had told her it had been worshipped as a Roman god.'

Gervase dutifully made a note and looked up. 'What happened to it after Vernon bumped off Larry? That question seems to have slipped everyone's mind, including ours. After all, Larry's main purpose in returning to the site on the Saturday night was to recover the figure.'

'Search me,' said Gervase who, Nelly had noted, was not at his best first thing until he was fed, watered and allowed to climb back in for what he termed 'a bit of the old how's-yer-father'. This, Nelly was usually gracious enough to grant.

Later in the morning, they hazarded a call on Detective Superintendent Bert Dalton who, predictably after the court fiasco, was in no mood to humour the hacks.

Nelly repeated her question. 'What happened to Larry Varnish's figurine?'

'Who knows?' said Dalton. 'Swept away with the rest of the temple, I dare say. Is there anything else? I'm busy.'

'Damn!' said Nelly, outside on the pavement. But Gervase, who had been tagging along out of devotion, had come alive. He said, 'I've had a blinding flash.'

Later still, they found Dr Bruce Stevens slumped in despondency in his office at Walker House. They took him down to the cavernous pub in the basement. 'I can't help thinking that my evidence helped get Gatling off,' he moaned, over his bottled lager.

'No point in scourging yourself. It's time to move on,' said Gervase. 'I've had an idea and I want you to confirm something for me. The bronze god statuette that Larry Varnish described to his wife – how much would it fetch on the open market today?'

Dr Stevens said dreamily, 'Ah, my little Mercury, I'm sure that's who it was. You're talking six figures.'

'A hundred thou? As much as that?'

'Easy – if it were in good condition.'

'It would be a hard thing to throw away, even if it were dangerous to keep?'

'Jolly hard,' said the archaeologist.

'Thanks. That's all I wanted to know.'

Being escorted back to their haven by an armed protection officer, Nelly said, 'What's with the statuette? What am I missing?'

Gervase said, 'Give me a couple of days. Then I may be able to tell you.'

Millie Moses's photographic studio off the Portobello Road, Notting Hill, was in its usual state of pigsty chic, with hypo-stained walls, the detritus of a thousand assignments and drying lines that could decapitate the unwary visitor.

Gervase ducked under and around the hazards. Millie was at a bench cropping prints with a guillotine that made a noise like a bacon slicer. Gervase gave her a hug. They'd not seen anything of each other since he had become entrapped in the life and times of the Gatling family.

'Remember that weekend at Vernon's country place when you shot a portfolio for Tabitha?' said Gervase, coming straight to the point. 'I left you to it. You shot inside the house – posed her against the paintings and furniture? I remember she showed me the best prints.'

'Yeah. She wanted smudges of herself in all her fancy clothes plus all the new interior decorating shown to best advantage in the background. She wanted to make an album up to please dear Daddy.'

'Did you keep a set of those prints?'

'You bet your ass. When darling Tabitha comes to trial they'll be worth gold dust to the tabloids.'

Millie opened a long drawer and pulled out a black portfolio folder. 'There are about thirty of the best shots and I have another hundred or so in contact print form. Help yourself.'

Gervase found what he wanted among the contacts and he waited impatiently while Millie made a ten-by-eight print. Tabitha looked radiant. She wore perfectly fitted Jimmy Choo riding breeches and leather boots, a yellow waistcoat and stock. She had posed with one leg forward of the other, a riding crop resting against her elegant thigh, as she gazed boldly from the frame, daring any man to soil her.

Gervase began to laugh uncontrollably. 'What?' said Millie, puzzled. She looked over his shoulder but could see nothing in her work to promote mirth.

'Got the bastard!' chortled Gervase. His finger jabbed at the background. The interior decorator had built a decorative plaster niche into the wall behind Tabitha to accommodate one of Vernon Gatling's pieces of statuary. The greenish figure appeared to be made of bronze and answered in every detail, from height to 'funny hat', the description of the Roman god Mercury that Larry Varnish had supplied to his widow-to-be.

Gervase and Nelly took their peace-offering to Bert Dalton. He immediately showed Millie Moses's photograph to Dr Bruce Stevens who became extremely excited. 'Oh, my goodness, that is the one. A dear little god complete with the traveller's sun hat that is called a *petasus* – though I'll need to examine it to be absolutely certain it isn't merely a copy.'

Dalton telephoned Ringrose. There was fresh hope in his voice. He then tracked down Vernon Gatling's interior decorator, Wensley Allbritton, pulled him in – a highly strung individual in a hat with an even wider brim than Mercury's – and invited him to go through the entire set of photographs Millie Moses had taken at Spear's End.

'Ignore Tabitha Gatling,' instructed Dalton. 'Just concentrate on the backgrounds and point out all the featured works of art you supplied as part of the interior-decorating programme.'

When Allbritton had completed the task, tutting and tsking over work that, with hindsight, he said he wished he'd done differently, the bronze figurine was among the leftovers.

'What about this little statue? Where did it come from?'

'My dear, our Vernon is a veritable Charles Foster Kane. I haven't the teeniest idea. He had all sorts of unloved *objets d'art* littering the place before I moved in with my team. If memory serves, I found that little chap in the attic, wrapped in sacking along with other souvenirs from his unfortunate marriage. Such a waste. It is a most charming piece, don't you agree?'

'Do you know what it is?'

'Well, it's obviously Roman or Greek or a copy thereof. It was not part of my commission to give him authentications or valuations. My job was to supply new works and display his existing best pieces to greatest advantage.'

Bert Dalton, at his most menacing, said, 'Mr Allbritton, you'll say nothing of this to anyone – and that includes your former client. Do I make myself clear?'

'Abundantly,' said Allbritton. 'Thank God my fees have been paid. I get the feeling more ordure is heading Vernon Gatling's way. Too bad. He's been a good client.'

Dalton telephoned Ringrose who was still beavering away in Kensington. 'Tom, if Vernon fails to supply a legitimate provenance for that statue, we'll have every justifiable reason for claiming it as Larry Varnish's missing booty.'

At seven next morning, Vernon Gatling was roused by his butler at his country home. Police officers, armed with a search warrant, were already storming through the house.

A policewoman, clutching a copy of Millie Moses's photograph, found the lighted niche and the figure of Mercury at the end of an upstairs corridor. Mercury gazed enigmatically at a highly agitated Vernon, ready to exact a harsh price from he who had wrecked his sacred temple.

Dr Bruce Stevens was escorted to the spot and rapturously pronounced the artefact genuine. It was then carefully boxed and impounded while Vernon screamed down the telephone at Sir Marcus Coombes.

'You may have been acquitted on one charge but the inquiry into the death of Lawrence Varnish and others is ongoing,' said Dalton bluntly.

The raid had taken place early enough to catch the evening papers and news bulletins. The breaking news had an unexpected outcome.

Dr Hector Crumley-Smith's state of agitation had grown exponentially since Tabitha Gatling's arrest and more so since Vernon Gatling's acquittal. The tycoon was now free to wield his power in his customary ruthless fashion against those who might harm him. Dr Crumley-Smith had begun to drink more than he should. He was wondering if Vernon would get round to thinking that host might include him.

Undoubtedly, Dr Crumley-Smith knew more than was healthy for the future happiness of the tycoon. This gnawing knowledge was having a disruptive effect on the Wimpole Street specialist's sleep patterns. He had prescribed Prozac for himself.

The doctor watched the late news keenly. The raid on Spear's End demonstrated forcefully that the police were not giving up on Vernon.

Dr Crumley-Smith had returned to London with a fine Riviera tan and a nervous stomach. His hands were clean – up to a point. All right, Tabitha had rushed him into signing her grandfather's death certificate. But he had no cause to suspect anything underhand had taken place. At worst, he could be accused only of professional haste.

Until . . .

Until, dammit, he had seen the London newspapers containing the photographs of the late Mr Ganz and the late Mr Beamish. There was no hiding from this. He was an eye-witness to the fact that these two killers had been in the company of both Vernon and Tabitha.

From that moment, Dr Crumley-Smith realized with terror, he was part of the conspiracy that the Gatlings had created around themselves.

At the end of the voyage, he had watched the entire crew of the *Black Glove* – Chinese, Turks, Indians – being paid off and placed on planes destined for their homelands, thus putting thousands of miles between them and the English-language newspaper headlines. Then the vessel had been handed over to the care of a marine security firm, while the captain, a Norwegian, had been sent by Vernon to report on South-American marina development possibilities.

All but two witnesses were safely out of harm's way. Dr Crumley-Smith was uneasily aware that he and his nurse were the only two people in England who could identify Mr Ganz and Mr Beamish as guests aboard the *Black Glove* just prior to their spectacular deaths in a south-west London suburb.

What would the newly liberated Vernon do about it?

To the doctor, there seemed three possibilities: 1. Vernon would do nothing, relying on his discretion as a medical man; 2. Vernon would shower him with yet fatter fees for bogus medical services rendered; 3. Vernon would have him silenced.

Dr Crumley-Smith pondered the odds. The first two choices might work for a time but, in the long run, Vernon wasn't the sort of man to let anybody have the power of a blackmailer over him. If the doctor wished to safeguard his skin, he realized, the only choice to be taken seriously was number three.

Trembling, he picked up the telephone and made an appointment to see Commander Thomas Ringrose of New Scotland Yard.

Ms Honor Pargeter wanted a private word with Ringrose. No, not in his office at New Scotland Yard nor at his temporary headquarters in Kensington. Absolutely not in her chambers. And, no, definitely not in anywhere as public as a pub or a restaurant.

'Where, then?' said Ringrose, intrigued but finally exasperated.

'What about in the rooftop car-park of Whiteley's shopping centre in Queensway?' said Ms Pargeter, into the telephone. 'And don't breathe a word to a soul – that includes Lionel Firth and Bert Dalton. My future is at stake here. I'm applying for silk next year.'

Ringrose located her Alfa as he drove slowly in. He parked and walked back. She had the passenger door already open to receive him. Ms Pargeter in off-duty mode presented a slightly softer front than of yore. The hair was looser, the pale face had benefited from an application of blusher, mascara and lip gloss, and the top two buttons of her business blouse were undone. Ringrose had no idea what to expect.

Without preamble, she said, 'Thanks for the discretion, Tom. Here's the situation. The day after tomorrow is the big get-together with the director of the CPS to agree how best to proceed with Tabitha Gatling and Big Daddy.'

'Right,' said Ringrose. 'I take it you'll be there?'

'Wouldn't miss it,' said Ms Pargeter. 'But I want to warn

you, the attorney-general is doing his oily best to put the fix in. There's not much he can do about Tabitha. The evidence linking her to those two apes is too solid for him to suggest reducing the charge to one of driving with faulty windscreen wipers. But he'd dearly love to save Vernon from another trial. With the prime minister's tacit approval, the attorney-general has that bullyboy of a Party chairman knocking the wig over his eyes. You can understand why. For the past eight years, Vernon has been worth a minimum of a hundred grand a year to Party funds. He would have received his knighthood in the last Birthday Honours list if little Larry Varnish had remained, like Pussy, in the well.'

'I'd heard about the cash for the Party and the pending knighthood,' said Ringrose, 'but how can you be sure the AG is out to scupper us?'

Ms Pargeter studied Ringrose solemnly. 'This is the top-secret bit, Tom. My significant other is also a lawyer. He works in the attorney-general's office. For the past month, I've given him the Lysistrata treatment. A week ago he cracked and told all.'

'Lysis—?'

'Spare my blushes,' said Ms Pargeter. 'Look it up.' She reached over to the back seat and produced à manila folder. 'I've been burning the midnight oil trying to locate something in the legal record that would give you a counter-attacking weapon.'

She waggled the folder in the air. 'This is it. The case of the Kentish Mercury versus Pook. As fine a piece of blackmail as the Lysistrata treatment. You study this carefully before you face the director of the CPS and we'll get that bastard Vernon Gatling yet.'

The director of Public Prosecutions himself took the top-secret meeting. Ringrose, Firth, Dalton and the prosecuting lawyers Mission and Pargeter were all present and all resisting an atavistic urge to assault the director with a blunt instrument.

The director was saying, 'The attorney-general is extremely unhappy at the turn this case is taking. He feels that adding

Vernon Gatling to the conspiracy-to-murder indictment alongside his daughter, and then additionally charging him with the murder of Lawrence Varnish, is tantamount to placing him in double jeopardy. There's a hint of the vindictive about it.'

Andrew Mission, controlling his contempt for political meddling, said, 'The charge he was able to beat was confined specifically to the concealment of Varnish's body. The charge the police now propose is that he murdered Varnish, an act that Vernon Gatling's own counsel was careful to separate from the body-concealment charge. In doing so, it may well turn out that Claud Collingwood has been too clever by half.'

Ringrose broke in, 'Thanks to our two tame journalists, we now have the evidence – the statue of Mercury – that ties Gatling directly to the killing. We can prove Varnish was unlawfully killed and we can now prove Gatling had to have been present when Varnish was battered to death. That grisly event and Gatling's need to bury the evidence provides the motive for everything that happened more than forty years later. The jury in the concealment trial probably acquitted him because they were puzzled by an absence of a convincing motive. They had a dead body but no one in court would tell them how it came to be a dead body. They probably felt they were being short-changed. We'll never know. But that motive is now clear for all to see. While Vernon Gatling has presented a bold, brassy front to the world for all these years, he has concealed murder in his heart.'

'Hmmm,' said the director, uncomfortably.

Bert Dalton butted in, 'This is not the vindictive pursuit of a rich man. The new evidence from Vernon Gatling's doctor and nurse ties both father and daughter in with the American killers. These new witnesses' testimony is cast-iron. There is no way the Gatlings can walk away from it.'

'And remember,' added Ringrose pointedly, 'it was one of Vernon's hirelings who discharged a shotgun directly into the chest of one of my officers. I don't recall the attorney-general expressing his extreme unhappiness at that. Or does he reserve his condolences only for those who fund his Party?'

The director jerked forward in his chair and thumped the table. 'That is grossly out of order, Commander Ringrose.

This business is entirely divorced from political considerations. The attorney-general is acting in his independent capacity as a law officer of the Crown. He would be furious to hear such accusations.'

'Then don't tell him,' said Ringrose, bluntly. 'In the past, I've had my fill of finding Whitehall's grubby fingerprints all over my case files when high and mighty friends of the government were involved. Do I have to remind you, as I've already reminded your colleagues, that there are two national journalists at the heart of these investigations? Take it from me, if you and the attorney-general refuse permission to include Gatling in the indictment, the public uproar they create will be highly damaging to your office and the attorney-general's future political prospects.'

'Nonsense,' snapped the director. 'There are perfectly sound libel laws to keep Meredith and Tripp in line.'

Ringrose looked across the table at Ms Honor Pargeter, who had suddenly found cause to examine her fingernails. 'Ah,' said the commander, 'I have something to say on that point. If the law fails to call the Gatlings to account, Meredith and Tripp's publishers have already agreed to include in their book all the evidence that failure to prosecute will have hitherto concealed from the public. And that includes Gunner Gatling's taped testimony that it was his son who swung that bricklayer's hod and crushed Lawrence Varnish's skull.'

'That's impossible,' snorted the director. 'Gatling would have a civil case for libel damages running into millions.'

'In theory, I agree,' said Ringrose. 'But a little birdie tells me' – Ms Pargeter was still finding something riveting about her nails – 'that Chantry's, the publishers, will rely on two interesting legal precedents. The first happened quite recently, in 1997, when the *Daily Mail* published the names and photographs of five young men and roundly declared they had murdered a black youth in a racial attack. The five were never brought to book in a criminal court but the *Daily Mail* invited the five to sue for libel in a civil court where allegedly incriminating statements inadmissible in a criminal trial would have been aired. The five declined to sue. But the *Mail*'s challenge forced a judicial inquiry.'

The director waved an arm impatiently. 'I'm familiar with the case. What's the other legal development you believe the publisher could rely upon?'

'Oddly enough, this took place in the same area of south-east London – Eltham – but a hundred and thirty years previously. A sixteen-year-old housemaid named Jane Marie Clousen was found fatally battered. Before she died she was asked if she could name her attacker. She was able to utter a moan that sounded like, "Pooooh". 'She had worked for a well-to-do family named Pook and was a few months pregnant. The evidence pointed to the son of the house, Edmund Pook, as being the culprit – the girl's aunt said he'd sent a letter inviting Jane Marie to a rendezvous, there were bloodstains on his clothing, he fitted the description of the youth who'd purchased the murder weapon, a lathing hammer, and a whistle was found near the spot belonging to the suspected youth. Despite all this, the youth denied everything and was vigorously backed by his family's wealth.' Ringrose went on relentlessly, 'In court, the police evidence was botched and – rather like old Gunner's tape in our own time – certain incriminating testimony was ruled as hearsay and therefore inadmissible. Young Pook, like Gatling, was acquitted.'

'And?' said the director shortly. 'Is there a punchline to this heartrending tale?'

'Most certainly,' said Ringrose, ignoring the sarcasm. 'There followed a great swelling of public outrage. A poor girl had been done wrong and a rich kid had been allowed flagrantly to get away with it. If the attorney-general gets his way, that will sound rather like the case of Lawrence Varnish and Vernon Gatling, wouldn't you say?

'There the matter would have ended but for the editor of the local newspaper, the *Kentish Mercury*. He was determined to see justice of a sort done. He most courageously published the full story, naming Pook as the murderer and, like the *Daily Mail* in the next century, invited Pook to sue.

'The Pook family was shamed into taking up the challenge and a writ was issued on young Pook's behalf. At the civil trial all the evidence that had earlier been suppressed during the criminal proceedings was revealed. The jury found for Pook, of course.' The beginning of a triumphal smile began to cross the director's face until Ringrose added, 'And then awarded him one farthing damages. Young Pook's reputation was ruined.'

'You'd better leave all this with me,' said the director, darkly. 'We can't take the decision today. There are ramifications . . .'

Ringrose, Firth and Dalton walked down the hill to the Bell in Fleet Street. Over his pint of ale, Dalton said, 'Tom, I'm amazed. You twisted the director's arm off at the shoulder with that libel-action stuff. When did our young hacks come up with that little stunt?'

Ringrose grinned and said, 'They didn't. They don't know about it yet. But they will . . .'

'So who's the genius?' asked Firth.

'A Greek celibate,' winked Ringrose, who'd been peeking in his encyclopedia.

Chapter Seventeen

There is little long-term loyalty in politics. There was no more emphatic advertisement of this truism than the official announcement that the attorney-general in person would lead for the prosecution in the trial of Vernon and Tabitha Gatling on a charge of conspiracy to murder.

Realpolitik dictated that Vernon Gatling had to be ditched. Better still, there was political capital to be made by the government of which the tycoon had been such an enthusiastic supporter. The attorney-general's active participation would demonstrate that here was an administration that could not be bought, no matter how rich and influential its erstwhile friends.

Sir Marcus Coombes brought Vernon the ominous news

that he'd been thrown to the wolves and sat helplessly watching his client pace up and down, ranting and raving at the greed and hypocrisy of politicians.

When Vernon had collapsed, drained, into his chair, the solicitor said apprehensively, 'Vernon, under the rules of disclosure, I've now seen the bulk of the prosecution's evidence. I'm afraid the time has come for some painful decisions to be made. Listen to me. I want you to give Ringrose another interview that you may rely on later in court.'

'Saying what, for fuck's sake?'

'Saying that it was your father who accidentally killed Lawrence Varnish and that you only helped him conceal the body out of filial love.'

'I've just faced trial and denied that until I was blue in the face.'

'Nevertheless, that is what has to be done if we are to save you. Against any other defence, the police have assembled a formidable case. It was extremely unwise of you to keep that statue. Did it not occur to you that one day you might be asked for the provenance of such an historic object?'

'Knock it off,' said Vernon. 'The fucking thing was put away by that mad wife of mine. I'd forgotten all about it. Then that poofter, Wensley Allbritton, creamed his pants over it and I was too preoccupied with my business to rein him in.'

'Most regrettable,' said Sir Marcus. 'The statue is unique. We cannot say it was a casual purchase. The prosecution would bring in experts from the British Museum who would rip our evidence to pieces. We have to own up.'

'Where does all this leave my little girl?' yelled Vernon, so loudly that the warder opened the door of the interview room and peered in to check for trouble.

Sir Marcus waved the man away and lowered his voice. 'You go into the box and swear it was your father who hired those appalling Americans to kill the witnesses – something you discovered only later – and then your father invited them aboard the *Black Glove* to accompany him while he was recovering his health.' He warmed to the scenario as he spoke. 'Tabitha was her grandfather's innocent go-between. You reveal to the court that it wasn't some American business acquaintance who asked you to accommodate Ruttmann and Iwasaki at Cheyne Walk but your own father. And it was he who asked his lovely granddaughter to be their guide on their first trip to London. She had no idea why they wanted to go to Chiswick. She sat in the car while they were inside the house . . . She was grief-stricken when she found out later what had happened to those poor women who were unfortunate enough to get in their way . . .'

Vernon looked wildly at him. 'Could it work? It contradicts almost everything we've said before. The bastards will fling it all back in our faces.'

'I agree,' said Coombes. 'It's a high-risk strategy. But what else do we have? We're down to our last box of ammunition.'

'That's a fine fucking metaphor, I don't think!' said Vernon. 'You'd better go and see Tabitha. Give her my love and make sure that if we're gonna have a new tune we'll both be singing from the same hymn sheet.'

'Don't worry,' said Sir Marcus Coombes. 'There will be many a rehearsal of the evidence before the big day arrives.'

The solicitor was about to tap on the door to be let out when Vernon said, 'Hey, Marcus.'

He turned back. 'Vernon?'

'You and Claud Collingwood . . .'

'Yes?'

'Legal fees aside, I'm making out four personal cheques, each in the sum of £2.5 million. If one of us walks free, each of you guys gets one cheque. If we both walk, each of you gets two cheques. Get out of here and earn the money, Marcus.'

Ringrose, Firth and Dalton studied copies of Vernon Gatling's new statement with growing concern. The tycoon had volunteered it in one long gut-spilling session but Sir Marcus had thereafter refused to allow the three detectives to pick over the details and question his client. There was a horrible plausibility about 90 per cent of it.

The following day at Holloway prison there was a similar performance from Tabitha, who looked pale but composed and still beautiful in khaki slacks and a charcoal polo-neck sweater.

Afterwards, Ringrose telephoned his FBI liaison, Marty Groot. 'Marty, I need help. Vernon Gatling is now trying to stick his dead father with all the wrong-doing. He's saying Gunner hired the killers so I need to prove the link between Vernon, that Mafia guy Albert Penn and the two hitmen he loaned out to Vernon and didn't get back.'

'I see the pit of boiling shit over which you dangle, *comandante*,' mused Groot. 'You need the Bureau's Costa Rican phone taps between Vernon and the egregious Albert, plus the photographs showing Ruttmann in Albert's company. Then you'll need one of our fine, upstanding young agents to testify to same before an English court.'

'Perfectly put,' said Ringrose. 'What are the chances?'

'None, if the RICO operation is still in progress. I'll get back to you.'

Five hours later, the answer was a definite no.

'*Comandante*, what can I say? The director says he won't sleep tonight knowing that he has perforce to let down his good friend, Ringrose. But regretfully he says he cannot alert the rascal Albert Penn to the likelihood of his imminent arrest in order to provide a morsel of evidence that, in any case, you should not need if your cause is righteous and your case strong. The Bureau has so far invested six million dollars in attempting to nail Albert Penn and associates. We can't let that kind of money go down the tubes on a favour – especially not on a favour to the people who burned down the White House.'

'Shit!' said Ringrose.

Chapter Eighteen

Beneath the parapet of the dock, they sat on their hard wooden chairs and bridged the gap, holding hands like lovers, a fact clearly seen from the gallery and reported.

In their latest incarnations, Vernon Gatling was now the loyal son sorrowing over his father's perfidy and Tabitha the bewildered, naive daughter who had been ill-used by evil men.

'Has old Coombes been taking a drama coach into Holloway?' said Ringrose. He looked at the jury and was not reassured that they were seeing the charade for what it was.

Ringrose thought Collingwood was getting the better of the joust. But, then, everybody knew the attorney-general might be a wizard on the greasy political pole but was bloody useless as a trial lawyer – the worst, it was said, since Manningham-Buller.

In having Collingwood represent both Vernon and his daughter, rather than providing her with separate counsel, the defence had knowingly surrendered a small advantage.

But when Sir Marcus Coombes had raised the matter of splitting the defence, Vernon had been adamant. 'Claud Collingwood is the best, and my little girl and I will accept nothing less.'

Tabitha had said stoutly, 'Daddy and I are as one. Our flesh and blood will not be divided.' Sir Marcus had been rather taken aback by her intensity.

The two Gatlings were jointly charged with conspiring to murder the Chiswick two, Melanie Lamb and Esther Keen, and complicity in the attempted murder of Police Sergeant Alan Passingham. Vernon alone was charged with the murder of Lawrence Varnish.

Because the only evidential link with the contract hitmen was the method of asphyxiation, Ringrose had agreed with the CPS that the name of Wes Lake be omitted from the indictment.

The dead blagger's friend, Waxy Bates, when he heard, had

appeared on the boil in his sharp Mark Powell three-piece suit at Ringrose's HQ. 'Do you mean to stand there and tell me that cow and her father won't be answering for Wes's death? It's diabolical, guv'nor. It's well out of order.' In his indignation Wes almost popped the buttons on his form-fitting waistcoat.

'One verdict of guilty on one count is all we need,' said Ringrose. 'Don't worry. Wes will be avenged. They'll go down for life. And if I know the judge he'll be recommending a minimum of twenty-five years apiece. Vernon will die behind bars and Tabitha will be a middle-aged woman before she sees the outside again.'

'Oh, yeah?' said Waxy, cynically. 'Well, balls to that. It'll be life in an open nick for her, with daily aerobics classes and Harrods hampers and bent screws waiting on her hand and foot. Maybe she'll do what all those rich pricks do – get some dodgy quack to certify that she's suffering from a terrible illness and get her sprung early to enjoy her millions after she, surprise, surprise, makes a miraculous recovery.'

'Trust me,' said Ringrose.

'Trust a copper?' said Waxy, eyes bulging in disbelief. 'Where d'you think I was born? Fucking Disney World?'

Ringrose had done his best to fill the gap left by the FBI's refusal to make the Vernon Gatling–Albert Penn connection.

Abbotsbury, our part-time MI6 Man in Costa Rica, had been summoned to London and given by the judge the imaginative pseudonym 'Mr A.' He had testified from behind a screen as to Vernon Gatling's telephone calls from San José to the Trapani Athletic Club of Brownsville, New York.

The FBI had finally shown Ringrose a small mercy by persuading the NYPD to send over to London a detective lieutenant to testify that the club was owned by one Albert Penn who had on two occasions been summoned to appear before congressional committees investigating organized crime and, in particular, contract killing.

Claud Collingwood put him though the mincer.

'Tell me, Lieutenant' – the QC immediately gained a laugh at the policeman's expense by pronouncing it looootenant – 'is the athletic club a properly run business? I mean, there isn't a back room full of desperadoes playing the numbers game, whatever that is?' (Another laugh.)

'No, sir. Not that I'm aware,' said the lieutenant impassively.

'In fact, Looootenant, isn't it true to say that Mr Penn owns a number of perfectly legitimate businesses – principally in hotel supplies – and has a number of contracts with Mr Gatling to supply clean towels and bedsheets and so forth for various of his establishments?'

'That is so, sir.'

'Isn't it also true that Mr Penn, apart from some trivial offences usually involving traffic misdemeanours, has never been convicted of any criminal activity of any sort? Indeed, has never even been *charged* with any such thing?'

'Yes, sir. That is true. But it is also true that Albert Penn has appeared before congressional committees to be questioned about organized crime.'

'Why do you think that was?'

'My understanding is that he was called because he is a known associate of prominent criminals.'

'Hmmm. Your understanding? Mr Penn is an Italian-American, is he not?'

'Yes, sir.'

'Is it not the case that Italian-Americans have been forced to set up an organization in your country to protect the good name of their fellow countrymen who are so frequently and unfairly depicted in a bad light in films, on television and in books?'

'There is such an organization, yes. Whether Italian-Americans are treated badly depends on who we're talking about.'

'Let us take those congressional committees. What was the outcome of their deliberations?'

'There was no outcome, as far as Albert Penn was concerned. Nothing ever came of it.'

'Precisely!' said a triumphant Collingwood. 'So Mr Penn returned without a stain on his character to run his perfectly legitimate businesses?'

'I wouldn't like to say one way or the other.'

Collingwood wasn't about to settle for that. 'I take it, Looootenant, that in the United States of America it is still the custom to regard a man as innocent until a jury of his peers has found him guilty?'

'That is so, sir.'

'So why have you been hauled across the Atlantic Ocean by the prosecution to smear the name of a man who is guilty of nothing beyond having legitimate business dealings with Mr Gatling?'

'I'm not here to smear anyone, sir. I'm here only to offer such assistance as the New York Police Department can give this distinguished court.'

'Very commendable. And very pointless, if I may say so. It all comes down to this, does it not? Did Vernon Gatling have perfectly legitimate business reasons to make telephone calls to Mr Penn whether he was in Costa Rica at the time or in Timbuktu?'

'Well, I . . .'

'Yes or no, Looootenant!'

'Yes.'

'Thank you. One last matter, Looootenant. When my learned friend questioned you, you testified that the dead hitmen, Ruttmann and Iwasaki, were unknown to the American police before they were shot in London. Is there any evidence you can produce for this court that proves these men were associates of Albert Penn?'

'Well, there does exist . . .'

'Just yes or no, Looootenant. Let's have no hearsay,' said Collingwood before the witness could mention the FBI photographs.

'No, sir, there is no evidence on that score I can supply to this court.'

'So, if Penn didn't know Ruttmann and Iwasaki, Vernon Gatling would not have been telephoning Mr Penn to secure their bloodthirsty services.'

'That is correct, sir – if Mr Penn didn't know them.'

'If, as Vernon Gatling says, his father hired the two killers, there is no evidence whatsoever you can produce here today that this was accomplished with Albert Penn as the intermediary? Nothing on paper? No phone records? No one within earshot?'

'That is so.'

Collingwood shook his head sadly. 'You don't really know much at all, do you, Looootenant? Unless the police have promised to show you Dr Crippen's pyjamas from their Black Museum at New Scotland Yard, I'm afraid you've had an awfully wasted trip to London.'

Apart from the prosecution team, everyone hooted and Mr Justice Quarmby, presiding once again, said testily, 'That's enough, Mr Collingwood.'

The defence counsel sat down, smiling. It was, indeed, enough.

For the benefit of the jury, Mr Justice Quarmby allowed an example of the alleged murder weapon, a bricklayer's hod, to be brought into court. The prosecution junior counsel had quietly advised the attorney-general to fumble and 'accidentally' drop the crude wooden apparatus to get the message across as to just how heavy it was and what an impact it would have on the human skull.

'I'm not here to mimic Collingwood's cheap tricks,' snapped his master.

To counter Vernon's version of Larry Varnish's killing, in which Gunner swung the long-handled hod round his head and caught Larry before Vernon could prevent the disaster, Ringrose produced an orthopaedic surgeon, who testified that Gunner's wartime shoulder injury would have made this physically impossible.

'My dad was in a panic,' said Vernon when he came later to give his testimony-in-chief under Collingwood's careful steering. 'It was quite dark but he saw Varnish had something heavy in his hand – it turned out to be the Roman statuette – and my dad grabbed the nearest thing to hand to defend himself. That was the hod. Fear of being hurt must have given my father the strength of ten to overcome his disability because from where I was standing I could see him clearly lifting the hod to shoulder height.'

Vernon actually placed a sincere hand over his heart. Sir

Marcus Coombes, sitting behind Collingwood, frowned and made a mental note to warn Vernon about overdoing the dramatics.

Vernon was saying, 'Believe me, no one could have punished my father more than he punished himself. I told him that what had happened was self-defence not murder. But he was afraid to go to the police as I urged because he did not think he would be believed – and what is being alleged in this court now more than suggests he was right! In the thirties he'd once been reported for striking his carthorse and he was afraid the police would cite this as evidence that he had a bad temper, which wasn't true. He was a sweet man who loved ballroom dancing.'

'It's all lies, isn't it, Gatling?' said the attorney-general, contemptuously, as he climbed to his feet to cross-examine. 'All the evidence is that Varnish was a slender, non-violent young man. The only person at that scene on that April night built powerfully enough to wield that hod in the fashion you have described was yourself. You killed Lawrence Varnish. You are simply blackguarding your father to cover your own wicked act.'

'No, sir!' shouted Vernon. 'I have protected my dear dad's name all these years because what he did happened in a brief moment of lost control. As a result, he suffered feelings of guilt and remorse all his life.'

After that sudden flare-up Vernon, perhaps sensing he had revealed too much of his own inherent aggression, assumed a contrite expression. 'However, I have to blame myself for one thing. When he became old and his mind was not as clear as it once was, I refused to let the doctors reduce his quality of life by drugging him.' Vernon turned tearfully to the jury. 'I had no idea his mental faculties were deteriorating so badly that, inside his head, he was concocting the appalling plot that involved the Americans and, most grievously, my lovely daughter. I bitterly reproach myself. If I'd consented to the drugs, his last years might have been more tranquil and the serpent would not have entered his brain and told him to do these terrible things.'

Vernon began to sob, long, shuddering sobs that brought an usher to his side with a glass of water.

'I don't know if Sir Marcus took a drama coach into Holloway but he most certainly took one into Brixton,' murmured Firth to Ringrose. 'That's vintage Olivier.'

The two detectives started. Across the packed courtroom rose an anguished eldritch wail. Someone was in terrible mental pain. 'Oh, please don't cry, Daddy. Please don't cry. You did the best you could.'

They looked across to see Tabitha Gatling, face contorted in misery, being pulled back into her seat in the dock by a female prison officer. Tabitha was outdoing her father in the crying game.

Mr Justice Quarmby peered peevishly over his gold-rims. 'Mr Collingwood, would you tell your client to control herself or I shall be obliged to send her downstairs.'

When the hubbub had subsided, the attorney-general continued his cross-examination. 'Now, let us see if I have this right,' he began comfortably. 'You lied about your part in the circumstances surrounding Varnish's death all through the months of the police investigation?'

'Yes – but, as I said, only out of consideration for my father's memory.'

'You continued to lie throughout a previous trial in this very courtroom?'

'Yes.'

'You lied under oath on that occasion – the same oath you swore when you first stepped into the witness box yesterday?'

'Yes.'

'The jury believed you on that first occasion? And acquitted you?'

'Yes.'

'And your word was worthless?'

'I regret to say, yes.' Vernon bowed his head in contrition.

'Why should they think other than that your word is worthless now?'

'They say truth will out. I can only swear that what I am now saying under oath is that truth.'

'Really?' said the attorney-general, turning to the jury with an expression of profound disbelief. 'You've heard Professor Dart give evidence that Lawrence Varnish was turned sideways to his attacker and possibly even moving away. That does not fit your description of Varnish advancing on your father with a weapon in his hand, does it?'

'You had to be there,' said Vernon gruffly. 'Professor Dart won't be the first clever-clever expert in this world to get things wrong.'

'Have you ever had medical or first-aid training?'

'No.'

'How could you be sure Varnish wasn't still alive after his skull had been crushed?'

'I wasn't. I rushed down the slope to my father's side, took one look at the figure on the ground and said, "I'll go and ring for an ambulance." But my father grabbed me. He said, "Save your breath. The little fellow has gone."'

'Meaning he was already dead?'

'Yes. My father had pulled many bomb victims from the debris during the war. You could say he was an expert in that area.'

'Not one of those clever-clever experts you describe who sometimes get things wrong?'

'Score one for the prosecution,' murmured Ringrose.

Vernon looked down at the floor, despite having been sternly instructed to keep an honest man's eye contact at all times with judge, jury and counsel.

The attorney-general said, 'Whose idea was it to toss Varnish, who may have been still alive, into the well?'

'Father's. We had a long argument about it but I let him persuade me. I was young.'

'You were twenty years old. Old enough to make up your own mind – indeed, old enough at that time to hang if you had been found out!' thundered the attorney-general.

'My lord,' said Claud Collingwood, 'I really must protest. Does counsel have a question for my client or is he making his closing speech?'

Unruffled, the attorney-general asked Vernon, 'Did you remove Varnish's clothes to make identification more difficult?'

'No, that was Father.'

'Then you mutilated your victim?'

'What?'

'You covered him in slaked lime to burn away his flesh?'

'Absolutely not. I took no further part in any of it. I was sitting with my head in my hands. I firmly believed my world had come to an end.'

'Your father, with his bad shoulder, moved the heavy altar stone, and blocked the well on his own, did he?'

'No. I helped with that but I then went home leaving him to cap the well. For days I could barely believe what had happened. I felt I was living in a nightmare.'

'But not so much of a nightmare that you forgot the vital business of covering your tracks. You did, did you not, return to the scene of the crime on the Monday to commit vandalism by assisting your father and your foreman, Mr Fling, in destroying a major archaeological find?'

'I'm afraid Mr Fling has let his imagination run away with him. There was nothing on that site even remotely indicating the existence of a Roman temple, apart from the altar block and a single run of stone wall that could have come from any period.'

'Did Varnish conjure the figurine of Mercury out of thin air? The altar was dedicated to Mercury. Wouldn't you say there was good reason to suspect the existence of other archaeological remains yet to be unearthed?'

Vernon shook his head. 'I'm simply not qualified to say.'

'Just as you weren't qualified to say Lawrence Varnish was dead when you callously cast him into the well?'

Vernon remained silent and the attorney-general turned a few pages in his bundle to come at Vernon from a new direction.

'You say your wicked father must have hired the killers, Ruttmann and Iwasaki. How did he do that?'

'I was out of the country. I don't know.'

'He wasn't in the sharpest of mental health?'

'No, but he did have his clear-headed episodes. Quite often he could still remember a great deal from the past.'

'Too bloody right,' whispered Ringrose, bitterly reminded of Gunner's taped testimony, now lying useless in his safe.

'You've heard evidence that all his telephone calls from the Aitkin-Adams Home are innocently accounted for. How did he contact the killers? By mental telepathy?'

Vernon pretended he had not caught the scorn. 'As I say, I'm baffled. My father had friends and business contacts in America right until the end of his life. The only possible explanation I can offer is that he had a go-between down in Bournemouth – perhaps someone on the staff at the home who would push him in his invalid chair along the promenade and leave him to make outside international phone calls.'

'The police closely questioned the clinic staff on that score. Your father was rarely taken out of the grounds. No one can remember him making outside calls.'

'Well, they'd hardly be likely to confess once they realized what harm they'd done, would they? Believe me, I would appeal even at this late stage for that person to come forward. He – or perhaps she – has it in his ability to clear my daughter and myself of these terrible charges. It may well be that my father tricked that person into helping him in the same way he tricked my daughter. That person should know he has nothing to fear if he acted in ignorance of what my father was plotting to do.'

'Shut him up!' hissed the junior behind the attorney-general's back. 'He's making a speech.'

Lionel Firth whispered to Ringrose, 'Jesus wept. Is that idiot prosecuting or acting as Claud Collingwood's bumboy?'

The detectives could see new life in a jury that had become progressively slumped. Here was a fresh, intriguing possibility. A go-between yet to come forward? They were sitting straighter in their chairs and paying full attention.

Claud Collingwood's high-risk strategy put Vernon into the witness box to answer for both himself and his daughter. Sir Marcus had expressed doubts about her stability and, at the last minute, had changed their minds about exposing her to cross-examination.

'There is sometimes a strange light in her eyes,' said the solicitor. 'I find her most unsettling. It is a light I once saw as a young man in the eyes of the notorious murderer Donald

Hume. I've never forgotten. I don't believe we can rely totally on Miss Gatling maintaining a coherent story. If she cracks, love him or love him not, she will take her father down with her.'

Chapter Nineteen

The trial ended on its nineteenth day. The police had piled in every evidentiary morsel they were allowed and the attorney-general had botched perhaps only 10 per cent of the ammunition he had been offered by Ringrose and Dalton. By his courtroom standards, this was a triumph.

Claud Collingwood's final address had been masterly. His face had a Churchillian gravity as if France had just fallen. Here was the betrayed daughter who, no matter what the outcome, would face a life for ever blighted. On cue, Tabitha began to weep quietly into her lace handkerchief.

In the cells below she had earlier confided to Sir Marcus that she thought at least two male members of the jury and one female had fallen in love with her. He had patted her hand, said, 'Well done, my dear,' and fled, shaking his head.

Collingwood, not forgetting for one moment Tabitha's previous starring role in tabloid gossip columns, told the jury, 'Here is a young lady who is blessed with good looks and a veneer of sophistication. Indeed, these attributes have contributed a great deal to her prominence among a certain set of young people in society – as I am sure some members of the jury will be aware. But please do not be misled. Beneath the physical appearance and the exuberance of youth, there is a woman lacking in a certain self-esteem because she had been unable to live up to her father's expectations for her.'

To Tabitha's fury, she'd had to consent to her unimpressive scholastic record being broadcast to the great unwashed.

'She failed to get into a university and was in that state of drift and confusion that so many young people experience when they are on the threshold of adulthood. The company she found was often transient. People wandered in and out of her life. Tabitha Gatling was renowned for her hospitality and generosity. She did not ask for their jobseekers' CVs before giving them a bed for the night in her father's house of many beds. On the occasion that has pitched her into this dreadful affair, it was good enough for her if they said they were her beloved grandfather's friends just passing through London . . .'

Collingwood hammered home the incontrovertible truth that, throughout the murderous rampages of the hitmen, Vernon Gatling, in Costa Rica or on his yacht, had been as remote from the action as it was possible for any man to be.

Collingwood suddenly asked the jury, 'I wonder how many of you know someone who has been in difficulties with the law?' He chuckled. 'Given the world we live in, I'd guess that most of you and most of the rest of us in this court including, I dare say, his lordship,' sly glance at a stone-faced Quarmby, 'would have to raise our hand and own up.'

The smile dropped off the end of his chubby chin so abruptly that several members of the jury flinched. 'And that is the truism that the prosecution has sought to exploit here in order to blacken Vernon Gatling's reputation. Alas, most of us know someone dishonest. These are scoundrel times we live in.

'This man Albert Penn in New York may or may not be a criminal who has so far escaped punishment. We still don't know. The American policeman the prosecution flew in at vast public expense to give evidence on that matter had nothing more than tittle-tattle to offer. What is true is that this man Penn owns legitimate companies that do legitimate business with Vernon Gatling's legitimate companies. The prosecution concede that fact without peradventure. Frustrated, what they have then attempted to prove, by smear and innuendo, is that Mr Gatling has other, criminal, links to Mr Penn, who has been portrayed here as some kind of underworld chieftain.'

Collingwood looked amused. 'Members of the jury,' he continued with infinite, tired tolerance, 'we've all seen the movie, haven't we? If memory serves, the role was played rather splendidly by Mr Marlon Brando. The prosecution has attempted to paint a lurid picture of Penn as a man to whom you would go cap-in-hand if you were shopping for contract killers. Unfortunately for them, after the looootenant had completed his evidence the picture was more a blank canvas splattered with mud than a scene from *The Godfather*.'

All twelve smiled.

'Shit!' said the attorney-general's junior.

Collingwood flung his arms in the air in a gesture of despair. 'The absurdity of it! Here is Mr Gatling, a celebrated builder of skyscrapers and vacation resorts. A public figure widely admired for his support of many charities. A man instantly recognized wherever he travels in the world. A man who cannot walk through an airport without attracting the attentions of a shoal of photographers. We are not in a movie now. We live in the real world where it is not remotely conceivable that a man of his stature would engage in anything as lunatic as a sordid murder plot with a don, or whatever they are called, from the world of American organized crime. The only explanation a bewildered Vernon Gatling can give now for his father's actions – and we are far from certain exactly what form they took – is that he suffered a moral collapse when, as Vernon Gatling so graphically put it, a serpent entered his brain.'

Claud Collingwood was on his feet cajoling, thundering, flirting, scorning, damning for five hours. The attorney-general had ploughed through his closing address, icily eschewing any of his opponent's pyrotechnics.

With the occasional jury, this contrasting quiet approach is sometimes most effective. The technique is based on the promiscuous actress's preference for the calm of the marital bed following the hurly-burly of the *chaise-longue*. A jury, overdosed on drama during a long, wearying trial, will doggedly remain impervious to all seduction.

But, on this fraught battlefield, Ringrose wasn't so sure. One had to admit that old Collingwood gave value for money. Unlike his opponent, that frozen fish-finger, the attorney-general, the defence counsel was a great entertainer with his jowls flapping and those caterpillar eyebrows signalling everything from disbelief in the current witness to the monstrous unfairness to his client of the judge's various rulings. The wig would slip and the white tabs at his neck point every which way. There was something reassuring about his shambolic appearance, which, in truth, was as manufactured as his expensive dentures. His sleeker opponents somehow seemed less trustworthy.

Mr Justice Quarmby's impeccable summing up gave no viable toehold for an appeal. 'If ever a man lay in an unquiet grave, it was Lawrence Varnish,' he told the jury. 'His shade has been with us for the past three weeks, trying to make itself heard through the welter of evidence and the arguments and counter-arguments of learned counsel. Beyond doubt, the death of Laurence Varnish, however caused, triggered a chain of events that has stretched through nearly five decades, embraced many people, darkened reputations, and sadly brought us all here to this courtroom. It is an extraordinary, tragic story, the various versions of which I am going to examine with you. I shall then give you guidance as to the law and then you, and only you, shall go away to decide the guilt or innocence of the two people in the dock.'

Mr Justice Quarmby paused to draw breath before subjecting all twelve jury members to a severe look. 'Here I must add a warning. The ghost of Lawrence Varnish cries out for belated justice but I have to remind you, most emphatically, that Vernon Gatling and his daughter, Tabitha, are entitled to the same consideration. Your natural sympathy for a life cut tragically short must not cloud your judgement when you come to weigh the explanation the defendants have given for their actions. If there is a reasonable doubt in either defendant's favour, then you must acquit and Lawrence Varnish's ghost must wait patiently for justice in the highest courtroom of all, where all sins shall be laid bare and a second death in the lake of fire and brimstone awaits those who murder.'

Over on the press bench, Nelly Tripp whispered to Gervase Meredith, 'Quarmby's got his head in the Book of Revelation. Did the old fart have Claud Collingwood write this stuff for him?'

'It was either crafty Claud or the Archbishop of Canterbury,' said Gervase.

Mr Justice Quarmby spent the remainder of the day picking through the evidence. The jury was finally sent to an hotel for the night at six p.m.

Ringrose, out on the pavement with Firth and Bert Dalton, said miserably, 'I'm getting bad vibrations about this. All that Bible-bashing crap from Quarmby about leaving judgement to a higher court. What the fuck does he think we're all here for? The jury was lapping up every word. Even the guy who swore by the Koran.'

The jury began their deliberations at ten the next morning. At midday they sent a message to the judge asking if the hod could be brought to the jury room so that members could feel its weight.

Quarmby refused, pointing out that the model displayed in court was not the alleged murder weapon but something similar and produced only for purposes of illustration. The original – if, indeed, there had been an original – may have been identical. Or lighter. Or heavier. Besides, he wasn't going to risk a juryman swinging the thing round his head and inadvertently clobbering a fellow member or a court official.

At five p.m. the jury was summoned back to court by the judge. The forewoman told him they were agreed on a number of counts but had so far failed to agree on others.

Mr Justice Quarmby said, 'If you go back for further deliberation, is there any chance of a unanimous verdict being arrived at on all counts?'

The peekaboo blonde forewoman whose skirts had become noticeably shorter as the trial progressed, said, in a North London whine, 'It's very unlikely, my lord.'

'I'd be happy to accept a majority verdict on those counts still unresolved. That means at least ten of you must be in agreement,' offered Quarmby.

She tossed back the side-hanging curtain of her tresses and said, 'That might be possible, sir.' She half turned and glared at a grey-haired woman member, dressed in a quiet, oatmeal suit, who was staring off into the mid-distance and pursing her lips.

Mr Justice Quarmby sent them back, while Ringrose, his team and the lawyers trooped across the road to the Magpie and Stump for a livener.

The pagers began bleeping all around the bar of the Stump a few minutes after six. The jury was on the way back.

Vernon Gatling's perma-tan had faded during his months on remand. Under the overhead lights both he and Tabitha appeared gaunt-eyed and ashen as they were ordered to stand and confront their fate. They gripped hands so tightly that their knuckles appeared to be lines of naked bone. They both looked at Claud Collingwood for enlightenment. He nodded sagely in a way that defied interpretation.

The clerk sought verdicts one at a time on the counts against Tabitha Gatling. But from the moment the forewoman intoned, 'Not guilty,' to the first, it was inevitable that complete acquittal would follow.

As a roar of surprise went up from the public benches, Tabitha fainted clean away. She slumped into a woman prison officer's arms while Vernon screamed, 'Tabby!' but was hauled back by his jailers.

The public roar of astonishment turned to bedlam. But suddenly, another voice, stentorian and raging, was heard from the gallery and all eyes swivelled to locate the culprit.

Waxy Bates was on his feet, arms flailing, as he yelled at the jury, 'You bunch of wankers. That fucking bitch murdered my mate and you're letting her walk. I hope you all die from cancer, you bastards – and soon!'

Quarmby banged his bench. The judge was not in the best of tempers. 'Remove that man from the gallery and hold him for contempt,' he snapped at the court duty inspector. He turned towards the dock. 'Miss Gatling is free to go. Please help her down.'

In the pandemonium, the shaken forewoman looked around uncertainly. She had the slip of paper with the remainder of the jury verdicts crumpled in her hand. The court clerk shouted across, 'Wait where you are.'

It took five minutes for a clucking Sir Marcus Coombes to

organize the carrying out of Tabitha by four helpers. By this time she was already showing signs of revival. Meanwhile, police officers stormed the packed gallery, shouldering spectators aside, to drag Waxy, spitting and cursing, down to the Old Bailey holding cells.

Finally, the judge was able to snap, 'Let's get on with it.'

The clerk rose once again. Vernon clutched the dock rail as the man intoned, 'How say you?'

The forewoman said the jury had been able to reach 10–2 majority verdicts on all the conspiracy-to-murder charges against the defendant. He was not guilty.

The court broke into renewed uproar. Mr Justice Quarmby shouted, 'If this noise doesn't cease instantly, I shall clear the court. The final verdict will not be given until there is order.'

The hubbub died down. Vernon peered around wildly. His shortened hair had fallen across his brow in a sharp dagger-shape. He caught Claud Collingwood's eye. His counsel was smiling broadly. As well he might. Every lawyer and policeman in court had already grasped the logic of the situation: if Vernon was not guilty of hiring the hitmen, Ruttmann and Iwasaki, then the guilty party must have been his father, Gunner, covering up his own ancient crime of which his son was but an unhappy witness.

Vernon Gatling was about to walk free.

Except . . .

The clerk said, 'In the case of the murder of Lawrence Varnish, have you reached a verdict?'

The forewoman looked embarrassed. 'No, sir. We have failed to agree.'

A stunned silence fell upon the court as if all the air had been instantly removed.

Mr Justice Quarmby barely suppressed his sigh. He thanked the jury for their diligence and dismissed them. As they filed out, he turned to the attorney-general. 'The charge remains on the calendar. Any thoughts on retrial?'

The crestfallen legal officer said, 'I shall have to examine where we stand on this matter and return to your lordship.'

'Yes,' said Quarmby. 'Do that!' He turned to defence counsel. 'Mr Collingwood? I'm sure you have something to say.'

'I'm obliged, my lord. I'd say only that to put Mr Gatling through the ordeal of a third trial would be a monstrous misuse of the judicial process and I would earnestly press the attorney-general to bear this in mind. One other thing: my client has now been held without bail for ten months while these matters have been proceeding through the courts. In view of today's verdicts, I would plead with your lordship to grant bail while the Crown Prosecution Service considers its next course of action.'

'Yes, no need to go on,' said Quarmby. 'Bail is fixed in the defendant's own surety of two hundred and fifty thousand pounds. Are the police holding his passport?'

'Yes, my lord.'

'Let's leave it like that for now.'

Collingwood rose again. 'On the question of costs . . .'

He got no further. 'No, Mr Collingwood. Absolutely not. Mr Gatling was awarded costs by me at his first trial. In view of what we have heard here about his testimony at that trial, there is much I could say. But, as there may yet be further proceedings, I'll hold my tongue. There will be no costs awarded either for Mr Gatling or Miss Gatling. Don't over-stretch your luck, Mr Collingwood.'

As the stunned prosecution team moved out, they passed a dishevelled Waxy Bates being wheeled in front of the judge for a dressing-down.

At the end of the sensational murder trial that had filled acres of newsprint and hours of television time around the world, the only person to go to prison was an unknown man, described as a company director, from South London.

For contempt of court, Mr Justice Quarmby ordered Waxy Bates to be held in the cells and not released until the following morning.

Chapter Twenty

The crowd waited like a glowering beast, frustrated and angry. Never for them would there be the orgasmic swish of the guillotine blade or the crash of the trapdoor and judder of the stretched rope. Now, in these namby-pamby times, there was not even the consolation of seeing the high and mighty tumbled and led off in handcuffs to face the petty humiliations of imprisonment.

In their delirium, Vernon and Tabitha Gatling believed they would emerge from the Old Bailey like survivors of a monstrous oppression, arms in the air signalling heroic victory to the waiting mob.

But the mob, unlike the jury, had been fed its information through the filter of wink and nudgery in the tabloid press.

Now all those weeks of promise of the retribution to come had culminated in bitter disappointment and collapse. The mob had been cheated of their due. Once again, the rich with their lying, slimy lawyers had proved they could brush aside with contempt the laughable desires of the little people for blood sacrifices from on high.

Vernon had wanted to burst forth from the Central Criminal Courts arm-in-arm with his beautiful daughter – now recovered from her fainting fit – and proclaim for the waiting cameras their innocence and his belief that they had been the victims of a cruel persecution on the part of business rivals and political enemies. He wanted to tell it to the world.

'It's our turn on the big guns,' he said below the dock, as Tabitha nuzzled his neck and wept happiness. His mouth was drawn in a straight thin line and his eyes blazed hatred. 'It's pay-back time,' he grated.

But Sir Marcus Coombes, not anxious to see his clients deflated before he received his two cheques, said, 'Listen to me, Vernon. You will do no such thing. There is still one count of murder hanging over you. There is a large crowd with a great many media people waiting outside. The police will hold them back, and you and Tabitha will cross the pavement and get into the waiting car without making any comment of any kind. You've been locked away. You are in no position to understand the mood of that crowd.'

Vernon looked at him angrily. 'What the fuck does that mean? They should be glad for us.'

Sir Marcus stared at his client. Was the man unbalanced? They say it is possible to blot from the memory all traces of shocking events. Had Vernon achieved this buffer-state of unfeeling and then substituted the sophisticated defence that had been mounted on his behalf?

'Vernon, you have to trust my judgement on this. You have to concede that it has so far served you well. Please do not attempt to do this foolish thing.'

The solicitor looked around to enlist support from Claud Collingwood, but the Queen's Counsel, having received the justified hosannas of his legal team, had headed for the bar mess.

To achieve headline brevity and a hint of mockery, several tabloids throughout the trial had referred to the Gatlings as the Chelsea Two. Now the Two emerged from the hulking greystone Old Bailey, hand-in-hand like a starring couple at a film première. They each raised their free hand in greeting to the throng.

The first shouts to reach their ears were from the media. 'This way, Vernon . . . Over here, miss . . . Say a few words, sir . . . Kiss your daddy, Tabitha . . .'

Then shriller, harsher voices intruded.

'You wicked bastard . . . whore . . . murderer . . .'

The sound that then rolled over the individual voices began as a low murmur at the back of the crowd over by the Magpie and Stump where a grim-faced, impotent trio, Ringrose, Firth and Dalton, stood alongside their raging hacks, Gervase Meredith and Nelly Tripp.

The sound gathered strength like an avalanche and surged forward through the crowd, growing in volume until, by the time it reached the front, it had become a gale of booing that swept all before it.

Vernon and Tabitha froze as the wall of hate smashed into their faces. Then Tabitha flinched and Vernon's face darkened in anger as he realized what was happening. He mouthed something that was lost in the mob's sound and fury. He felt a push in the back. 'Dammit, Vernon, keep moving,' screamed his solicitor.

Vernon threw a protective arm round Tabitha's bowed shoulder and, at last doing Sir Marcus's bidding, rushed for the waiting Daimler.

Despite police attempts to prevent it, the limousine was pounded, rocked and kicked until it turned the corner on to Holborn Viaduct.

'Why did they do that to us? We were *acquitted*.' Vernon bellowed at Sir Marcus who had slipped into the front seat beside the chauffeur. 'Look what they've done to my little girl. Her heart's broken.'

The lawyer twisted his bulk with difficulty to see Tabitha huddled in a foetal position. 'I'm sorry, Vernon. I have little influence on what appears in the newspapers once they are in full cry, baying for blood. Most of the press coverage of the trial has not been friendly. Some of the yellow press have barely escaped contempt-of-court proceedings. And I fear there will be worse to come in tomorrow's editions. For a start, inevitably there will be accounts of the booing. Then, I am told, there will be feature articles turning a light on Albert Penn. The tabloids have been harassing and photographing that gentleman – much to his fury. And I'm sorry to say there is a great deal about his activities that is, to say the least, unsavoury. Thank God the rules of evidence kept it from the jury.'

Vernon sat dumb as the car sped along the Victoria Embankment. As they approached Westminster, he said suddenly, 'Can't you take out injunctions? Stop the scandal sheets libelling Albert? He's going to be extremely pissed off with me.'

Sir Marcus shook his head. 'He is not my client. He has his own remedy in law – if he feels secure enough to face someone of Claud Collingwood's calibre in court.'

'Can't you do anything?'

'The something I am going to do is to do nothing. It is called masterly inactivity,' he said.

'What fucking use is that?'

Sir Marcus tried to keep the weary note of condescension out of his voice. 'I'm rather relying on the tabloid press to be frightfully unpleasant about your friend Mr Penn. This, of course, will reflect badly on you.'

Vernon stared at the back of his large, round head and his wispy hair. 'Marcus, have you gone nuts? Why are you letting this happen?'

The old crocodile turned once again in his seat to smile thinly at his client. 'At the moment it is about fifty-fifty that the director of the Crown Prosecution Service will decide to re-try you for the murder of Lawrence Varnish. Once the tabloids have shat all over you tomorrow morning and for the following few days, a fair trial will be an impossibility – a representation I shall make most forcefully to him. Where will they find an untainted jury? I am relying on the gentlemen of the press not to disappoint. The price of your future freedom will be that you have to endure a passing embarrassment. Then memory will fade and your troubles will be over.'

One week after Sir Marcus Coombes's prediction, the Crown Prosecution Service announced that it would not be in the interest of justice to re-try the construction tycoon. As Coombes had anticipated, the tabloids had risen magnificently to the task of highlighting the dubious activities of Albert Penn and friends.

'A just decision,' declared Sir Marcus in a press statement. 'Vernon Gatling may now return, with his head held high, to serving his shareholders and his twenty-five thousand employees, whose future welfare has been uncertain while Mr Gatling has fought to prove his innocence.'

Vernon Gatling watched him on the television news, oiling the restive media vipers, and reached for his cheque book. Couriers delivered his personal cheques to both Sir Marcus and Claud Collingwood. Tabitha placed a single red rose with each.

Then, with their passports grudgingly returned by the police, the Chelsea Two disappeared abroad to recuperate from their long ordeal.

Chapter Twenty-one

Gervase Meredith and Nelly Tripp stepped warily into Chantry's boardroom. Gervase, on his original commissioning visit, had been dazzled by the summons. He hadn't appreciated then how oppressive the floor-to-ceiling oak panelling was.

The room was the publisher's showpiece, transported in its entirety to this glass blockhouse in the Battersea prole-land south of the Thames from the cramped Dickensian premises Chantry's had occupied for a century in Bloomsbury.

Gervase felt unsettled. Too much like the beak's room at school. The boardroom was decidedly minatory, the kind of place where they gave you stick. As if to reinforce this impression, Chantry's legal adviser was already seated at the table. A towering white pile of paper that the intrepid writers recognized as their hard-won manuscript was stacked in front of him.

Long John Silver, who was also now acting for Nelly, had warned them on the phone that trouble of an unspecified nature was brewing. 'They're calling it a crisis meeting,' said Long John.

'Crisis? What crisis?' Gervase had asked. 'We've delivered a book that'll sell a million copies in hardback alone. How the rich get away with murder. Chapter and verse. Why don't they just get their presses rolling? It's two months since we handed in the golden words.'

'Yeah, yeah,' said Long John. 'Do you think Woodward and Bernstein were cry-babies, too? Let's just go along quietly and see what Chantry's have to say.'

The chairman, Raymond Dilke, was not present to say

anything. There was no warm, enveloping beam-and-chuckle routine to flatter the ego – and no sherry either. Just the lawyer, a narrow-faced picture of sobriety with a five o'clock shadow, and Rodney, the elongated Old Etonian editorial director. His bald patch had spread since their last meeting. Either that, thought Gervase, or he should change his barber.

Long John ushered his clients to the table. The lawyer was introduced by Rodney: 'This is Quentin Carberry who would like some enlightenment from our authors.'

Rodney seemed out of sorts, as if someone had mistaken his necktie for Old Harrovian.

Quentin placed a manicured hand flat upon the manuscript. 'An extremely hot potato,' he said gravely.

'Enid Blyton it ain't,' nodded Long John, and was ignored.

Turning to Gervase and Nelly, the lawyer said, 'Tell me, can you back your claim that the FBI photograph exists showing the assassin Ruttmann in the company of Albert Penn? If it exists, it would have changed the course of the trial.'

Gervase said, 'It exists. The FBI declined to send it to London, that's all.'

'Yes,' said Quentin patiently, 'but what is the source of your information?'

'Ah,' said Gervase, 'you've got me there. I can't say.'

A week after the collapse of the prosecution of both Gatlings, a still seething and frustrated Ringrose had summoned Gervase to meet him in a pub in a Knightsbridge mews. 'Leave your tape-recorder at home,' instructed the commander.

In a corner nook, Ringrose had told him off the record about the photograph, the libel case of the *Kentish Mercury* versus Pook, and of the Los Angeles Police Department's reopening of inquiries into Gus Meldrum's death. 'There's only the smallest amount of forensic evidence. In Meldrum's hotel room, they recovered a short synthetic fibre that may have come from a cheap wig made of artificial hair. Our scientific examiners recovered similar fibres when we searched the Gatlings' house at Cheyne Walk. But there was no sign of the wig itself. We've established that the fibre is manufactured for numerous purposes, apart from wig-making. The LAPD will detain Tabitha for questioning if ever she is unwise enough to set foot again in California, but they'd never get extradition on what they have so far.'

Quentin Carberry was patting down the manuscript as if it were attempting to rear up and bite him. 'The absence of the FBI photograph is hot potato number one,' he said.

'Try us with number two,' said Long John.

'There is the innuendo that Tabitha Gatling killed our authors' predecessor in Los Angeles.' He puffed out his bluish cheeks. 'I can't think of a more monstrous libel.'

Nelly Tripp, who so far had sat silent, maintaining an unwavering stare of suspicion into the lawyer's face, broke in, 'Apart from that dim-witted jury, the whole world knows that the Gatlings should both now be serving life behind bars. What do you think all that fucking booing outside the Old Bailey was about?'

'That's as maybe,' said Quentin, 'but who's to say the Gatlings would not be fortunate enough to find another dim-witted, celebrity-adoring jury in a libel action against Chantry's?'

'*What!*' bellowed Gervase. 'After we play them the tape of Gunner Gatling describing how his son murdered that kid Varnish?'

Unmoved, Carberry said, 'I know for a fact that Vernon Gatling still has Collingwood on a massive retainer. I can just imagine what scorn he would pour on that tape. He'd have experts doubt its integrity and authenticity. In court he'd produce an actor to impersonate Gunner's voice to demonstrate how easy it is. He'd say the evidentiary chain had been broken and, therefore, the tape was contaminated. Oh, old Claud would have a lovely time with your tape.'

'We're not censoring the book,' said Nelly doggedly. 'My flatmate and landlady are dead because of me. The Gatlings have to be called to account. We have to use the only weapon left to us. Like Winston Churchill during the war, we have to mobilize the English language and send it into battle. The Gatlings must be brought to their knees, driven from society and Vernon Gatling's empire destroyed.'

She came out of her seat and rounded the table to place herself at the nervous lawyer's shoulder. Her eyes flashed fire. 'The pair of them, father and daughter, must be turned into outcasts wherever they go. And if Chantry's hasn't got the balls to publish, we'll take our book elsewhere.'

'Who said anything about not publishing?' said the lawyer mildly.

'So what's all this shit about hot potatoes?' said Nelly.

'In Britain,' said the lawyer. 'That's where the potatoes are hot. Too hot. We can't do the book here.'

The visiting trio all opened their mouths to speak, but Quentin Carberry added hurriedly, 'We thought the United States would be a better bet. Much safer. Freedom of speech. First Amendment to the Constitution and all that. Put the Atlantic Ocean between the book and old Claud. You two journalists should know better than most what a horrible gamble libel actions are in Britain. The Gatlings could walk away with a farthing, as in the Pook case you cite, or they could be handed millions by way of damages. The risk is too great.'

'So what's the deal?' said Long John.

'We propose to establish a new imprint in Manhattan, backed by a modest amount of capital, with the sole purpose of publishing *How To Get Away With Murder*. You, as authors, will consent to be released from your Chantry's contract and you will sign on again with the new imprint. In this way, Chantry's will be completely ring-fenced from any legal action the Gatlings might take.'

'And who's to ring-fence my clients?' demanded Long John. 'They'll have a bundle in royalties if the sales are all we hope. Suppose Vernon sues them for every penny they make?'

The lawyer smiled for the first time. 'In the land where freedom of expression is enshrined in the Constitution, that is highly unlikely. Did Richard Nixon sue Woodward and Bernstein or the Hollywood studio that made the movie from their book? In any case, I gather from Miss Tripp's outburst that our two stalwart authors are on something of a personal crusade. They must bear in mind that when they send words into battle they must expect to suffer reverses. If memory serves, Mr Churchill never flinched from facing that likelihood.'

'I'm flinching already,' said Long John. 'Ten per cent of these two heroes is mine. My piece depends on them remaining in one piece.'

'It'll work out just fine. You'll see,' soothed Quentin. 'Everyone will get their piece. My only regret is that I won't be there to witness the look on Claud Collingwood's face when he gets the news that he has been checkmated.'

The book was handled as if it contained the plans for the invasion of Normandy. Only one plant in upstate New York was contracted to do the printing and binding, and there was heavy perimeter security that included the body-searching of employees as they left the premises. Chantry's was not about to underestimate the power of Vernon Gatling to suborn staff and get his hands on the galley proofs.

All copies were cling-wrapped the moment the dust jackets were added. The cover showed profiles of Vernon and Tabitha hovering darkly above an abstracted female figure with a plastic bag over her head.

Gervase Meredith and Nelly Tripp had both objected vigorously to this penny-dreadful vulgarity. They argued that they had produced a serious work of investigative journalism, an outstanding contender for a Pulitzer prize. They did not need to promote their achievement in such a low fashion.

'This is America,' said the hustler who had been hired for the one-off job as sales director. 'Subtlety ain't in our dictionary. I'd ring the cover in neon tube if I could figure out how.'

He was a horrible person but his organizational ability could not be faulted. The must-have frenzy he so skilfully generated had unsettled Manhattan for a week before the couriers were despatched with the first copies to book critics and media panjandrums.

The launch party took place at the Metropolitan Museum of Art on Fifth Avenue on the same evening.

Twenty-four hours later the young English authors were television chat-show celebrities, interviewed to soundbite exhaustion.

Vernon Gatling ranted and raved through every room of his vast Manhattan penthouse, terrorizing the staff and making even Tabitha cringe nervously. Chantry's had outmanoeuvred him. It was far too late for Vernon to send in his army of lawyers to seek injunctions and bribe judges.

Gatling's portfolio of companies, including the umbrella parent, Gatling Construction, had all suffered stock-market reversal during the months he had awaited trial when it was clear that the driving force of the empire was preoccupied with matters of life and death.

Publication of *How To Get Away With Murder* now provided the push that sent the stock into catastrophic decline. Share prices were given a further downward shove by Senator Jackson Davis's announcement that his committee on organized crime had issued subpoenas for both Vernon Gatling and his daughter to appear before it.

Forced by the revelations in the text, the incompetent Los Angeles Police Department hurriedly announced they were issuing a warrant for the arrest of Tabitha Gatling on suspicion of murdering Gus Meldrum. The *Wall Street Journal* immediately despatched a team of Gus's old colleagues to California to help keep the LAPD's renewed investigation ongoing.

Within two weeks of publication, the rout of Vernon Gatling was complete. His spokesman announced that the chairman and CEO was retiring and placing the future of his group of companies in the hands of the main board. The spokesman refused to be drawn either about the book or the media blitzkrieg.

An hour before the press conference was held, Vernon and his daughter had sped in a car with smoked-glass windows to Newark airport. Their protection goons and cops on the payroll had hustled them out on to the tarmac and they'd made an ignominious departure in his private jet. The spokesman, when asked, professed not to know the current whereabouts of his boss.

Fearing subpoenas, Vernon had instructed his pilot not to risk a refuelling touchdown anywhere in the United States. The pilot filed a flight plan for Nassau in the Bahamas.

After a fraught night stopover, during which the couple left all the talking to their two bodyguards, they flew onward to Costa Rica where a limousine was waiting on the tarmac of Juan Santamaria airport to whisk them to the last building project remaining under Vernon's personal control – the Arenal vacation complex he had been surveying while Rutt-mann and Iwasaki first went about their bloody business in London.

Tabitha hated the country with its moist, clammy heat and its hammering rainfall. She'd never seen so many varieties of bug and serpent in her life. They repelled her. 'Daddy,' she whined, 'can't we go back to London? We're in the clear there. No one is pursuing us.'

But Daddy said bitterly, 'It's all over. There's no going back. Those Fleet Street hacks have fucked us over good. More copies of that book are crossing the Atlantic than bottles of duty-free booze. We'd be spat at in the streets. We have to make a life here for a while. Then we'll see . . .'

They were lying side by side on a bed in a newly built *cabaña* in the grounds of the complex where a giant aviary, designed to display in minimal captivity the many exotic bird species of Costa Rica, was nearing completion. Vernon had lost interest.

Tabitha gazed at him sorrowfully. He had lost weight, and his lovely silvering hair its lustre. A light had gone out. For the first time Tabitha could recall, her father looked his age.

She turned on her side. His skin was slack and his face pouched. His tan had deteriorated leading an unhealthy jaundiced tinge to his skin. He needed a decent haircut, and there were days now when he could not be bothered to shave or let himself be shaved – a task she had often delighted in doing for him, whipping up the lather in the mug and pretending to wield the bone-handled cut-throat razor like Sweeney Todd. Not for him the effete Tiffany safety razors that he scattered around the *Black Glove*. Her daddy was so manly.

She sidled across the wide mattress until their bodies, over-cooled by the fierce new air-conditioning, were touching. She slipped an arm under his neck and half climbed on to him, sliding one glossy leg across his lower torso. He stared emptily at the slope of the timber ceiling and did not seem to notice when she pressed her soft lips against his beloved, neglected cheek.

'Don't worry, Daddy,' she whispered. 'Whatever happens, it'll always be the two of us. Wherever we go, we go together. Never apart. Tabby will look after you. You'll see.'

Chapter Twenty-two

It took much to wipe the merry smile from Albert Penn's beefy face. Life had been good to the great-nephew of Albert Anastasia and he didn't see why he had to maintain a front of gravitas like some whitebread chump from the Chamber of Commerce. He had other ways of impressing people.

He'd looked up his name in the index of the book those Limey schmucks had written. So the Feds had photographs of him and Oscar Ruttmann. Big surprise! Oscar had been selling him toys for his kids. That would be the story, if asked. Right?

The Feds had a tape of Vernon Gatling calling him at the athletic club? Oh, wow! Excuse him while he cried for his momma.

At his trial Vernon had adequately explained their perfectly legitimate business dealings. The Feds could take the Washington Monument and shove it right up their Ivy League asses. Albert Penn was smart. Albert Penn was clean.

Albert read the paragraphs in which he starred, then tossed the book at his mouthpiece, who got paid to do boring things like read books cover to cover. All the same, the Pen Man was currently not his usual sunny self. The day had begun with a big jerk of a United States marshal stopping him in the street

– Albert's protection had both begun sliding hands under their armpits – and serving him with a subpoena inviting him for a return gig in front of the Jackson Davis congressional committee.

Then at noon the newly restructured main board of the Gatling enterprises had summoned him to an uneasy meeting to inform him that it would be wiser all round if Albert's contracts were not renewed and, er, his future association with Gatlings held in abeyance.

That was how the pot-bellied weasels had put it: held in abeyance.

Yet none of this was as alarming as the third ballbuster of the day. His mobile phone trilled and a voice that did not announce itself but which he knew well said, 'Carmine would like to play *bocce*. Five o'clock.'

Carmine did not play *bocce*. Had never played *bocce*. Had no intention of ever playing *bocce*. But Albert had his driver hit the road for Long Island early. You were not late when Carmine wanted to play *bocce*.

At the estate, everything appeared normal. Albert, as was always expected, left his protection at the gate-lodge and proceeded alone up to the house. You didn't insult Carmine by trailing your hired muscle over his fancy carpets.

Ushered into the presence, even a pachyderm would have felt a flicker in the gut. Jeeesus! Carmine was not alone. He sat flanked by two other members of the council, a copy of the Limeys' book set four-square on the desk in front of them.

They hardly gave him time to finish paying his respects before Carmine said, 'Alberto, this shit with the *inglesi* must stop. You did them a favour and did yourself no favour. Your name is everywhere.'

Albert groaned inwardly. His name was even more 'everywhere' than they yet knew. The subpoena was eating a hole in his pocket. He had not had time to bounce it off his lawyer's head. He drew it out and placed it under their noses. You couldn't flim-flam with these men.

'I was hit with this today,' he said, humbly.

The three read the legalese and Carmine said sternly, 'This only underlines the council's concern.'

The boss of bosses paused and looked at Albert strangely. Finally, he added, 'Alberto, isn't there something else you wish to discuss?'

For a moment, Albert was puzzled. The three had raised eyebrows. They were expecting something. What?

Christ! They must already know about the Gatling board putting him 'in abeyance'.

Albert hurriedly brought the trio up to speed. They nodded, satisfied. Yes, they had definitely known. Albert shed a little sweat. He had almost blanked them, thinking he could fix his woes before coming clean.

Carmine's watery eyes drooped sadly. 'The termination of these contracts will seriously damage family revenues. We are paying a heavy price for your generosity towards these *inglesi*. Were you screwing the beautiful daughter? Did she mess with your head, Alberto? It is the only reason we can see for your lapse of judgement.'

'I've never even met the bitch,' yelped Albert. 'I've heard she has a thing going with her own father.'

The three old men reacted as if he had brought news of the death of their first-born. Three crevassed faces turned to granite. Between them they had eleven children and six grandchildren.

They stared wordlessly at each other. Then Carmine said, 'This is a *peccato* beyond forgiveness. They will burn in hell.'

He looked at his two associates and they both nodded. A unanimous vote had been taken.

Carmine pushed the book across the desk and spun it round. Albert looked down. Before his eyes they made his decision for him. Carmine took a felt-tipped pen from a figured silver pot and, with a fierce flourish, circled the heads of both Vernon Gatling and his daughter.

'Go away, Alberto. See it is done,' said Carmine. 'And then you go back to those old women at Gatling's and tell them it's business as usual. By then they will have come to understand the true meaning of putting someone in abeyance.'

Chapter Twenty-three

The Costa Rican government wasted no time in asking the State Department in Washington if they could fly in experts to investigate the killings. The forensic skills available in the tiny republic were not, the government had to concede, of the highest order. If the growing tourist industry was to be reassured, speedy and decisive action needed to be taken.

Even before the preening FBI team landed at Juan Santamaria, they were wearily resigned to finding that the *policia* and morbid sightseers would have contaminated the crime scene. Cops of the Latino persuasion were so *excitable*. They gave their relatives *guided tours*. Hopeless!

However, the special agents were gratified to find a police chief in charge who was a cut above the giddy throng. The trampling of the evidence had been shortlived before he arrived at the Gatling vacation complex, kicked ass, cleared the area and sent for two photographers to make both a still and video record of everything as it had been found.

Of course, he could not be held to account when, three days later, a selection of these photographs found their way into the newspapers. This was happy-go-lucky Central America, after all, not stern Singapore. A *peon* had to make a living.

Immediately the photographic record was completed and everybody even remotely connected to the events of the previous evening rounded up, the bodies had been removed to the mortuary to await the arrival of the FBI. In such an oppressive climate, this was regrettable but necessary.

What remained, the physical damage, the blood splatters and groupings, told their own story.

The Gatlings' own compound, deep inside the 20,000-acre site, had been deliberately designed not to be of an obviously defensive nature. High walls and watchtowers would have struck a jarring note in this carefree vacationland.

Trees, foliage and grassy embankments marked the boundaries. Behind them an invisible chain of electronic beams encircled the main house and Vernon Gatling's guest *cabañas*.

Unfortunately, the system was in its test stage where the operatives were still learning to distinguish between human intruders and the larger mammals.

When it occurred to the police chief to inquire why the goddamn system had not raised the alarm, an underling was sent to investigate. He found the night operative slumped over his monitor board, a bullet in the back of his head. The intruders had not risked being mistaken for human beings.

Despite the elaborate security arrangements, Vernon Gatling had no cause to sense a specific imminent physical threat either to himself or to his daughter. They knew they were world-class pariahs on the O. J. Simpson scale, especially now that the book had included every damn word those bastards from Fleet Street had wormed out of Gunner. But the hostility was generalized, not *mano a mano*.

Vernon's only pressing worry had been Albert Penn. He had cost Albert two of his best men and had made him the target for much unwelcome publicity. Vernon had waited three months for the trial hysteria to die down before risking a call to him.

There had been the usual rigmarole. Ring later. Where are you? He'll ring you. Maybe. Yeah. The silence lasted a whole uneasy month.

Finally, Albert had connected in his own cautious way and had brushed aside Vernon's profuse apologies. He had been surprisingly affable.

'Those Limey cops surprised the shit out of all of us, huh, Vern? Still, you go hunting tigers, sometimes the tiger turns and bites you in the ass.'

'Fortunes of war,' said Vernon helpfully.

'You said it,' said Albert. 'Which reminds me, there are two widows who need looking after. I'd say a million bucks a head should see they get their widows' weeds from Oscar de la Renta, wouldn't you, Vern?' Albert guffawed.

As far as Vernon knew, the killer with the Nip name didn't even have a widow. But there is a time when it is better to be clipped than clouted. Vernon was just happy that, against expectations, Albert was not coming at him like a homicidal maniac. 'I'll get the money ready,' Vernon said promptly.

'Keep the bills small,' said Albert. 'I'll have one of my guys call to collect. He keeps hitting on me for a vacation.'

The guy who arrived four days later was a darkly handsome Italian-American named Bobby. Like his boss, he was a sunny fellow, and when Vernon showed him the two valises containing the widows' compensation, the guy told Vernon to put the money back in the safe. He'd rather like to relax for a few days.

'Be my guest,' said Vernon.

Bobby had played tennis with Tabitha, put the moves on her – delicately rebuffed – made full use of the health centre and gym nearing completion, taken a bath in the black mud heated by the hot stones from the Arenal volcano, horsed around with the security guys, and all the while made careful, discreet notes on the compound set-up.

Finally he departed, a heavy valise swinging at the end of each arm, flashing his fine white teeth at the staff and working the snake hips on his way down the path as if he could hear 'Stayin' Alive' playing in his head.

The FBI team were unanimous that the hit squad had had a good grasp of Gatling's layout and state-of-the-art alarm system.

After avoiding all boundary obstacles and despatching the surveillance system operative in his bunker – the electricity feed wire to his air-conditioning had been cut and he had left his bunker door ajar to catch some cooler night air – the assassins had headed directly for the *cabaña* that was the Gatlings' temporary home while the main house was being decorated.

The outside guard was found rolled under a jacaranda tree with his throat cut. His inside counterpart had been lured to the kitchen door by the sound of a parakeet screeching on the patio. He discovered the bird tied to a post with a small screwdriver thrust into its body.

The parakeet was still alive; the bodyguard wasn't.

Vernon and Tabitha each had a spacious bedroom with the connecting double doors wide open between them. From the gory evidence of the blood pools soaked into the satin sheets, spurts up the walls, and absence of blood on any clothing, it was possible for the FBI blood-patterns expert to deduce that Vernon had been lying naked on his own bed when the intruders had burst in and jumped him.

In all probability they had given him time only for the briefest of screams before they slashed his throat so severely with a machete-type weapon that his head was half severed.

At this moment of retribution, Tabitha, in her silk panties, had been seated at the dressing-table in her own room. Unlike her father, she had managed to put up some resistance. The damage to her right ankle, hands and arms denoted a ferocious flurry of counter-attacking and defensive blows, delivered by foot, hands, forearms and elbows. But these had not saved her.

The FBI team estimated that, given her skills in the martial arts, it had taken at least three people to overwhelm her. They would all now be nursing bruises and, perhaps, some broken bones.

Despite the opportunity for rape, they had not removed her panties. A trail of blood blobs, later identified as her own, showed they had lifted her bodily and rushed her through, still alive, to her father's room where they had forced her to witness the act that, in death, left Tabitha's lovely face contorted in an expression of total horror.

They had then carried her back and held her down while they forced her lips apart before slicing open her creamy neck.

The killers had taken their time. Before leaving, they'd all changed out of their undoubtedly blood-drenched clothing, showered and presumably dressed in their back-up kit. They'd taken all their soiled garments and weapons with them.

For amusement, perhaps, or to destroy bloody prints on the flesh, they had carted Vernon and Tabitha on to the internal courtyard built like a Roman atrium and dumped them in their own bubbling mudbath.

Later, when the FBI pathologist first caught sight of the two bodies in the mortuary, even he grimaced. The mud had caked and crazed on the flesh. In death, Vernon and Tabitha Gatling resembled excavated victims of the Vesuvian lava flow at Pompeii.

The pathologist bent over Tabitha. There seemed to be a

considerable mud accretion around her mouth. He began to dab with a damp swab. What he uncovered caused him to grimace for the second time that morning.

The local police chief had done his best to cover the airports and seaports but the killers had almost certainly arrived and departed via the Pan-American Highway. By now they could be in Mexico, drinking tequila and letting the sunshine take care of their bruises.

The information released to the world's press, storming in by scheduled flight and private plane, omitted one unappetizing detail that the FBI team leader judged unfit for public consumption.

But Our Man Abbotsbury had been in Costa Rica a darned sight longer than the FBI. They could be as prissy and namby-pamby as they jolly well liked but Abbotsbury was made of sterner stuff.

All the same, he did say, 'Yuk!' and 'How absolutely beastly,' when his police joe, giggling obscenely in his ear, passed on the morsel that within days would be whispered throughout London clubland and other high places.

Abbotsbury beetled round to his phone-in-a-box at Edificio Centro Colón and made sure his handler was apprised before he shared his goodies with His Excellency, Her Britannic Majesty's ambassador to Costa Rica.

'Nasty,' said his handler, Mr Sinker, shortly. 'I seem to remember that was a joke unfriendly Arabs used to perpetrate if they caught one of our chaps unawares in the desert. I didn't know it was a Cosa Nostra speciality. Must be one of those frightful Sicilian things – that'll teach you not to play doctors and nurses with your own daughter. What?'

Abbotsbury's handler cut the secure line to Costa Rica and rang upstairs.

'Here's a good one,' he told the deputy director-general. 'They found Tabitha Gatling with Vernon's shrivelled dick in her mouth.'

Chapter Twenty-four

A certain Ozymandian irony on the question of memorials emerged in the aftermath of the bloodshed. Given the climate of hostility towards the Gatling family that was universal in civilized society and the widespread feeling that justice had been done, albeit in a thoroughly uncivilized way, it was felt by the trustees of the Gatling estate that a family tomb in, say, Highgate cemetery would have invited early defilement.

It was Sir Marcus Coombes who persuaded his fellow trustees that cremation was by far the better course. A small party of Vernon's closest friends and associates – Tabitha was considered not to have any of sufficient weight – was flown to San José for the ritual scattering of the ashes. They found the *Black Glove* waiting for them in port at Limón.

The group was puzzled to be confronted by three bronze urns until it was explained that old Gunner's ashes would be joining those of his son and granddaughter.

They'd heard the rumours and *sotto voce* there was some tasteless ribald speculation: one urn contained one small, charred part of Vernon and all parts of Tabitha.

The jokers were careful not to voice this within earshot of Sir Marcus who, after all, was mourning the loss of a client worth an annual seven figures to his firm and was in no mood for bad jokes.

An Anglican chaplain had not been available but Sir Marcus had recruited an Episcopalian substitute from the local Church of the Good Shepherd. The scattering took place on a radiant day, far out in the Caribbean where there were pelicans in the sky.

The *Black Glove* hove to. The sea was calm, the dark blue water moving in shallow rolls.

For a few moments the contents of the three urns lay on the surface like grey scum doing a slow rhumba. Then Sir Marcus tossed overboard a single wreath of frangipani and broke up the *danse macabre*. The mourners lined the rail and watched, fascinated, as the last of the Gatlings disappeared into the depths. Then they turned inboard where the champagne was waiting.

When the *Black Glove* returned to port, the associates went their respective ways to begin the discreet task of removing the Gatling name from Vernon's SkyCities, shopping malls and holiday resorts.

The emperor's name was about to be chiselled from his monuments.

In London, the coroner finally resumed the adjourned inquest on the late Larry Varnish, aged twenty-two. On direction from him, the jury returned a verdict of unlawful killing by person or persons unknown, thus frustrating their unanimous instinct to name Vernon Gatling.

By now everyone had read copies of *How To Get Away With Murder*, flown from the United States and sold in Britain at a premium price pending a British edition. The Costa Rican killings had made British publication legally risk-free. Albert Penn, unwittingly, had done yet another favour for the Limeys.

Only with the jury's directed verdict was Lorraine, Larry Varnish's widow, at last able to claim him for a Christian burial.

Both the City of London and Metropolitan Police officers who had taken part in the long investigations organized office collections so that Lorraine would have sufficient funds to do the job properly. Many attended the service in the Southwark Roman Catholic Cathedral, conducted by the Archbishop himself.

Lorraine, with Ronnie Sims, her second husband, dutifully at her side and not quite knowing what his role should be, was bewildered by all the attention. She thought that a small service at St Joseph's, where she had been married, would have sufficed.

But in contrast to the furtiveness, sniggering and cynicism that marked the disposal of the Gatlings' earthly remains, the people of the Borough had simpler emotions for their own.

On the day of the funeral Lorraine burst into tears when she saw the hundreds who had turned out to line the pavements to show respect for her Larry. Almost none in the crowd had known him personally but he was a South London boy who had been ill-used by rich men and rich men's lawyers. The brotherhood of the poor needed to be demonstrated.

Mr Smith, the undertaker, was inspired in his response. The deceased, he ordained, would have a working-class funeral of the magnificence he could have expected in 1955, the year he died. Instead of wheeling out the Daimler hearse of modern times, the magnificent horse-drawn hearse of yesteryear with its cut-glass side panels and filigree trimmings was dusted off and refurbished.

Thus Larry Varnish, like an emperor, was hauled to his final rest by four Belgian greys with black feather plumes fluttering above their manes, and leading a column of flower-covered Rolls Royces, Daimlers and elderly Austin Princesses.

As the procession, headed by Mr Smith on foot in his black top hat and flourishing a furled umbrella, reached the great road junction of the Elephant and Castle, where Larry had seen *Hue and Cry* eight times all those years ago, passers-by who knew nothing of the day's event stopped to gape.

The spectacle was so grand that some thought it must be the funeral of a gangster.

Months later, the Gatling trustees made a gesture that was considered entirely appropriate in the circumstances. On what would have been Larry Varnish's sixty-fifth birthday, a small group gathered in the Weston Gallery at the British Museum. Among those present were Sir Marcus Coombes, representing the trustees, the widow, Mrs Lorraine Sims, the three senior detectives, Ringrose, Firth and Dalton, Ms Honor Pargeter, now a QC, and the newly rich authors, Gervase Meredith and Nelly Tripp.

They gathered round a spotlit glass case mounted on a basalt base and Lorraine, embarrassed at being the centre of attention, mumbled a few words to say how happy her Larry would have been to be there, and tugged a gold cord to reveal a small statue of Mercury in his travelling sun hat.

The printed legend at his feet read:

THE ROMAN GOD MERCURY (*c.* 150 AD).

THIS FIGURINE WAS EXCAVATED IN 1955 FROM A SITE IN BISHOPSGATE IN THE CITY OF LONDON BY AN AMATEUR ARCHAEOLOGIST, MR LAWRENCE VARNISH.

Afterwards, Nelly and Gervase hugged Lorraine, shook hands warmly with 'their' detectives, Ringrose, Firth and Dalton, then stepped out into the sunshine of the great courtyard.

Nelly took her fiancé's arm, sighed, and said, 'Old Shakespeare got it right, didn't he?'

'What?'

'Gods kill us for their sport. Poor Larry Varnish. Nobody told him that bit.'